Edited by - Sara Berzinski

Cover art by – Ashley Seney

CONTENTS

THE DAUGHTER OF ORACLES

GRAVESTONE BOOK THREE

By Amber Darwin

AUTHOR'S NOTE

I WRITE GRITTY, RAW, sometimes disturbing gothic/dark fantasy/paranormal romance. The heroes do villain-type shit, and the villains are not always what they seem. Everyone is morally gray. Some find redemption. Some never will. These characters are not human and won't always behave as you or I would expect, but I hope you see something in each of them that speaks to you. And through their struggles, I hope you find those jagged pieces of yourself and learn to love them for what they are.

This is the third and final installment of The Gravestone Trilogy. Adult fantasy (18+)
It contains scenes that may depict, mention, or discuss: abduction, anxiety, attempted murder, blood, death, emotional abuse, fire, kidnapping, murder, occult, PTSD, torture, war, graphic sex, gore, foul language, dysfunctional relationships, miscommunication, and cliffhangers. If any of these themes are damaging to your mental health, turn back now. This is not the book for you, and that's okay.

To my readers. Sorry about that last cliffhanger...
Just kidding, I'm not.
Cheers, to the only book in this trilogy that answers the
godsdamned questions!

CHAPTER ONE

THE MORTAL FOREST

"I MADE THE DAMNED portal as you asked! So why is it necessary to follow you through it? Filthy earthlings…" Kalliope gripes as we hike down the flagstone walkway into a gray-swept forest.

"Hey, Venom Tongue, I love some of those *filthy earthlings* you're talking shit about!" I purse my lips at her unwarranted opinion.

Kalliope turns her unsettling catlike eyes toward me. "Love is a useless emotion."

"Haven't you ever listened to The Beatles? Come Together. Let It Be. Love is all you need! Goddess on fire, Kalliope… I thought *I* was bitter, but you're in a whole extra category." I scowl as we approach a cluster of naked trees with limbs reaching out like splintered finger bones.

Sisters are a pain in the ass. Yeah, I said it. Like itch bane in your undergarments, the gift that keeps on giving. And don't even say it; I already know what you're thinking… *'But Vivi, you could never shut the fuck up about saving her and then becoming besties. You were going to ride off into the sunset on unicorns.'*

I remember what I said.

Maybe this is my karma for being an insufferable sasshole or payback for that time I didn't tip my server enough. Then there's the whole executioner thing I did. So this has to be my penance for one of them, if not all.

The three days after Kalli opened her eyes, we spent in silence. Whatever happened in the Bone Keep, leaving her half-beaten to death and hidden beneath a tangle of thorny vines, must have been horrific. If she had been mortal, she would have died. But she isn't, so she didn't, and she's chosen to make that everyone's fucking problem.

My sister is eerily beautiful, scary brilliant, and twelve gallons of madness in a six-gallon cauldron. She is chaos personified. Her mother passing on the body-hopping mojo of the Goddess of Love might make you think she's somewhat pleasant underneath all her venom, but that's just not the case. I get it. Her mind is fractured; emotional wounds bleed too. Except those aren't as simple to heal. But for the love of everything sacred, she could at least pretend there's something in her chest besides petrified rocks!

I stayed by her side. In fact, I even tried to convince her to cry, scream, rage, or break shit. Something to help her release the proverbial demons that were clearly haunting her. I could see them in her vacant eyes. We did everything possible to help her, but she only stared at the walls, nearly catatonic.

The first twenty-four hours revealed it was a waiting game. Kalli would come around when she was ready, not a minute earlier. Finally, two days later, she did. Once she spoke, it was like conversing with an older, more jaded version of… me.

Deacon always told me growing up that getting anything through my thick skull was like nailing faery pudding to a tree. Unfortunately, he never got the chance to meet Kalli. Reasoning with her is like trying to swallow iron spikes. This girl is impossible! If the universe planned to teach me a lesson in patience, I hope it's today. *Goddess, please let it be today.* Because in just a few minutes, I'll embark on my first official mission for the Nether Realm. They've chosen me to deliver a Netherling child to the new headmistress of Underhill Academy. The first in history.

The council forbid it for decades. Any non-witchling was not eligible to attend Underhill. Only those with pure witchling blood, and a few wealthy exceptions, were given access. Funny, isn't it? I've been a halfling this whole time, and it was overlooked or exploited. I imagine it was a mixture of both.

It has been tricky to get to this place in history. The council has discriminated against supernaturals for centuries. They have killed some for the impurity of their blood and who their parents loved. Too many innocent lives have been lost. Even those who weren't killed have been treated as lesser for decades.

That all changes today. So yeah, opening the Academy to all magical beings is a big freaking deal, and Kalliope is coming with me.

What was I supposed to do? Leave her to wander the fortress? Or worse, keep her locked up until I get back? No. I don't trust her yet, but trust comes with opportunities to make it or break it. I want to believe there's something worth saving in her, something that can be salvaged from her dark soul.

My old therapist would say that I look so hard for it in her because I secretly hope there's something worth saving in me, too. I may or may not agree with that. Either way, convincing anyone to agree to her tagging along with me was more complex than I imagined.

'She's too unpredictable.'

'She may be a spy.'

'Nobody knows what her intentions are.'

I was surprised when Lincoln, Ansel, *and* Killian fought me over it. I mean, Killian? That's not shocking in the least.

Right now, I think the Dark King disagrees with my entire existence. Not that I blame him...

We're locked in this star-crossed dance, him and I. We find each other in the right place but at the wrong time. Or the right time for the wrong person. We are drawn to each other by something bigger than ourselves, but are unable to make it work in any type of functional way. Our ships pass each other, but the inevitable crash into watery destruction is never far behind. We're the relationship equivalent to the fucking Titanic.

About this Kalli thing, though? I didn't expect Ansel and Linc to agree with him. The filthy traitors. Whose side are they on, anyway? Sometimes I wonder if they have half a brain to share between them. It's not like she's going to burn the Academy down. Newsflash, I already did that.

I doubt Kalli will go feral and eat the children, even if she *has* threatened to do just that. But it's only theatrics. She's a wounded soul, and wounded souls lash out to keep themselves protected. I should know because I do it, too. Now, I'm not saying she isn't powerful enough to be scary. I'm just saying she's not a total monster, no matter what she would like everyone to think.

Plus, a little empathy never hurts. I mean, think about it. Kalliope is in the fortress of her father's enemy, surrounded by people they have taught her to hate. So, of course, she's going to be on edge. Her world just got flipped. She needs to experience something beautiful. A reminder that not everyone is a total asshole, and days like today exist. Not only do they exist, but they're worth fighting for too.

So, I argued my case like Elle Woods. I'm a Demon Goddess from Hell. Kalli is a Demon Goddess from Hell. Shadowlings have been raiding the outer edges of Netherworld territory for weeks now. There's no sense in not having a backup, especially when the two of us have proven that we're like supernatural cockroaches. We're almost impossible to kill. Other than their suspicion of Kalli, none of them had a valid reason to deny me. So, I won.

They don't have to be happy about it, but here we are. A foul-mouthed witch, a problematic demon, and a rare supernatural child walk into the Mortal Forest...

It's like we're a barroom joke waiting to happen.

I find the name 'Mortal Forest' a strange choice for this section of the Netherworld. We are in a forest. That much is true, but here's nothing mortal about it. This is a Forest of the Dead. I sense restless spirits here. Watching, waiting, eager. As for mortals? That's a hard no. No mortal would have the balls to come here. Their human nervous system would override their limbs to run in the opposite direction. Hell, I doubt many supernatural beings would enter here either. Not willingly, at least.

Even though Kalliope doesn't mention the ominous atmosphere, her subtle change in pace suggests she is just as unsettled as I am. We are not welcome here.

"We shouldn't linger any longer than necessary," I comment.

Why did Kalli choose this forest? Creating a permanent portal to the Academy could have been done anywhere on the property. Had she done it because no one in their right mind would enter this creep show? If so, it's fucking brilliant.

Did she have something else in mind?

My head shakes as I reject the intrusive thought. For a moment, the men in my life have temporarily clouded my mind, but I can make my own judgments about what she is and isn't. Kalli is an asshole, for sure, but that doesn't make her a liar or a spy. I will not condemn her for something she had no control over. I know well enough what that feels like.

Mordred shaped my sister into who she is, just like Faustus Culpepper shaped me. I don't know her brand of darkness, not yet. But I know mine, and if I can claw my way back from being abused to the point of thinking that I was a great evil. From killing innocent women... and children. Then she can come back from whatever the fuck her story is. Everyone in this fortress can think I'm a dumbass, and that's fine, but if there's a glimmer of hope left for my sister, I *will* find it.

"It would be a shame if the wraiths got a taste of our souls," Kalliope muses, smirking to herself as she approaches the gently churning blacks and purples of the portal she created.

Admittedly, it would be a lot easier to put faith in her if she'd stop saying shit like that!

"Would you zip it? There's an impressionable youngling standing right here. Remember?" I protest, looking down at the half-demon girl traveling with us.

"And?" Kalliope shrugs and smiles.

She leans her petite frame against a gnarled tree trunk, looking every bit the assassin that she wants me to believe she is. Kalli was raised by uncivilized beasts. I won't deny it, but I recognize pure evil when I see it, and it's not her.

I kneel in the brittle leaves, face to face with the girl. "Don't fret, little Eira. Sisters are biologically programmed to argue. It's how the universe keeps us from joining forces and taking over the world."

Eira's eyes sparkle with amusement. Then I whisper, "And there are no wraiths."

This time she nods, but I don't think she bought it. Smart kid! I'm bluffing about the wraiths. I have no clue if they roam this forest. I'm not even sure what they are beyond the basic stuff. Unfinished business and whatnot. Do they eat souls? I hope not, but this child is only nine years old. I think the soul-sucking monster discussions can wait. I suspect she'll have plenty of time with monsters later in life, up close and personal.

The minute I laid eyes on Eira, I suspected she was chosen for this coveted position for reasons other than her academic merits. I recognize that look. You know the one… the expression that says, *'my name is trouble, and I bring pandemonium in my wake.'* It's a look I'm intimately familiar with. This child has fire in her soul, and she's going to light the world up with it one day.

Goddess, pray she chooses her powers for good.

After I saw the little spitfire who would be in my custody until the exchange, my curiosity got the best of me, so I asked Marlow to help me work some smarty-pants magic, and we kind of ransacked Killian's office. He locked the documents in a cabinet, so we liberated them. According to those slightly stolen documents, Eira is an orphan. Amethyst couldn't find anything about her parents except that her mother was a demon.

A vampiric spirit known for its ability to shift into different forms, an Aswang. After digging into their species, it did not surprise me to find that the Aswang causes havoc wherever it goes. Make no mistake, there's a teacher somewhere in the Netherworld having a shot or two in celebration of Eira's departure. I'd bet my best pair of boots on it. She'll give the new headmistress a worthy challenge.

My mind turned back to my sister, remembering what she was trying to do. And if razor blades could shoot from my eyeballs, she would be in bite-sized pieces. I take a deep breath, hold it for three, and exhale. I will not strangle her. I will not suffocate my shithead of a sibling who terrorizes children for her own entertainment…

Meditation breaths or whatever.

"Hey asshole, you think we could declare a temporary truce? Don't worry, we can deal with all the broody family drama later." I look at Kalliope expectantly, and I'm met with silence.

"Please, Kalli?" I tinged my voice with desperation at this point. She is too exhausting.

Several tension-filled moments later, Kalliope rolls her eyes and says, "Fine."

That's all. Nothing to see here. Just... *fine*. She then dives headfirst into the portal between the Creeping Aspens, not bothering to leave me instructions on how not to die on my way through.

CHAPTER TWO

GRAVESTONE ACADEMY

EIRA AND I LAND on the velvety grass surrounding the infamous academy courtyard, and I sigh in relief. Checking us both over. We're in one piece and in the right place. Thank the goddess and all the baby gargoyles.

Feeling this grass against my skin again stirs messy emotions inside my chest. A flashback, a vision of blood bubbling from the ground invades my mind, and I shut it down. I'm weirded out to be back at the Academy. That's fine. That makes sense. We went through a war together, this house of horrors and me. The battle of adolescence. The struggle between good and evil. Except the latter was the only choice I ever had. This place turned me into a thing of evil, took more from me than words can ever explain, but it strengthened me too. The battle for my soul happened right here on this spot. If I ever had one to begin with…

Even as a former bastion of evil, this land is magical in a way that defies explanation. I can't resist taking a moment to stare at the imposing yet elegant iron gates and the trimmed hedges lining a grand, former castle with the most magnificent towers. It smells of the salty sea mixed with forget-me-nots. A nostalgic scent that brings me an odd brand of comfort.

Kalliope snorts, "You look like a pathetic dreamer."

"That is not a term I ever imagined being used to describe me, but whatever you say, Jackass." I hiss.

Despite her teasing, I do have things to be optimistic about. We've disbanded the remaining Elders and their followers. They're placed on Thornfall's most wanted list. The crooked council no longer exists. They're fugitives. They will be hunted down and discriminated against in the harshest sense of the word. When captured, punishment for their crimes against supernaturals and humans alike will be doled out in the Netherworld, where the real monsters live.

Do I feel remorse? Nope.

If we do not eradicate the poison, it will grow and spread.

This is a new era. In this Thornfall, everyone gets a representative and a seat at the table. Even the humans who have suffered at the hands of the elders, just as we have. Tuition has been abolished to rid the new council of breeding greed. Now that the Netherling children are welcome, Killian offered to bankroll the entire Academy. He gave up his right to vote to not be a conflict of interest. Who knew he had a bleeding heart under that broody mystery mask… and enough money to fund an entire school for the next millennium, apparently?

We cannot erase the history of what has happened here. That's impossible. Evil leaves an imprint that cannot be scrubbed from the land. The damage from the past won't be eliminated overnight, but I think these measures will help us heal with time. Pain has tainted this Academy for years. The road to healing will be as just bending as the path to destruction, but at least there's a road now. A place to start.

Fresh memories are already being created all around us. Supernatural children are running and playing. Their giggles fill the courtyard with a sound that I imagine being like the warmth of sunbeams. This is something worth taking the time to appreciate. It warms my arctic heart to think that all of this was all accomplished by a group of supernatural fuck-ups.

It's ironic to feel this kind of hope while standing on the spot where my world once shattered. The granite likeness of the first man I ever loved stares down at me. There's a sense that he's listening to the words inside my heart, which eases the ache. The humble inscription on the statue's base catches my attention as I tread closer...

'Deacon Harwell–Warrior. Mentor. Father.'

This is where Deacon belongs. Regardless of his many faults, he was a born protector. Lincoln, Marlow, and I were shielded by him for so much of our lives. Now he'll protect the children that pass through these halls for eternity. I couldn't imagine anyone better for the job. Crouching on one knee, I place my fingers to my lips and press them against the cold stone. A moment of reverence to my crazy old guardian, my bonus father. I hope he sees what we've done here and what we'll continue to do. We're building the future he gave his life for, and I hope we've made him proud.

Moisture makes its way down my cheek, and I allow the one tear to make its way to the edge of my eye before I shut it off. *Alright, that's enough. Unfuck yourself, Vivi...* this is what Deacon would say, after accusing me of having rocks in my head, because that was his love language.

I never thought I'd miss someone's insults quite so much.

"I love you, you grumpy bastard." I smile as I whisper my faded grief. It's not healed and never will be, but it doesn't hurt to breathe anymore.

<hr>

As I mentioned before, being responsible for burning half the buildings down, I am interested in the new construction. A rounded chapel catches my attention as I scan the grounds.

This must be a recent addition. A stunning, elegant tower straight out of a fairytale. The sight of this beautiful thing where the bane of my existence once sat hits me with alarming force. I went full Firestarter inside the Academy. It could have gone badly, and I'm lucky I didn't.

A smirk forms on the corners of my rosy lips. "I said I was going to burn this motherfucker to the ground. Didn't I?"

My whisper is barely noticeable. I do not intend my words for an audience. I just want to reveal to Faustus in Hell, or whatever level of purgatory the gods threw him in, that I keep my promises.

"Queen Genevieve! We weren't expecting you until later this afternoon," Iris calls out from the carved wooden double doors at the entrance to the Academy.

She smiles as she makes her way down the steps to meet us. A procession of small ones trails behind her like little ducklings in a row. Pureblood, halfling, mixed orders, all following their new governess anywhere she leads. And I grin. This was always the correct answer. Iris will nurture the children, show them how to love, and teach them at a young age that not all strength looks the same. Loud or quiet, bravery is strength. Iris will care for the wee ones until it is time to learn the more brutal truths, and they will be better for it. A new generation that doesn't value violence above bravery.

A future worth ending the Shadowlands for.

"Well, hey there, Mother Goose." I smile, and Iris chuckles. "I've brought you another duckling by the name of Eira. She's honored to be the first of many Netherling children to attend the freshly sanctified Gravestone Academy."

So yeah, we changed the name. It only seemed fitting since Deacon gave his life to defend it, to protect us all.

Eira catches my eye as I glance at her. As I suspected, her glittering eyes flash defiance with an undercurrent of fear, but she nods. "I am honored to be here, Mistress Crowe."

I smile and nod my approval at her courage. Leaving everything she knows, being thrown in with supernaturals that she has been warned to hate, trusting her *Queen* with the course of her future. This little one has enormous mettle. She will give her professors a taste of hell. I know it. But I'm confident Eira will thrive here.

"You allow this... this... atrocity to exist?" Kalliope sneers, twisting her face like she's smelled something rancid as she eyes the children of various realms and orders.

Son of a fucking swamp witch! Godsdammit. Our father is a spectacular fuckwit, and everything he taught Kalli about the rest of the realms is dead wrong. "Forgive her. She isn't house-trained yet." I distract from the utter nonsense escaping my sister's mouth while glaring at her complete lack of tact or empathy.

"Shall we go inside and get Eira settled?" I break the uncomfortable silence.

"I think that would be wonderful." Iris shares a warm grin.

We move toward the all too familiar main entrance. The moment we enter the hall, I forget all sense of decorum and squeal, sprinting into the foyer. "Agnes!" I wrap my former aide in an enthusiastic hug.

"Well, let's have a look at ya, child! It's not every day we're visited by a Queen!" she exclaims, chuckling at my outburst.

When Agnes grins proudly and bows low, reality hits me in the temple. I don't know what I despise more: the ruse everyone believes or the reality nobody knows. I am not a Queen, and I'm not built for pretending.

While speaking with Eira, Agnes squats down. I don't know what they spoke of, but it doesn't take long before the sour girl smiles and grabs her hand. Agnes has a way about her. That woman could tame The Wild Hunt and still have time to wash bedding afterward. Not to mention, Miss Agnes has always had a kinship with the firecrackers. Eira waves as she follows Agnes to the student dormitories. Holding up my hand, I wave back.

Goodbye and good luck, little one. You'll rattle the realms one day.

Once they are out of sight, we travel further down the main hall. As Iris comes to a halt, she ushers her little ducklings into an enormous five-star cafeteria.

"Have your treats. I'll be back shortly."

And like pixies in a windstorm, they cheer and scatter.

"Everything seems to be running smoothly," I make casual conversation as we venture into the rest of the new section.

"We're doing well, dear. With the help of the supernaturals from both Thornfall and the Netherworld, our sanctuary is nearly finished with construction. There is peace here. Children don't know hate if you catch them young enough. It's the rest of the world with its head up its ass." Iris grins.

"I can't argue with you there." I chuckle.

In silence, we make our way into another corridor. Finally, we're inside the business and governing side of the Gravestone Academy. The decor is bright, clean, and modern. Mixed with what they could salvage from the fire. This melding of antiques and modern elements has a *gothic in white* vibe. Fresh, like a brand-new book. Ornate like the great castles of the Fae Realm. Or what I've seen in picture books, anyway.

"Wasteful," Kalliope mutters to herself, not so quietly.

See, I told you. Kalliope from the Shadow Court is a royal pain in my ass.

I deliver a sharp elbow to her rib cage, a quick reminder of what we talked about before leaving today. This is a diplomatic mission between the two realms. We cannot afford to piss off the new headmistress on the first day. Especially *this* one. From personal experience, I know she can be a nasty adversary.

My nerves kick in as we turn the corner. The last time I saw Willa was before I went back to The Night Fortress. Lincoln and his shifters had handled the move from the catacombs, while Amethyst handled contact between realms. I'm ashamed to admit I was too busy denying anything queenly to do those things myself, although it *was* technically my job. It is an oversight I'm hoping I won't be paying for when I cross into Willa's office.

Upon entering, Willa sits behind a sleek desk. Her head bowed as if she was reading something official. Her unseeing eyes move back and forth across the paper, and I realize she's employed magic to interpret scrolls. Bloody brilliant!

The slate-gray pants suit she wears is stylish and commanding. As if she's always belonged where she is, and perhaps she always has. Who knows what could have happened if Faustus hadn't banished her to Tanglewood Manor so many years ago? I wouldn't be surprised if she was more powerful than Faustus, which is why he imprisoned her.

"Look what the demons dragged in. Not one, but *two* abominations." Willa looks up to give me one of her famous unseeing glares, but it lacks any real animosity. *Thank you, goddess.*

I hold back a snicker, and my lungs tingle. Willa's position of power hasn't changed her a bit. She's still the same old auntie sunshine. Meaner than the Furies, and I love it.

"Yep, two demon goddesses from hell. Come to visit the new headmistress in her marble tower." I bow dramatically.

Iris gasps. "Now, you stop that. You are a queen, Genevieve! Act like one."

She's correct, or at least she thinks she is. And I must remember that aside from our immediate inner circle, that is how everyone views me. A queen. I cannot continue to mock this crown. But, for everyone's safety, I should mind my sarcastic impulses. At least in public. Not for Killian, but for the people he is sworn to protect.

Willa, Iris, and I converse about the Netherworld news for a few moments. My eyes dart to Kalliope occasionally, gauging her reaction to what peace could look like if we took back The Bone Keep together. I don't know when I decided that was something I wanted to do. I'd always pictured myself going back to The Gravestone once the Academy was secure, and the Shadowlands were no more. Back to my shifty apartment and slinging drinks to the Thornfall patrons. Except none of that feels right anymore. I thought The Gravestone was Deacon's legacy—but it wasn't, was it? He was only there for my mother. For me. The Netherworld was his home.

Iris reaches for Willa's hand, their fingers interlacing as we make conversation, but I can't help being distracted. I've never seen them so happy. I can't imagine what it must be like to see their life's work laid out before them. From smuggling mixed order supernaturals through tunnels while exiled in a psychotic house to living out their dreams of unity in Thornfall. They'll have their struggles to come in the future. Of course, they will. Nothing worth having is perfect, nor should it be. Perfect leaves no room for growth.

I think seeing it for myself, being part of its creation, is what turned the tides in my mind. Because this can be done in Thornfall, it can be done elsewhere. Everywhere. That is what I want for the Netherworld. It's been a long time since I've thought about my future. Or what it would even look like. But I know it now. I want to go home. To my real home, and I want my sister with me.

Wrapping up our meeting, we discuss the most important subjects: supply chain, food sources, magical barriers, restructuring the Rune Force, staffing the Academy, and the quality of education that is expected.

That part isn't really my message to Willa. It's Killian's. I'm the messenger, and by the looks of it. Willa wants to kill me. It's easy to diffuse, though, when I explain that Killian is more than willing to bestow another donation to hire qualified teachers who have no societal standing. In other words, real teachers. No more brainwashed pure blood puppets paid for by pretentious elders. And the only thing he asked in return was to be included in regular progress reports.

After the formalities, Willa's milky eyes move in my direction, and I already know what's coming next…

"What has my niece been up to in that Dark Fortress?" she asks.

I was waiting for this. There are two stories I can weave. One involves Daddy Dragon and my suspicions about what Jagger and Lowe do (together) when no one is watching. The other is less salacious, probably more appeasing. It may save me from being hexed by an enraged Moonfall Priestess. Considering the choices, I think I'll go with door number two.

"She's doing well. Loving the new job and learning a lot about the history of the Netherworld." I respond.

Killian assigned Marlow her own office in the library and gave her the title of Netherworld Historian. After everything she has endured, it is nice to see her have the things she has wished for. A dragon boyfriend from her smut books. A massive library filled with thousand-year-old manuscripts. It's like Marlow's wettest dream. It's hard to tell what turns Marlow on more. Jagger or the smell of old paper and bindings.

"Relay a message from me." Willa says threateningly, "If she doesn't visit her family soon, I'll march into your King's extravagant library and drag her out by her ears."

"He's not my...."

Oh, fuck. I'm an idiot.

What was I going to say? He's not my king... yeah... great idea, Vivi. I have to get my shit together before it happens in front of the wrong person, and Mordred realizes it. We'll be in a world of trouble then.

"Apologies. I'm still learning how to be a queen. It's been quite the undertaking, I'm sure you can only imagine. I just meant to say my king's sense of humor could use some work, but I bet he would be entertained to see that." I stammer.

"Oh, bullshit." Willa scoffs at my attempt to speak like a queen.

I know this temper will be my death someday, but the sound of that stolen title triggers my 'fuck off' response. *King Killian*, what a crock of shit. I don't even care about the godsdamned title or what he thinks he needs it for. It's deeper than that for me. He lied to me. Again. I don't even know why I'm surprised, hurt, pissed, or whatever. I knew better. I always know better.

What do you do when love and lies exist in the same space? Do you forgive and forget? Pretend the lies don't exist. That sounds nice, but it's not reality. Love can conquer many things, but without trust, what's left?

What do you do when you love a man you cannot trust? Question of the fucking year.

"We just miss our Marlow, and her mother isn't adjusting as well as we had hoped," Iris says, misreading my pained expression.

We only had Judith with us for a few days. Despite the grim circumstances, our time together was wonderful. But Judith is human, and sadly, we all agreed that the Earth Realm would be safer for her. I suspected she would have trouble coping without Marlow.

"I will pass the message along, of course," I reply.

"Thank you, Genevieve." Iris nods as she lays her free hand on Willa's shoulder.

As I prepare to leave, my mind starts to spin. "Have you had any backlash from the humans in Thornfall? Security issues? And the old portals we closed, no activity? What about staff? How many stayed. Were they properly vetted? Have you found the remaining Elders or their sympathizers?"

Willa tilts her head, diagnosing the state of my mental health, I'm sure. Then, after a few moments, she gives me a disapproving scowl. "No, no, no, twenty-seven, yes, and no."

"I'm sorry. I know I sound neurotic. It's just that everything seems too peaceful. I'm on edge." I offer her an apologetic wince.

"My father doesn't want this... *dump.*" Kalliope interrupts, turning up her nose.

We may need a ball gag for Miss Chatty Pants over here.

I mean, it's great to hear her say something (anything) about what Mordred is planning. I'm relieved to know he doesn't have his sights set on an academy filled with children in the Earth Realm. But did she have to say it like *that?*

"Oh, my goddess, Kalliope! Just shut the fuck up." I blurt, and then promptly close my hand across my own mouth. I cannot believe I just did that.

Willa's cheek twitches as if she's holding in laughter. "Queen of the Netherworld, indeed."

Whew, the goddess must favor my stupid ass today.

Anyway, as I was saying about the barrage of questions. I've been soaked in uneasiness at night. Perhaps it's my upbringing and the constant need to be on guard. Or the fear of shoes dropping all around me. Maybe this is just paranoia, and it's nothing, but the uncertainty of what I'm feeling makes me itchy.

The Sight has been untrustworthy as of late. I don't know if it's something magic-related or if I've done it to myself, but until I can say with certainty that I'm not glitching out on the psychic plane. I have to trust gut instincts, and my gut says that life in my world is never calm for long. I don't feel prepared for whatever comes next.

"Genevieve, we are fine. Safe and secure, this is not a place of evil any longer. As soon as you two leave the grounds, anyway. Now, off you go. I have better things to do than listen to you babble." Willa pats my arm with her wizened hand.

"Thank you, Mistress Willa. For everything." I squeeze her fingers.

"That's enough dawdling. Go give your king his update." She smirks.

A year ago, I would have said I didn't believe in miracles. But what can be more miraculous than Willa expressing affection? To me! Her assurance that everything is fine makes me want to believe her. If only my dreams weren't so dark. Like a thunderstorm building just out of view. I can't see it yet, but the wind has stilled, and the birds have gone silent.

Trouble stirs. My blood knows it.

I have spent many lonely nights in my gilded rooms. The darkness seeps into the walls like an illness I can't pinpoint. The Dark King sleeps only steps away from me, but those steps have seemed like miles. The door might as well be a mountain. Every day, that distance increases.

Are we truly fated, cursed, or crossed by the stars? If so, these miles will come with a price. Destiny *always* has a price.

CHAPTER THREE

THE NIGHT FORTRESS

FEELING CAUTIOUSLY TRIUMPHANT, I return to the portal with Kalliope. Eira is safe. I have good news for Killian for once, and Kalli was pretty tame in Willa's office. At least compared to what she could have been. So, despite the ominous clouds that hang over our heads, I'd call our mission a success.

This might even be my golden ticket out of the Real Housewives of the Netherworld. I am ashamed to admit it, but they have transformed me into a lemming. I never imagined someone would ask me hundreds of questions about new fabric patterns and glassware to use when serving guests. Still, here we are… like I have a fucking clue which plates should be used for VIP court members? Until a pair of stormy turquoise eyes trampled my life, I ate my meals out of plastic bowls and take out boxes.

The makeup, the dresses, the luncheons with snooty night creatures. It's exhausting, and I'm not slamming the people who like this stuff, but I'd rather be training. Or learning to ride Calypso! She's big as a horse in her Shadow cat form and isn't entirely against wearing a saddle.

Kind of…. let's just say we're working on it.

Regardless of my complaints, I don't mind humoring Selene and her incessant talk of decorating and making the fortress in my image. It's the least I can do for the woman who saves my ass and regularly brings my friends back to life. Goddess knows she's the only pure thing in the realm, and I would do just about anything to please her. But there was always an expiration date on this wedding arrangement, and I cannot help but feel as though the members of this family are prolonging it.

The silent stares when they don't believe I'm paying attention, the stolen glances when I ask the wrong questions. I love these people who have become family, but I think we all know what lies ahead, whether or not it's openly discussed. Soon, I will have to make a choice, and I already know which one I will make. The only one I *can* make. My father is killing the entire realm with his Shadow Court and its oily rot. It seeps into the ground and poisons everything in its path. So how can I not feel a calling to undo it?

I'm biding my time, gathering my power, and going through the motions until it's time to take the Bone Keep and end this.

Kalli and I continue down the forest path in silence. She's uninterested in speaking, and I'm also lost in my own thoughts. I need to ask her some questions, but the idea of asking makes my stomach twist. My brain wrestles between wanting to respect Kalliope's space and knowing that the information she conceals could save countless lives. Somehow, I've found myself divided between the family that chose me and blood that isn't quite family yet.

My thoughts return to the present, and I note the change in our surroundings. Every time I step outside the fortress walls, I end up on a path I haven't traveled before. This realm is a godsdamned labyrinth. Nothing is where you would expect it to be, even if it was? Look again because no, it isn't.

In my previous explorations, I've found some sort of spiritual monument. A river. Another river. Yet *another* river and a dead garden someone must have loved at one point, but that time had long passed. I swear we're in an orchard straight out of a horror movie this time. The trees are misshapen, and the skies are lifeless. Rotted fruit hangs from overgrown twigs, disfigured worms feast on the corpses of fallen apples, and my nostrils burn from the sickly sweet aroma.

To my right, I spot a monstrous creature nestled in its web. Shaped like a spider, its humanoid eyes and tiny hands adorn each end of its spindly leg. I do not know what this creature is called, but I hope it doesn't have a taste for a couple of sisters who don't know where the fuck they are going. I don't mind spiders, but with a curse out to kill me, this is the absolute worst location to be going for a stroll.

I give Kalli 'a look,' and she raises a questioning brow.

"Let's go!" I whispered, tilting my head towards Aragog and Golem's love child.

"But aren't you it's Queen?" Kalli replies sarcastically.

I choose not to acknowledge that. I recognize manipulation when I see it. Kalli is not hiding the fact that she's looking for reasons to hate me. Poking and prodding, waiting for me to lose my patience and strike back, because then she can justify her hostility. Jokes on you, sis! I'm not giving her the ammunition. Not happening. I speed up, and she reluctantly follows until we cross into the Netherworld version of fall.

I'm not sure how to explain the spooky girl dreamscape Killian's lands have become since I've arrived. The closest I can think of is eternal Halloween mixed with Sleepy Hollow. The Johnny Depp version, not the cartoon. The pumpkin spice, haunted hayrides, and mystical witchery with a darker twist. As if the Netherworld had to add a little flair to the mix.

A deep breath of cool autumn air fills my lungs. It smells of campfire and cloves, awakening my inner witch and soothing my soul. I take it all in while Kalliope stares at me like I'm destined for a padded cell.

In their spiritual language, the crows call out to each other, speaking their omens into existence. Leaves fall from the branches like October rain, yet the trees stay full of multi-colored foliage. The assortment of gray mums lining the rock path reminds me of a printer that ran out of ink in the middle of a gorgeous mural. Or a warped children's book… *Edgar Allan Poe–for kids. What a beautiful disaster that could be!* The thought makes me grin.

"Why do you smile?" Kalliope asks, "You are also a prisoner here, are you not?"

I need a few moments of reflection before giving her an honest answer to such a complicated question. It's true that a man I wasn't fond of brought me here unconscious, and without permission. And I spent a ridiculous amount of time unable to leave my rooms. But when I left this realm, nobody tried to stop me. So this time around, nobody is keeping me here but myself.

"In some ways, I suppose I am… but I chose it."

"You chose it?" she repeats my words back with a puzzled expression.

The lack of eye contact tells me she's not talking to me. Perhaps she's talking to herself. So, I continue walking. Gazing at the colorful sky until the questions flooded back to invade my mind. Should I give her more time? Is there any time left? What if I…

"I will not fight my people for you." Kalliope states. Her face is a portrait of calm.

How do I forget she can do this? But, of course, she can hear my thoughts… I don't know how to turn them off.

"That's not the only thing I wish to know, Kalliope."

She answers inside my mind, "You want to know if I have come to destroy you? You questioned my intentions when I did not ask to be here. You're desperate to know about Father. Although you disguise your personal curiosity with a sense of duty. You wonder if the Oracles speak to me, and you think I know who your mother is? You are in an arranged marriage with our father's greatest enemy and would like to believe it's strategic. But your love grows...."

"And that's enough of that!" I plaster a false grin on my lips like she didn't just make my heart plummet into my asshole.

"I can go on if you'd like."

"I'm glad you're speaking over two words at a time now, but please stop talking in my head," I say.

That's it. I'll be making a trip to Dante and Bane's Den of Debauchery as soon as possible! All the nasty-nasty that goes on down there, there's no way they listen in on each other. Right? That's just too weird, even for the twins. They've got to know how to block each other out. I want that answer, pronto.

"Now you ask me to stop speaking in your head after you begged for months?" Kalliope bites back.

I gasp for air, and my voice shakes. "You knew? You fucking heard me all those months and left me alone in the dark? You fucking knew. I tried blood magic, cursed herbs, dark things I had no business touching, Kalliope! I needed you!!"

"And look what it cost me to come to your aid!" Kalli trembles now. Rage consumes her glowing pupils.

My Goddess. That's why he hurt her?

Mordred maimed my sister and left her to suffer from helping *me*.

We blast through the fortress gates like a pair of thundering Minotaur twins. I could hear each of us muttering under our breath as we stomped through the grounds, our mouths splitting in a thin line. By the time we reach the entrance, our elbows and hips clash. The power struggle spills into the foyer, where we knock into an elegant vase and the mirror above it. Knocking it from the wall. As glass rains from above, a jagged shard narrowly misses slicing through my neck.

"What the fuck, Kalli?" I exclaim.

Instead of receiving a response, Kalli's icy white hair whips across my face as she zips past me and stomps her way up the double staircase. When she reaches the top, she turns, pinning me with her emerald stare. And then she sticks out her tongue, her TONGUE! Mocking and sneering before entering the hallway to her rooms.

"Childish! Is this what it would have been like to grow up together? Fucking ridiculous."

"You big crybaby!" I shout before turning in the other direction toward my own rooms.

My door stretches open, and I slam it behind me. My veins are boiling. That woman drives me crazy! I have changed my mind about Killian being the biggest thorn in my side. Kalliope takes the cake for the most problematic person I have ever encountered!

Having made my way across the room, I collapse on my bed.

Nothing ever comes to me the way I imagined it in my head. It was supposed to be that we were kindred spirits, bound by hatred for our father. She was going to be my light in my darkness. Our meeting was meant to be a supernatural event. Instead, I get the Netherworld version of fucking Maleficent. What the hell happened?

Stupid bullshit prophecy...

Rolling to one side, I slam my fists into the pillow, burying my face and letting out a strangled scream. What a swamp hag! Does she believe she is the only one who has suffered for no reason? Have a look around, Sis. I've been living in purgatory right alongside you. First, trapped in a Victorian dream castle with an irresistible yet manipulative prick. Next, used as a bargaining chip, then a lover, and a pawn.

No matter how beautiful the handcuffs are, they *are* still handcuffs. They made hers with shadow, but the stars have slapped mine around the wrists. Or a boiling hot asshole did it. I'm still undecided. Who knows what's real and what Killian wants me to believe? I certainly don't, and that's why everything is an absolute shit show. Lies, curses, blurry boundaries. Impending fucking doom.

Doesn't she know I did this for her? That I'm here because of my endless quest for answers about where she was. It led me to the academy, which led me to a dungeon, a boat, and into my cage. Yes. I left, but I was fooling myself when I said I wasn't coming back. Because here I am in even deeper shit than I was the last time I tried to walk away.

An overwhelming sense of guilt merges with the burning rage. Kalliope must have known what helping me would cost her, yet she still did it. Our father is a bigger monster than I ever imagined. The punishment for disobedience is the beating of your life and being dumped to live or die, whichever the Gods decide. Even for the God of War, that's fucked up. And under all those prickly thorns, Kalli cares. Despite being raised by that tyrant, she still has something worth redeeming. We couldn't be more different in appearance. But, like mirror images reversed, we're perhaps more alike on the inside than we want to admit.

The worst part about this argument was that everything Kalliope said was correct. Those *are* my innermost thoughts and fears. She pegged me, and it hurt. I'm only irritated that she dug inside my head and found the baggage I've worked to hide.

What kind of sister does that make me? A shitty one. Deep down, this outburst is so much more than a few indignant words. I'm looking for reasons to hate her, too. I'm angry with the sister who saved my life because she showed up too late to save Deacon. As ruthless and despicable as he may be, Kalliope still has a father.

And I don't.

Did I want to make her hurt for that? I don't know. My darkness, my demon. She craves things I don't understand. But I see now that my sister has already paid the price for entering my life. It's the one everybody pays for. You'll never know a moment of peace when you're with me. Shit, maybe we've been searching the realms for what was in front of our faces all along. Perhaps *I am* the curse?

"I don't have time for this. I need to train." I speak aloud to an empty room, then take out a pair of leggings and a sports bra from the drawer. Putting on the pants and boots. I need to punch things, shoot targets, and let my power loose. Since becoming a socialite, I haven't had an outlet, and I feel it bubbling over.

The nagging in the back of my mind intensifies, and my skin prickles. Wait… an empty room. My room is empty, and it's quiet in the fortress today. Unusually quiet. My heartbeat picks up the pace. Kalli and I caused so much racket with our grand entrance I wasn't even aware Calypso hadn't greeted me.

Kalli and I tussled through the foyer, smashing shit, and nobody shrieked or tried to break up the fight? Was the hall empty when we got here? I wasn't paying attention. Shit! On such an important day for the future of Netherling children, no one waited for our return? That can't be right.

Crossing the room, I glance at Killian's doorknob. The ring of forewarning permeates my mind. I push the door open, listening to the creaking of the hinge as I feel horror creep into my toes. The bed is unmade. A tumbler of amber liquid sits on the nightstand, untouched. A book lies open on the rug with its pages bent and smashed.

Killian's uptight ass would never, could never, leave his room in this state. He would short circuit before he left his room in this state. Something has happened. My heart races as I rush out of his door and into the hallway.

As my fear intensifies, my hurried steps turn into an anxious jog. I rush through corridors and pop my head into the richly decorated rooms. Then, one by one, I check for the others. And there's nothing, nobody. Not even the Brownies. By the time I circle back around to where I started, I'm genuinely terrified.

"Marlow!" I scream. "Anise! Are you here?"

Fuck, fuck, fuck.

"What are you shouting about?" Kalliope rounds the corner, coming to a stop next to me.

"There's nobody here, Kalli."

Listening, her expression turns icy. "They have infiltrated your borders."

My hands go clammy, and my throat constricts. Lincoln, Marlow, Anise, Jagger, Amethyst, the twins, Grim, Lippy, and… Killian! Where are they?

"FRANK!!!" I shout.

Too many moments pass, and my mind goes blank. There is no coherent thought, only panic. My fingers are numb, and my legs are made of putty. I forgot how to breathe, so I'm just standing here—breathless, shaking, stunned.

Kalliope stares at me as if I've lost my freaking broomstick…

"GODSDAMMIT, FRANK! Where the fuck are you?" I scream, slamming my hand to the damask wallpaper. My insides twist in a painful realization.

The dark goddess isn't coming to help me. So, I am on my own. So, I have two choices. I can sit on this floor and fall to pieces, or I can woman up and find my friends. But I can't do both.

I can't do both…

"I'm going to find them. If you're coming with me, you'll need weapons." I call out as I pull myself together and rush back into the hallway.

Before Kalliope can respond, I'm racing back to my rooms. Then, like a wild thing, I delve into my arsenal and rip apart my closet. I already had my daggers with me, but I grabbed some throwing knives and tucked them into the waistband of my leggings.

I recognize that I'm frantic, but I'm also trusting my instincts. As each second passes, I feel the dread rising in my throat. Tell me Marlow is with Linc or Amethyst, that they're somewhere safe. And I'm not sure what this thing is between Killian and me. Even when we're tangled in each other's sheets, I hate him, but my monster tears to the surface when anyone threatens him. She's roaring now.

Stepping back onto the throne room floor, I'm startled by Kalli leaning on a stone pillar. She's wearing a thick leather top and holds her wicked scythe. We don't have time to stop, so I move past her and through the front gate. Hoping she follows.

"I thought you said you wouldn't fight your own people?"

"I did."

"And now you've changed your mind?"

"Did I say that?"

Oh, for the love of the godsdamned stars! I close my eyes and drown her out, letting all the tension go. I ground my body and spirit into the earth. Imagining the soil between my toes and the taste of ozone on my tongue, I can feel it all in my mind, the realm calling to me, offering me her gifts. As I float above myself, my vision narrows…

A massive crack in the earth is visible from my position on a hill. The men and women were not prepared. They focused their attention on the camps, and it blindsided them. Shadowlings inside the grounds. Calypso attacks. A dragon screeches. Steel, blood, screams.

CHAPTER FOUR

THE KILLING FIELDS

SHREDDED BODIES LITTER THE fields. Shadowlings? Netherling? I can't tell. The smell of sweat and copper is heavy in the air. Kalli and I exchange glances, unsure of what the other will do next. I don't have the time or patience to babysit her eccentricities because my insides are screaming. I'm close to losing control, and I have to move. All I can do is trust that my sister still has a light inside her, and I don't find myself on the other end of that scythe. Again.

Trying to locate my people, my eyes scan the scene. I immediately see Calypso leaping from one shadow guard to the next, shredding into them without mercy. She is deadly grace in all her destructive glory, and my chest heaves.

Thank the goddess, she's okay. I won't survive losing her again.

Next, I spy a crimson-haired hellion with her dainty hands wrapped around a man's neck at least three feet taller than she is. Anise's face is lit up with a wicked grin as a manticore writhes in agony under her spell.

A violent roar booms from above. Rows of flame blaze through the trampled grass, incinerating everything in its path as Jagger's scales glimmer through the sky. The twins stand back-to-back. Snakes coiled round their heads, ready to strike, ready to kill.

Where is Killian?

As I step onto the battlefield, I draw the daggers from my thighs and slice through the shadow guards in my path. If guards are what you want to call them? The Shadowlands' beasts are just as poisonous as their territory. A distorted version of themselves. I have no idea how to explain it. They're just plain wrong.

From a few feet away, a Spiny Waterbuck charges straight at me. I drop down and scrape my palms against the hard ground at the last possible second. My heart battles against my rib cage. Bile rises in my throat when the Waterbuck skids to a halt. I needed the monster to leap over me so I could stab from below. Shit! I don't have a Plan B, and right now, I'm looking good and fucked.

Backing up, I'm reassessing my options when a massive red-coated wolf leaps at the beast and knocks it to the ground. Then, he removes the creature's head with his powerful jaws, flinging it like a rag doll away from my path.

Thank the fucking Forest Gods for Ansel; always on my six.

"Hey, thanks, Cornflakes!" I call out to him. I could kiss that stale-breaded lumberjack right on his mouth for being so godsdamned dependable.

If Ansel is here, Linc and Marlow must be okay, because he would never leave his alpha's side if they were in danger. Lincoln ordered him to fight with the rest of the Netherlings, which is a good sign. A wave of relief washes through me. Knowing it won't be one of their bodies that I stumble over. Standing back up, I wipe the dust from my leggings and notice a rip in the thigh. *These were new!*

I weave between the fallen bodies, checking their faces, searching for the king. My daggers sing as they cut through necks and stab through the hearts of my enemies. The violence becomes a dance, with no music, no sound. Only the monster who lives inside me performing her graceful waltz. My foot catches on a stray piece of bloodied armor, and I lose my balance. Just as I'm about to face dive into the mud and entrails, cool fingers wrap around my arm, yanking me back up.

"I knew you liked me." I grin while slashing my daggers, cutting through the wave coming toward me.

Kalliope sneers, "I owe the shadow cat."

She deflects a shadow guard with her foot, kicking him squarely in the chest, but does not use her deadly scythe. Staying true to her word, she is not fighting against her people.

"Owe her what? I'd love to hear. Is this the medieval land of the Fae? Do we do life debts in the Netherworld?" I ask as I fight off a towering ogre.

Kalliope doesn't respond, but flashes an irritated stare.

"What? Can't fight and chat at the same time?" I tease. Little does she know it's just something I do to keep my mind from spiraling out when shit is bad.

Looking around at the carnage before me is sobering. The more time passes, the more questions I have. Curses, prophecies, oracles, and fate. How do we all fit into this blueprint of the Gods? Is there a choice at all in this? Or are we puppets for the old ones to continue their petty feuds? This is senseless. All this death. But I suppose it's neither time nor place to ponder the universe's mysteries.

"The least you can do is get over here and stand with your back to mine," I yell at Kalliope. "It makes no sense to get murdered for nothing."

"You really think they'll murder *me*? Worry about yourself." She scoffs.

"I don't see any of them coming to your rescue, Kalli. Pretty sure they're swinging their axes at you too! I'm just pointing out the obvious." I grunt, getting hit in the stomach by a red-caped asshole.

Much to my surprise, Kalli's eyes go dark as she marches toward us. If I was a gambling girl, I'd say she might even look protective. Fuck that, though. I give in to the urge to prove I can take care of myself by dispatching the shadow guard in one smooth movement, splattering its blood across my face.

Kalli stops in front of me, assessing the situation, and then she snorts. Her chest is shaking as she puts her back to mine. Laughing? Is she seriously laughing at me right now? What a lunatic! But before I know it, a small huff of amusement exits my lips. Of course, it helps to have a dark sense of humor amid complete mayhem, right? Right.

It doesn't take long for us to get in sync before we know it—we are working together like it's always been. Kalliope kept her word. She isn't killing anyone, but I'm betting 30,000 amperes of lightning bolt to the chest will knock you on your ass for a good long nap.

The battle sounds fade with the extra backup and my mind races. How did this happen? If my Sight is accurate, some of these Shadowlings got past the fortress gates. Was there another spy involved? Do they have scouts we're not seeing? Nothing was amiss inside the fortress itself. Common sense says whatever happened, it happened outdoors. What were they looking for?

An ear-splitting screech startles me back to reality. Anise is wailing like a banshee, and she has metaphorically sewn herself to the shadow guard's back. Her eyes become wild as she stabs the guard. I can't resist the urge to laugh despite this severe situation. *Goddess alive... she is terrifying!* I am forever grateful to be her friend since I damn sure wouldn't want to be her enemy.

As I watch Anise in all her chaotic glory, I notice something behind her. A faint blue light paints the sky in the distance, and my heart skips a beat. "KILLIAN!" I scream, and then I sprint at a breakneck pace.

My inner monster propels me forward as the world slows to a crawl. Instinct takes over. I duck and dodge the weapons and magic, delivering bursts of violet from my palms like flaming cannonballs. My magic is doing things I didn't even know I was capable of; I can feel myself stretching on the inside. The monster inside me unleashed. I am her, and she is me. My legs pump with vigor as I climb the crest of a grassy hill and skid to a halt.

Killian. My Killian is in the low land, battling a Grendel the size of a fucking giant. My eyes drink every inch of his body, instinctively checking for injury. Just as much as I'm drooling over the corded muscles of his back while I watch him in action. He is gracefully lethal. Stunningly dangerous. The battlefield is his canvas. It takes my breath away, and it breaks my heart into jagged pieces. Despite being a lackluster *husband*, he is a true king. I will not rob him of that.

He becomes ferocious when he senses my presence, his jaw going rigid. Killian gathers his crackling blue demonic power in the palms of his rough hands and slams them into the massive, deformed troll's chest. Blue streaks rip through its veins and disperse through its body like an explosion as the creature stumbles before sinking to the ground.

Killian turns to face me. His eyes are magnetic, primal, and not of this world. We may not be in a good place. I resent him for too many things to list, but no matter what I do, Killian will never be erased from my mind, my memory, or my skin. I can hate him until the rapture comes, but hatred isn't the only strong emotion I feel towards him. The Binding ritual ensured that.

Sex Magic. And stupid ocean eyes can get a girl in heaps of trouble.

We stand in suspended animation, unable to break our intense eye contact for what seems like lifetimes, until a flicker in my peripheral grabs my attention. As I break free of Killian's hypnotic gaze, my blood freezes. Although it should be dead, the Grendel is no longer on the ground. Instead, it's been magically altered. I can smell the tainted sorcery in the air. This is Mordred's doing. I know it is.

Fear grips my throat as I strangle out a hopeless cry, wishing I could alert him in time, but I already know it's too late. I watch as a knifelike claw rips through Killian's torso as he sinks to the ground. Helpless to do anything about it, I drop to my knees and dig my fingers into the earth, splitting a fingernail through the middle, but I can't feel a thing.

The beast howls its victory, and I release a scream that pierces the realm. One second, my king is lethal grace and beauty, and the next... Killian's blood is streaming from those enticingly kissable lips. I lean over and wretch, emptying what little was in my stomach, and then every molecule in my body ignites.

I move down the hill toward the creature. Feeling myself evolving into something darker than all the pits of hell. Savage and untamed. The guttural growl that escapes my lips is a sound I have never made before. I step closer to the Grendel and bare my new jagged teeth with no fear. My body bursts into violet flames, and my fingers itch to destroy. I move down the hill toward the creature.

You will not leave this field living, and that is a promise.
But first...

"JAGGER!" I scream with my voice *and* with my mind. If he doesn't hear my plea, Bane and Dante will. Someone will come.

I don't know if Killian has a fighting chance to survive this. I don't know how anything works with the immortals. Is that supposed to be literal or figurative? All I know right now is that he is not breathing, and if there's a chance? I will move the stars and moon to give it to him.

Standing toe to toe with the Grendel, my rage intensifies. In all honesty, I should subdue this motherfucker, drag it back to the fortress, and elicit answers by any means necessary. In my head, I know that, but my arms still rise, and my flames blaze free, burning the Grendel. Starting with his feet and moving up with perfect precision. Watching every agonizing minute as the beast turns from flesh into charred bone. It's only when the flames reach his neck do I stop. I've got plans for what's left of him.

Goddess, I truly am a monster.

"No more a monster than I am." Kalli's familiar voice comes from behind me.

If I had the energy or the will, I would be satisfied right now. Killian has been avenged, and I finally got what I wanted. Kalli let the guard down for a split second. And she was my sister. I should be elated, but all I can think about is *him*. I don't look her in the eye on our way back to the fortress. I'm too frightened by the answers I'll find.

CHAPTER FIVE

VIVI

IT FEELS WRONG ON so many levels to sit in Killian's office without him. My ass is in *his* chair as I look over *his* view of *his* domain from behind *his* desk. I don't want this. I've never wanted it, but it doesn't matter what I want. Now that everyone is safely inside and the fortress is secure. It's my responsibility to determine what happens next and decide our course of action.

Bust out the big girl panties, Vivi Graves. Lock it up.

Ansel and Lincoln both lean up against the dark burgundy wall. Anise is sitting on the leather couch with Amethyst and Sybil. Jagger paces the floor. Marlow sits on the edge of the desk, looking at me as though I'll shatter any second. Like a baseball catcher, ready to grab the exploding pieces. The silence is unsettling, full of tension. I stroke behind Calypso's ear as I reach down. Goddess knows I need my brazen familiar right now. Give me strength, Murder Kitty.

"Tell me what you saw." I project my voice to everyone in the room.

"The attack came as a surprise; we have eyes on all the camps and there's been no movement. This was carefully planned." Jagger gives his insight.

"We were divided. Someone wanted inside the fortress." Amethyst adds, and Sybil agrees.

"This was only a diversion. The Shadowlings were testing our defenses." Lincoln adds.

"It was a recon mission." Ansel states.

"I think we can all agree this was Mordred. The question is, why? What is the motivation? The scouts were out, the fortress was guarded, and although they got past the battlements, they did not make it inside the fortress itself. Nothing has been disturbed. How many?" I ask.

"There were two. Dante and Bane sensed them inside the barrier walls and alerted the king." Lincoln answers, "I took the staff and those who aren't trained to fight into the undercroft, per Selene's instructions."

What the fuck is an undercroft, and how did I not know we had one?

Marlow must have noticed the furrow in my brow because she speaks up. "It's like an underground cellar. Storerooms, a weapons cache, that kind of thing. It has ocean access, and there are row boats down there if we need to escape. It's also where they keep a vault. That's where we were. Linc and Amethyst stood guard outside."

I nod. "Only two? So, the ambush happened after Killian (my voice shakes, and I almost lose it just using his name) followed them beyond the gates? Was it to lure him from the grounds?"

If the Shadowlings attempted to enter the Night Fortress, they were after someone. Would Mordred send his twisted creations to collect Kalliope? Me? Or could it be an object that he's seeking...? At the thought, my skin tingles, and I assume my intuition is speaking.

"Is there anything inside this fortress besides Kalliope and me that Mordred might want?" I address the room, but I'm looking at Jagger. He shakes his head, frustration evident in the veins protruding from his neck.

"You think they were looking for something," Anise says, not a question but a statement. My arms are tingling as she is reading me with her siren abilities.

"I do, and I think it's time to find out what it is before they get their hands on it."

***

Rather than return to my chambers after the meeting, I wander the halls. I just need a moment, lost in thought, away from prying eyes and nosy powers. I don't know where to start. I suppose the beginning is as good a place as any...

How much do I know about Mordred? Very little.

Mordred created Kalli and me as weapons against the original King of the Netherworld from what I've put together. Kalli's history is sketchy to me, nothing concrete, and she isn't sharing. I assume her mother is not around, and my mother fled when she became pregnant with me. Did she see his endgame? I think she did, and whatever she saw scared her enough to force Deacon and Rowena into a blood oath, keeping me hidden. Why? I bet the answer to that question would tell me what Mordred is after.

The old Vivi would pack a bag and sneak away into the night, ignoring all logic and throwing caution into a dumpster. Then, she would march straight to the gates of The Bone Keep and demand answers. And by sundown, the old Vivi would be knee-deep in a shit storm of her own making. But I'm no longer the old Vivi, am I? It crept up on me through loss and maybe even through love. A ton of mistakes and many brushes with death later. The old Vivi died, and I hadn't even noticed.

The undercroft piqued my interest, and I was headed there. But after entering yet another hallway, I pause, confused as shit. I swear I was under the fortress, but the moving wallpaper spreads out before me, making little sense. This is two, maybe three stories up, and I do not remember climbing any stairs.

What the…?

The hallways are all so similar here, but this one is unmistakable. It's the story of the Netherworld. The Maiden. The First Queen. She looks different today, not as calm as usual. Her smile no longer reaches the corners of her eyes. The maiden looks up and motions to me as if she has something to say. I pray this is the Sight and not a mental breakdown. It could easily go either way.

A couple of months in the Netherworld, you think walls can talk. Not insane at all, Vivi. I'm sure the grippy socks are nice and soft where I'm going to end up.

But I can't really argue with what I see right before me. Until now, I have never seen the wallpaper interact with anyone. It's like a memory that plays over and over, a residual haunting. It's not supposed to be sentient, and with everything that's just happened, this can't be a coincidence.

"Can you tell me what I need to know?" I ask.

The maiden nods to say yes, her cream-colored skirts fluttering in the breeze. Shocking me half to death.

"Holy shit."

She waves her arm in the air like someone's frustrated mother, talking with her hands. As I just stand there in utter disbelief, mouth gaping open. She huffs and stomps away as if *I'm* the one who's being unreasonable. After a few paces, she stops, tapping her foot. The universal sign for… are you coming or not? And I know I've said it before: this could really be the dumbest thing I've ever done, but how could it get any weirder than it already is? So, I follow the maiden and pray it's not to my own demise.

With each step she takes, the flowers wilt and fall behind her. Which is concerning. Death blooms in her wake. And from the tales passed down, I think she's supposed to be

a living embodiment of spring. The maiden *gives* life. She
doesn't end it. So why would they wilt in her wake? It's the
land. She's trying to tell me the land is dying.

"The land is dying," I say aloud.

The maiden stops. Her piercing gaze penetrates my soul.
There is a deep, profound sadness that robs my breath. She
lifts the hem of her dress to show me her leg. A black tar-like
substance covers it up to the shin. She carries the wounds
within her. She is poisoned and dying…

Omg, the maiden, she holds the magic that keeps the
Netherworld alive. Fuck. This is bad, really fucking bad.
I continue to follow her through the dimly lit corridors
of the fortress until I find myself at the end of a hallway
I don't recognize. Standing in front of an ancient-looking
door. There are bars across it, not just the kind you pick up
and move. This door is reinforced like the last Horcrux sits
behind it, ready to unleash havoc upon the world.

What the hell could be so important it needs this kind of
protection?

The maiden waits, watching me as she stands at the end
of her mural. Would she like me to open it? Because I don't
know about all that. There are stories on the television about
stuff like this. Girl finds ancient relic in her garden, the girl
opens a box she should have left alone, girl unleashes hell on
earth while everyone says, *"put that back right now!"*

This door doesn't seem friendly. Does that make sense for
a door to feel like a sentient thing? Because this one gives
off all the red flags. What if it tries to eat me or turns me to
stone…?

Oh, for star's sake. Doors are inanimate objects, Vivi.

On the other hand, I'm already talking to the woman in
the wallpaper. I've already embraced the crazy, and what are
the odds I end up in front of this door after inexplicably

teleporting three stories higher than I intended to be? None of this seems like an accident.

"Eh, screw it," I say as I approach.

There's no knob, nothing to hold on to. Argh! I'm tempted to give the wallpaper maiden a dirty look. Still, I think I will refrain from arguments with inanimate things for now. I mean, who has that kind of time? So instead, I take a step back and eye the demon door. Maybe there's a button. Or an incantation that makes it light up like the one in the Lord of the Rings? The only problem is that I don't know any Netherworld incantations to test that theory with. So I'll start with the obvious.

"Libero!"

Which means 'unlock' in Witchling, but it doesn't work. As my frustration builds, I throw my shoulder into it. Nothing. Flames burst from my palms, slamming into the thick grainy wood. They don't leave so much as a scorch mark.

"Stubborn fucking door. What secrets do you keep?"

"This is the end of the line, huh?" I ask the figment of my dark imagination living inside the wallpaper. But the maiden shakes her head, no.

"What do you mean, no? If I can't get through the door, it's the end of the damn line, right?" I exclaim.

Oh, I'm really doing it. Of course, I'm arguing with the fucking wallpaper...

But she nods in agreement, the shadow of a smile crossing her lips.

"What's so funny? I'm in this dead-end hallway looking like an actual psychological hazard right now. And you think it's amusing?"

The maiden shakes her head again and moves her hands in a prayer-like motion. She repeats. And again. To be honest, she looks like a tweaked-out faerie princess trying to play charades.

"Are you saying this is the beginning?"

If my imaginary friend could speak, I think she might cuss me out for taking so long to interpret her nonsensical messages. Instead, she pulls at her hair and shakes her head enthusiastically. Yes.

Well, that's just awesome, isn't it? I'll be adding that to the ever-growing list of shit that makes no sense in this gothic nuthouse. What I seek is behind a magic-resistant door with no knob. Why wouldn't it be?

"What should I do next?" I turn back to ask what the maiden suggests, but she's gone.

As in, nowhere to be found, and I am in a perfectly normal corridor. The one that leads to my rooms. Am I losing my fucking mind? Ansel stands guard with the dry cereal expression he always has on his handsome bearded face.

"You should smile more." I mess with him.

"Hilarious, my queen." He gives me his best dead-eyed stare.

I enter my room and head straight to my dresser. I did the queenly thing and then the haunted house thing, and now I just want sweatpants. My cozy black joggers catch my eye, then I select a random t-shirt from the drawer above. Looking in the mirror after I put it on, I can't hide the smirk. The shirt says, "In my defense, the moon was full, and I was left unsupervised."

My shoulders bounce as I chuckle to myself. The universe has a sense of humor. I'll give her that. When I move to the side of the bed and sit down, my shoulders slump. I'm just totally tapped out, exhausted in more ways than one. Calypso adjusts herself next to me and digs her claws into my blankets, kneading them until they feel right. She then falls dramatically into her 'nest' and closes her eyes. Grim must be with Anise tonight.

"Some guardian you are, Lippy." I rub the rough skin underneath her chin. "Always sleeping on the job."

I glance at the door that separates me from my husband's chambers with a deep sigh. Killian has not invited me into his private rooms in a long time. Do I dare enter without an invitation? Will I be able to handle what's on the other side? I've been compartmentalizing this all day. Just trying not to think about it. My nerves are raw. I'm so angry, confused, afraid, and worried.

Getting up and crossing the room, I inhale; then I grab ahold of the latch and slide it open. I put my foot through the threshold first to ensure it hadn't been spelled. You may wonder, do I really believe Killian would put a defensive spell on the door between us? The answer is... maybe.

You don't know what it's like here since I pulled a Runaway Bride. Twice. Let's just say that dry ice seems warm compared to how he treats me now.

I step in, and it takes everything inside me not to run to him. His broken body lies in his bed, covered in herbs and pastes. There's sweat beading on his forehead, and his bare chest is every shade of purple and green.

As my heart cracks in two, I say the only thing I can think of. "You look like shit."

"You whisper such sweet poetry, *wife*." Killian tries to sneer, but it falls flat when he winces.

"You're welcome, *husband*." I flash him a crooked smile.

Throughout the time I've known Killian, his skin has always been a perfect sun-kissed shade. Unfortunately, it has a gray tinge now, and his cheekbones are too sharp. His hero hair has become a greasy mess. Killian is a straight-up wreck. He almost appears... human. Something about this unfiltered realness sends a thousand bees to swarm inside my belly.

"My son is a stubborn mule. If he doesn't restore his power, he won't heal for months." Selene's stern voice interrupts my thoughts. I hadn't known she was in the room.

Selene purses her lips in the way only a frustrated mother can, and Killian flinches, just a little, beneath his mother's disapproving gaze.

So, the Dark King has a weakness, after all.

"We don't have months. There may not even be days. The king belongs on the throne, leading his people. So why would he choose not to heal?" I ask Selene, but direct the words at Killian.

"Have you told her?" She asks him accusingly.

"Told me what?" I question.

"Mother," Killian warns.

"That boy will die keeping his secrets! Killian has refused to feed for quite some time now. His power is depleted, and therefore his body is not regenerating in the manner it should. Without a food source, he will go into a state of hibernation. And we will be without a king." Selene casts a devastating look at her son. Her skirts whoosh as she turns on her heels and sweeps out of the room, closing the door with a solid slam.

"Is that true? A revolution begins, and you're starving yourself? Eat." I scold.

"No."

"What is the purpose of this? Lilia? I don't give a damn about that bitch's flame-broiled bones. I was jealous and immature, and I didn't know shit about the world. Surely, you've fed since then?" I ask.

"No."

"Have you forgotten the rest of the English language, Killian?"

"No."

"For star's sake, I already said I don't care if you feed. Pull your head out of your ass and go get healed. A giant egomaniac is knocking on the doors of the realm you protect! If you need to bump and grind with a random woman to heal yourself, do what you need to do."

"I am a bonded man, Genevieve."

Oh, I was expecting a different response, and I'm not sure what I'm supposed to say to that. My stomach is doing weird shit to me, and suddenly avoiding eye contact seems like life or death. So this is about the binding? I swear it was the most disastrous decision I have ever made. I can feel him, even when I don't want to. Especially when I don't want to! But it doesn't matter because wherever I go, there he is, taking the word stalker to a whole new category. Wait, what's with the nice guy act, though?

Is he mocking me? I bet he's fucking mocking me.

"Oh, give me a break. You haven't acknowledged my existence or spoken to me since that Bonding Ritual. What happened to it being sacred, Killian? Or is that only when it's convenient for you? Because none of this is convenient for me! Whatever. We have no time for this. Find someone to feed on today."

"Who walked away from whom?" Killian accuses.

"We are not having this conversation. There's no point. You know why I walked away from you. We both do. Just feed, and let's finish what we started so we can get on with our miserable lives."

"And if I sent all the feeders away?"

My heart skips.

"Why would you do something like that? Are you trying to prove a point? Let's see, how can Killian manipulate me into doing what he wants? Hmm, what a mystery. Oh, I know. Pull a stunt where he dismisses his feeders, and the stupid witch will fall into the trap! And yet you continue to underestimate me. You're a handsome devil, Killian. Find more. Or I will climb up there and do it myself." I warn.

His eyes go full midnight. "Are you saying you want to feed me, Kitten?"

CHAPTER SIX

VIVI

I STORM OUT OF Killian's private quarters in a blaze of crazy. Furious and flabbergasted. This is what he does, classic Killian. He breaks my walls down just enough to get a bit of trust, a small glimpse inside me. And then he destroys it. But is it really him, or is it me? Who keeps letting it happen? I do. I can't get him out of my skin, and the bond only makes it worse. I don't know how to snuff it completely, but I am a witch. I know enough.

Looking over my shoulder, I bite my lip as if I'll find him standing in the doorway. This is the right thing to do, or it's really fucking not and I'm about to make a terrible mistake. I can't think, though, not knowing he could be feeling it. I'm suffocating here. I need an open window. I need space. I need…

I need to do a spell.

Just a mild one. Like a mute button.

I have to, or I'll go insane.

As I crush the herbs and light the candle, something that feels like heartbreak fills my chest. I could have cried tears of joy when I saw he was alive. I could've cried tears of joy and thrown myself into his arms, knowing he was okay. And in ten minutes, I'd rather smother him with a fucking pillow. I swear he does this shit to me on purpose. This is the right thing to do. It must be. This hesitation creeping through my body is just nerves. That's it, that's all.

He was made for me… ha! That much is accurate, as my personal nightmare.

"I'm a bonded man, Genevieve."

"And if I sent them away?"

"Are you saying you want to feed me, Kitten?"

What an insufferable ass. Killian looks at me like I'm the most precious thing in his world and touches me with reverent hands. He kisses me like he'll die without me. Then, every fucking time, he stabs me in the chest. I have to do this, right? I do. I really fucking do.

He punishes himself by punishing me. I don't know why, but Killian wants to feel that pain when he looks at me. He chooses this chaos. How the fuck do you break that kind of curse? The answer is simple: you don't. You just die inside trying. Breaking yourself against his jagged edges until there's nothing left.

I can't love him. I can't hate him. I can't accept him. I can't erase him. I can't purge him, and it hurts. All of it. It aches to have a part of his soul entwined with mine, but it would destroy me to have him torn away. So here we are. Cosmically screwed. And I'm just so tired of thinking about it that I could scream.

As the last bit of the incantation settles in the air and I feel the spell lock in place, a silent sob tries to escape from my throat. *No. No, Vivi. It's done.* There's nothing more to say, and now the fates will do what they please. The Fates. The vindictive, petty life-ruining fucking fates.

I need a beer and a lobotomy, but I'll settle for a hot bubble bath.

I don't bother closing the bathroom door as I draw a hot bath with lavender oil and valerian tea leaves. I wait for the tub to fill; I look in the mirror. I run my hands through my hair and over my cheeks.

Rowena taught me a faery soul cleanse when I was a child. You look in the mirror for ten seconds and explore anything that makes you uncomfortable. I've used that method many times over the years. It's how I check my internal crazy meter. I do that now. Only this time, I can't even make it one full minute before I turn my head away in shame.

"You can't even look at yourself right now, Genevieve. Explore *that*." I glance at my reflection one more time, sickened by her weakness.

Slipping into the hot water, I try to loosen my muscles and relax. To be fair, not everything is doom and misery. There are some positives. I made progress with Kalliope today. She was my sister for a passing moment. I smile as I wash the negativity from my skin. Today, I saw a thread of hope for Kalli and me to have a future, and that's something. I picture Marlow in her library. Amethyst and Sybil were together, no longer hiding. After so many generations of violence, Lincoln led his people with love and respect. Willa and Iris are free from banishment. All the children have a fighting chance because *everyone* has sacrificed something.

I don't have the market cornered on pain.

Mordred's plans are set in motion. I can feel it in my bones. Today was just a prelude. We must be ready for anything. Or… we need to strike first. A spark of an idea forms in my mind, and I think I know what I can do. I can push Mordred far enough to show his hand. Did Daddy Deadbeat give me the fiery temper? I think we can find out, and I think we can use that information against him. As far as the rest of the mysteries that live here? Perhaps it's time to dig a little deeper. I was born of darkness, but I don't want to live in it anymore.

Although my muscles feel amazing after soaking in the bath, my mind is still a wreck. If I sit still, I picture Killian's face, and he is the last thing I want to think about. So, I pace. And I pace some more. Moving to the closet I demolished earlier, I pull out some artillery and place it on the floor. The next thing I know, everything has been polished and sorted according to ease of access.

I've flipped through some trashy reality shows, but nothing is keeping my attention. I tried moving my bed for better energy flow, which ended in disaster. I had to ask Ansel to help me fix it, which was mortifying.

After that, I called Maius and asked for comfort food, but the term *comfort food* was impossible to explain to my small Netherling friend. When I said, "carbs, just bring me anything with carbs," she looked at me like I had asked her for the keys to Narnia.

She came back with chocolate covered fruits and human wine… close enough, I guess. *Oh well, if I can't eat my boy problems away, maybe I can drown the bastard.* I join Lippy on the plush mattress and swig straight from the bottle.

Who needs a glass? Not me.

"If they could see their queen now, a pillar of virtue." I laugh. Calypso chuffs, burying her head in the mountain of blankets.

Virtue. What an utter crock! I am supposed to be upholding appearances as their fake queen. Instead, they stuff me in dresses and parade me around as a symbol of decency. It's almost comical when I factor in what I've seen with my own eyes inside that hall. What a bunch of hypocrites. We argue about color palettes and who gets the finest crystal, but there are literal orgies in that same room when the lights go dim. Maybe I'm a little tipsy, but after watching the lords and ladies on their knees with dicks in their mouths, among other places, I don't see why our tapestries and table manners are relevant.

"I guess they have to draw a line somewhere, and they picked fancy silverware as the hill to die on. Tits out? Sucking dick in public? No problem, but don't forget to curtsy! It's considered vulgar." I giggle at my astute observation of Netherling politics.

Calypso groans and rolls to her back, demanding tummy scratches, and I burst into full blown belly laughs. Fucking Calypso. She still doesn't listen to a godsdamned word I say, and I love her for it. I laugh until my side hurts, and when I run out of excuses, the tears come.

"You know what's the worst, Lippy girl? It's like he's under my skin, and I can't get him out. Tunneled right in there like a pest. It's so stupid because I feel sorry for him. Are you kidding me? I'm sitting here feeling sympathy for the jackass who is determined to ruin my fucking life. And *that* is why we are doomed." I wipe my damp cheeks with my sleeve and hiccup.

I'm buzzed, weeping, and muttering nonsense to a demon cat. Is this my life now? Is this what I've been diminished to?

That familiar anger builds inside my chest, spreading fire through my limbs. Screw this. I'm nobody's plaything, and I am far from helpless. It made sense to go through with this bonding. It was a good plan, even if it hurt. This is what we need to do for everyone's sake. Killian and I don't have to get along. We just need to defeat Mordred before the cost is too much to bear.

Fuck, I hate him so much! But... I can't stand to think of him in pain on the other side of that door. It must be the alcohol in the driver's seat, liquid courage, but my feet move as if possessed.

I've already opened the door before I've even had time to think through my actions. I'm standing in his archway dressed in a raggedy t-shirt, with a wine bottle dangling from my hand, looking like a half-deranged zombie Snow White.

Killian is awake and not at all shocked to see me in his room. Which is infuriating, but before I can decide on words—he quirks his brow and then nods toward the bottle.

"Share," he commands.

That wasn't the reaction I was expecting, but I get it. I look like a fucking lunatic, and he should probably get on my level. I shuffle over to his bedside and hold my arm out. He reaches up and takes the bottle, bringing it to his lips.

It's only seconds before he's spewing the wine from his mouth like it's burned his tongue. "That tastes rotten. Have you poisoned me?"

I burst into a fit of hysterical laughter. "Technically, it *is* rotten fruit. Fermented is the scientifical term. And I only wish I knew how to poison you! Count yourself lucky, buddy."

"Scientifical isn't a word. And... buddy? Is that right? Interesting take on our relationship." Killian teases.

"What relationship?" I flash him a sarcastic grin.

The king takes another swig of wine despite just complaining about the taste, then hands the bottle back to me. "So, what brings you to my bedchamber half drunk and in a nonsensical riot, *my Queen?*"

"You."

"Care to elaborate?" Killian asks.

"I am not drunk, by the way. But I am lubricated enough to abandon the filter in my mouth, and yeah... *I think I am going to elaborate, MY KING." I pause to get my footing.*

"Are you aware of how infuriating you are? I don't trust you. You're too pretty. I think you're fucking with my head, and I need you to know I'll stab you in your sleep before I agree to be controlled. Oh, and I hate you." I continue.

Killian opens his mouth, but I hold up my hand.

"I haven't finished yet. I could talk all night, until my lips turned numb, about all the things you do that make me crazy. But I can't deny this either, whatever this is between us. So, in conclusion. I can't stand being your fake queen, but I won't let you do this to yourself."

"That was quite a speech," Killian smirks.

"Shut up, asshole." I set the bottle on the rug and plopped into his reading chair.

We sit in silence. Me with my emotions spilled all over the floor. Killian was wordless, as usual. I don't know what I expected coming here. Maybe I wanted to see how much the spell worked? I don't know. Perhaps if I let myself feel what flows between our bond, he would feel me for a change instead of being distracted by his own emotions, obsessions, whatever.

I know better. I should be angry, but I only feel despair.

"I'm trying to feed you, stupid." My voice cracks, barely above a whisper.

I watch his body go rigid.

"The Netherworld needs a protector. You can give up on me whenever it suits you. I've come to terms with that. But I can't allow you to give up on your people, so I'll do it. I will feed you. All I ask is for one thing in return."

Killian watches me with primal intensity, his stormy eyes searching mine. "What do you want, Genevieve?"

"I want the truth."

Killian's stupefied look is damn satisfying, but when his eyes go to all molten galaxies, my knees buckle, and I rethink my decision-making skills. I was never any good at this self-preservation thing. Does he know I tried to mute the bond? I don't even know if it worked.

"And what sort of truth do you require?" Killian replies.

He's back to mister upright citizen, using sentences my language arts teacher would be pleased with. Which means he's nervous. Good. I know that the more anxious he gets, the more proper he becomes. Finally, something worked out the way I hoped it would. I'm not so foolish to believe I can coax all his secrets in one night, but if I fluster him enough, I think I can steal a few.

I'm learning how to play his game, and he does not know what's about to hit him.

"That's not how this works." I take a step closer.

"So, tell me. How do you want it?" His eyes gleam with lustful suspicion.

Damn him! He could recite the alphabet and somehow sound like a depraved fantasy. Fucking incubus.

"First, I want to know how it works," I say, ignoring the goosebumps all over my body.

"This is the truth you're asking for. Do you want to know how I feed? I imagined something more creative." Killian replies, clearly amused.

"No, I want you to tell me how you feed, and then you will tell me the truth. Whatever I ask." I inch closer, brushing my skin against his.

It's easy to seduce a man you can't stop fantasizing about. The promise of what he might do has me just as eager as I know he is, and I resent my body for not following the guidelines. But I've really stuck my foot in it this time, and it looks like I'll have to clean up the wreckage he creates after I follow through with what I started.

"I'd start by touching you, right here." His fingertip trails along my cheek, moving a lock of hair behind my ear. Our lips are so close that I can taste his power on my tongue. The internal shiver hits me like an enchantment.

"And then, if you are my chosen, we would share a kiss." He runs the tip of his nose along my forehead and back down, bringing our lips impossibly close.

"Your chosen?" I whisper breathlessly.

"I do not fornicate with my food, Kitten. Sex while feeding is sacred, only meant for my chosen mate. However, I absorb lust in *other* ways." He murmurs as he nips my neck.

He thinks I'm a puddle in his hands, calling me his mate. I smile like a predator. "Nice try, Killian. What is the *other* way?"

"Kiss me." He replies.

There's no sense in denying the heat between my thighs or the change in my breaths. Killian knows my body responds to him the way he wants it to, but he doesn't know the depth of my pigheadedness. So, as I lean over his broken body, propped on a mountain of pillows. I brush his silky lips with mine and speak softly. "Show me the other way. I want to know what they felt."

Before he can reel in his anger, his face turns a fascinating shade of red. *Now we're getting somewhere...* when he looks into my eyes again, I'm unsure what I'm seeing. Nervousness, hesitation, distress? Maybe all three. But I stare back, unwilling to bend.

"Give me your hands," Killian growls.

The moment his skin touches mine, I am in an unfamiliar place. It's like a grotto. There are two chambers in the cave. The bed I am sitting on is in one, and the hot spring is in another. Killian is on his knees in front of me, peeling the straps of my tank top down my shoulders and revealing my breasts. My fingers weave into his hair, loving the feel of his body near me. He lowers his mouth to my nipple and wraps his tongue around my puckered flesh with precision. I arch my back under the intensity of his tongue.

A husky moan escapes my mouth as I press myself into him. Sweat beads at the back of my neck, and his swirling galaxies meet my eyes as his tongue travels between my breasts. He trails a finger along my hip, and it blazes an electric path straight to my core. I pulse once, twice. A silky layer of heat pools between my thighs.

A sensual groan escapes Killian's throat as he works his way up my neck, taking his time to reach every nerve ending on the way. My breath grows raspy as he grabs my cheeks and gazes deeply into my eyes. There is no part of me that does not want to be near him. I would fight the gods themselves if they thought to take him from me.

This warrior is mine.

Our lips crash, and his kiss is what I've always dreamed of, the kiss I laid beneath the stars and fantasized about when I was still too young to be curious about kissing. Everything is right, so right that I can't imagine not wanting it. Everything he offers, whatever he needs...

He presses his knee between my thighs with just the right amount of force. His hands tightly grasp under my ass cheeks as he pulls pull me closer, grinding himself against me. The feel of skin-on-skin floods me in all the right places, and I am ready for him. Everything he can give me, more than he thought I could take. His answering rumble makes me want to wrap myself around him, fitting him in every corner, every spot, until we become one. Souls and bodies. He will be my new god.

Did I just say he would be my god?

My subconscious mind sets off alarms, and it takes every ounce of my willpower to pump the damn brakes, but eventually my vagina stops calling the shots, and common sense returns to my body. We aren't in a cave near the ocean. Killian is far too injured to be on his knees, let alone what I think he was about to do next.

"This isn't real." I cry out, and the illusion fades.

I find myself sprawled on top of the real Killian, with a very real erection pressing against me. Gasping to catch my breath, and turned on beyond all sense of reason.

"What the fuck?"

"You're the one who demanded to know the *other* way," Killian replies.

"The *other way* is MIND CONTROL?!"

That's so fucked up. But I don't know what's worse, my anger at him hiding this ability from me? Or that I liked it. I am so screwed. So, so epically screwed.

"I have never taken a woman without their consent, Genevieve, for food or otherwise," his voice has gone from resigned to straight-up dejected.

I don't know if he is reading my expression, my body language, or if he has been invading my mind, and I have been oblivious the entire time. But the tears threaten to spill over again, and I look away.

The old Vivi would have created a scene, but I guess I already had my moment in the spotlight when I burst into this room half-buzzed on human wine and feeling incredibly daring. So creating another scene just seems redundant at this point.

"Well, that's one way to keep your body count low." I fake a laugh, trying to hold myself together with the equivalent of one janky bobby pin and some chewing gum.

"You asked me for the truth. Some secrets don't permit themselves to be told, and then there's what is best kept in the dark." He tries to explain himself, but I already get it.

"No, you're right. I asked you to show me, and you did. I appreciate your honesty. Did we? You. Me and you…." I'm tripping over my words like a drunken pixie on the solstice.

"Oh, for fuck's sake. Did I feed you, at least?" I finally blurt out.

Killian's eyes go wide, and he clears his throat as he runs his hand through his inky hair. "Is this reverse psychology? Why aren't you yelling at me?"

I remove myself from Killian's lap, careful not to put too much pressure on his mid-section. When my feet touch the floor, I'm sure he's doing okay. I lift his bandage and peek underneath.

If he doesn't want to answer the question, I'll find out.

Killian's angry, puckered wound isn't healed, but it looks a hell of a lot better than it did before. I guess that answers the question. I fed him at least a little. Perhaps Killian was telling the truth when he said he never fucked Lilia. If I understand him correctly, they never even kissed, but why does my chest hurt at the thought of him entering her mind in such an intimate way?

"Genevieve?" Killian says my name like it's a question and a prayer combined.

"It's okay. We're fine. Your wound is already healing. By tomorrow morning, you will be as good as new. All broody darkness and serial killer charm." I piece together a broken smile and see myself out.

Call me the girl who lost her nerve, but I think I've had enough truths for tonight.

CHAPTER SEVEN

THE FORGOTTEN GARDEN

AFTER TOSSING AND TURNING for hours, I fall asleep. A smoky jasmine scent unique to only one man filled my dreams. I arose several times during the night, drenched in sweat and breathless. While I didn't stay in Killian's chambers long enough to see how fast he recovered, I couldn't bear to close the door this time.

He's a bastard, and I hate him, but what if he called out for help in the night? What if nobody heard him?

As soon as I smell coffee, I poke my throbbing head out from beneath my covers. "Maius, I love you."

I don't see her, but that doesn't mean she isn't here. There is a common misconception because of their fae-given name, but the Brownies aren't brown. At least not all the time. They blend in with their surroundings, making them cooler than ninjas and chameleons combined.

The events of last night's alcohol-fueled bravery come flooding back, and I fear it will embarrass me for the rest of my life. I have two choices. Melt into this mattress or change my identity. Can I just live here now? In my bed. Unfortunately, my bladder feels like it could burst.

There go my dreams and aspirations.

I groan and drag my battered carcass to the bathroom. It's so awkward to pee. Have you ever noticed that? There you are, sitting in the silence, watching the paint peel off the walls, with your business all out in the open…

As I'm finishing up, I hear muffled voices echoing through my rooms. It's generally frowned upon to pee with the door open. According to Marlow, it should be illegal. But in this case, my lack of shame might just prove helpful.

"It's not supposed to be happening." I hear a warm female voice. It's Selene.

"We cannot ignore this. A single occurrence is just a coincidence. Maybe even two, but we're far beyond that. I think it's time to face the facts. The curse is attempting to kill both of them." A voice I don't recognize replies.

"No. There must be another explanation. This is not how the curse was created. The oracle was clear. It takes your true love." Selene says.

What the hell. True love? As if.

A troubling thought swells between my ears, something I should remember. Instead, my eyes go out of focus, and I'm transported back in time with Killian.

I am a bonded man, Genevieve.

And if I sent them away?

Only seconds have passed, and my vision returns. Is Killian my mate? No. That's not a real thing, is it? I think that's just for wolves. Do demons have mates? I don't know. That sounds kind of suspect. But then again, I grew up with vengeful sprites who hexed strangers in a coffee shop for entertainment. So I should know that stranger things exist. It's more believable that I just don't want to accept it.

Can someone who makes you want to commit homicide several times a week be your true love, though? Because that sounds toxic to me. Shouldn't it be all frolicking teapots and singing candlesticks? Prince Charming announces his intentions through a dancing montage? I don't know, something less tragic.

Only a vengeful god would decide that this prick is the perfect man for me and then tie our souls together so we can torment each other for eternity. On second thought? Yeah, that sounds about right.

Fuck.

Although I should be angrier about this revelation, the anger never comes. I think my other half, the darker half, already knew. He said as much last night. It's not his fault I didn't want to hear him. It makes sense, and nobody has ever said we'll like or even get along with our soulmates. There must've been a disclaimer somewhere in the user agreement about that. Probably next to the no return policy. No one ever reads those.

I take in a lungful of air and release it. Bringing my hands to my face. I'm not sure if I'll have a breakdown or maybe cry. But when a stifled giggle escapes my lips, I roll with that instead. I don't know how it happened, but within minutes, I'm laughing like a maniac with my hand over my mouth. The tears drip down my face, and my stomach clenches with the fits.

I just realized Killian was my mate while spying on the toilet. Signs from the mother fucking universe! I swear someone up there has sick a sense of humor, the dirty bastards. But I can respect that.

Despite the absurdity of it all, this was still a productive morning. I've learned more in fifteen minutes of accidental bathroom spying than I have the entire time I've been here. Like, actually valuable information.

Based on what I could overhear. After the bonding, Killian had a few accidents requiring healer's skills, and what a shocker... he hid them from me. However, my accidents have been fewer. There were no errant branches trying to remove my head or creatures straight from my most horrifying nightmares, scratching me with poison-tipped claws. So has Killian altered the curse? Or worse, taken it upon himself?

Selene's voice sounded worried. The words "since the binding" were mentioned during their hushed conversation, but I couldn't hear everything she said. The mystery deepens, I suppose. It *is* concerning that an immortal being can put their life on the line by loving somebody. They're supposed to be… immortal. But isn't the whole point of being immortal not dying?

There are some fucked up curses hovering over the Netherworld. These assholes don't mess around with their hexes. I can't just sit back and see what happens. What if the next attack is Killian's last? There must be a way around this.

Selene's words echo in my ears, "Haven't you ever read a fairytale, Genevieve? Curses are made to be broken."

———◆◯◆———

Once I've finished my coffee and stretched, I head toward the library. Whenever you have questions, the only logical person to find is Marlow. I have all the faith in the world that if answers can be found, my best friend will find them.

Inside the library, luxury floor-to-ceiling windows surround Marlow's office. Her walls are covered in mounted maps and art from lost civilizations. She wears an elegant white blouse and a sensible skirt. Having grown up with Boho Marlow, the change is jarring at first, but I love it.

Jagger leans over her shoulder, fascinated by whatever they're discussing. There's a good chance she's looking up the names of plants and creatures found in this new environment. Marlow's irrational fear is that she will get a rash or suffer an allergic reaction that will cause her throat to close. She's been obsessed with the problem since childhood, and that's how she copes. We're all afraid of something, right?

She's probably explaining the intricacies of anaphylaxis. By the green tint to Jagger's face, she's at the part where she describes the involvement of the mucous membranes. I've been in his shoes, and I have to give him credit. He's listening and validating her fixation like a champ. Sometimes her research gets creepy and unreasonably graphic. It warms my chest that my bestie bitch has found someone who loves her for who she is. It's like Jagger and her were grown on the same cloud. Weird as a fuck and dirty-minded as they come, both of them.

"Sorry to interrupt this sexy librarian fantasy, but I have a pressing request of our historian." I wink.

Amethyst's disembodied voice appears from out of nowhere. Her blonde waves hang around the edge of a far-off shelf. "I can pull some books!"

I look at Marlow, raising a brow in confusion. I swear, for being such a thick amazon baddie, Amethyst has the stealth of a fucking jaguar. Color me impressed, and a tad confused...

"Okay? That was weird. Anyway, I need you all to dig up anything you can find about this curse. It must have a name, an original text lying around somewhere, or the identity of the enchantress who cast it. I need to know everything."

Jagger's eyes bug out of his bearded face, and I can't deny the satisfaction in my soul at seeing his reaction. I've been thinking a lot about the truth lately. They say it sets us free, and I can get behind that. But I wonder if it also holds us captive? Everyone in this fortress has secrets. I can't speak for them, but I know mine has haunted me for years and made a mess of my life. So, I've decided... fuck secrets.

"I don't know everything, but I know enough, Lizard. Now put your eyeballs back inside your head before you have an aneurism." I smirk as I address Jagger's shock.

He adjusts his crazy eyes and closes his obnoxious mouth. That might be a first, but it's for the best.

"Amethyst, Sybil," I call out, knowing they're hidden between the stacks. Listening in like a couple of gossips. "I know you're both confused as fuck right now, but Marlow will explain the curse. I am grateful for any help you can offer."

Marlow's eyes shine with excitement, "You're going to break it!"

I nod in agreement. "I'm going to try."

"Anyway… Jagger. This was perfect timing because I was going to come to find you next. So, what are you up to today?" I offer a mischievous grin.

"What's up, Little Monster? More dastardly plans in motion?" he chuckles.

"I have a mission for you if you choose to accept it. This one might include some mild troublemaking." I wiggle my eyebrows and give him a saucy wink.

His face twists in something that resembles concentration. I wonder if it physically hurts him to think or if he plays it up to be funny? I think he does it to be a nuisance, so nobody takes him seriously. Crazy like a fox, this one.

Jagger eyes me suspiciously. "Does my brother know about this plan?"

"Does your brother need to know everything?"

"I guess not. If it's as devious as I think it might be? You know I'm in. I have to tell him, though." He replies.

"Tell me what?" Killian swaggers in looking like a million bucks.

How does he appear from thin air like that? He's like a spicy Houdini.

I see little point in trying to hide my intentions, so I turn to him and smirk. "We're going to drop a dismembered Grendel head in the Bone Keeps Courtyard. Say hi to dear old dad and return his lost property. Nothing crazy."

If you ever want to shut an entire room up, suggest dropping a giant severed head in the middle of someone's courtyard. Works like a charm.

"Can you expound upon that? Mostly the part where you said you want to drop a severed head in Mordred's courtyard." Killian asks.

"I said what I said."

Why do I need to explain myself to him? He does whatever he wants, no explanation necessary. Am I not the *Queen?* I don't have to say shit. And in theory, all that sounds good, but the argument that will surely follow makes my head hurt just thinking about it. It doesn't take long to decide it's not worth the dramatics. Plus, we've turned a new leaf, right? Everyone is telling the truth.

"Okay, fine. Mordred's greatest weakness is his ego. He gets high off the destruction he can create and the power he can steal. He won't be able to resist a challenge to his superiority complex. We don't sit and wait for the next attack. We bring the fight to him."

"Psychological warfare." Jagger nods appreciatively.

I nod. "We strike and wait for him to react. People like him are creatures of habit and more predictable than they seem. We have to push him far enough and make him so angry that his narcissism enters the chat. Then we can see who really lives behind the curtain."

"Is Kalli on board with this?" Amethyst asks, chewing her lip.

She must have come out of the shadows when I called her name. At first, it bothered me that Kalliope seems to have clicked with Amethyst and Sybil. When you've wanted something for so long and sacrificed so much only to be snubbed and then replaced, that shit hurts. But I can't deny the sense of peace it gives me that Kalli has someone to talk to.

"Kalliope won't accept the truths she needs to face, so she must see it for herself. I know it's important to be gentle with her after everything she's been through, Amethyst. But we don't have the time for much more of that. The truth may be painful, but it is always the right choice," I explain, giving Killian a pointed look.

No, I don't believe some truths are better off hidden, as he suggested last night. That's how people get hurt. That's how lives become endangered in a place like the Netherworld.

"She's gonna be pissed." Amethyst hisses through her teeth.

"Most likely." I shrug.

Yes, Kalliope is going to be jumbo pissed. But I'll show my sister the true monster living in the Bone Keep because I have to, and then we'll find out which path she will choose.

The looks I receive range from confusion to anger to enthusiastic smiles of agreement. *Ahem, Jagger...* he would probably jump into a volcano if it spiked his adrenaline. The man loves chaos. Anyway, I believe my job here is done. Marlow is on the case, along with Amethyst and Sybil. They'll come up with something I can work with.

Does Killian look pissed off? Thoughtful? Perhaps a little amused... it's hard to tell with Captain Mood Swing. So, I put very little thought into it. But all I need to do is pull one thread in this tangled web, and the rest will unravel. I know it in my bones.

"Jagger, go grab that Grendel head, dirty it up, and drop a package in the heart of the Bone Keep."

"That's it?" he questions. Like it's not dangerous enough.

"Don't get caught."

"I'm on it!" He kisses Marlow on the cheek and whistles a tune as he joyfully exits. Marlow and I exchange amused looks. That dragon is a certified lunatic, but he sure burrows under your heartstrings.

Kilian lingers in the doorway to the library as I finish writing my list. A guide for Marlow, Amethyst, and Sybil to get started. I'm interested in the origins of this supposed prophecy. I need to know more about that door and what's behind it. This curse needs to be dissected, and we need to figure out its inner workings and dismantle it, because Mordred is zeroing in, and right now, we do not know what he wants. Or why?

In my experience, it's dangerous to have a blind spot. Not knowing his motivations is a major disadvantage. How the fuck do you plan against an attack when you don't see the target? I silently thank Deacon for all those tedious hours of tactical instruction. I suspect he knew I'd need it someday.

I'm guessing *My King* won't be leaving soon. Since his stormy eyes and stupid, chiseled jawline won't get the fuck out of my peripheral vision. Doesn't he have work to do? A realm to run, perhaps? I mean, c'mon. How am I supposed to act like a badass when he's clouding the doorway with all of *that* going on? The sexy bastard.

"Is there something I can assist you with? Or has stalking become a fundamental pastime for you?" I ask.

"Would you mind putting your lethal tongue away for a moment and walking with me? There's something I'd like to show you." He half-grinned, mischief written on his lips.

"Fine, but on one condition," I say.

"Ah, trying that method again? Go on. I adore these *conditions* you keep demanding. I've thoroughly enjoyed the results." His eyes turn dark and highly unprofessional.

"Are you even supposed to be out of bed?" I roll my eyes.

"I am the King, and as you pointed out last night, I have responsibilities. Unless you'd like to accompany me back to my sickbed. I *could* be persuaded." He replies, dripping with incubus charm.

And it would have worked, it would have jump-started my libido like it always does, and I would have been struggling to fight against it. If it weren't for his use of the word: 'King.' My anger spikes at his haughty use of it. Yeah, he's the King, alright. To get there, he only had to be charming and give a few mind-blowing orgasms to some dumbass Demon Goddess to get there...

"Well, let's go see what you've got up your sleeve today, Stalker. Wouldn't want to take up too much of your time. I'm sure your court is waiting for you."

"It's your court too, Genevieve."

"Killian, the only way it will ever be my court is if I marry you for real, and I don't see that happening in our lifetime."

"Why is that?" He brings his fingers to his chin and rubs them against his stubble.

"Have you met yourself?" I laugh, and Killian responds with that maddening smirk I love to hate.

Old habits die hard, I suppose.

———◦◦◦———

We arrive at the remains of a dead garden. I stand looking at a rose bush encircled by an unkempt bed of thorns. A fountain stands on the front right side of the garden, although it might as well be a birdbath by now. A few messages are carved on stones scattered around the dirt, inviting visitors to read their stone-washed riddles. Even though that makes no sense, this place has a sense of familiarity.

Strange that Killian brought me here. It's been on my mind since I came across it days ago. "Who took care of this garden? What happened to them?" I ask as I try to move carefully around the remains.

Hexes can be hidden anywhere. All you have to do is trip one, and you are fucked with a capital F. I'm not taking any chances.

"It once belonged to the Goddess of Night, the Dark Goddess. Back when she spent a lot of time in the Netherworld." He replies.

"You knew her?!"

"Only in passing. But my father did, and my mother... if I tell you a secret, will you promise to keep it?" He moves around the dead vines, observing them as if they'll magically pop back to life at any moment.

"I'm feeling generous." I can't contain the snark, but I am curious. Killian voluntarily giving up a secret is such a rare event.

"I think my mother and the Dark Goddess practiced together. Here, in this garden."

"Like magic?" That is one profound secret. I couldn't imagine Selene tarnishing her light with the Queen of Darkness, The Mother of Witches... but it offers more pieces of the puzzle.

That night, the first time I saw Kalliope in the Great Hall. While I was standing on the dais next to the throne, Mordred made that speech about bringing me to the Shadowlands, and I feared the worst. But, a few seconds before the Dark Goddess burst through me like a demonic possession gone wrong, Selene whispered in my ear that I should trust her. Selene made the deal that solidified mine and Killian's betrothal. And she made it with the Dark Goddess, my ancestor. It never occurred to me that they were acquainted. I should have recognized it.

"I'm not sure how to respond to that."

Killian nods his head. "I assumed you'd be interrogating me about a curse and a door you shouldn't have been able to find. So how *did* you find it? The door, I mean."

I don't think anyone can blame me for the adrenaline that courses through my body at that question. Suddenly, this whole scene looks a little different. Killian is kind to me, offering secrets when he's always held them so tightly, taking me far from the fortress to a place filled with things that had once been alive. He knows I know about the door...

"Are you going to kill me?" I blurt.

"Kill you? I bring you to a place I believe you'll feel a connection to, and your first thought is that I'm going to murder you? I was trying to be romantic, Genevieve." He shakes his head, pulling his fingers through his unkempt hair.

"What do you mean, romantic? How the fuck am I supposed to know that? Your intentions haven't been pure with me. I don't know. Maybe I'm getting too close to the answers you want to hide?"

"And what is it you think I'm hiding?" he smirks.

"Why did you need me to agree to the binding, *my King? And don't you dare say it was for love.*" I snarl.

Killian's eyes fall to the ground, and a pained expression dominates his beautiful face.

"Nothing to say? Or maybe you just think I'm stupid. You'd be right, you know. About me being stupid. I was stupid enough to believe that you wanted to help me. Stupid enough to fall into your bed." My voice quiets, "Stupid enough to let you into my heart."

When he looks up again, his eyes are uninhibited thunderstorms.

"I have never wanted that throne, Genevieve! Do you think I desire the obligation of fixing everything my father ruined? Do you truly believe my life has never been my own? I never had a choice. And since I don't have a choice, the least I can do is a better fucking job than he ever did." Killian's voice booms.

"You think I don't know about choice? I've been someone's pawn my entire life! Cry me a river. Killian. So, they took your choice from you, and you think that gives you the right to steal mine? WHY?" I scream, tears streaming down my face.

He stands mute. The only indication he's heard me at all are the galaxies swarming under his lashes.

"WHY?!! Answer me, you fucking prick." I shout.

"You want to know why?" Killian laughs in that maniacal scientist type of way, taking a step toward me with each word. "I did it to save you!"

If Rowena were here, this would be the moment she would tell me to close my gaping mouth, or a mythical creature would steal my tongue. He's rendered me speechless, and that's not a simple task. Hurt, anger, confusion, and a crumb of foolish hope wage war just under the surface of my skin.

"Oh, and I suppose you saved me with your magical cock?"

Anger wins.

Killian closes the distance between us and holds my face in his hands. "I wanted to destroy you because of who you are, who your father is. I took you, and then I used you as bait to guarantee peace. I was going to hand you over, and I didn't care what happened. You were never my business, Genevieve. Only a means to an end. I couldn't do it when the time came to release you to Mordred. Not even for my realm."

I open my mouth to interrupt, and Kilian shakes his head.

"I tried to stay away from you, and when I wasn't strong enough to do that, I pushed you away. I treated you like a prisoner. I did it all so I could to make you hate me. I tried to pry you out from under my skin. None of it worked, and the moment I admitted it to myself, I cursed us both! To be a king, you must bond with a queen, it's true. That is customary in the Netherworld, but I didn't do it to control you, Genevieve. I bonded us to dampen my father's curse until I can break it. Because I can't lose you." He admits.

We stand in silence, eyes connected, breathing heavily but not making any moves toward each other. Neither of us trusts what may happen if we do.

"You could have told me instead of breaking my heart repeatedly. Pulling me back in and then pushing me away. You could have trusted me, but you wrapped yourself in lies, leaving me alone in the darkness to fend for myself. How am I supposed to forget that?"

"I don't want you to forget it, Genevieve." He drops his guard and stares into my eyes, his soul laid bare, and my knees shake.

I'm no dummy. There's more to this story, but it only takes one look into his turquoise depths, and I know he's finally telling me his truth. I no longer know if it's enough, but Killian does love me.

CHAPTER EIGHT

VIVI

THERE'S NOTHING QUITE LIKE the night sky in the Netherworld, where the universe spins backward. It's like someone poured ink on a canvas and then shook it. Stars dance across the pitch-black backdrop, glowing like embers in a fire or rubies. Great shimmering rubies. The faint red glow permeates the shadows in my soul. I could stay on this balcony, wrapped in the finest silk sheets, for many lifetimes.

Killian brings a cherry cola with him, leaning into me as he sets the glass on the table. His warm chest presses against my back and strong hands lean on my bare shoulders. I could stay like this for many lifetimes, as well.

We haven't worked all of our shit out, and neither of us knows what the future holds for the Netherworld or for us. We disagree about practically everything, but there are two things we can finally agree on. First, we must show a united front when fighting against evil in the Shadowlands.

And we're done battling this thing between us. Curse or no curse, the bonding strengthens us when we're together. We don't have trust, not yet. And I'm sure the universe means to tear us to shreds before it gives us any happiness, despite all that. We will fight this evil side by side. What comes after will just have to meet us at the finish line.

It turns out Killian doesn't mind telling secrets at all, especially in the bedroom. Not only have the Netherlings within the fortress suppressed their natural eating habits for more earthling-friendly options because of me, but did you know they hold court at night? At night! This whole time, an entire fucking kingdom has been traveling in the middle of their bedtime (daytime) to accommodate their queen from the Earth Realm, and I never even knew it. Have you ever heard of such nonsense? If we weren't in the position we were in when he told me, the outcome might have been much more flammable. Because seriously, who does that?

I feel like the biggest asshole, and I owe this whole realm an apology for having to adjust their lives to suit me. Since I can't apologize individually, the next best thing is to change it. Starting now, today. If I am to be the Queen of the Netherworld (false or otherwise), I will adapt to accommodate *them*. A leader is the humble servant of their people, not the other way around.

It's not really Killian's fault he doesn't understand how things are supposed to work. He's from a different realm. Or rather, I'm from a different realm. It doesn't matter. I'll teach him to be a more compassionate leader, and he can teach me how Netherworld politics work. It will come in handy for me to run the Bone Keep with Kalliope when the time comes.

"Are you ready to hold court, my queen?" Killian's silky voice caresses my insides.

"Well, I'm almost ready." I smile seductively as I stand, dropping the silk sheet. My naked body bathed in crimson starlight. "But I need a promise."

Swaying my hips across the narrow walkway, I round the corner of the terrace to a magical invention called a private outdoor shower. I'm afraid it has spoiled me for an eternity. Entering the open-air alcove, I grasp the elaborate iron handles and twist until warm rain floods from the oversized showerhead above. It's like showering in the rain, under the stars.

"And what sort of promise do you require, Love?" Killian says, standing at the entrance.

Love? I pin him with a sharp stare and smile with my teeth. "You will never lie to me again. I am gifted, forged from war, and if you betray me again, I'll cut that beautiful cock off and mount it near my bedside table."

I feel his electrical energy before I sense his warmth creeping up behind me. That delicious ache between my thighs bursts to life. He pushes his body against my back, guiding us toward the stones.

"Is that so?" He growls.

My chest heaves with the need for him to fill me. "It is."

Pressing my aching breasts against the soft rock wall with his body, Killian brings his lips to my ear and rumbles a seductive promise. "I'll give you anything you want. How shall I apologize?"

"You can start by washing my feet." I tease.

"No, Kitten. I don't think I will. I'd rather tattoo my name on your soul while I worship every inch of your body." His chest rumbles as he urges his hardness against me.

I hum in agreement because my vocal cords have stopped working along with the bones in my knees and my internal thermometer. *But, goddess, this man is addictive.*

Killian's arm snakes around my stomach, applying gentle pressure with the palm of his hand. Fire blooms in the wake of his touch, and then he slowly lowers himself, placing kisses across my wet skin all the way down my back. When I feel the heat of his breath on my throbbing sex. When I lose my footing, he's there to steady me.

"Grab the wall." Killian groans before placing his sinful mouth between my thighs.

The thought of Killian on his knees behind me, on his knees *for* me, makes me feral with need. His mouth closes around my swollen clit, and I writhe, sensitive and scorching with heat. Then, finally, my hands give way, and my body thrusts forward into the wall. The sting against my chest, mixed with the assault of pleasure between my legs unexpectedly sends me over the edge.

Then, with no warning, I'm coming undone for him. I feel as if he's exposed every nerve at once. I don't think I can handle even one more touch without my spirit escaping my body.

"Killian." His name sounds like a prayer to my lips.

His laugh is dark and wicked as he replies. "Don't move."

He stands, running his expert hands across the skin of my back until I can feel him at his full height. His fingers dig into my hips, and he turns me around—and I drop to my knees, taking his hardness into my hands. Disobeying him. Killian groans, and that sound makes me absolutely feral. I flick my tongue against his tip, watching his eyes close and his head fall back.

"Do you like this, my king?" I hiss, running my tongue along the backside of his erection.

His eyes meet mine, dark as night. And he growls, giving me all the answers that I need. I take him inside my mouth, slowly guiding him into the back of my throat. Never letting my eyes leave his. I want to watch what I'm doing to him, the muscles in his stomach tensing, every erotic expression that crosses his face. I want to see it all. My mouth wraps back around him, and I move faster.

"Oh, fuck. Kitten… your mouth feels too good." he moans and pulls himself out. Slamming me against the rock wall as he lifts me in the air. Instinctively, I wrap my legs around his waist. Grinding my wetness against him with abandon.

"Please." I moan, and my legs shake with need.

Killian lines himself up and thrusts hard. "Mine, Genevieve. I'm going to fuck you so hard you'll feel me in every lifetime."

My mouth captures his as he pounds into me, tongues mimicking each stroke harder than the last. Tension builds in my core, and I clench around him, throwing my head back.

"Not yet, Kitten." He grunts as he moves inside me like a man possessed. His tongue moves to my neck as me takes me hard, and I gasp with the intensity of my body shivers. Killian clamps on my neck, and he bites down and then whispers. "Come for me."

And I scream, my body igniting in violet flames, engulfing us both.

⎯⎯⎯⎯◇⎯⎯⎯⎯

This evening's dress leaves my shoulders bare, flowing into a delicate scoop neckline that highlights my breasts. The tight fit is slightly uncomfortable, but the slit revealing my smooth leg up to my thigh makes me feel powerful.

Killian is seated on his throne, clad in a midnight suit jacket that fits him like a glove, just like a tailored fucking glove. The wildly inappropriate thoughts racing through my mind make my mouth water and skin prickle. His smoky jasmine scent reaches me right to the core, and all I want to do is feel him on top of me. Inside me.

Who is this man, and what has he done to me? I'm like a succubus in heat.

Killian leans into my body. "I can still taste you on my lips."

My cheeks burn, and my panties have morphed into a slip and slide. Is this what he's like when he's not hiding things from me? Because holy shit, Killian is dominant, and the confidence he exudes while saying filthy, sexy, forbidden things to me… whew.

A buzz of exhilaration envelops the Great Hall. Perhaps that's because the court is holding according to their customs once again. They must feel relieved to get back to normal, and, to some extent, I think it builds their trust that I have accepted their lifestyle.

Have I accepted it?

I hold on to Killian's hand, and he stands. He fills the room with a boom in his voice. "Citizens of the Netherworld, my queen and I invite you to our court. Please proceed."

The room quiets as they bow and form an unorganized line, waiting their turn to address Killian. And now, I guess me too.

Even though I have sat in court with Killian before, this is the first time I have done so in the middle of the night. As compared to previous situations, tonight is relatively mild. Just another typical day at the office. They robbed centaurs of hay, a changeling was on the loose, and a wild pack of teenagers vandalized a portion of the forest. The strange nature of Netherworld crimes is becoming more familiar to me, so I am not as inclined to giggle as I used to be.

I'm just about to have an inner yawn when two guards burst through the door with Anise in tow. A man with a severe widow's peak and a nasty scowl follow them. I turn a questioning eye to Killian.

"What is the meaning of this?" Killian calls out to his guards.

Anise is quiet, and I'm taken aback by the lack of screeching and kicking. She stands before us with her cherry-red hair an absolute mess, and her head hung low. Which immediately activates my 'I'll cut a bitch' reflex. What did this asshole do to her?

"Your Majesty." The tall, ugly man addresses Killian and *only* Killian. But, judging by the change in eye color, the subtle jab at me didn't escape his notice.

"First, you enter the hall with my sister in chains. Then, you insult my queen. Mr. Pavonis, I suggest you get to the point and do it fast before I lose my patience." Killian's words hold a threatening tone.

"He cornered me in the hallway and put his hand under my dress without my consent, so I took over his mind and made him squeeze his balls until he screamed and pissed himself." Anise interrupts.

Her face is resigned, her posture stiff. I don't understand. Mr. Pavonis is a fucking pervert, and he got what he deserved. What is the problem?

"I formally charge Anise of the Night Fortress with the crime of using her Siren Spell to cause harm." Pavonis sneers, looking pleased with himself.

This is a fucking joke, right?

Molesters are the scum of the universe. They don't deserve mercy. He's lucky it wasn't me, because I'd have torn his dick off and fed it to Calypso.

I'm surprised to find him upright. Anise isn't known for having patience or forgiveness. What am I missing? I glance over at Killian, and the look on his face makes my stomach drop. He's clenching his jaw so hard I'm afraid it might crack.

We're serious right now? Anise is in real danger of being punished for this. What the fuck? My nerves unravel as I hold my breath, waiting for Killian to say something.

"Do you have a witness?" Killian's rage is barely restrained.

"This guard witnessed the assault." Mr. Pavonis replies.

Jagger shifts behind our matching thrones, the thrum in his chest getting louder by the second. Dante and Bane stand creepily still, unblinking. Where is Lincoln?

"He's on patrol, my queen." A voice echoes inside my head. That's Dante.

When Anise shakes, I can't take it any longer. I stand, giving Mr. Pervert Dickface a glare that could melt steel. There is no way this will happen, not while I'm standing here. Over my dead, fucking body.

"Mr. Pavonis." My voice carries through the Hall. "Do you deny the attempted sexual assault of a member of the king's family?"

"My Queen, this urchin is not of noble blood." He replies.

"That is not what I asked," I reply with all the menace I'm battling.

The man doesn't know how close he is to death. My blood heats and the flames from deep inside me stir. This motherfucker thinks he can feel up on my friend and then have her punished when she kicks his ass for it? Sentenced to… wait, I don't know what the punishment is.

"What is the sentence for the use of a Siren Spell?" I ask.

"Fifty lashes." Killian bites out.

Oh, I think the fuck not!

My pulse goes erratic. I may hyperventilate. Willing Anise to look at me, I stare at her gorgeous face. It takes a moment, but she lifts her eyes. When she acknowledges me, I push my emotions toward her with all my might.

I will not let this happen.

"May I have a moment to speak to you in private?" I address Killian.

His eyes go wide, so I'm guessing that's an unusual request, but a quick dip of his chin says he'll humor me. We both walk to the side of the hall into a small chamber room. The moment we're both out of hearing range, I lose my shit.

"Killian, you can't do this! She's tough, but she's too fragile for this. Her mind will fracture… please do something!" I'm shouting in my desperation.

"I am Dark King of the Netherworld. This is the law. I cannot show leniency, especially to my sister. I cannot ignore this." He hangs his head, eyes rimmed with red.

"And he gets nothing? He confessed! Your sister defends herself against an attack, and she faces the whip. But he gets nothing?! What the fuck? Can you change laws, Killian? This one has GOT to go. I'm so fucking serious." I stop to catch my breath. "This is not happening. I don't give a shit what we need to do. I will burn him where he stands before that whip ever touches her skin. Test me! Just fucking test me."

The killing calm settles over me.

Jagger pokes his head in. "Everything okay in here?"

"Yes." "No." Killian and I both answer at the same time.

"Okay then, well, they're getting restless out here." His forehead creases as he backs away. "You're on fire, little monster."

I am? Shit.

I look down at my ruined dress and sigh. I don't know why I even bother at this point. Selene really should have my dresses made from flame-resistant materials.

"Are you going to do this?" I bring my attention back to Killian.

"I have to." He looks stricken.

"I will take her place."

"You will not!" He looks at me with a seething rage.

"I can handle it. Anise doesn't deserve this. You love her too much, Killian. You're the only thing she has. You are her hero! Look at Kalliope and me. I fight to have what you and Anise have. Don't break it, Killian. Don't break her." My eyes are welling up now.

The silence is deafening. Shadows fill the room as the war rages inside his mind.

"As the Queen, can I do this? Legally. Can I take her place?" I interrupt his brooding.

He hesitates before answering, "The Dark Queen of the Netherworld has the power to make that determination under special circumstances."

"Then it's settled. This is a special fucking circumstance, Killian! Anise will confess, and I will accept the sentence on her behalf. End of story."

"No!" He sets his jaw. I will not sway him.

After several more minutes of intense debate, Killian and I compose ourselves and return to the great hall. Where it is getting out of hand. While we were arguing it out privately, the rest of the court was doing the same, but publicly. And it's no surprise Lincoln Blackwood is in the center of it all, teeth bared and ready to fight.

I knew he felt something for Anise. I fucking knew it! If we were in different circumstances, that thought would make me smile, but what he's going to hear next won't help the situation in the least.

"Bane? I have a favor to ask of you. I need you to get Anise, Lincoln, and Calypso out of this Hall. Right now."

"My Queen?" Bane questions.

"No time to explain. Just please get them out." I plead.

Killian stands at the edge of the platform. The crowd pays him no attention. The argument is too heated. Electricity fills the air, and the hair on my arms stands at attention. Blue streaks crackle above their heads, an obvious threat, and the crowd settles.

I whisper to Killian. "It's time."

"Silence!" Killian booms, and the hall quiets. "Anise, do you confess?"

"Did I use my powers to make him squeeze the shit out of his tiny balls? Yes, but I was captured before I could remove them and have a snack." She replies.

That's disturbing as fuck, but perfect for an insanity defense.
I guess that's my cue. I stand next to Killian, head held high. "Anise, we have deliberated and found you guilty."

A mixture of horrified gasps and savage cheers breaks out.

Holding my hand up, I make the universal signal to stop. "I am not finished! You are guilty of your crime, but we have determined that you are unfit to receive your sentence. Therefore, I will act as a proxy."

If I thought the crowd was rabid before, I was mistaken. Anise looks like she's about to go nuclear, and the only thing I can do is make eye contact with Linc. I know he's fucking fuming right now, but I hope his feelings for Anise supersede his protectiveness of me. I beg with my eyes.

Go with her. Take her and Calypso somewhere safe.

As I move down the steps and onto the execution block, I realize I'm glad they have holed Kalliope up in her rooms since our last encounter. I'm not sure how she would feel about this. Part of me holds hope it would upset her. On the other hand, the more logical side of me says she'd pull up a lawn chair and crack a beer for the show. Either way, she should be elsewhere. Marlow, Amethyst, and Sybil are sound asleep.

As I sink to my knees, my heart breaks.

"Queen Genevieve, our realm has long awaited a powerful ruler to stand beside its King. One who not only protects our citizens on the battlefield but inside the halls of this fortress as well. You have shown bravery, but you have also reminded us that mercy is not a sign of weakness. For that, I reduce the sentence to twenty lashes." Killian announces to the room.

Brave my ass. I'm shaking in my fucking heels, which I decide to remove for this. Call me strange, but something about these gorgeous red-bottomed heels witnessing something so brutal makes my stomach clench. I think my brain is trying to escape what it knows is coming.

Bending over the block, I feel the first lash across my back, and it's hot. The next few lashes sting my skin like razor blades cutting my body. I've broken out in a cold sweat when I reach the fifth. Every time a lash penetrates deeper into my skin, I feel the urge to cry out, but I remain silent. The tenth lash finds me staring holes through Mr. Pavonis, imagining all the ways I could torture him to death.

The agony is unbearable, and I crumble to the ground. Struggling to regain my strength as I feel Killian's misery through our binding. His pain gives me the boost I need, stumbling back up to my knees. Tears stream down my cheeks as I shake and sweat, but I remain silent. Lashes sixteen and seventeen blur my vision, and my body convulses.

Death would be kinder than this.

I have been tortured, beaten nearly to death, and experienced many unspeakable horrors. But I have experienced nothing like this.

Killian delivers the final crack, and my knees give way, causing me to fall. Unable to move, unable to breathe. With the cold stone against my cheek, I struggle to stay conscious. Before losing the fight to stay aware, the last thing I hear is a blood-curdling battle scream.

The smell of electrical fire fills my nose, and the world goes dark.

CHAPTER NINE

KALLIOPE

EVEN AFTER EVERYTHING I have done to prove to my father that I am not a mistake. I believe he has betrayed me. Is he really leaving me with his enemies? As if I were yesterday's garbage. Could it be that I am here to complete a mission? A mission I do not know of. There are no false pretenses in my case. I am aware Genevieve is his favorite, his greatest accomplishment. I am the failed prototype, the wrong sister.

My mother's power was not strong enough to create what he was seeking, and she paid for that with her life. I miss my mother, what little memory I have left of her. She was the only person I felt safe and loved around. The time for that is long gone. I've learned to survive on my wits and sheer willpower. The palace that raised me knows only one truth: power is everything. And those who lack it? Perish. Either by weakness or stupidity. I am neither of those things.

It's strange to be inside the dreaded Night Fortress. Other than the fact that it is the one place I never thought I would find myself, it is not as horrifying as I first imagined. This is quite contrary to everything I've learned about the other side of the bridge. Father's enemy is brutal. Evil by definition. He slaughters for power, for entertainment. He is the son of The Dark One himself, and he is ruthless.

This is my understanding of The Dark King's son. This…
Killian. Yet, I hear no screams echoing through the halls. I
see no Shadowling bodies hanging from the ramparts.

My nerves are frayed. Is there anyone here I can trust? Not
a chance with most, but two witches have been friendly to
me. I am treated as a guest in this gilded room, with all
the finery I can imagine, rather than a traitor. My rooms
have never been entered without my consent. I have not been
punished, abused, or assaulted. This makes no sense, and I
remain suspicious.

One or both silver-haired men guard my door. Initially,
I thought they would be the first to enter my rooms and
harm me at night, but after days and days… still nothing. I
am unscathed. I am greeted with courtesy by the fascinating
men who stand outside my space. It's almost as if they guard
me rather than keep me hostage.

The one called Bane sometimes speaks to me with the
same power I possess. He enters my head, telling me stories
unlike those I've known since birth. He mentions my sister,
as well as his king. Praises them. I find it infuriating. As if all
I've ever known has been a lie, as if I don't even know my
mind. I'm tempted to think these handsome men are capable
of mind control, but my mental shields are ironclad; I've
yet to encounter a Shadowling who could penetrate them,
including my father. I doubt a lowly Netherling could do it.

Aside from one. Genevieve, the "Daughter of Oracles,"
is father's ultimate weapon. Her power can penetrate my
defenses. She can do more than that, but she hasn't yet
unleashed her potential. Does she realize that her blood holds
the key to complete control of this world and all those
that follow? The sorceress Morgana, the sister of my father,
supervised the process. Naturally, father was right by her side.
However, I know something neither of them knows…

I can feel electricity crackling at my fingertips. My sister is all he cares about. I am torn between hating her for everything he did to me or hating her for the freedom she gained by slipping through his grasp. The freedom I never had. I don't know why I hate her so much. I just know I always have.

She sat by your side, Kalliope. She never left, even when you pushed her away…

My thoughts chase themselves in unending circles. Father never told me the item he needed from this fortress. Yet, I just know it's here. Am I meant to find it, or is my fate already sealed? My stomach sinks at the thought of what my intuition tells me.

Does my sister realize she's a weapon? Can she see she's a pawn? While I pace the red and gold-trimmed room, I notice the differences from my lodgings at home. This is a far cry from the darkness I spent my life in. Instead, I occupy a stark, black chamber in The Bone Keep. Aside from one item, which is hidden where no Shadowling can find. Here, I have toiletries. A television. Things to read, and even a set of charcoals and paper to draw.

I've never told a soul that I love to sketch. Did Genevieve steal it from my mind? I worry that this kindness is a distraction. Or worse, it's like father's tea - steeped by his dark witch. Designed to control.

I stand in the fancy bathroom attached to my sleeping quarters, taking it in. What I wouldn't give to climb into this obsidian tub and soak for hours. I've never had such a luxury. Which is why I'm convinced they have spelled it. I've seen the Goddess that lives here. I've noted her power level, as well.

They aim to drain me of my magic, and that tub is my first suspicion.

The proximity to my sister and everything about this fortress fogs my brain. It tests my loyalty. I grow more curious and less determined to destroy her every day. What kind of woman is this who speaks of sisterhood? Of family? I haven't been able to figure out what she wants. What's her angle? We argue day after day, but she assures me she wants me by her side. And she wants nothing to do with father. In fact, she wants to destroy him.

Is that it? Is this another one of father's tests? He is obsessed with loyalty; his paranoia consumes him. He tests everyone in his circle. Nobody knows when it's coming. But if they fail? Their life is forfeited. I can't let my guard down. I've already done so twice, and that will not escape punishment when I am called back to the Bone Keep. If I am called back…

My senses register my jailer's absence outside the door now. Should I risk it? Am I allowed to leave these rooms? I am filled with questions, and my curiosity gets the best of me. I discovered a cloak in my closet days ago. I could cover myself. My face would be hidden. Perhaps I could spy on those around me. Father would surely reward me if I learned something of value.

As always, I am driven by curiosity. I rush to the closet, searching through the fancy dresses and tactical clothing until I find the dark cloak and pull it over my shoulders. Taking meticulous care to conceal my face. The moment my hand touches the doorknob, I feel uneasy.

<hr />

The Netherlings are holding court. I watch from under the cloak in the back of the hall. Listening intently. I must admit, the court in the Netherworld is dreadfully dull. Stolen hay, land disputes, rogue teens, and vandalism. Again, nothing like I had expected. I think of heading back upstairs. Amethyst is asleep, but the thing they call television is more entertaining than this…

Really, no bloodshed? Not even one beheading. Lame.

I turn to leave, disappointed by the intelligence I've gathered, when I hear a commotion. I spin on my heel to see the crimson siren dragged by guards into the hall. Netherling guards. Now, this is interesting! How will this noble King handle the accusations? Does he execute his sibling? Does he show mercy?

Despite being a Netherling, I like this red siren. I've heard the rumors of her broken mind, the bastard daughter of a dead siren whore. She's feisty, feral, and violent. In another life, we could be friends. It will be a shame to watch her perish. This scrawny man lies. I can feel it on my tongue. The siren will pay for naught, but such is the way of our realm.

My thoughts are interrupted by a blast of murderous power, and my eyes are immediately drawn to Genevieve. I snarl in a fury at her distress. My chest tightens. It has happened to me more than once. I don't understand this reaction. Though we might not be friends, our monsters are connected. Hers is pacing, raging, and erupting. As I mirror her, my thirst for violence intensifies… she whispers to her King. His face tightens, and they both stand, leaving the thrones empty. That has never happened in the Shadowlands. Does she question him openly? Is she challenging a king in front of his court? This seems unwise. Is she craving death? Maybe she's more unbalanced than I realized.

My monster does not like this uneasiness.

In their absence, the crowd grows rabid. Fights break out. A gargoyle and a basilisk exchange heated words. Groups form behind each, picking sides. It seems this court is divided. I tuck that information away for later, watching it unfold. Of course, father will want this information. A smirk forms on my lips. Today isn't so wasteful after all.

As a voice booms throughout the hall, I am struck by The Dark Prince's power. It is staggering... supercharged. I detect Genevieve's power mingled with Killian's forceful persuasion. It seems they are soul-bound. Father underestimates this king, and it will be to his detriment. The situation is much more complicated than it appears. The Gods have meddled here.

When Genevieve remains standing, my body stills, and my blood ices over. I search her face. What I find there makes my skin shudder... resolve. I see the bull-headed resolve in her lavender eyes. By the Goddess, what has she done?

Genevieve steps to the platform's edge and attracts the red sirens' attention. Something passes between them. In an instant, the siren is being dragged out by the silver-haired men, followed by the wolf and the shadow beast. Time slows. Genevieve removes the shoes from her feet and descends the steps, kneeling at the execution block. My monster stews and I must take extra care to keep myself concealed.

The false king speaks. My heart speeds up in my chest. The misery emanating from him was suffocating. Can nobody else sense it? Panic grips me as my sister tenses. What did he say? I was distracted by the unfamiliar sensations battling within me. I missed it. And then I see the cat-o'-nine-tails hanging limply in his hand.

An emotion I cannot identify fills my heart. Tears fill my vision. I cannot understand them. I think my heart will burst into pieces; my mind will surely break. Genevieve is willing to accept this punishment to keep the red siren safe? She would endure the pain at the hands of her soul bound to protect her people. That is not possible. I have never witnessed such a selfless act. Suddenly, I am filled with a strange sensation. It's as if my heart has opened and something crawled inside.

She crossed into the Shadowlands to save me…

A resounding 'crack' echoes through the hall, cleaving the silence. My muscles are tense as Genevieve bites back a scream. Another wet-sounding lash has my monster pacing within me. With every sound of the whip, my rage grows. Minutes pass slowly and quickly at the same time. Genevieve's back is flayed open, and tears mar her face. I'm ready to do whatever is necessary to end her pain. I move within range to strike the false king, but the determination on Genevieve's face gives me pause.

The Dark Prince looks as if he'll be sick. This is not the monster who revels in the pain of others. This is not the beast who ravages his subjects for entertainment. The anguish at doling out her lashes is written plainly in his features. No, this isn't punishment. This is a show of power, the public unveiling of their untested queen, and her first act of leadership is mercy at her own expense. I cannot interrupt.

I train my eyes on my sister's withering frame. Blood flows from her flayed skin. She'll lose consciousness soon. Lash fifteen, sixteen, seventeen, eighteen… Genevieve sways and then rights herself, still fighting to stay lucid. Still showing her willpower for all to see. This is unbearable to watch. My palms twitch, and my insides boil. I follow Genevieve's line of sight. What is her focal point? What's keeping her awake and defiant through this exhibition? And then I see where she stares with malice in her eyes. The ugly man smirks with satisfaction at her pain and humiliation.

My control splinters.

Without a thought, I throw back my hood, revealing my presence. Stalking ever closer to where my sister lies brutalized in front of the Netherling court. If I can't save her from this, I will make him wish he had never been born.

My power gathers in my palms, filling the space with the calm before the storm. The scent of ozone fills the air as exhilaration fills my bones, building... building...

Genevieve falls to her hands on the bloodied stone, struggling to pull herself back up and failing. An inhuman growl erupts from my body and electricity dances across my skin. Then I consume the perverted motherfucker from the inside out. Frying his organs as he feels every nerve ending turn to dust. A smile gathers upon my lips as the Netherling guards tackle me to the ground.

CHAPTER TEN

VIVI

I AWOKE YESTERDAY MORNING, blissfully satisfied and at the center of Killian's expert attention; I never imagined in a million years that it would end in my very public display of insanity. One of my greatest weaknesses is that I can't stand by and watch my loved ones suffer. And now, every creature in the Netherworld knows that about me.

My eyes are heavy. Even my hearing feels muted. Am I drugged? Spelled? I have been in and out of consciousness, so far as I can tell. How long has it been? My blankets are infused with the aroma of smoky jasmine, so I know *he* has been here, between my sheets. The thought of that somehow excites and unnerves me all at once. Was he wrapped around me like a protective cocoon? Or did he spend his time brooding about something I gave him no choice in?

It was Anise or me. I knew Killian wouldn't have the strength to punish Anise without hating himself afterward. Of course, he hates himself now, but it's nothing compared to what he would feel if he had broken their bond. He is everything to her: a savior and a hero. If I had to do it over again, I would. Anise is worth every ounce of pain.

Not that I'm feeling anything but stiff and a little sore. Thanks to a shitload of Killian's healers, I imagine.

So, what happens now? If I move, if I open my eyes, I'll have to deal with reality. I'd rather bathe in griffin shit than face any of them. Not until the stink of dumbfuckery wears off me. *Maybe I could pull a Sleeping beauty minus the enchanted kiss.*

"Open your eyes, Bitchface. I know you're awake by the way your fingers are twitching." Marlow's voice is filled with amusement.

"Unfair home-court advantage," I grumble and pull the covers over my head.

"Come on now, Warrior Princess. We all know you don't have any sense of self-preservation. Out you come." Lincoln's comedian voice is back, and I'd tell you I love that for him, but he may be suffocated first. He grins and whips the blankets around, exposing my shameful 'PJs and lunacy' look.

"I hate you both." I groan, over-exaggerating the amount of pain I'm in.

The smell of mocha and magic beans drifts into my nostrils as Marlow smirks. "I guess this mocha latte is for someone else then. I bet we could get Kalliope addicted to the nectar of the Gods."

"Shut it, Hooker." I smile, realizing I do not know how long it's been since I've brushed my teeth. They're probably wearing fuzzy sweaters by now. Whatever, I grab the coffee anyway.

We'll just add that to the mortal embarrassment list…

Now that I've crawled out of the pit of despair hidden within my bedsheets, I scan my room. It's just Marlow and Linc, both staring down at me like I've gone batshit.

"Sorry to interrupt this lovely intervention, but where is everyone?" I ask.

It turns out a lot has transpired while I was unconscious. That electrical smell I remember just before losing consciousness was my sister. Taking a page from *my* playbook and electrocuting people to death in the middle of the great hall. Well, not people: a pervert. Which concerns me and makes my heart swell with pride at the same time.

Being a mysterious woman from the Shadowlands didn't work in Kalliope's favor. Words like 'traitor' and 'Shadowling whore' were thrown around, which landed her in a cell for a night. Until Anise broke her out, got caught, and was now in the middle of an epic banshee-style meltdown. According to Lincoln, it must be impressive because it's kept all four of her brothers busy for about two hours.

"Is Kalli okay?" I ask.

"She's fine. Anise has been kicking the shit out of your *husband* up and down the halls for putting Kalliope in a cell in the first place, and she's pissed that he whipped her friend. So, they all have their hands full right now. Kalli's been holed up in her rooms with Amethyst and Sybil for hours." Marlow fills me in.

There goes that pang of jealousy again. I still wish it was me she wanted to bond with, but I'm glad she's not alone. Anise, on the other hand? That's fucking hilarious, and Killian deserves it… a little. Girl power and all that. I note the fingers tensing in Linc's hands, and my heart hop-skips. There's really something there between him and Anise. It's clearly killing him. He's not there to soothe her. I can see it in his body language. I can feel the tension he's trying to suppress in the air.

"Lincoln Blackwood! Why don't you just come out and tell her you love her already? Make that shit official. Then it could be you holding her right now, calming her, loving her back into herself. I always said you were perfectly made for someone and that someone is Anise." Tears form in the corners of my eyes, and I wipe them quickly. "I'm not crying because I'm mad about it, by the way. You have my wholehearted blessing, Wolf."

His face softens, and I know it's about to get sappy, but for once, that's okay.

"From the first day we met, you took good care of me, Viv. You were there when I didn't have a dime to my name or a shirt for my back. You loved me when I was the most unlovable. And you were right. I misunderstood that love. The day you stepped into the portal, and away from Killian, I realized it. When I saw the pain on your face, I knew you weren't mine, but I didn't want to accept it. Now someone looks at me like that. The way I always wished you would. She lets me protect her, but she can stand on her own. Her mind is a mysterious place that few can comprehend. She's everything I never knew I needed. Fuck, I think I'm beginning to trust all this destiny crap after all." Linc gives me one of his quirky smiles, and something in my chest clicks into place.

Peace.

Linc leans in to give me a gentle hug, and I whisper. "What are you waiting for? Go get your girl."

Once he's left the room, I scoot closer to Marlow, groaning at the soreness leftover in my back. My nerves are so raw, and I've missed her so much. I want a moment of the old days, back in the apartment. Drinking tequila and watching trash tv, laughing at each other's stupid jokes.

Everything that's happened in such a short time, it's changed us both in ways that defy explanation. I don't even recognize my former self. That short-tempered, jaded girl with a chip on her shoulder the size of the moon. I thought the world owed me something for everything I'd endured, and now I understand how life works. It's beautiful, and it's complicated. Most of the time, it's just plain messy and painful. But even if we can't see them etched on their skin, everyone has battle scars.

Marlow wears them in her eyes now, and instead of making her appear broken, I see the quiet strength behind that dirty mouth and quick wit. Every blow strengthens her. We lay watching a movie I couldn't care less about for a few moments, saying farewell to the old life we'll never have again. Savoring just one more minute before we must travel back to reality and face our real-world problems. When the credits start rolling, I turn to my best friend. My voice lowers because I'm not sure who may be listening...

"Tell me what you found."

"How did you know I found something?" Marlow asks.

"Come on now, we've been friends since childhood. I know that sparkle in your eye. You have a secret, and it's a good one, by the looks of it. I'm guessing it's curse, door, or prophecy related. Unless you handed the vCard to Daddy Dragon?" I smile, and Marlow's cheeks redden.

"Did you use the vCard, Marlow Culpepper?!" I exclaim.

"No, well, not like the *whole* card."

"So, a partial card? Interesting." I smirk. "Which part?"

"We found some information." Marlow changes the subject.

And just when it is getting entertaining...

"Okay, fine, keep your secrets." I laugh.

According to Amethyst, the prophecy is sketchy. Like, really sketchy, and thousands of years old. Now, that's not saying it isn't about Kalli and me, but if it is? It's almost impossible to decipher what's the original text and what's hearsay. There wasn't a lot of writing going on back then. Information was passed down by mostly word of mouth. So, it's a dead end. Or a nonfactor. Unless it comes up to one of us and introduces itself, we can't be sure.

Well, that sucks, but there's better news.

The curse has a little more information. Unfortunately, the most essential parchment they found was flimsy, and some words were indecipherable. Still, Amethyst and Sybil gathered enough clues to put some chess pieces in motion. Basically, it's the Sleeping Beauty spell on steroids, mixed with a bit of death and destruction. Any witch who's powerful enough to pull it off forfeits their life when the curse is completed. And it's not like they immediately drop dead. Instead, they live their lives knowing death is around the corner, and it always finds them.

"That's wicked evil," I comment.

"Seriously, next-level shit, but there's a purpose for that. The death of the caster cements the spell." Marlow adds. "Like a human sacrifice."

"Death magic? DARK blood magic?!" I clarify.

"Bingo." Marlow's forehead creases.

"Damn, that's outlawed everywhere, in every realm. So, how do I get around it?" I grin.

Marlow smiles. "You can't. There is no way around it. That's why it requires a living sacrifice. But there is a loophole, of sorts. It's just as fucked up as the spell itself, but it *is* a loophole. Kill the victim, kill the curse."

"Murder Killian's father?" I question.

"If you can figure out how," Marlow replies. "There were a series of words that appeared over and over in the texts. It was written in an ancient language, but it closely translates to... blood of the oracle. And something about a weapon forged in love? Or maybe sex? Amethyst and Sybil are at odds with the translation."

I shake my head at Lowe. Some things never change. She has my brain spinning, though. I know very little about the relationship between Killian and his father. It's not like he's been open and honest in my time here. I know *who* he is because of Willa and Iris. He's the God of Death, but I don't even know his name.

Sometimes I think Killian's father was his hero, but there are other times, like in the dead garden. When his mask slips, I can see hatred in his eyes. It bleeds through in his words. Selene's too. There's another layer to the story, and my gut tells me when someone receives a curse like this one. He must have provoked it. What could The Dark King of the Netherworld have done that was so fucked up? Or is Mordred just twisted enough that he uses blood magic death curses for entertainment? My skin prickles at the thought.

I don't know the answer, but it suddenly feels like life or death that I find out.

"Thank you, Lowe. I know I can always count on you. Did you find anything about the door?" I ask.

"There was nothing in the fortress blueprints about a creepy hidden door, and we walked the halls for hours trying to find it. I can only guess, but I think that's your mystery to solve." Marlow wiggles her foot like she always does when she's nervous.

"My Sight says whatever is behind that door reeks of evil," I admit.

"Then you need to watch your ass, Vivi. Someone wanted you to find it, but we don't know why. Keep your perky tits out of trouble, and don't get possessed. Okay? I don't know what kind of monstrosity would need to be locked away in this realm, but nothing good can come of it." Marlow worries at her lip.

"No promises." I grin, only half-joking.

Marlow rolls her eyes and snorts, making me laugh until I'm hit with a wave of unstable magic. Then, my inner monster perks up, tracking the signature that could only belong to Killian.

An unfamiliar voice rings out in my head. *"Mine."*

Killian bursts through my door, taking it off the hinges. He's Killian, but... not. His stormy eyes are obsidian galaxies, his smell is off, and the elongated fangs I can see in his mouth are a new development.

"Um, hey?" I give him a lopsided smirk.

The look in his eyes intimidates the shit out of me, and Marlow takes the awkward opportunity to exit the room.

"So, this is your true form, then? I like it. Kind of murdery, though." I joke.

"You think this is funny, Genevieve?"

"Depends. Are you going to attack me with those fangs? Or just look pissed and super fucking hot?" I giggle.

"I would never hurt you," Killian whispers with his eyes pointed to the floor.

Damn, I know what this is about, and I bet Anise poured salt on his wound and then mixed it with lemon juice. Vicious little creature, she is. I'd rather swim with an angry nymph than have this conversation with him right now, but here we are.

"I know that, Killian. I compelled you to do it. I figured out how to use my magic through the bond. You flat out refused, and I saved you from yourself. I saved you and Anise from that pain." I tried to explain as best I could, knowing I was about to receive the icy side of my husband.

The sting of betrayal he's feeling hurts like a bitch. I know because he's done it to me. Don't get me wrong. I wasn't being hateful about my decision, and I didn't do it for revenge. I just couldn't watch him destroy himself. I had no other motive. It was really that simple. He won't believe that, but it doesn't make it any less true.

Killian tenses his jaw and then shouts. "You didn't save me from pain!"

"Oh, but I did. You're just too angry to see it, and that's okay. I understand now. When faced with an impossible choice, you do what you have to do to protect the people you love." A sad smile adorns my lips, my first admission of what I feel for him, and it's wasted on this moment.

Killian strides across the room, and my instincts come to life. *Goddess, please don't make me fight him.* But he only leans down, kisses my forehead angrily, and then turns and walks away. Shutting the door between us.

I deserved that.

He'll see it as betrayal, and I don't know if he'll forgive me, but Anise called me her friend that very first day I sat at their table. She has protected me with a fierceness that defies logic ever since. What kind of queen would I be to stand by and let someone degrade her like that? Even more importantly, what kind of friend?

CHAPTER ELEVEN

VIVI

SWEAT BEADS ON THE back of my neck, and my legs feel weightless. As I wade through the fog, I realize I am in the fortress. I don't know what's happening. The door creaks on its hinges, opening slowly to reveal a dimly lit hallway. As I take a tentative step forward, the sensation is so sinister that I lose my nerve, turning back toward my ...

Where is my fucking door?

Continuing forward is my only option, so I step further into the hallway. Though I am familiar with it, it seems... foreign. A warped version of the hallways I've walked a thousand times. The mood is darker and more threatening. Rather than the moving wallpaper, dead vines are hanging. They drip a black oily substance, as if someone poisoned the flowers that once bloomed there. I never thought I'd say this, but I think I prefer the spooky maiden.

Further down the hall, my eyes are drawn to the iron lanterns that illuminate the walls. They flicker before they move, twisting the iron into threatening faces. Is this like a "Nightmare on Elm Street" situation? Am I sleeping? What the fuck...

To avoid the horror of what awaits me on the walls, I put a bit of pep in my step, but the more I walk, the worse it gets. I eventually find myself lost. The flickering flames of the lanterns have transformed from faces into snakes. According to *the triangular shape of their heads and the aggressive hissing? Venomous snakes. Fantastic. I really hope this isn't real.*

The whole damn castle has become a full house of horrors. Words escape me. This place is a maze on a good day, and today it isn't a good one. Honestly, I have no clue what's going on right now, but I didn't come all this way to die in a hallucination. So, I run, taking this turn and that. I'm trying to find some way out when my foot gets caught, and I land on something soft and... sticky. The thought of opening my eyes makes me nauseous. My heart is pounding so fast I am afraid it might burst. Fear grips me as I attempt to pull myself back up, only to have my hand slide further and touch bone. Oh, my goddess, my hand is inside a chest cavity, and it smells like roses. I don't know if that's more or less disturbing than what it should smell like.

Looking around, I see the floor of the hall is littered with dead bodies, and they aren't random ones either. These are the bodies of my loved ones. As bile hits the back of my throat, I look down and see my sister's face. I'm removing my hand from Kalliope's chest.

No, this isn't real. None of this is real. It can't be. Wake up! Wake the fuck up right now! Returning to my feet, I continue to run, intending to escape this twisted nightmare, vision, alternate reality. Whatever it is.

I run until everything looks the same, as if I've been on a haunted treadmill this entire time. I go on until I come to a dead end. My body is shaking, and my throat is like the desert. I can't let this beat me. I won't give myself over to the fear. I raise my head, knowing what I'll find…

The Door. Like the last time I found myself in front of it, the evil emanating from the wood itself feels malevolent. What the fuck is the deal with this door? Why is it so important? I already tried to get it open. Magic, fire, elbow grease. Nothing worked. The damn thing has no knob.

"Look again, child." A female voices whispers, the dark goddess.

I'm not even going to get into where the fuck she's been or why Frank is missing in action. Because honestly, right now, I'm so scared of this door I might pee myself. And from prior experience, when the goddess shows up, it's for a reason. So I'm going to guess and say this demonic door is about to become my problem.

"I already tried to get it open…." I'm making excuses, but I know that's shitty and not warrior princess of me in the least. The lack of response from the dark goddess confirms it. Fuck.

"Fine." I take a deep breath and look.

A heavy bronze metal hand now adorns the door, and it appears to be reaching out for me. My hand trembles and my fingers twitch. I can be reckless sometimes, yes. But this seems pretty sketchy even to me. What if it pulls me into an even more horrific hellscape than this one? Although I'm not sure I could dream a worse one up than the one I'm currently in, I've learned my lesson about what can and will get worse.

It only takes a moment to weigh my options, and I don't see a scenario where I have a choice. Therefore, the only way out is through. Right? So, if this is my way out, then I'll confront whatever monster needs its ass kicked on the other side. I have a moment of hesitation as my fingers brush the iron hand, but it's too late. Metal fingers clamp around my hand, making a fist. Holding me hostage.

Well, I guess there's no going back now, Dipshit.

"So, what happens next?" I speak to a whole lot of nothing. So, I'm not surprised when the nothing doesn't answer back.

Let's twist the hand, then. Otherwise, I might pass out from the stress. I do as I am told. I push the medieval-looking slab of wood and iron forward. Almost immediately, the seal cracks with no resistance. A sharp pain radiates through my forearm, distracting me from the faint movement behind the door. I believe I saw a streak of gold move across a vast mausoleum. It's dark, so it's hard to be sure.

My forearm feels warm, and as I look down, I see that a clean, straight cut has ripped the skin, and my blood is dripping onto the floor. Rivers of blood. More than any individual can contain inside their damned body. I struggle to keep my balance, and my vision becomes blurred. As I watch the crimson stream down the hall, I cannot help but stare. Streams of dark scarlet trickle down the walls, soaking the magical wallpaper and spilling into the fields.

This is too bizarre.

I return my attention to what's behind the door as an enraged voice surges through the cavern walls, but it speaks a language I cannot understand. My Sight flares to life, telling me that the voice is ancient, and it is not someone I want to pick a fight with.

—◇—

My throat constricts, and I gasp, sitting up too quickly and smacking my head against a very real headboard. The dull pain radiates in a circular motion around my skull before it dissipates. Calypso jumps, whipping her flaming tail as she hisses towards the bathroom.

"I'm sorry, Lippy girl. It was just a nightmare. A really fucking twisted nightmare. No more chocolate before bed, huh?" I laugh.

You are injured.

I haven't heard Calypso inside my head in so long. It startles me for a second.

"Injured? What are you talking about?"

Stupid witches get eaten by bigger monsters…

"I love you too, Calypso."

Your arm bleeds.

Oh shit! I yank my arm from under the covers, inspecting it, and sure enough. My forearm bears the same cut it did in the dream that Freddy Krueger directed. The cut *is* concerning, but given the rest of the shit show we are all living in right now, I'm not as worried as I should be. Besides, it's already healing, which is good because there's something I'm far more concerned about. If the cut from my nightmare was real? Then I need to check on my sister, now. My heart constricts at the thought of her lying there, lifeless and decaying. I'll never be able to erase that sight from my memory.

I'm up and putting my clothes on in a flash. Something unusual is happening in this fortress, and it calls for my signature black leather pants and heeled boots. I sneak across the cold floor to my closet and grab my thigh straps and reach for my daggers in a hurry. When I realize there's only one in the box, I stop moving. How the fuck did I misplace a dagger? Maybe I went to bed with one. I strap the single blade to my thigh and rummage through my blankets, lift my pillow, and run my hand under the side of the mattress. Nothing… hmm. Well, I guess I can find it later. My need to see Kalli alive and breathing overpowers my compulsion to search for it.

Making a quick pit stop in the bathroom, I do a shoddy job brushing my teeth. After that, I don't bother with my hair, and then I'm headed toward the door when Maius steps in. Her eyes widen as I nearly trample her.

"I am so sorry, Maius. I'm just… in a hurry this morning. It's not your fault, I promise." I'm talking like I was raised by an auctioneer.

Shit! Did I just give a promise to a Fae? Yes. Yes, I did. Can't wait to see what the universe hands me for that colossal fuck up.

"You've given me the highest honor, my queen." Maius coos at me, her push pop orange-tinted skin glowing.

"Yeah, awesome. Okay! I need to go now. Big meeting. Many important things." I sound like an idiot.

As soon as I slip past Maius, I walk as fast as possible without appearing like I'm trying to run down the hallway. I slow when I reach the staircase leading to the lower quarters. These halls differ from ours, less fancy shit and more comfortable looking. It always made me jealous until I remembered my giant tub.

Standing in front of Kalliope's door, I get a wave of unexpected nerves. Oh goddess, please, just tell me she's okay. She can be the bitchiest bitch of any bitch that ever bitched, and I would love her for it. No more complaining, I promise.

There I go with the promises again.

"Knock, knock," I call out as I tap on Kalliope's door.

Footsteps move beyond it, and I release the tension in my jaw. She's here. Nobody murdered her in a vine-covered hallway. Of course, a dream is just a dream, or maybe a vision, but I'll worry about that later.

"Open the door, asshole. I can hear you." I smile, waiting to see her angsty face.

Kalli opens the door with her usual sour patch expression. "Are you crazy? Do you have any idea what time it is?"

Nope, sure didn't.

"Too early. That's what time it is." Kalliope snips, tapping her foot like someone's pissed-off teenager.

I ignore her as I breeze into the room, heading straight for her disheveled bed. I plop myself onto her mattress. "Dang, this thing is comfy," I swear if looks could kill, I'd be a goner. And I'm just so happy to see her alive. I don't give a shit. I lay on my stomach, swaying my legs back and forth in a crisscross motion. I'm waiting for her to finish verbally slapping me around. Ready for the insults to fly…

Imagine my shock when the bravado leaves her face, and she climbs into her bed next to me. I think it's an honest to goddess miracle.

"You're afraid." Kalliope remarks.

"I was, yes. I had the most horrific dream that something had happened to you." I reply.

"This fortress houses a great evil. All is not what it seems."

"I was hoping you wouldn't say that, but I had a feeling you would. Okay, so. There's this creepy door." I begin…

I explained the wallpaper and the strange maiden as she listened. I could picture Kalli dead on the ground with my hand inside her chest, and I cracked. Everything inside my soul comes pouring out like a verbal waterfall. I couldn't stop it even if I wanted to and despite the risk of her using it against me. I tell her everything.

What Killian's original plans were for me, and how I'm still not sure how I feel about it. I think I love him, and I don't know if I'm lucky or really fucking stupid. I admit to my worry that Frank has been missing in action, and although the Dark Goddess has saved my ass a few times, I don't know if I should trust her. My Sight is useless with her. I don't know what she wants, and I'm unsure if everyone wants to use me for my magic? Or if I've just had the worst luck in all the cosmos.

I tell her about my childhood and what Faustus had done at the Academy, that Deacon died. At the same time, I was still upset with him for being dodgy with any answers about my life. I know that's fucked up because he was under a binding blood oath and probably literally couldn't tell me anything that might cause me to be hurt. I tell her how I blamed it on her for not answering my call when I knew she could. I apologize for not knowing what it would cost her. But then, I broke down about Rowena missing for so long and Bronwyn.

Letting the tears well up and fall over, giving her an unguarded front-row view of my soul. I tell her how hard I have fought for her. I left it all on the pretty purple bedsheets, just me, laid bare and asking for a sister. I'm fully aware that I face rejection, but I'm just not able to summon any more fucks. I saw her dead, and it broke something inside me.

I didn't ask her questions about father or The Bone Keep. It wasn't the purpose of my visit, and I needed her to know that I was giving this to her without expectations.

The room was silent for what seemed like an eternity. So long that my stomach dropped, and I could no longer keep eye contact. I don't want to watch the hatred fill her eyes again. If she tells me to fuck off, I don't want to see it coming.

So, I scan her room instead. It's simple, but somehow it fits her perfectly. The walls are burgundy and gold, minimally decorated. Everything is in meticulous order, from her clothing to the toiletries. Everything is in its place, so she's a type-A personality. That's good to know.

"I'm sorry too," Kalliope admits quietly, and my soul lights up.

"For what?"

"I'm sorry I killed your cat."

"Yeah, that was shitty." My voice cracks. I don't know why I want to laugh at the most inappropriate times.

"I hated you so much I couldn't see past it. Imagine living your life confined to a castle full of monsters. Knowing you were just the backup, a failed creation, but your sister? She's the one father got right. The one he scoured the realms for, the one he wants more than anything. I thought you got away and lived a happy life while I had to stay with a tyrant. I was nothing more than a chained pet to unleash on his enemies. That's all I've ever been. I didn't know what was happening to you. I didn't know you were living in hell, too." Kalliope sniffs and wipes at her face.

"Before you ask, I don't know the details of what father wants with you."

"I wasn't going to ask." I smile.

Kalliope regards me awkwardly, shifting sideways on the sheets. I think she might be fidgeting, which is fascinating to witness. I don't think I've ever seen her vulnerable while conscious.

"I don't wish to be your enemy, Genevieve." She says quietly, almost in a whisper, but not quite.

"Well, I'd say the first step to being sisters is to drop the formal bullshit. Right? My name is Vivi." I smile.

"Okay, Vivi."

She thinks I don't notice the flash of light in her eyes and the subtle smirk at the corner of her mouth, but I see her. I see her more than anyone else does. She wears that layer of Teflon over her skin, not because she doesn't want to be loved. But because she's loved too much and only ever got pain in return. She's the girl who doesn't think she can smile because someone might see behind her mask.

Snatch out my heart and put it in a blender. I think it would hurt less than seeing myself behind her eyes right now. My big sister, my mirror. In all the worst ways. How did we spend our lives apart but still go through the same hell? Are the gods really this cruel? I don't need to think very hard about that to know the answer.

Absolutely, they are.

A wave of protectiveness washes over me with stunning force. And I know I may get punched, but before I can overthink it, I reach for my sister. Wrapping my arms around her gently. When she brings her arms around my shoulders and hugs me back, I can't hold back the tears.

"I love you, Kalli," I whisper as I wipe my eyes and carefully reapply my own mask.

"Where you go. I go," Kalliope replies, just as Amethyst knocks on her door and peeks in. Which seems like the perfect timing for my next stop on the apology tour.

I'm not looking forward to hunting Killian down after our last train wreck of a conversation, but it doesn't matter much what I want. A conversation needs to happen, some type of resolution, a cease fire, white flag, something. I don't know what it is about us, but we cannot get it right. I don't know how the fuck we're supposed to be fated for each other when we can't even get through a conversation without fireworks.

I don't have any of those with me this time. No harsh words, no accusations, no excuses. I betrayed him. I did it knowing what the repercussions could be. Killian has every right to be angry about me using the bond to manipulate him into whipping me. He's right to be furious. But I'd do it again. For Anise, I'd do it a thousand times over. Because I know she would have done it for me. He doesn't have to understand it, but if we're going to restore this realm together. He has to accept it.

So, I set about the fortress to find him and whatever personality he's wearing today. My frustration level is at maximum capacity after checking every likely place he could be and coming up empty. I'd asked around. Nobody seems to know where he is.

Since I've already scoured the fortress, the gardens or the training arena would be the next most obvious place. I make my way toward the grounds, passing all manner of netherlings on the way. They smile, nod, and some even curtsy. It's such a stark contrast from when I first arrived here. It seems like so long ago; I was half-dead in a rowboat crewed by two ridiculous demons who had no business trying to keep me alive. And now? I don't know what's happening now, but I've never felt more real. Here in the Netherworld, in this fortress. It's the freest I've ever been.

I wander the gardens, keeping my eyes open for a gorgeous, broody incubus. While observing the savage vegetation in all its glory. The flowers are poisonous, the leaves sting, and the stems have fangs. This realm is truly beautiful in a dark paradise kind of way. Before long, I realize I've wandered a little too far from the central gardens, and I'm lost as shit again. This is becoming a regular occurrence for me, but I'm not even sure I'm still inside the grounds this time. Nothing looks familiar, not that that means much of anything. The realm is alive in the most literal sense. Things shift as they please.

A movement on the left draws my attention, and I hurry to catch up. It doesn't take me long to recognize his walk, the way his muscles move under his clothes. I've memorized Killian's entire body.

There is no way for me to call out to him in this forest. I'm too far behind. Keeping quiet is always best since you never know what may lurk. Killian turns toward another path, and I follow him. Hopefully, there isn't another one around the corner that I cannot see. Wouldn't want to lose him.

It makes me wonder why he's out here. Could it be the same reason I wander? To clear my mind. After what I'd done to him, I understand his need for that. Whether he has done it to me as well is irrelevant. Pain is pain. A betrayal is a betrayal. To the person suffering the aftermath, the reason rarely matters. I hope he'll be able to see with time that I never meant to harm him. Maybe if I just got him to listen for a few minutes, he would see my point of view. That doesn't mean I'm holding my breath, but I have to try.

As soon as I reach the next turn, I realize it leads to one of those rivers I'd seen on many of my excursions into the Netherworld. I couldn't say which one, though. To me, they all look the same. As I reach the end of the path, I see Killian pulling a black t-shirt over the top of his head, exposing his corded back muscles. I bite my lip and clench my thighs.

Goddess, bless the realms and all the fucking stars. He is criminally hot. When he pulls down his jeans and reveals a pair of boxer briefs, I might combust. Images of us in the shower before it went awry play through my mind. Whenever I touch his skin, it's like being in a dream. The sounds he makes inside me and how his fingers clutch my skin. A split second before I'm about to explode, he jumps into the water.

I step off the path with a smile on my face. Already tugging at my pants and tank top. There are worse ways to have this conversation. Perhaps our lack of clothing will diffuse some tension, and we can mix frustration with pleasure. And if not? At least I can splash the shit out of that stubborn bastard.

As I approach the bank, Killian turns toward me and smirks. Apparently, he's done with being pissed already. So maybe today won't be as challenging as I thought it would be...

"Well, hey there," I call him, my husky voice.

The intensity of those stormy eyes creates a waterfall between my legs. "Okay, fine, play hard to get. I'll come to you this time. I owe you that much."

I concede and step onto the bank. Dipping just the tip of my toe into the water, I can already tell it's cold. So, I don't waste time trying to acclimate. Instead, I crouch down on my knees and jump.

Before my body collides with the chilly water, a desperate scream shakes the forest. "GENEVIEVE, NO!"

CHAPTER TWELVE

THE SHADOWLANDS

A SINKING SENSATION SETTLES into my gut, and my arms flail while I attempt to catch my bearings. Water rushes up my nose and into my mouth, cutting off my supply of life-sustaining air. I am made of instinct and adrenaline, pumping my legs to gain momentum. I need to breathe; I need to breathe. I need to breathe! My foot thrashes, fighting against something unnatural trying to pull me under. Then, in the cold, murky depths, a pair of vicious sea-green eyes stare back at me, its mouth opens to reveal rows of serrated teeth.

Whoa, what the fuck?

I kick and jerk until the sound of bones cracking, muted underwater, makes its way to my ears. Loose flesh squishes between my toes, and I shudder. Fucking gross. My chest burns, spasming for the air I have deprived it. I push off with all my might, looking up toward the surface, praying to the goddess I can make it just a few more feet. My vision blurs, and my body jerks. I'm sinking…

"*You must survive.*' A female voice rings in my head.

Not my voice, but somehow familiar. I kick again, dragging my strength closer to me. I'm about to break the surface when a stabbing pain slices through my thigh. I gasp, stupidly allowing water into my mouth. I swallow it and try not to cough. Looking down, I know what I'll find—the sea-green eyes of a monster, and if the water doesn't kill me? The monster will.

"Survive," the woman's voice echoes…

My face breaches the surface, and I struggle for air. Choking on the water trapped inside my throat. I propel my body toward the shore with my last bit of energy. Throwing my half-drowned body onto the muddy edge and digging my fingers into the rocks, dragging myself onto the yellowed grass.

Sweet baby Cerberus, I almost died!

I cough and gag, expelling the murky water from my throat, and then retch as it evacuates my stomach. I lay there with my cheek pressed into the dirt until time didn't have meaning. Then, when my breathing becomes steadier, I roll to my side and shrink in on myself. I'm naked, cold, and seriously fucking confused. How did I end up in a monster infested river, and why is there a monster infested river in the Earth Realm in the first place?

"By the gods. Are you alright, dear?" A deep male voice calls out, startling me. I scramble to a sitting position, covering my breasts before I twist myself in the voice's direction.

I didn't expect to find myself in a stare down with a tall, dark-haired man. His hand is extended as if to offer help. But his eyes are red as rubies, and I don't know of a single supernatural with red eyes who has ever had good intentions. The warm smile adorning his face is off-putting. My first instinct is to back away. Far, far away. I subtly adjust my butt cheeks, readying myself to slide backward out of his grasp should he come any closer, but before I can move, the mysterious red-eyed man laughs. Surprisingly, it's not a sinister sound.

"I understand your predicament better than you know, dear one. You've left your clothing on the bank near that tree. There's no reason to climb back into the freezing water and what dwells within. I don't intend to hurt you, and I'm not ogling your nakedness."

A forward man, one who speaks plainly. I can respect that. Sure enough, glancing at the tree in question, there are clothes strewn across the ground. I don't recognize the outfit but based on the bralette peeking out from under a pant leg and us two being the only people in this clearing. So I'm going to say they're mine.

"What do you want from me?" I question.

He grins and shakes his head. "You'll catch your death out here. Will you allow me to approach you? I have something to offer you extra warmth."

That sounds nice, and I am cold…

Despite the tremors coursing through me, I nod. He turns his chin up respectfully and removes his cloak, placing it across my shoulders to cover my nakedness. I pivot my back and wrap the cloak around my body, rushing to the pile of clothes and dressing myself lightning fast.

I don't know what's worse, the embarrassment of being a drowned rat on a riverbank in front of this well-put-together stranger, or that I'm tits out in the middle of a forest with no clue how I got here.

"Um, thank you?" I know it sounds like a question because I'm out of my depth here.

The man turns his head and nods once. "We should get moving. There are far worse things in these woods than what you encountered in that river."

Hmm. Stay here with the swamp monster or follow the man with the red eyes? I mean, neither is the most superb option. But as the slice in my thigh pulses in pain, I think I'll go with the red-eyed dude. What can I say? He gave me a cloak. So, I fall in step behind him. Toward what? Goddess only knows.

As I trudge along a leaf-strewn walking path, I take in the view. The sky is streaked with scarlet, a mixture of dark shadows and ominous warnings. The sharp grayish spire of a towering castle pierces the fog behind us. It is hauntingly beautiful in all its rough edges against the softness of the sky. I feel my heartbeat quicken. Then, I'm overcome by melancholy as it fades out of sight.

"What part of the Earth Realm is this?"

"We are in the Netherworld, dear girl. On our way to the Bone Keep of the Shadowlands," he responds to that second part with pride.

The WHERE?! Did he just say Netherworld? As in, the one you must enter a portal to get into. The same one that's utterly impossible because the portals haven't been opened in decades? What kind of fuckery is this guy up to? I decide to let it slide for now. I don't think I'm in danger, but it's always wise to keep your mouth shut when bodily harm is in question. At least, I think it is.

Mistaking my silence for something other than suspicion, he continues. "Many nightmares slither and crawl through the forests of the Netherworld, but you needn't worry. The border is just ahead, and then we'll be in the safety of the Shadowlands."

Call me crazy, or call my seventh-year history teacher crazy, but I believe what I learned about the Shadowlands back in school. Unfortunately, what I learned suggested the opposite of safety. In fact, I think I could describe the whole of the Nether Realm as a treacherous hellscape filled with unlimited ways to die.

The man's crimson eyes slide over me. "My name is Mordred, and you are?"

My brows crease. The answer dwells in my mind, but when I try to focus, it slips through my fingers. What is my name? I tremble as my heartbeat spikes. I shake my head, attempting to jolt something loose. "I'm sorry... I... I'm not sure."

"A dark power lives under the surface of the Lethe. Perhaps your mind will thaw when your body does." Mordred lends me a reassuring smile.

"I'm sure you're right," I respond, but I'm not sure. Not even close.

We leave behind fall's crisp smells and sounds for something more bizarre. As we cross a makeshift footbridge, I know darkness has contaminated this land. The ground bubbles with a thick black liquid, as if it's seeking to rid itself of the disease that has taken hold.

My instinct to eradicate this wrongness comes roaring to life. Fire. I want to destroy it with fire. My hands glow, and I shove them underneath the cloak. Mordred hesitates, and my internal storm fizzles out. My whole being screams to keep my magic to myself. My subconscious whispers how essential it is that no one knows. At the same time, I experience a vision. Me. Standing in a cafe, with steam curling from my fists. And a face, a beautiful brown freckled face.

The vision fades as quickly as it appeared.

How did I learn that? And how did I end up in this situation? Somewhere inside my head, memories curl in on themselves in a way I can't reach, pressing against a wall of spiderwebs. I focus until my head throbs, but nothing comes. A broken shard, a fragment of emotion, a scene that looks like a damaged film. There is a bar. There are shadows and smoke. Hypnotic cerulean eyes the shade of wild, raging storms.

"That's quite the dagger you have." Mordred's eyes slither to my thigh, breaking my train of thought.

Dagger... what dagger? I feel my pulse race. It had never occurred to me that I would be armed. I was likely too shocked to pay attention to what was in my pile of possessions.

As I gaze down at the blade strapped to my thigh, my mind flickers to a pair of violet eyes and flowing black hair. The woman in the lace robe distorts her face, but I believe she gave me the dagger. I want to keep this to myself, just as I want to keep the forbidden magic from others.

"It was a gift," I respond, trying not to give myself away.

Mordred's eyes narrow before another warm smile resurfaces on his lips. "A splendid gift, indeed."

While avoiding eye contact, I glance upward, admiring the canopy above. It is a mixture of deciduous and pine trees. Kind of? Imagine a world in which pine trees ooze a tar-like substance from their bark, and their needles resemble knives. The Netherworld is just a twisted version of the Earth Realm, as far as I can tell. Except this place smells of decay.

We come over the crest of a hill, and I glance into the distance. A second castle looms ahead. The closer we get, the more I can see. My instincts kick in, and I feel compelled to study every detail. They lined the outer walls with black stone. There is a tower at each corner. Unlike most castles I've seen in books, these seem to be spread out over a large area instead of climbing toward the sky. All the construction was done with this black stone. I can feel its repellant energy even from a distance.

I don't have to remember anything about myself to recognize that this is an impenetrable fortress. So the question is, am I a guest or a prisoner?

On the towering gate are two enormous black snakes entwined like intricate carvings. Though I know they're made of metal, their lifelike appearance gives me pause. Like poisonous daggers, their onyx fangs poke threateningly from their mouths as beady eyes follow every move I make.

Not my idea of a welcome sign.

As we approach, two monstrous beasts with dripping tusks and leathery skin stand on each side of the gate, holding long spears. "Welcome back, my King." They speak in unison.

King?! The king of what? Because this looks like the basement of Hell.

Mordred's matte-red eyes draw mine in. "There's nothing to be concerned about, dear girl. I thought to tell you on the way, but you have been skittish after your ordeal. Welcome to the Bone Keep."

After my "ordeal,"… okay? What an intriguing way to explain finding myself drowned in a river with no memory of who I am. And when I pulled my disheveled ass up the muddy bank, a king was waiting for me. Strange coincidence, I tell you. So who is a nobody like me to a king in the Shadowlands?

The gates open, and my jaw drops.

Across the grounds, night creatures stand at attention, arranged in orderly rows. There are thousands and thousands of them. They stretch as far as the eye can see. I am immediately suspicious; this is a legion. A sizable one at that! What does this King of the Shadowlands plan to do with them?

Another thing I notice is the black obsidian. Everything from the sidewalk to the benches to the castle itself is made of it. Black obsidian absorbs energy, and it's a powerful protection stone. And if this is all raw obsidian, then that mountain in the distance isn't a mountain. It's a volcano. Witches can draw dark power from volcanoes. Is there a witch inside this castle? My mind has more questions than I can keep up with.

This castle is unlike anything I've ever seen before. As I suspected, it doesn't climb to the sky. Instead, it's about three stories tall. All that distinguishes it from the rest of the buildings are the looming Gothic windows and columns in the shape of snakes at the front entrance.

The Bone Keep is already bustling with attendants when I arrive at the polished foyer. Throughout this short but macabre adventure, there has been a recurring theme... . demons.

I am surrounded by demons.

Speaking of demons. I stand before two extraordinarily beautiful women dressed in dark silks and long, untamed hair. Their eyes and teeth are black as night. A third woman stands beside them. A sweeping lace veil obscures her face, so I don't know what she looks like, but the magic she radiates makes me sick to my stomach. Darkness is her nature. She's a witch, no doubt about it, but it never occurred to me that Mordred had a sorceress.

Not someone I plan to cross paths with on purpose, that's for sure.

The last man. How can I even explain him? The man is gorgeous. He has golden eyes, so I recognize him as a demon. Still, he's not as threatening looking as the creatures I encountered lining up on the grounds. He is tall, lean, but muscular. Dark brown waves brush his shoulders, and he oozes carnal energy from every pore. I take a deep breath and tell my lady bits to relax. That man is definitely a sex demon.

"Una and Marta will show you to your quarters, where you may bathe before our meal. Hunter is my best warrior. He'll be your personal escort for your time with us in The Bone Keep." Mordred nods to his team of handlers, an apparent dismissal. And those words must signify the beginning of a godsdamned circus because that is what ensues.

The two women grab my arms and whisk me down corridors so fast I'm not sure what I'm seeing. Everything is shiny, black, or monotone. As far as I can tell, it's modern. There is some taxidermy on the walls, but not the kind you see in hunting lodges. They have fur, but I cannot determine what kind of creatures they are. There's a bit of a 'weird doctor' meets 'cemetery chic' vibe taking place in these halls.

Considering my feet aren't touching the ground, I'm willing to guess these demon-eyed ladies are flying or floating. I'm not sure which. And trying not to worry too much about Hunter following indecently close behind us, because my lower bits are tingling in his proximity. Second, because how the fuck can he keep up with these fast-flying lunatics?

I feel like the pasty girl in the middle of a demon sandwich.

Una or Marta, I'm not sure which, talks to me endlessly about her doll and asks if I can play with her. It's almost like she hasn't ever seen life beyond the castle walls. While I like her, I get the impression that *I am* the doll she refers to. Which is creepy, but I don't think she means to cut me up into pieces.

The other Una or Marta, again I'm not sure which, stares at me with daggers in her eyes. It's obvious. This woman is bloodthirsty. I don't know why she wants to hurt me, but the intensity of her hatred is unmistakable. I can feel her claws pressing on my arm, but they don't pierce my skin. Mordred probably told her not to harm me, and I think that might be the only thing keeping me from an unfortunate speeding accident. I'll be sleeping with one open eye while in the Shadow Court, that's for sure. And Hunter? Hunter is sexy as fuck, but just as with everything else in this mind-bending place, there is something off about him.

Not that I dislike the view; I'm just stating an intuition-approved fact. This guy has *I'm here for a good time, not a long time'* stamped on his forehead. The man is the definition of a walking red flag.

Why do I get the feeling red flags are just my type?

Ugh. Yeah, this is a fucking circus.

Una and Marta produce the most awful shrieking sound in stereo to prove my point. The deafening shrieks of their brain melting yowls cause me to jerk back, nearly falling on my ass. Then, as smooth as a used car salesman, Hunter catches me.

I can't help but wonder whether this is all staged. If it isn't? What in the Tim Burton film is going on with my life?

The wailing resumes before I can ask questions. The women sure have some pipes. Trying to find the source of this epic freak out, I squint past the bleeding eardrums when I see a dark angel in the middle of their path.

He. Is. Stunning. There is nothing sexual about it. Nothing at all like that. He is more like a dangerous explosion of beautiful chaos. A silver-haired Adonis of total darkness. I peer over Marta's (or Una's) shoulder, and he makes eye contact with me. Something is enchanting and reassuring in his sky-blue gaze. I'm reminded of a waterfall, but the sharp rocks below his surface hide a wild and captivating menace.

"Fuck off, Sylas. Mordred assigned me to escort our mouthwatering guest." Hunter's voice sounds like warm honey being poured all over my body.

"Ask me if I give a shit." Sylas's blue eyes gleam. "I've only come to introduce myself."

"I gave you an order," Hunter growls.

A conspiratorial grin slides across Sylas' face as he turns to me. Oh, and he's funny too! I get the feeling that getting a rise out of Hunter is the highlight of his day, every day. A small smile appears on the corner of my lips. His eyes light up.

This one is a troublemaker. Straight to the core.

"I had been preparing to welcome you to the Bone Keep before being so rudely interrupted. Let me try again." He clears his throat as obnoxiously as possible.

"Hello, Little Monster!" he exclaims. "My name is Sylas, as I'm sure you overheard."

Goddess, I hope he's not an axe murderer. I think we could be friends.

I smirk, cocking my head to the side. "I'm having some technical difficulties with my memory. So, my name is… I have no fucking idea?"

"Sure, you do." Sylas winks. "I just told you. It's Little Monster."

How do I know those words? They settle into a familiar place inside my stomach. I'm just about to ask when my attendants intervene…

"Our guest needs to bathe before dinner, Sylas." One psycho-screamer cuts in.

"Yeah, she reeks of bog water and desperation." The other screamer adds with a cackle.

By watching the conversation, I believe the nasty one to be Marta. Though Marta looks almost identical to Una, she carries herself with the aggression of a predator. I feel like I should file away that information for future reference.

"I'll see you soon, Little Monster. Remember to bring your claws to dinner." Sylas remarks before strolling away, grinning at Hunter like an incredibly satisfied asshole.

Bring your claws. That's an odd thing to say to a stranger, right? Who says that? But despite the unusual remark, I feel heat flicker deep in my chest at the sound of his words. A memory trying to push its way through the fog...

"Shall we get this exquisite body of yours washed and ready for dinner, Sweetness?" Hunter asks, his words dripping with innuendo.

My face heats as my lips twist in confusion. I don't think he means what I think he means, does he? Hot or not, this doesn't happen within a few hours of getting to know each other. Does it? Suddenly, I'm picturing some downright indecent bathroom counter action I wouldn't mind...

Hold on. Where did that thought even come from? OMG. No.

"Off you go, Hunter. You'll see our lovely guest at dinner." Una interrupts, guiding me past him.

CHAPTER THIRTEEN

THE BONE KEEP

I watch as Marta pulls out a skeleton key from inside her flowy silks as Una takes over, holding my hand. Pictures flash through my mind as I watch her slide it into the lock. *A wilted field. A dragon. Snow-white hair. Flames. Blood. Death.* Then comes the pain. Excruciating, all-consuming, blistering... pain. As the ground races up to meet me, my ears ring, body contorts, and knees buckle. I feel a warm sensation trickle down my chin before being swallowed up by the shadows.

A loud voice echoes through the void. "Get up! I said GET UP, WHORE!"

I blink a few times to clear away the confusion as my eyes flutter open. I'm trying to reconnect my head with my body. My skull aches. I think I passed out. Did I? I recognize those images, but what good does that do? This whole recognizing but not knowing a thing is getting old.

My hip shifts, and that's when I realize I'm lying in an unfamiliar bed. The bed isn't huge or fancy, just a full-sized bed with a slate-colored sheet. A greyish braided rug covers the rough stone floor. There are glossy black stripes on the walls, with matte black accents. There isn't much to see in terms of embellishments, just some jars of herbs and bleached skulls. Unrecognizable creatures...

Wait, did Marta just call me a whore?

Pushing past the throbbing in my head, I snap back. "Awfully judgmental, assuming I'm a prostitute, Marta. I mean, who knows? Maybe I am! But that's not the point. Obviously, *someone* didn't get the female empowerment memo, and that someone is you."

Marta doesn't trouble herself with a response. Instead, she flashes her blackened teeth at me and stalks off into a side room, to the bathroom, I'm guessing.

"You've been unconscious for quite some time. Bathe now, before we are late." Una's pleasant voice graces my ears.

Well, I suppose if Una is asking, I could be cooperative. I slowly swing my legs to the edge of the bed, pulling myself upright. A sharp stabbing in my head causes me to sway, but I catch myself with an arm propped on the mattress.

"Just give me a second to get my shit together," I comment. Then, both screamers burst into inhumanly fast cyclones again.

As far as I can tell, they're preparing for the bath. In an attempt to assess my surroundings, I take a few moments to observe. It feels like a habit, something I have learned. Of course, I can't possibly know who taught me without knowing who I am, so I let the pointless questions go for now.

I don't think I have much time left before the screaming banshees come to collect me, so I try to use it wisely. What stands out? A well-stocked bookshelf is the first thing I notice because it's the only color in this room. Next, I'm intrigued by the antique-looking lantern on the plain black dresser beside the fireplace. The room lacks personal items, but one hand drawn piece of art decorates the wall. This picture shows a key surrounded by fire and lightning. It stirs an emotion I can't define.

A creaking door interrupts my train of thought, and four tall, misshapen female creatures walk in with towels and soaps. Iridescent sheer gowns sway in the breeze as their legs move. What is this, a nudist colony? Does the Shadow Court frown upon covering genitalia? I'm curious, but I suppose asking is probably frowned upon.

As the women set their packages down on the small table beside the tub, they move on. Without speaking a word, they leave as quickly as they arrive. They don't even glance at me as if I didn't exist. Then I hear a 'click' behind them.

"This question may seem stupid, but why am I being locked in if I'm a visitor?" I ask the screamer sisters. They may not be sisters, but they look alike, which is why they earn the nickname.

Marta glares. "None of your business, parasite. Get in the tub and keep your mouth closed."

"You're a friendly one." I beam obnoxiously.

"And you're a stain on this realm." She replies.

Alright, so much for the small talk. Maybe she's just hangry? Or there's always the possibility that she's possessed.

"Marta!" Una's eyes widen, and she hisses. "You are to follow orders."

Before I can ask what all these elusive *orders* are, several figures pass through the wall carrying oils and candles. My mind is so puzzled at their sight that I forget all about orders and crude, screeching women. These are specters. Ghosts. With sunken eyes and tattered rags for clothing. Their translucent skin hangs loosely off their bones. Some still carry phantom wounds from a former life. My stomach churns. This is blasphemy. What sort of monster enslaves restless souls to an eternity of delivering toiletries?

"Get. In." Marta snarls.

I don't like her; however, I have limited options at the moment. After stripping naked, I step into the bath. Although I wish I could say that I wasn't fuming inside, that would be a lie. I don't appreciate being forced, and I don't love the insults. As I feel my temper rising, a plume of smoke curls from my fingertips. The screeching psychos step away from me, fear written on their supernatural faces.

Shit.

"I don't know what's happening," I whisper, looking down at my legs.

Okay, so that's not completely true. I know why my fingertips are smoldering. Anger. I have magic, and it's somehow tied to my darker emotions. When my temper flares, my skin feels like it will melt, and then the fire show begins.

However, they don't realize that, and I think it's better to let them believe what they see. Mordred is sure to become involved in this now, and I would like to minimize the damage as much as possible. I wash my body free of the mud and river muck, thinking through my options. If I act like it's not a big deal, others will follow suit. Seems like a solid plan to me, not that I have many to choose from.

Yes. That's precisely what I'll do.

I smile, rinsing the bubbles from my skin. "I'm done with my bath."

The moment I step out of the tub, Una and Marta attack me with oversized bathing towels. As if the awkward community washing event wasn't mortifying enough.

No regard for personal space, I tell you. None. Privacy ... what's that?

Anyway, they drag me to a closet after the unwanted rub down and throw open the doors. There's an assortment of sweaters, jeans, leather, dresses, and shoes. All black, or some variation of it. And I thought I embodied the 90s grunge era already. Clearly, I have some competition. There are things that I know instinctively, like my preferred choice in clothing, but the majority of my memories are out of reach.

"Tonight, you'll wear an erotic dress." Una smiles as she rifles through the racks, a mischievous look in her black eyes.

"Um. I'd rather not wear a dress if it's all the same to you." I reply.

Marta sneers, "I don't give a fuck what you'd rather do. Una wants to decorate you, and the orders were formal dresses for dinner. You don't want to be presented to the King looking like a common whore, would you?"

And that's the second time she's called me a whore in less than twenty-four hours. "Excuse me?"

Marta plants her hands on her hips, exhaling like I've inconvenienced her. "Was there something you didn't understand?"

Though I briefly consider starting a fistfight, I'm not sure it's worth the trouble. I'll repay her *kindness* at some point. Our time will come, I'm sure of it. A grin passes over my lips at the thought.

After taking a deep breath, I nod to Una, allowing her to approach me. Minutes later, I'm standing in front of a mirror admiring her handiwork. I'm in a black dress, made with a fluid fabric that moves with my body like a second skin. It's a very Grecian goddess number. The neckline is extraordinarily revealing. I could do without that, given my current situation. But the joy bursting through Una's pitch-black eyes almost looks like stars against the midnight sky, and that's at least partially worth it.

After getting dressed, we took part in another speed drag race through the corridors. Fortunately, we covered a shorter distance this time, and I think I might even recognize a few things as we whiz past. Maybe this memory of mine isn't so broken after all? What if I could memorize the movements and not the scenery? Hm. That's a thought.

The universe must not enjoy me having thoughts because when I have a good one, every time—something interrupts. This time I am unceremoniously dropped into a small dining space. I struggle with dizziness that threatens to empty my stomach all over the floor. As I double over, my skin hums with strange magic. Looking down at my feet, I notice a complex mixture of what looks to be glowing stellar runes and an unfamiliar language scrawled across the glossy black tiles.

This is sorcery.

"Are these markings to keep something out or lock something in?" The words are already free from my mouth before I realize I've spoken.

The chilling sorceress from the foyer twists her neck at an unnatural angle, like the unsettling young lady that crawls across ceilings in the horror movies.

"Uh, never mind. On second thought, I don't need to know." I mutter without screaming and running in the other direction.

Sadly, the next horror is just around the corner. In the distance, there is a striking girl with short lavender hair and a freckled nose. Her oversized eyes meet mine, and my blood freezes. A dark fae. The most powerful kind there is. Is she... is she really locked inside an oversized birdcage hanging in the corner of a dining room? What the fresh hell is going on here? Do they make a habit of humiliating strong women for dinner entertainment? What the fuck. The fire in my veins grows hotter, my magic swells, and the earth rumbles beneath me.

The pretty fae stares at me with the wildest eyes I've ever seen. Her expression is not one of fear but of pure rage. Then, a moment later, her face becomes blank and non-threatening. Finally, she mouths something to me before anyone else looks at her. I think she said something like... Beebe? When I try to figure out what that might mean, my river-water-addled mind does somersaults. There is still sludge unfurling there, swallowing most of who I am and everything I know.

Beebe?

She took a dangerous risk trying to communicate with me. There must be a reason for it. I mean, just think about that grotesque cage. It couldn't get any worse, could it? But I think I know the answer to that. There's something sinister about The Bone Keep. As if the walls themselves are woven with a menacing undercurrent. The way these guests sit mute at this table, they all look as though they'd rather saw off their arms rather than be here. I can't imagine that's a sign of anything good.

"Let's all be seated, shall we?" Mordred announces.

I draw my eyes to the long table dotted with candles and artfully arranged oddities. Initially, I was a tad surprised. It may be impossible for me to remember, but I am not aware of any meals in my past that included jars of wet animal specimens. Those and various skulls are arranged as decorative centerpieces. Are those real skulls?

Note to self: strong stomach required to dwell within the Shadow Court.

There are only a few spiral-shaped platters on top of one another that I can see with anything that looks edible. I think it's fruit, but nobody has reached for plates yet, and I don't know what table etiquette in Hell's Basement looks like. So, I wait.

More specters deliver chalices and trays as they glide through walls. The smell of steaming meat fills the air, but I feel the darkness within me. Displaced spirits are being used as servants. The disrespect ignites embers in my soul. This practice is inhumane and coldhearted. This is a crime against the stars, against the gods themselves.

I know I should mind my business, but I'm not sure I can. The longer I sit, the hotter I burn.

"Freakshow's eyes are glowing." Marta casually speaks to Mordred.

Is she talking about me? Am I freakshow? I curl my lip at the insult.

"It pains me to see you unhappy, dear. Would you mind telling me what's bothering you? It seems your magic is expressing its distaste." Mordred's fingers curl into fists as he speaks.

My... magic. He already knows I have magic.

Hunter runs his fingers along my arm as he moves closer, and I melt into his presence. When he places his hand on my thigh, I feel a tingle between my legs. Yet my magic bucks against it, almost as if it were driven by its internal desire to resist him. I think the heat in my skin rises, sweat forms on my neck's back, and then Hunter is jerking his hand away.

I look into his golden-flecked eyes apologetically. "Sorry, I didn't mean to burn you."

In response, the sorceress tilts her head again. Although I cannot see her face behind the black lace cover, I know she looks at me. I feel cockroaches and worms crawling over my grave under her scrutinizing gaze.

In a gravelly voice, she says, "The King asked you a question."

A gentle grin graces Mordred's lips. "You are dismissed, my muse."

His muse?! That woman is vile, not to mention fucking petrifying. The only thing I see her inspiring are night terrors! Mordred raises a brow at me, and for a moment, my gut wrenches. Shit. I hope he can't read minds.

Screw it.

"I was thinking about your servants, King Mordred. They're restless spirits. Why do you hold them where they can never find peace in the afterlife? Why are they enslaved?"

"That is a story I will share with you at a more appropriate time. But, for now, would it please you if I send them away?" His eyes flash bright red.

No, not really. But before I can answer, he's already waving his hand. The undead servants scatter back into the walls as if they'd never existed. And that upset me just as much.

"I hope you can find your place here with us in the Bone Keep. I imagine it's difficult with no memories of your former life, no identity, no name. Perhaps it will soothe you to be given a name?" Mordred studies me.

I'm not all that keen on this idea. I have a goddess-given name, the one somebody assigned me at birth. Remembering it. That's what would soothe me.

"I think we should call her Sweetness." Hunter offers his suggestion, bringing his hand back to my thigh. His smile is confident, almost to the point of cocky, as he leans closer and runs his nose along the curve of my neck, making me shiver.

Is it creepy that he's *this* into me? Or do I think it's kind of hot? I can't decide, and I don't know what that says about me as a person.

"What about Sparkles?" Una suggests.

"What's wrong with Freakshow?" Marta sneers.

Sylas sits across the table, ripping meat off the bone with his bare hands. He looks at me and smiles, baring his sharp teeth. *Okay, I guess Sylas is keeping his opinions to himself.*

I should have expected that, since someone had already convinced him that my name was Little Monster. Or he could be fucking with me. I guess that's a possibility too.

Thoughts of lilac fae drift into my head. She has a name, too. I wonder how she got herself in such a bind. Does she have a history of killing people? Is she a thief? Can those actions result in imprisonment and humiliation in the Shadowlands? How does the Shadow Court operate? What justification could anyone give for trapping a fae like a pet in a fancy dining room?

I look up, about to run my mouth some more. But Sylas' icy blue eyes are drilling into me with laser precision, telling me not to look at the pretty little fae or draw any attention to her. He stares at me threateningly, but I don't flinch. Something tells me it isn't personal; I think he might be protecting her.

Hunter brings his hand to my cheek, overwhelming my senses. "You look tense, Sweetness. You've barely touched your meal."

"I don't know this meat," I respond, hoping that's enough of an explanation, and then I avert my eyes. Checking out the rest of my surroundings.

This is not the main hall. Considering the size of the castle, it's not nearly as large as it needs to be. Even if it is spread across the land instead of into the sky. What is this space? Is it the family dining area? I smirk at the thought.

Dysfunctional family dinners in Hell's Basement.

"Surprise, surprise." Marta snips, "Her Highness is fussy about her food too."

And I think she's said enough! Despite my efforts to be patient, quiet, and keep a distance from this asshole, every girl has her limits. I suddenly don't care that I'm in a strange castle with an eccentric king. He already knows about my magic, so why does it matter? I level a murderous glare at

Marta, letting my eyes glow brightly with pride. "Is there a specific reason you're being such a miserable bitch? Or were you hatched that way?"

Sylas's eyes go wide. He blinks twice and adjusts his head a fraction. I'm sure he's telling me to shut my mouth, but I've already lost the ability.

"If you have something to say to me, Marta. Then fucking say it!" I continue.

She grins, her blackened teeth on display. "Big mistake, you foolish whore."

"You know what? I'll show you a *whore…*." I stand up, willing the violet flames to my palms.

"Enough!" Mordred rumbles, filling the room with inky darkness. His power slithers over my skin, binding me into submission, and I sit back down at the table. When Mordred's ink clears, Marta is missing.

Una stands, giving a slight bow. "I apologize, my King. She has not been herself."

Mordred shifts his gleaming red eyes to her. "See that she visits Thane's lair. Now."

Thane's… lair? As in a place where dangerous animals live? That's not terrifying or anything. And who the fuck is Thane? Is that the lace-faced sorceress? I bet it is.

Una nods and excuses herself from the table, and Mordred sets his sights on me. "Would you mind joining me for an after-dinner walk? I believe we have much to discuss. Don't you agree?"

No, I'm not sure that I do, but I suppose it would be unwise to decline the invitation after what I'd just witnessed.

CHAPTER FOURTEEN

VIVI

SOME MIGHT CONSIDER THE crimson sky above the castle grounds to be sinister, and that's a fair assessment, but something about it soothes me. The darkness of it, something is intoxicating about not knowing your surroundings but seeing them as they really are. That happens in the dark.

Mordred and I wander in silence. I'm not sure if it's a comfortable one or not. This red-eyed demon is hard to read. Such kindness he's shown me, but there is something that skirts along his edges. Invisible and deadly, this man is dangerous.

Our stroll eventually brings us around to what would be courtyards, I think? If this were a normal castle. But because normal it is not, we come upon the sea of monstrous creatures. Lined up in perfect symmetry as far as the eye could see. They stand at attention, still in the linear, organized fashion they were in when I arrived. Do they ever sleep?

"Every king has enemies, child. I am no different." Mordred states as we stride down one of the many rock paths.

"I see."

"Have you recalled anything about your life in the Earth Realm?" He asks as we pass a towering statue that looks like the castle's lace-covered sorceress.

Mordred erected a statue of his muse. I'm not sure if I find that incredibly romantic or seriously fucking disturbing.

"I know the portals have been closed for years. The council banned the other realms from accessing them after the war. So, I'm still not sure how I ended up here. I've had a few flashes of faces, people I think I love, but they only happen as flickers in my mind. It's not enough to create a full picture."

Nodding, Mordred puts his hands behind his back and smiles. "The Netherworld has been at war for centuries. Like your realm, we've had our share of internal strife."

"That makes sense. The Netherworld is synonymous with horrors meant to torture souls who've earned a place with their evil deeds." I huff. That must be one of those things I just know, because I'm not sure where it came from.

Mordred chuckles. "You have strong opinions, girl."

"I suppose I do." My cheeks flush.

"As we speak, a self-proclaimed king sits upon my throne. That Dark Prince, they call him. The son of an old friend who plotted against me. Betrayed me. I was exiled from the heart of my realm, of course. But not before I took this expanse of land for myself. I built a civilization here in the Shadowlands. My sorceress harnesses the power of a volcano. Our forces grow stronger. I will not be an exiled king for much longer." He watches me as if gauging my reaction.

I haven't been here long, but he often looks at me that way. I didn't get the memo if I'm supposed to freak out about something he said. Why does he give a shit about my opinion? I could be 100% full of shit, and neither would know the difference. But I understand betrayal. I don't remember the specifics of my own life, but I know the pain. My heart tightens for him.

"This Dark Prince. He has done this to you?" I ask.

"His father, and then the son. He's done worse." Mordred extends his hand. I accept it, ignoring the involuntary shudder that runs down my spine.

We stroll back toward the castle in silence once again. I guess he's a man of few words. But as we come to the end of our walk, the nagging question in my head claws its way out of my mouth. "Mordred, do you know how I got here?"

His face doesn't seem taken aback; he doesn't seem to have a reaction at all. "Sadly, I do not. I was exploring when I came across your predicament, but I am grateful to have found you in time to spare your life."

That is a lie. I don't know how I know it is. I just do. It's at this moment that I remember the cut on my leg. It hasn't hurt since my bath. Odd.

The part of me still underwater wants out, furious at being deceived. If this Dark Prince was on the other side of the bridge, Mordred would not be exploring there alone. Why would a king go into enemy territory without guards? I didn't see any guards until we entered the castle. He may not know how I got to be inside this realm. I have no way of knowing that, but he was not *exploring* next to that river.

With a whisper of a smile, I reply. "Well, I suppose the answers will come when they're meant to. But, if it's alright with you, I think I'd like to get some rest."

"Of course, you must be exhausted. Let's get you to your quarters. We will resume our search for explanations tomorrow afternoon. Join me for tea in the garden."

"Um, sure," I reply.

He wasn't asking a question, and it didn't escape my notice. With another wave of his hand, my personal escort appears.

"Hello, Sweetness," Hunter murmurs as he approaches.

I don't bother with a reply. He can see how I react to him, the way my eyes dilate and my hips shift. I don't have to announce it. I'm not even sure if I welcome it. Plus, it's been one hell of a screwed-up day. My patience is running thin, and I'm running low on fucks in general.

"Hunter will escort you to your attendants. I assure you there are no hands more capable inside the Bone Keep as his." Mordred smirks.

"Goodnight, Mordred," is all I can muster in response.

Hunter takes a step closer and leans into me, letting a lock of his dark brown hair fall onto his forehead. Goddess, he is handsome, but this guy will be a thorn in my side. Him *and* his capable hands.

When he offers his arm, I allow him to lead me through the castle. We pass the dining hall, noting the pretty fae curled into the corner. Still in a fucking cage. My blood simmers…

"I know your secret."

With four words, Hunter ends the heat that was climbing my throat. He douses that flame and replaces it with fear. My secret. Those words let cyclones loose inside my stomach.

I chuckle. "You're going to have to be more specific. I have so many secrets to choose from."

Hunter grins, watching me eye him up. "Your ability to distract me is unmatched."

"I aim to please?"

"So, about that secret." My heart paces at his words. "You have a bleeding heart. I can feel your anger at the treatment of the traitor. Of all the traitors. It's a good thing to have compassion. A favorable trait for motherhood, but it's best to leave war decisions to the ones waging it."

First, thank the goddess, he does not know I've remembered anything. Second, I'm sure he just told me my place was barefoot and pregnant in the kitchen, but nicely.

Third, the motherhood comment is strange. Maybe he has a breeding kink or something? None of my business. This traitor business, though.

"Traitors?" I ask.

His mouth twists. "Those who aim to harm our King."

"He's not my…." *King.* Why did I say that? It's almost like I've said it before.

Hunter's gaze burns through my skin and into my bloodstream.

"Sorry, I just meant that I don't know him yet. Anyway, about that motherhood thing? I'd wait on the jury to see what sort of creature I am first. Some supernaturals eat their young." I joke, hoping to change the subject.

Hunter laughs, those perfect teeth gleaming. "You're funny, Sweetness."

Mission Accomplished.

Hunter and I pass through one chandelier-lined corridor after another. The design is similar in every one. Several ornate doors, dark walls, and obscure artworks depict debauchery in countless forms. I stop and tilt my head when we come to a picture of a woman and four men engaged in what looks like a great time. I just wonder where… well… where are all the dicks fitting? Simple biology says that supply doesn't meet demand. If you know what I mean.

I still have my head tilted, looking at it from a different angle when Hunter clears his throat. "See something you like?"

"Oh! Oh shit. I'm sorry, no, I just." I can't finish that sentence.

"You just?"

Oh, for fuck's sake. He's really going to make me say it. "Fine. I was trying to figure out how one woman could disappear four dicks. You know, because three holes. But four dicks."

Kill. Me. Now.

Lincoln would have a field day with this! Lincoln. Who is Lincoln? Linc. I have a memory! He's my friend. He is one of my friends! At the thought, my chest tightens, and I feel a tremor that causes Hunter to stop and stare at me. I don't want him to know about this. I try to tame my expression back to a combination of fatigue and curiosity, hoping it's enough to keep him at bay.

"You look like you've had a revelation." Hunter grins, running his tongue along with his perfect teeth.

I have! But, oh goddess, he thinks I've had a revelation about the dick equation. Hunter thinks that look of awe on my face was inspired by a confusing orgy. The version of me before the river must have been a terrible person to deserve this kind of karmic fuckery. I've been sitting here too long without an answer. But, goddess, now he really thinks I'm fantasizing about multiple dicks.

Stop saying dicks right now. Think, think, stupid girl. With a bashful grin on my lips, I lean closer to him. Through his thick jacket, I can feel the warmth of his body. "I just realized why you are my personal escort."

"Have you?" He grins.

"Well, you're very handsome. Am I right in thinking that perhaps Mordred wants to play matchmaker between us?"

The tip of Hunter's tongue runs along his lip as his gaze becomes hooded. "We can easily test that theory."

"Perhaps," I reply.

It doesn't matter who I am or what my name is. It doesn't matter what I know about myself, because one thing is universal. Give an interested man extra attention, and his brainpower will migrate straight to his dick. So it turns out the medieval wall porn helped after all.

Was that fair of me? Not really, but then again, what does *fair* mean? That's right, it's just a carnival. I need to remember that around here.

"You must use the weapons available to you. The mind is a weapon. Just as sharp as a blade, if you use it correctly."

Someone taught me that, my father, I think.

Hunter and I arrive at a platform, and he turns toward me. His bright eyes glistened, his hands running up and down my arms, creating a body buzz that vibrates straight through and below. I feel like I'm floating. My head swells with all the sensations he awakens within me, and the earth trembles under my clumsy feet even though they don't feel like they are touching the ground.

Hunter grabs my waist as I sink to the ground, and he pulls my body flush against his. His lips are impossibly close to mine. I can smell a minty sharpness on his breath. We stand here for much longer than we should, the tension coiling in us. Then, finally, my eyes close at the sheer pleasure of his touch.

When I am about to lean into it, a pair of angry storm clouds form inside my mind. Turquoise eyes are so intense that I can hardly catch my breath. There's a sharp tug on my insides, scratching at my core. Suddenly feeling overwhelmed, I look away from Hunter and step backward. No. This feels wrong.

"I enjoy the chase, Sweetness. Let me catch you, and when I do..." Hunter lowers his eyes to the area between my thighs.

"Would you look at the time?" I half-squeal. "Una and Marta will wonder where we are."

As Hunter moves to the side, he sighs. "They'll meet us here."

"Oh. Okay." I fidget with my hands, willing myself to stop thinking about those eyes. Those soul-consuming eyes.

The shape is circular in this part of the building, like the sun. In the center of the platform, the halls extend like beams. I imagine it's hard to keep your bearings when you are inside. Then I realize that's why they have recruited me to their drag race circus. If I don't know how to get from my door to the exit, I can't escape The Bone Keep.

Una and Marta appear ahead of us as if on cue. Hunter whispers into my ear before handing me off to my attendants. "I can't wait to taste you."

Whoa, okay. You know what? Wow!

I step toward Una and Marta, allowing them to whisk me away.

CHAPTER FIFTEEN

KILLIAN

"What do you mean, she vanished?" Marlow shoves her fist into my chest.

"I mean, I felt Genevieve about to wander outside the protection of this fortress from the… it doesn't matter where I was. I felt her. I followed her through the wildling woods. When it dawned on me what she would do, I panicked. But before I could tackle her to the ground, she stripped down and threw herself into the river Lethe!" I explain for the third time.

"I know what you believe you saw, Killian, but that is impossible. Vivi is a witch. She is hard-wired to sense magic. She would have felt that kind of dark magic from miles away, like a cosmic bitch slap right on the ass. She wouldn't have gone anywhere near it." Marlow replies.

"That's just it. She didn't seem to react to magic at all. Not hers, or mine, our bond, nothing. Someone nulled her, Marlow. She's spelled. I followed that river for miles, and she did not resurface. Our bond was muted and faint, but I can still feel her now. She didn't exit the river, but she is still alive."

"Alive in the river Lethe? How is that possible?" The twins asked in unison.

Marlow let loose another snarl. "You are mistaken!"

We've been back and forth for hours, but I know what I saw. Genevieve wandered through the forest as if she was following something I couldn't see. Genevieve didn't respond to my voice, magic, or our bond. And she jumped into that river. Our feisty historian refuses to believe me. She would rather lash out than think her friend is in enemy hands. I would feel the same if I were in her shoes. Although that isn't entirely true, I know I would do much, much worse.

I replay the memory in my head. It was like she was in a trance. Sorcery seems the most likely explanation, but I know of only one sorceress who can nullify. The most monstrous witch in the Nether Realm. Her name is Thane, and she is Mordred's mistress of terror. I can't entertain the thought of Genevieve in her clutches. No. Because even the idea of my queen anywhere near that perversion of nature makes my stomach churn.

"None of it matters now, Lowe. I know you're going to hate me for saying this, but you need to calm down. If Killian says she's alive, that means she is alive. The longer we stand here arguing, the further away she gets. If Killian thinks Mordred has her, he's right. We have to find her and get her out. End of story." Lincoln Blackwood attempts to referee our verbal sparring match, while Marlow only glares at him.

Anise bounces on her heels as Calypso snarls on one side and Grim on the other. She has been pacing and bouncing (and cursing my name). Muttering about hexing my nether regions and hanging slugs from my entrails as I beg to die. Among other colorful threats. Anise has many quirks, some of which are unpleasant, but nobody would ever accuse her of being disloyal. Even against her own brother, she fights for her friend. For her queen.

They all do, and I understand their anger.

None of them is angrier than I am with myself.

I was deep in the underbelly of the Night Fortress, behind the door that Genevieve had been desperately trying to unlock. How she found it is a mystery to me, but I have my suspicions. Meddling ancestors can cause so much turmoil, and for what? There's no way she's getting through. That door is spelled to the Fae Realms and back.

I'd been standing there for what felt like hours, staring at the root of all her suffering. Of mine. Of the entire realm. My father's cursed body.

Genevieve betrayed me. She cut me bone-deep. Did she know? Did my little mate understand what my father had done to us? Did she know about his twisted appetites? The Mad King is what he *should have been* titled. Lascivious, homicidal, vicious, and unpredictable. If she knew the things he'd done and then chose anyway…

Forcing me to become the one thing I vowed never to become. I channeled the worthless, vengeful God of Death. I became my father. I flayed her porcelain skin to the bone in front of the Night Court. I debased my queen in front of an audience.

Wicked thoughts swirl and fester in my mind, warring between anguish and hatred. Memories crashing against my broken edges. I looked upon my father, and after all he's done. Every scar, every horror. My loyalty remains. Maybe he spelled me too. I have never faltered in carrying out his plans. Not until her.

In the end, I found what I was looking for through that doorway. I found clarity.

If there was a way to put an end to my father. I would do it. For her, I would do a great many things. I had planned to visit her right after. To apologize. In fact, I would hold her tight and not let go.

I felt a slight tug at our bond as she departed the perimeter of my protection. The moment she passed them, I knew

I needed to act. I should have been on her dainty little ass before her toes crossed that line, but I hesitated. I was afraid she was trying to leave me. Would she just disappear into the forest without a word, explanation, or a goodbye? Did she really care that little for me?

I faltered because of my wounded pride, and I fucking hesitated.

Yes, I was livid with her. Yes, I was destroyed. But I would never risk her life. I'd rip the fabric of the realms apart to keep her safe. I'd lay down my sword, my powers, my immortal life. I'd forgive anything, anything at all. I'd choose her. And I never told her.

Jaggers's voice pierces my recollections. "She's tough as nails, Bro. Don't count her out."

He leans against the wall while he picks his nails with a dagger. He's right, of course. My girl is a blood born warrior. Jagger, as the voice of reason. Our world has been flipped on its end. I sigh, running my fingers through my disheveled hair.

"If he lays a finger on her, I'll fucking gut you, Killian. King or not, I will gut you and walk to the guillotine with my tits out smiling!" Marlow shrieks as Jagger drops the dagger back into its sheath and drags her tightly against him.

Protective, but of who? I smirk at what I think the answer might be. I guess my brother and I are not so different after all.

A hush settles over the hall as Kalliope descends the left side of the split stairwell. She's been calm since learning the news of her sister's disappearance, unnaturally so. Yet, her behavior has suspicions at an all-time high. Allegations of treachery float among our circles. Some believe she sold her sister out. I do not.

If Kalliope had set Genevieve up to be captured, she would have fled. There is no logical explanation for her to remain inside my fortress. Mordred has had his sights set on tainting the entire realm with his dark sorcery for as long as I can remember, and now he has Genevieve. If the prophecies are accurate, he now has the weapon he needs. But, no. If she were loyal to Mordred, she would have stolen away in the night.

Kalliope faces me as if she can read my thoughts. "Father has Genevieve. If she has no memory of who she is, I promise he planned it that way. He does nothing without motive. She won't understand the power she holds, nor will she be able to wield it. He'll keep her distracted. He'll attempt to breed her with one of his creations, and then he will take her blood. Her blood is the key."

"Anyone who lays a finger on her skin is fucking DEAD!" My voice carries like thunder. Blue streaks skitter across the marble. The fortress trembles under the intensity of my rage.

"Killian," Jagger warns. "Chill out."

"Her blood is the key to what?" I cock my head, wrath thrumming through my veins.

Kalliope looks at me as though I'm daft. "To the curse, of course."

No. I refuse to accept this. Is it true what my mother has been saying all along?

They make curses to be broken.

The fates have plans, and we don't dare interfere.

You cannot escape destiny, my son.

My body hums with electricity, energy begging to be freed. I am fearsome. I am the strongest being in the realm. This is true, but I have a secret. One that few are privy to. I am not quite the all-powerful ruler I am advertised to be. That is an impossibility because the rest of my power lives within my father's body. Not alive, not dead. My ancestral birthright hangs in suspended animation, and I believe Kalliope just said that Genevieve is the one to set me free.

"What do we do?" Amethyst bites her nails as she listens to Kalliope.

"I don't know," I reply, my stomach full of lead.

Kalliope plants her hands on the banister, leaning in. "He designs his children for specific purposes, but you already knew that. Didn't you, Nether King? Just like you know, if she does not submit to him, he *will* bend her to his will."

I recognize that truth, and my chest plummets. Genevieve will not yield. She may not understand who she is, but the gods crafted her soul from the same thing an inferno is made of. She will not bend. She will not back down. He'll attempt to break her, and she will destroy herself to prevent it from happening.

"Father didn't expect you." Kalliope cuts back in. "He doesn't understand love, the power it holds. And that is your advantage."

In the past, I would have blanched at her blatant use of the "L" word, but that doesn't matter anymore. I didn't understand what I had. Kalliope believes I can reach her. The idea tumbles through my head as it settles into my rib cage. First, I'll find my girl and help her remember who she is. Then, I'll bring her home.

Genevieve may not be my queen in truth, at least not yet, but I intend to fix that after I have crushed everyone who stands between us. I have made every mistake. I have taken every wrong turn. But I will spend eternity correcting it if it takes that long.

CHAPTER SIXTEEN

THE BONE KEEP - WEEK ONE

AFTER FALLING INTO A paranormal river, a few pleasant walks with a possible homicidal maniac, several dinners straight from hell, and all the unexpected sexual attention Hunter lays on so thick, I am exhausted. It seems to all be catching up with me tonight, and I am ready to dive face-first into oblivion and sleep like a mound of buried bones.

Marta and Una don't linger in my quarters this evening. I would say I'm disappointed, but I would be lying. I haven't had many moments alone since I pulled myself from the muddy riverbank of doom, and although I am thoroughly done with life at the moment. This is one of the few opportunities where I can exhale, relax, and meditate without the buzz of background voices.

I've learned the hard way that forcing memories is painful, also stupid, and requires hand scrubbing blood droplets out of my clothing with salt paste and my own toothbrush because that is what's available to me. I can't ask someone else to clean them because I don't want people to know what I was doing to make them bloody.

I don't want them to know that I know some things…

A few nights back, I got pretty godsdamned sick of saying the words *"I don't know."* And there was something about this room that awakened a connection. I can't define or explain it, so you'll just have to take my word. The chamber calls to me when I am alone. I've followed the call, inspecting walls, drawers, and hidey holes in floorboards. All the perfect places for stashing dirty secrets.

I was right, by the way.

Well, I was right in the sense that there are things stashed in this room. Not so much about the dirty secrets. I found a sketch pad and some charcoals inside a closet hidey-hole and a space under the rug where the rock is cut in a perfect square.

It's the sketch pad and charcoals I climb into bed with tonight. There are several used pages, although they aren't sketches. They're the deeply haunting words of an incredibly lonely girl. I've taken to pouring over them at night, looking for... I don't know. A spark. A closer connection to this broken girl. She's like putting a mirror up to my face. The memories stir when I read her words, and I believe they'll come back to me one day.

My fingers trace the paper lightly as I devour the enchanting words, repeating them by heart.

"Fire in the darkness. Watchers of the shade. From the stars we came to the stars we defy. The first, the last, the eternal. Daughters of shadow. Bound by nothing. Conquered by none."

What brilliant mind crafted these words that wrap tendrils of light around my spine and squeeze? Whose broken soul bled this poetry into parchment? Sometimes I think I can feel her here, my invisible muse. I flip to the back of the sketchbook, where I've added my own contributions.

My heart throws itself against my ribcage as I settle on my current work of art. A pair of haunting eyes. Tempestuous waves hold lightning and ether, passion and intensity, danger and deliverance. The eyes of the man who plagues my dreams. When I look at them, it's almost as if I'm torn in two. My body shivers and my mouth goes dry.

There's a water pitcher on the sparsely decorated dresser, along with crystal glass, but it's across the room, and I am already wrapped in a blanket burrito. The growl in my stomach makes me wish I'd eaten something when I had the chance. Maybe it's best I just roll over and try to sleep.

If overthinking was a superpower, I would be the queen of all the realms.

Today sucked, just like all the rest, but I remembered a name. I even wrote it on the back of the sketch pad. That's where I've been squirreling away bits and pieces of what I remember. Which isn't much, not yet anyway. I know I should sleep, but the nagging feeling makes me anxious. Maybe if I start there, something will jog my memory. Lincoln. I focus on the word. Images blur against the haze, and I almost see a face before it drifts away. I clench my fists and slam them on the thin mattress. Tears well up in my eyes as frustration and despair threaten to overwhelm me. The exhaustion is settling in, but I try to move past it. Focused on that single word.

Lincoln.

A dull roar fills my head as my body stretches and pulls. I feel strange, like I am expanding. Sweat breaks out across my top lip. My legs shake, and my spine bows. My palms tingle, and then they ignite. Violet flames erupt like an explosion of pure, undiluted power. Despite my depleted state, I smile. Mesmerized by the flames dancing in my palms. I have magic. I'm still fascinated by that, although I'm hesitant to show the full extent to anyone inside this castle.

A sharp pain explodes behind my eyes, and I scramble from the blankets. I barely make it to the fancy trashcan before losing what's left in my stomach. Then, with my hands shaking, I reach for the water on the dresser.

Taking a big gulp to wash the tang out of my mouth, I notice something is off. There's a hint of sorcery and crushed petals on my tongue, but it's already too late. Within moments, I am blissfully unaware of what I was so upset about.

My body calms, and then my most pressing thought is about slinking back under the warm blankets and finally getting some sleep. Hunter will collect me tomorrow, and maybe we can spend the day together. Wouldn't that be nice? It's the last thing I remember before drifting into the starlight abyss.

He fills my soul with all the heat I have been missing. His smoky, sweet scent permeates me with silky warmth. Rough fingers trail across my skin, leaving burning passion in their wake. The touch of his skin is divine. I dream of stormy turquoise skies. Soft lips caressing mine. Flames lick at my chest and scorch my nerves. My desire for him is beyond comprehension.

His hot tongue glides down my stomach, lapping, caressing all the way to the apex of my thighs, and I gasp. Galaxies whirl in the surrounding space, and the ocean churns with violent waves. He stares into my eyes and thrusts his tongue deep into my pussy, and I quake. It's him alone, keeping me afloat with pure pleasure. He consumes me. Burns through all my layers straight to my core. The heat builds to a crescendo, mixing sensations until I feel as though I will split apart. His firm hands hold me as I approach the cliff's edge. My heart swells, and I free fall. Euphoria floods me as I crash against the shore.

In a moment of clarity, a velvety male voice penetrates the illusion. "You are mine."

A burst of adrenaline jolts me awake. A thick layer of sweat coats my body. My heart races like crazy. I can feel it. Someone is watching me. They lurk in the shadows, waiting. The flood of irrational fear overwhelms me, and I become paralyzed. This is terror, like an old memory, trapped and alone in my bed.

The dark figure moves inhumanly, but it's only a shadow. My overactive imagination comes back to haunt me. I release a shaky breath, willing myself to get it together. I only need more sleep, that's all. Perhaps I can propel myself back into a fantasy with the literal man of my dreams.

I lay my head back down, turning toward the wall and denying my mind, when a phantom hand covers my mouth, and a gritty voice whispers into my ear. "Don't move."

I freeze in place, thinking of the dagger. What kind of dumbass goes to bed and doesn't put the dagger under her pillow?

Me. I'm the dumbass.

The voice persists. "I don't mean you harm, but you must listen to me. You are a queen; you have more power than you could ever imagine. Discover it, access it, and then use it. There is no one you can trust. Nobody. Remember who you are, Genevieve."

A gentle breeze moves across the bridge of my nose, and I swerve to discover who is trying to help me. *Genevieve.* But my ears fill with the sound of shattered glass. *Genevieve.* My water pitcher and the crystal glass. *Genevieve.* It's the strangest thing, as if they exploded.

By the time I return my attention to the spot he was in, it's too late. The phantom voice has escaped, along with any answers I'd been hoping to get. Fuck! I pull my sheet off the bed and lay it on the floor as a makeshift dustpan, readying myself to clean up the mess, when my door bursts off the hinges. Hunter.

"What did the door ever do to you?" I call over my shoulder.

Mr. Walking Red Flag is hiding an ugly side beneath that charming smile.

"What happened? I heard a struggle. Has someone attacked you?" Hunter's face is the picture of a perfect gentleman. Too bad I'm not so easily fooled. I already saw a glimpse of what lurks underneath.

"Only the clumsy bug." I fake a smile. "I got up to take care of some lady stuff… and I forgot to put the lantern next to the bed before I went to sleep. So I tried to reach for it in the dark, but I tripped and knocked the pitcher off the dresser."

I'm not telling him shit.

After watching me for a flash, he shakes his head. "You need to be more careful, sweetness. Come with me. Someone will get this cleaned up."

His boots crunch against the glass covered floor, and he lifts me up. His touch has a tingling sensation. He smells like vanilla beans. Was there something I was stressed about before? It doesn't matter. It can't be that important. While he carries me to his quarters, I lean my head against Hunter's chest, and all my worries disappear.

It hadn't occurred to me that Hunter had wrapped me in a blanket and not much else. The thin nightgowns they have provided for me leave very little to the imagination. For a moment, I worry this might look bad to Mordred. Are there rules on this? I'm so disoriented and drowsy, almost as if I'm drugged. I remember Hunter trailing his fingers over my skin and complimenting me until I must have fallen asleep in his lap.

There was nothing that crossed any boundaries, though I feel like I might have welcomed it. Hunter's touch carries the kind of oblivion a girl could get used to, but I'd be lying if I said I didn't drift off picturing haunting turquoise eyes.

What is wrong with me? Having those thoughts while I have a handsome man lavishing me with his affection? I'm an asshole for that, but whatever I felt in that dream, that's what alive feels like. That's what I want in my life. All consuming passion. The type of connection that stops time and commands the stars. I can't help but hope that man exists somewhere out in the universe because, gods damn, I want him for my own.

When Una knocks on his door to announce my room is cleaned and I can go back to bed, I hold back my sense of relief.

———————◦O◦———————

Breakfast is awkward. Let's just leave it at that. I'm guzzling coffee like a champ in between bites of strawberry pancakes. I guess I must be the only one in the building who has a caffeine habit because instead of minding their own business and eating like ordinary people, everyone is staring at me.

Sylas has blessed us with his presence this morning, and his shitty attitude came along for the ride. Una looks a hot mess, chewing on her lip and fidgeting. The only way Hunter could get closer was if he wrapped his entire body around me. And Mordred seems pleased by this. I ask myself why and I come up with no explanation. There is more going on than I currently understand. That ruffles my feathers a bit. I am discovering that I don't like to be kept in the dark. And Marta. Well… let's just say if I die here, I'm sure it will be because she smothered me in my sleep.

I need to remember who the fuck I was before I got into that river, and what I was doing there. Things are getting weird, with the pockets of empty time and unexplainable mood shifts. There's something wrong with me. I should regain my memories, according to Mordred. And I remembered a name a few days ago, but oddly, I don't recall it this morning. Which makes me wonder if I ever recognized the name in the first place?

They have returned the lilac fae to her corner cage. A majestic bird who's had her wings clipped. Sadness settles into my bones at the thought of her withering away.

Yet, today, something casts her eyes downward. Her body appears fine. There are no bruises or wounds visible when I sneak a glance, but something has wounded her spirit.

My arms and legs break out in goosebumps, subtle magic prodding my senses like being poked with a stick. With one glance across the dining room table, I lock gazes with a pair of sky-blue eyes: annoying. Sylas looks furious. With me! I don't understand what I did to him that warrants the stare of hatred, but okay then. This place is fucking strange.

Although his stare makes me uncomfortable, I can't seem to turn away from it. Mesmerized by his pupils, I peer further into their depths. A sharp pain jolts through my hand, and I look down. I'm convinced I'll find some type of rabid night creature taking a bite out of me. But there's nothing. Again, odd.

The lilac fae coughs. It's the first sound I've heard her make this morning. I want to turn my head and check on her. But I know it isn't safe. Sylas clears his throat, and I look back at him. He looks like he's about to pop an eye socket this time.

Okay, he's trying to tell me something.

I believe they both are.

I blink, following his line of sight. He's staring at my cup. Looking back into his eyes, something dark passes between us, and then I get it. I swirl the coffee inside the mug, shoving it to the side to be taken away.

CHAPTER SEVENTEEN

THE BONE KEEP - WEEK TWO

I CAN'T IMAGINE WHY walking is such a popular hobby in the Shadowlands. As far as I can tell, the only thing to see is tar bubbling up from the cold, hard ground. Death clings to anything that tries to thrive. It's all night creatures and nothingness. It's a bit of a wasteland, but I suppose the tea garden has a morbid beauty.

The towering willows don't hold any color, the gray branches that curve toward the ground contrast with the crimson sky. Yet, it makes me feel something. It's said that Weeping Willows symbolize death, which is fitting for a place as desolate as this, but to me, they look like art. A thing does not have to be pleasant to be beautiful. Even amid darkness, beauty still exists. If you know where to look.

"What's on your mind, child?" Mordred asks as he lifts our afternoon tea to his lips.

Mordred and I have a routine, or I guess you could call it. We spend our afternoons in the shadow garden, drinking tea under an iron gazebo among the fever rose and blood lilies, the only plants that thrive in this unforgiving landscape.

"Nobody knows anything about me. I'm nameless. Homeless. I don't have a purpose. Without a past, how can I see my future?" I finally responded to Mordred's question. Fishing a little.

Genevieve.

He regards me for a moment, and I swear I see a flash of satisfaction in his eyes. "Now, you can be anyone you wish to be. Isn't that also true? Who's saying you enjoyed your former life? How do you know you were happy? This may be the greatest gift to receive. The fates have intervened, and who are we to question them?"

"Yeah, I guess so." I lower my head, picking at my leggings.

Maybe he's right, maybe not. But I don't believe for a minute that I could be anyone I wish to be. Considering he knows who I am. *Genevieve.* Plus, I'm confined in the Bone Keep, repeating each day on loop, devoid of many choices at all. So I can't help but think what he really means is that I can be anyone *he* wishes me to be.

My forehead creases as I fiddle with my spoon. I can't remember things I knew *after* arriving at The Bone Keep. Things I know I learned here. Call me Nancy Drew, but the math isn't adding up, and I intend to discover why. So, I repeat the thing I cannot allow myself to forget. *Genevieve.* My name is Genevieve.

"You haven't had a sip of your tea." Mordred points out.

"Oh… yes, I suppose I haven't." I pick up the teacup and take a healthy sip. The aftertaste sits on the back of my tongue, bitter and sharp.

We converse for a few minutes, rehashing the same old subjects we've already discussed. For example, Mordred would like Hunter and me to be engaged. Something about lifting morale before they march on the enemy. Apparently, weddings are an effective distraction from the possibility of having an arrow shot up your ass. Or your head lopped off like the one that rots in the middle of the courtyard.

I recognize that giant skull as having come from a Grendel. Another thing that must have been living in the 'useless information' section of my brain. I don't seem to have any issue at all with those memories…

I've noticed how people perceive that skull as an offense. Their body language goes rigid, and their noses turn up. Yet they haven't removed it. I wonder why? I'm sure there's a juicy story there. I only wish I felt comfortable enough to ask.

Anyway, back to the original train of thought. Marriage. I about choked on my dinner the first time he mentioned it. What a way to find out they arrange marriages in the Netherworld! That it isn't about love or even attraction from what I'm gathering. In this realm, marriage is a tool. I remember learning about this when I was younger. It must have been in school. Although that part of my memory is still a relatively blank space, things have been filtering back in pieces, but there's no rhyme or reason. Most of them center on my earliest memories, anyway. So, they're not much help in this situation.

I do see the merit of arranged marriages. They could symbolize the promise of protection. Or pull someone from the dregs of poverty and elevate them to a throne. To power. I don't think I've ever cared much about any of those things, but to each their own. If I'm honest, I couldn't tell you what I wanted.

Stormy eyes emerge inside my mind, mocking me, calling me a liar. They've been a more and more persistent distraction through these weeks. Some nights, I can barely wait to go to bed and meet him in my dreams. I only wish I had remembered the details in the morning. But I suppose that's how dreams operate: cryptic manifestations of our wildest subconscious desires.

This line of conversation sours my mood. It's not like I can contribute power or advantage to the Kingdom of the Shadowlands. So, I'm not clear on what the point is? But Mordred is persistent. He wants my agreement, and he wants it fast tracked. Each time we discuss it, his frustration is more and more clear.

And then there's the other... um... what was the other thing Mordred is always talking about again? I take another sip of the bitter tea. Sometimes my mind feels hazy, full of fog, and I lose minutes. Or maybe hours? I'm not sure. There's no rhyme or reason with the empty spaces.

"I'm sorry. What were we talking about again? I must have been daydreaming." I ask Mordred.

He grins. "We agreed Hunter will remain your escort. Kings have enemies, dear one. You would be quite the prize for the Dark Prince, and you wouldn't want that now, would you?"

"No."

I shudder to think of it. Each day, after having our tea, Mordred and I sit and talk about the Netherworld. He's shared countless stories of the histories, the tales of how everything came to be, and of the Shadowlands. It turns out the Dark Prince is even worse than I expected, but there is one story that haunts me to my bones...

As Mordred explains it. In the beginning, kings did not rule the Netherworld. Gods and Goddesses ruled all. Aedonius was a god, the God of Death. And Mordred, too, the God of War. They were friends, but they loved the same woman. A dreadful goddess who was known for stirring discourse among men, and she excelled at what the cosmos created her to do.

It didn't come as a surprise to hear that their friendship was torn apart. The fighting between them was destructive. Death and War battling across the realm. So, the other gods and goddesses stepped in and made her choose. She chose Mordred, and they left the Night Fortress to build this stronghold beneath a volcano.

To make matters more complicated, this goddess becomes pregnant. Aedonius abducted the woman, held her captive, and cut Mordred's child from her womb in a fit of jealousy. Letting her die and keeping the child for his own.

How fucked up is that? But it gets worse.

In his grief, Mordred allowed himself to be weakened. He was overthrown and exiled. Aedonius declared himself King of the Netherworld and betrothed Mordred's stolen daughter to *his* son. The Dark Prince.

Not knowing his only son had plans for revenge. So at the first opportunity, the prince hexed his Aedonius to sleep for all time. Which I guess he deserved, if you think about it, but the prince turned out to be even worse than his father.

A true tyrant. He is an incubus king who uses sex and mind control on his own people while butchering Shadowlings in the streets for entertainment. Real dirtbag-type stuff. And that's the guy who's supposed to marry Mordred's daughter if she's even still alive.

No wonder Mordred is starting a war.

I mean, besides the obvious God of War thing.

———◆———

"Hey. Sweetness! Hello?" Hunter's voice pulls me from my contemplations.

I train my eyes on him, bewildered. Was I not just having afternoon tea with Mordred? Now Hunter sits across from me at the latticework table, and the light reflecting off the gazebo has shifted. How long have I been here? Shaking my head, I sigh. I lost track of myself again.

"I'm not feeling well. I'd like to go lie down."

Hunter's teeth grind. I can see his jaw tighten. Then, his eyes flash darkly, "I did not permit you to speak of the Dark Prince."

I didn't realize I was speaking about anything, but I was startled at his violent reaction. My instinct is to agree, if only to escape his anger.

"I said. You will not speak of the Dark Prince. Do you understand me?" His face reddens, spittle flies from his lips, and peppers my cheeks.

"Y… yes?"

The next thing I know, forceful hands are grasping my jaw tightly. "His filthy name doesn't touch your lips, and don't you ever *forget* it again!"

Holding back the tremor possessing my body is a Herculean effort. I can't decide if it's fear of what I may do, fury that will turn to fire, or murderous rage. It takes everything I have to restrain myself. But I know I must.

Hunter's face softens, like everything that just transpired was in my head. Then a menacing smile creeps back to his lips. "Walk with me, beautiful."

I don't want to walk with him. I want to yank his spine from his body, light his ass on fire, and dance in the fucking ashes. I'd like to snatch his balls and twist, pay back for the way he leers at me, like I'm something to manipulate. A possession to own. My palms sweat, and heat rushes through my limbs. Based on Hunter's expression, my eyes are probably glowing. Violet flames explode from my chest, scorching the tar-filled ground in a perfect circle around me.

"Good, good. You're getting stronger. Now, put them out. We wouldn't want to have any *accidents*, would we?" He asks. The question is obviously a veiled threat.

I don't have the energy to engage with this now, so I nod.

"Let's get you to bed," Hunter suggests as he lays his hand on the crook of my arm.

His voice is enthralling. Thousands of tiny needles prick at my skin, and my flames sputter out. The quiver that glides up my arm makes everything feel right again.

I let loose a deep sigh. "Okay."

CHAPTER EIGHTEEN

THE BONE KEEP - WEEK THREE

DAYS AND NIGHTS WEAVE together. Dinners and walks. Afternoon tea and endless conversation that I don't pay attention to anymore. It has become harder and harder to tell what is delusion and what is reality. I feel as though I'm constantly clinging to the ledge. Dangling by the tips of my fingers, and they slip. They always slip. The question is, would I follow myself into the shadows over that ledge? And what would I find there? I already know there is a darkness that dwells within me. She grows more powerful here. I grapple with the most disturbing thoughts.

Blood.

Torture.

Executions.

I think I might be a demon.

I get the distinct impression Mordred would love that. Walls are pressing in on me, and he thinks I haven't noticed them. I have. He started with isolation; he introduced me to acquaintances so he could take them from me. It's been days since I have seen anyone other than Mordred, the banshees, and Hunter. Then it was the repeated conversations among the blood lilies. The ones where he tells me half-truths, and I pretend not to notice. The memories have stopped flowing, but something else has taken hold of me.

I know things. I hear things. I feel things. My senses unfurl and search the air. They do it by themselves. Magic with no master. I'm more than what these people want me to believe, so much more. I imagine that's why Mordred has made no substantial moves to help me recover my memories. Just the same old promises. Thane is working on it, and he's sure they'll return with time. And if they do? I am to tell him everything I discover.

It is what it is. I have little hope of seeing my memories again. I'm getting acquainted with the idea of never knowing what made me who I am. Did my parents love me? I don't let the melancholy whisper to me. It won't do any good. There's no use in crying over spilled perfume, right?

What's gone is gone, but what's over the horizon hasn't been determined yet. I like those odds better. And all is not lost. I still have what's in the back of my secondhand sketchbook. Names, sentences, scenes that seem like visions. They're my memories. It's too bad that none of them make a lick of sense to me.

I'll confess it now. I riddled most of the pages with depictions of my storm cloud with skin and how our bodies may look if they were to be intertwined with each other. My dreams are an incredible inspiration. It might even border on obsession at this point. He comes to me every night, in technicolor. It's a shame the details fade after I open my eyes.

Just fantasies. What do I care? I am liable to lose my mind if I don't indulge in something at The Bone Keep. And I don't mean standing awkwardly in a hallway, staring at an orgy canvas. Besides, sleeping is a pleasant way to spend the day. Wrapped up in those dreams with a figment of my inappropriate imagination. And in the night, I make time for Hunter. He holds me and caresses my skin. His touch conjures an oblivion I can't get enough of. I'm nobody, nothing, and the void never felt so perfect.

I won't be intimate with him, much to his disappointment. I simply cannot do it. We're fine. Hunter is sexy, attentive, if not a little overbearing. He's fine. It's just... when I think about taking that next step with him... my brain goes berserk. It's not just my brain, though. It's more like my whole being. Body, mind, and soul. As if anyone having that part of me is unthinkable, sickening.

So, I guess despite the way his skin tingles on mine, the path his power takes when it's winding up my thighs, bringing me to arousal, it's doubtful that I will ever go farther. The satisfying numbness those amorous deeds offer? My soul is against it.

How can I argue with that?

I'll marry him, if that's what Mordred wants. To me, it doesn't matter because they are immortal. In other words, heirs are nice, but unnecessary. A woman can be a wife only in name. If it helps the cause, I'll go along with it. Mordred assures me that my union with Hunter will strike a devastating blow to the Dark Prince of the Netherworld. I don't see why a Nether Realm prince would give a shit about a nobody like me, but how would I know what provokes a tyrant?

Since I have become more "reasonable" (whatever that might mean), Mordred doesn't mind if I wander certain areas of the Bone Keep on my own. Mordred-approved areas, of course. Which only includes the dining hall, tea garden, my quarters, and now the library. Even though it isn't much, it's four places I can go to and be left the hell alone.

I've taken a liking to the library. Something about it feels comforting, like warm blankets and laughter with a friend. A friend. I don't feel like I have one here... but I think I've had one in the past. This library is small and not very well stocked, but there are plush chairs that soak you right up when you curl into them. And that is worlds better than the metal chairs in the gazebo.

It's raining today. Drops of scarlet fall from the sky onto the muddy tar filled land below. I take it in with more than just my eyes, noting the tiny details others often overlook. It reminds me of a battlefield where carnage paints the ground. So, that's what I draw. Battlescapes, either from my imagination or from another life.

Hunter noticed the sketch pad while loitering in my quarters unannounced. I remember my chest drowning in dread, my skin ready to turn itself inside out. But for whatever reason, he never opened it. So after that, I found a better hiding place. And Hunter must have misread the situation to my benefit, because the next day, I had several brand-new sketchbooks and top-of-the-line charcoals waiting on my bedside table. Since then, I've filled them with anything my mind can conjure.

A meek voice attempts to gain my attention. It's Una. "Miss Genevieve?"

I lift my head, wondering if I heard her correctly. "Who is Genevieve?"

"You are Genevieve, remember?" She regards me for a moment, most likely waiting to see if I'll throw a tantrum. When she realizes I'm too stunned to question her, she continues. "Our king extends his apologies, but he cannot join you for tea this afternoon. He requested I deliver yours."

I am Genevieve.

Una is fidgeting. Something has her spooked. I narrow my gaze and search her face for clues, making no attempt to hide my suspicion. "What are you so nervous about?"

Una turns, checking the area. I'm half-tempted to help her out by letting her know we're alone. She won't find anyone.

I'd worked out a deal of sorts with the king. I no longer have a twenty-four-hour escort following me while inside the walls of the Bone Keep. I agreed to fetch Hunter if I wanted to go outdoors, and in return, I got a small measure of peace. Which she is interrupting, I might add. I'm tempted to tell her that too, but my curiosity wins.

It's astonishing what people will expose when the silence becomes uncomfortable. And so I wait. Unwilling to speak, hanging on for the moment when she breaks down. Fortunately, it doesn't take long.

"Miss Genevieve." she leans in, setting a saucer and teacup on the table and making an odd face at me. Why is Una whispering? "I think you'll find today's flavor quite mouthwatering."

I laugh out loud. "Oh, I very much doubt that, Una! We have vastly different ideas of what makes a good tea."

Her paper white cheeks are warm with a hint of purple. "I don't mean to offend, but I think you should try it, nevertheless."

Interesting. Okay, fine. I'll play along.

Lifting the cup to my lips, I shoot another quick look in her direction. Am I being an idiot right now? Is this the part where the girl in the movie is about to be incredibly stupid, and everyone in the seats is shouting… "What the fuck are you doing?!"

I suppose it could be, but I'm going to do it, anyway. Do I have a death wish? No, not really. I'm already in the Netherworld, so I don't see much of a point. But I am curious about something. Una has been kind to me. And yes, she looks like she belongs in the bottom of a well or climbing out of someone's television with seaweed wrapped around her legs. But she has been kind, I'd even say friendly.

If there's poison in this cup, it will answer some of my growing suspicions.

If not. No harm done, right?

Smiling wickedly, I take a sip.

A pleasant, berry-sweet taste hits my tongue, and my eyes widen. This tastes nothing like the swamp water Mordred has been feeding me every day. "Una, I think it's time we have a chat. One where you tell me what the hell is going on in this castle."

CHAPTER NINETEEN

KILLIAN

THE RUMBLE AND CRASH of glass shattering has Jagger barging through my door again. It's not the first thing I've destroyed in a fit of anguish disguised by rage. Genevieve's mind is addled. She's too foggy. I can't break through to her from this far away, not unless she's asleep, but it's the same every time she wakes up. Her mind, our bond. They both descend into the darkness. I should be able to breach this thrall. But, instead, something is blocking me from her, something more than meets the eye.

"We NEED to act!" I grind my teeth, electricity crackling in my knuckles.

Jagger leans against the dresser. "No, what you *need* is a shower. When is the last time you drank something other than whiskey?"

"I don't give a fuck."

"Your mother raised such a gentleman." Jagger grins. "You already know what Kalliope said. All Mordred needs is for you to lose your shit and walk right into his trap, and then it's bye-bye Nether Realm as we know it. And I'm not usually one for pointing out the obvious, but you're doing a bang-up job of losing your shit, bro."

My brother pauses, looking for a reaction he will not get out of me.

"She's strong, Killian. Stronger than anyone I know." Jagger repeats the same thing he's said to me a hundred times.

"But she doesn't remember…." I whisper, letting the rest of that thought fade.

I don't know what transpired between my girl and Kalliope before she was taken. Yes, there was love hidden under all the claws and flying fur, but they mostly wanted to tear each other to shreds. They were on the verge of needing supervision. But on that last day, they didn't.

Something powerful happened between their visit to Gravestone Academy and when I woke up from my wounds. I don't know what it was, and Kalliope isn't exactly forthcoming, but it healed them.

Genevieve now has what she's always wanted: fierce and unconditional love from her sister. Her blood. She has a family, she belongs, and she's not even here to witness it. My heart thinks it's cracking in two, and maybe it is.

Kalliope moved into Genevieve's rooms with Calypso and Grim. I didn't have the heart to tell her no. The silence was deafening anyway, the emptiness filling every dark corner. To be truthful, I welcomed it. If only to lie in my bed and listen to the shuffling of movement between the doors. I can close my eyes and pretend it's her banging around in there, doing her best to drive me insane. It's not enough to quell the ache, but if I drink myself to stupidity—the memories help me believe she's moments away from wandering in with nothing but a t-shirt and a smile.

When I open my eyes, the illusion fades away, and I'm plunged back into the depths of melancholy.

Kalliope revealed to me she and Genevieve can communicate telepathically. It confirmed a suspicion I had when she first arrived. Something I've got Marlow, Amethyst, and Sybil working on. Those ladies are tenacious. I'd be willing to wager that their trio could unlock the secrets of all the realms if only given a few days and a bottomless coffee thermos.

Lincoln has made himself sparse these weeks. Holed up with Anise, avoiding me, but there is nothing under this roof I don't already know about. He's good for her. They have an understanding nobody else has accomplished. Not Jagger, not even me. He calms the cyclones inside her mind. I suppose I should be jealous, being replaced, but I don't have the heart for it.

My heart belongs in one place, the only place it will ever be. This feeling, mother calls it *helplessness*, is foreign to me. I rarely encounter anything I can't handle, but this is tearing me to fucking pieces.

"And I am to sit by and do nothing. Just wait while another man puts his hands on *my wife*! She doesn't know what's happening to her. My queen doesn't know ME!" I shout, shaking the windows as the door opens between Genevieve's and my room.

The sensation of eyes on me becomes overwhelming. When I turn to the source of that irritation, Kalliope stands in the doorway. Wearing one of Genevieve's shirts and a pair of jeans with ripped knees. She stares at me with disdain and my chest aches. It's the same defiant look Genevieve gives anyone who opposes her, especially me. I need that smart-assed, take no prisoners, infuriating woman. I need her like I need to breathe.

Kalli snorts, "Oh, give me a break, Romeo. You are going to sit here and wait with the rest of us. I know the Bone Keep front to back and sideways. There is no way in, only out. And before you get the clever idea that you're going to bust through the front gate on a power charge. They spell the obsidian."

"What would you have us do?"

Kalliope pauses, rolling her eyes. "If she's with Hunter, and I already told you, I suspect she is. He's suppressing her with physical touch. He's an incubus, like you, but father corrupts his toys. Twists them, distorts their powers. Hunter is father's pet psycho. He is an incubus, Killian, but he can do much more than he should be able to."

She stops, grabbing the whiskey bottle and pouring herself a shot. Knocking it back.

"There's nothing we can do. She must overpower Hunter. And she *can* overpower him; she can do much worse than that. It has to be her. Nobody inside this fortress can get inside the Bone Keep and go unnoticed. She must remember and break free of the stranglehold on her magic. I'm sorry, that's the truth. She's brilliant, though. Genevieve will come through this, but I'll cut you if you ever tell her I said that."

The Shadow Princess pours yet another shot of whiskey and downs it. The tink of the glass hitting the dresser is like hearing a pin drop. Right about now, she's more like her sister than she would like to admit, all hard stubborn edges and a smart mouth.

Kalliope runs her fingers through her snow-white hair. "Okay, fine. We have some things to talk about."

Jagger and I stiffen in unison. Genevieve's sister has been uncooperative, discourteous, and just as impossible as her sister from the moment she arrived. We've tried to get inside information countless times, and she has refused. Why now?

Kalliope pours another shot and slams it before she takes a deep breath.

"Mordred is not the only one who wanted us born. The oracles did not foretell us for a war of kings, Killian. They foretold us to be created by dark magic... to kill immortal gods." The weight of her stare makes my insides writhe.

"Are you saying you're God Killers?!" I ask, unable to wrap my brain around that revelation.

Kalliope nods and grins. "Well, she is. So, you better watch your ass, King of the Netherworld. I was a failed experiment, better suited for other purposes. My sister is his ultimate weapon. Did you think Father hasn't known where she was all along? He ordered Faustus to break her, mold her, and make her cold."

"Why?" I ask, fists clenched.

"Why does anyone create a weapon capable of untold destruction? Power. Control. Manipulation. All the above." Kalliope shrugs.

"I meant, why break her?" I ask, muscles coiled. An unfamiliar ache in my chest.

"If I were to guess, I'd say he's saving the best performance for last. He thinks that broken things are easily controlled. He's a dick. I don't know, pick one. If you could keep your phantom cock in your pants for long enough, maybe you'd already know."

Jagger coughs, attempting to hide his amusement, and I glare. My brother knows good and well that I cannot bring myself to correct or discipline her. I will not have Genevieve come back to me and hear that I've mistreated her sister. Regardless of how vexing and long winded she may be.

I have already caused enough damage as it is.

"Hilarious, Princess Kalliope. I visit her dreams. She doesn't remember when she wakes up." I explain.

"Do you realize I am no longer welcome in my home? I dislike that very much. But, unfortunately, the only person powerful enough to help me remove our father is currently his prisoner."

Kalliope steps further into the room.

"So here I am. Stuck with you. Oh, dreaded King of the Netherworld. So, it would be fantastic if you could sober up and get your shit together." Kalliope rolls her eyes and scoffs. She glances at Jagger and then back at me. "And the dragon is right. You need a shower."

I narrow my eyes and permit my demon to rise to the surface. My teeth sharpen and claws develop. "I can gather my legion and retrieve my queen!"

"Do that, and she dies. He'll get what he needs from her. You round up a legion at his front gate, and he'll do it violently. Do not put her in that predicament. Release her from his grasp through the bond, idiot, not her dreams." Kalliope taunts. "I'll be using our blood to contact her."

"Your blood?" I raise a brow.

Kalliope grins. "Did you think Genevieve and I weren't blood bonded? You underestimate my father. How else would he fulfill his lunatic prophecy?"

My breath hitches. "Are you telling me... what are you telling me, Kalliope?"

She rolls her eyes and places her hand on her forehead. "Would you keep up? I'm telling you *exactly* what you think I am. He's known where she was her whole life because he bound her blood to me."

And the secrets keep coming. Mordred once asked that I find the lost princess. He offered me peace between the realms if I collected and delivered her. And to hear this, that he knew where she was. That this was planned. He wanted her here in the Night Fortress until it was time to take her. Mordred played me.

Kalliope twitches in her spot. "Yes, yes, I'm a fucking villain. Deal with it. I was his eyes and ears, not that I had a choice. And don't you dare look at me like that! You don't know shit about me. You don't know shit about what I have or haven't done to protect her in my own way. We're all the monsters in someone's story. Remember that, Dark One."

"Does she know?" I ask.

"What do you think?" She places a hand on her hip, tapping her foot.

So, Genevieve doesn't know.

That will go over like a handmaiden humping a thornbush.

"So!" Kalliope claps her hands together. "Stop moping around, take a shower, and act like a fucking king! When the time is right, you can call upon your men and women, and we will retrieve her. Then The Shadow Princess and the Daughter of Oracles will take their home back and help restore balance to this realm."

They'll take their home back...

Kalliope's words, and their implications, cut like a blade through my chest.

CHAPTER TWENTY

VIVI

As I try to catch my breath, I press my back against the heavy door of my quarters. Hunter's questions were some of the most aggressive he has ever asked me. One minute we were cuddled up, and I was soaking in the void. The next, he was grilling me like a fucking prosecutor. The bruising grip he had on my arm hadn't gone unnoticed, either. He pushed and provoked me, forcing my magic to the surface, smiling like the swindler he is. Hunter basically did everything but flat out accuse me of remembering my past life.

This is bad. It's really fucking bad. I don't remember saying anything that would give it away. I've been careful. And I need at least another few days with the Tonic of Memoria in my system. I don't know how Una gets it, or where she gets it from. I don't ask questions and she doesn't provide explanations. It's a need-to-know basis, and all I need to know is when I drink it, I remember things.

The afternoon Una and I met in the library; she was right. To prevent me from remembering, Mordred and Thane had been adding Lethe water and dark enchantments to my tea—and everything else I drink.

Isn't that just fucking awesome? Enough to piss a girl off, that's for sure. He was going to help me recover my memories, my ass! The lying liar man was the one stealing them from me. For what purpose? I intend to find out. Until then, I'll be drinking hex-free beverages provided by Una when I can help it. And plotting their destruction.

Fucking Mordred. I really should have known better. All the signs were there. The missing pockets of time, remembering something only to forget it again, not knowing basic core memories that should be there: childhood, parents, the first day of school, friends, first love. I shouldn't be blank. Any number of those things should be there. So many indications that shit wasn't above-board around here, and I dropped the ball. No. Worse. I dropped it, tripped over my own foot, and then kicked it halfway across the fucking play yard.

The tonic is working. My magic is getting stronger. My mind is sharper. I'm barely reactive to Hunter's influence now. I don't crave his touch any longer. Quite the opposite. I think I'd rather drag my bare vagina across the lava rocks at the base of the volcano overlooking this hellhole than have sex with him. So, yes. I'd say it's working a little too well.

Mordred is a different story. I don't have enough of the tonic in my blood to overpower his control yet, and we can't stop him from giving me the hex water. Not completely. Una tries, but she can't be everywhere all the time. It's a wrench in the plan, a pretty fucking big one. The Tonic of Memoria is temperamental. So it must be taken gradually. Consistently. In doing so, my mind unlocks at a steady pace, nothing too noticeable. No power spikes. All things that keep us under Thane's radar. And believe me, I want absolutely nothing to do with that twisted bitch's radar.

I don't get the impression that I am a person who gets rattled easily, but Thane scares the ever-loving shit out of me.

And that's why I need more time, and we could also throw in some extra patience to act as a clueless puppet before my reckless mouth ruins it for everyone. It couldn't hurt.

Just a bit more time and I'm sure I'll remember everything.

We need to press rewind to understand where I am now, back to that first night in the Bone Keep. It turns out I wasn't crazy after all. It wasn't in my head. The shadows really were creeping past the matte black walls and crouching in the darkest corners of my room.

That wasn't the shocking part, not really. The shocking part is the *ghost* was Sylas.

After that first night and the pitcher of glass shattering to the floor for no reason, I'd convinced myself it was my overactive imagination. Then, when Hunter came for me, everything changed. My mind was numb. I had no recollection of Sylas giving me a message, and damn sure couldn't do anything about it, even if I had remembered at the time.

I spent at least a week in a complete daze with Hunter, maybe more. His every touch was exhilarating. At one point, I thought I might be smitten with him. I even considered... us. You know, in a horizontal way. All that attention he lavished upon me got to my head. He seemed perfect; I mean, there is something about a man who can verbalize his feelings and lay them out on the table. Not hiding a single thought from me. That shit is enough to make a woman go feral! Even if he's cocky about it.

What an impressive idiot I was.

Looking back, I understand now that Sylas was doing everything in his limited power to wake me up to the truth. It's not the river affecting my mind, not anymore. It's the veil lace faced sorceress and her dark spells, its Mordred's tea, and it's Hunter's incubus influence. You know the saying about if something is too good to be true? Yeah, about that. It's fucking accurate.

Una and Marta prepared me for bed a week ago, and shortly after they left my room, a shadow man appeared in front of the fireplace. To say it startled me is an understatement. I almost flame broiled his ass. If not for his considerable power, he would be barbeque right now. And that would be a shame, since the pretty lilac fae in the birdcage is his mate, and I'm guessing he'd have a hard time setting her free if I turned him to charcoal.

I thought Sylas was being a dick throughout these weeks, but it turns out he was just trying to grab my attention. Don't get me wrong, it still stands that my first impression was correct. He's a prick, but he's a prick I want on my side. Everyone knows that if you're going to win, bet on the asshole. They don't play fair, and they rarely lose.

Even though I still can't remember nearly enough, I was pleased to find out Una was the one who smuggled a pencil and notebook into my room a few weeks ago. How had she gotten away from Marta to do it? I'm not sure I want to know. And to think I thought Hunter was being thoughtful and sweet, bringing me gifts to make me more comfortable in the foreign place. Haha! What a funny joke. He doesn't give a shit about me, and the feeling is mutual. He just doesn't realize it yet.

Anyway, I've been penciling down what I can before it floats away to oblivion. Familiar words, sentences, and even some sketches. That way, when Mordred doses me with the bitter tea of forgetfulness, I can always come back and read the things I'm supposed to remember.

Here's what I've salvaged from the wreckage of my mind so far: Mordred is my father, and that is not a good thing. Una is an angel. Well, not literally. She's a banshee, but she's nothing like Marta and wants out of hell's basement, too.

The Sorceress, Thane, makes Cruella look like a godsdamned saint. Hunter is a deviant asshole who gets off on taking control of women without their consent. The lilac fae is called Bronwyn, and as I mentioned before, Sylas is her mate. Bronwyn and I were friends in my former life, close friends, from what I understand. I haven't remembered that part yet, but my instincts tell me it's true.

Oh! And I guess I'm a Queen. Which sounds horrific, but Sylas assures me it's not as catastrophic as it seems. He better not be lying because I'm not a big fan of dresses. Or husbands. So, this one must have been fucking magical. Like, world shaking, because I think that's what it would take for me to agree to something like that.

I think Sylas is full of shit. What king in his right mind would have me? I talk back. I've got a nasty right hook, and I don't listen. I'm not exactly wifely material.

As much as I hate to admit it, I'm at Sylas's mercy. At least for now. He knows who I am. He's got the details about my origins, background, and possibly even family. But it's not as simple as sitting down with me and spilling the details. If he reveals an event that trips Thane's spell or forces something from my subconscious that I am not ready to handle...?

"It will stir-fry your fucking brain." According to Sylas.

My burning question is, what in my former life was so traumatizing that recollecting it causes the threat of brain damage? My first thought was a serial killer, but then I realized it was more likely fire related. That had me envisioning the cute little girl with blonde hair who torches fucking everything like Satan's baby sidekick. After seeing that awesome visual, I decided maybe it's best that I don't know the details.

That would explain why I haven't remembered yet.

Anyway. I have a few friends in Hell's basement, although I use that term loosely. I don't get much time alone with

Una. Marta is always trailing along, but at least she's quiet now. Hasn't called me a whore since she visited Thane's lair. Come to think of it, she has said nothing since returning. Like, nothing at all. That only solidifies my thoughts on Mordred's fucked up muse and the terror that rolls off her in waves.

Sylas materializes in my room when it's safe to do so. We speak in code, dancing around the dark magic that invades my body, waiting to set off the alarms. Finally, some of my memories are becoming clearer. A bit too slowly if you ask me. But nobody is asking. So, I remain a partial mystery. I now have enough information to drive me insane trying to play detective. But I think I have our idea.

Hunter is looking for a mate. It seems like Mordred can't wait to throw me at his pet demon, like a sparkly new chew toy, and I think I've been looking at this all wrong. What if this is the opportunity I've been waiting for? We need a little more time, and I think I know how to buy it.

It's crucial that I miss dinner tonight for multiple reasons. I set myself to finding a nightgown and crawling under the blankets. It will not be long until Una comes to dress me, and I will have a migraine. After retrieving the tonic, she will inform the commander that I feel ill and need to rest. Hunter will check on me because he's so controlling that he can't help himself. When he does, I will give the performance of my life.

The stage is pretty easy to set. I lie wrapped up in soft blankets with the light dimmed. A cup of untainted water sits beside a cold washcloth on my bedside table. When the heavy door creaks on its hinges, I close my eyes and pretend to sleep. An echo of heavy boots fills the room. His vanilla bean scent becomes overpowering as he creeps closer.

This isn't the time or the place, but the thought crosses my mind, anyway.

When my mattress dips and the tingle of Hunter's fingertips move across my face, I roll toward him and open my eyes, remembering to wince. Hunter doesn't care about my discomfort, which is not surprising. His expression is cold and unforgiving, like it always is when he thinks I'm under his thrall. All those pretty words and roaming hands when I arrived. That's the mask.

"I invited guests." He bites out.

He really isn't the brightest, is he? I already knew that. It's why I'm faking a *migraine*. It feels so wrong to even think this thought, but I have ears in this castle. Sylas overheard Hunter and Mordred talking about this dinner and what they had planned… let's just say, I want no part of it.

"I'm sorry," I whisper.

Hunter releases a shuddering breath and clenches his jaw. "This is an important event."

Again, I already know that, and I don't fucking care.

"I really am sorry. I'm just not feeling up to it tonight. Please send my regards to your guests." I say as I run the tip of my finger along Hunter's forearm, holding back the smirk that wants so badly to make an appearance.

So, I'm genuinely surprised when Hunter grabs my wrist in a bruising hold and damn near yanks my arm out of the socket, pulling me to my feet. I expected him to be a jerk about it, but this is excessive. Instead, a snarl builds in my chest as he drags me like a rag doll to the closet. "How about you pick a dress?"

"How about you fuck yourself?" I reply without thinking.

I didn't even see his backhand coming.

Holding my hand to my heated cheek, I consider unleashing my magic upon his ass, but I need to watch myself. Understand me, if I could strangle Hunter to death with his own shoelaces and get away with it? I would. Oh, how I dream of that day. Stabbing him, incinerating him, burying him alive. It doesn't matter to me. But he shouldn't know that, so telling him to fuck himself was a monumental mistake. I'm not supposed to react to him the way I did. There are still plans to put into action. I cannot get caught until they're firmly in motion.

Shit.

CHAPTER TWENTY ONE

DOOMSDAY

THE DRESS IS A tight fit. I'm not overly blessed in the boob department, but the way they have stuffed me into this stretchy body sucking thing has my tits shoved almost to my chin. It's indecent. That's what it is! It's a test of my faith in Una's fashion sense. Friends don't put friends in plastic wrap and call it a dress. They just don't!

Okay, that wasn't fair. I'm just in a foul mood.

In reality, I'd rather wear a hundred of these dresses, with sequins on the inner lining, than sit at this table with a bunch of Court assholes. Naturally, they stare with judgment on their pinched faces. Corn cobs lodged in their asses, the whole group of them. I was surprised to see the usual suspects here. I figured Sylas, Marta, and Una would be locked away somewhere. Maybe strung up for aesthetics like Bronwyn, the dark fae in the corner. Those were the worst-case scenarios. Now, this? I'm not sure what this is.

Hunter tenses up. The grip he has on my thigh is painful. The man smiles and nods, talking with the guests at the table, showing off his best face. It takes an incredible amount of restraint not to call him out right here in front of everyone.

Wouldn't that be humiliating? But alas, I'm still playing the good little puppet.

I place my hand on top of his and squeeze. A bit more forcefully than necessary. I smile effortlessly afterward, like the picture-perfect bride with a controlled mind.

Please gag me.

Thane sits quietly, her face obscured as usual. Now that I'm not woozy from Mordred's twisted tea, I can feel her emotions churning. Clearly, she hates me. I'm not going to delve into her swamp of endless reek to analyze that. It's not like I sauntered in, guns blazing, and commanded her master's attention. That was his decision. This is not something I asked for.

Bite the tongue, Genevieve. Just shut your loose mouth.

My poker face is the difference between freedom and… something much worse.

"Welcome, friends and colleagues." Mordred stands as his booming voice carries; everyone quiets. "This is a momentous occasion indeed. We'd like to share some news!"

My eyes roam these guests. What species are they? I really couldn't say. There's a man with long bent ears sitting on each side of his squared head, which is covered in coarse hair. He reminds me of one of those naked rats masquerading as a dog. A woman sits next to him. Her dress is breathtaking, a real deal belle of the ball dress in canary yellow, but somehow the color compliments her flawlessly. Beautiful from far away. But up close, a heartless smile reveals blade-like teeth and a forked tongue. A handful of similar characters occupy the rest of the seats. This is one strange crowd. These must be the other leaders here, maybe a council? I can't envision Mordred having friends, only subjects he doesn't treat as cruelly.

My insides flip when the specters materialize through the walls with trays of champagne. We hadn't planned for this;

I was supposed to be in bed with a migraine and a harmless glass of water sitting next to me. Instead, I have no options because the flute that finds its way to my hand *will* be tainted. I spare a lightning quick glance at Sylas, but it's clear. He doesn't have a contingency plan; I wasn't supposed to be here.

Sorry to disappoint.

My palms go slick when Hunter stands, looking down upon me with an open smile and seductive eyes. It's happening, oh goddess, it's happening right now. My legs twitch, and the sensation of bugs crawling under my skin intensifies. I don't think I can do this. I can't pretend to accept this. I envision myself rubbing my hands along his arm. Kissing him in celebration after he makes the announcement. Bile rises in my throat. No. No, I definitely cannot do this.

My pulse roars inside my ears. The room narrows at Mordred's face. The world moves in slow motion. I draw my gaze to a hand. It's stretching out for me. I follow along its arm and up to a face. Hunter wishes for me to stand at his side while he asks a question I cannot answer because if I do? I'll ruin our plans. My eyes fixate on his outstretched hand, frozen with indecision.

I don't know what to do.

In times like these, we always think we will react a certain way. People say it all the time. If I was ever in that situation, I would (fill in the blanks) with some heroic story about how we saved the day. Nobody really knows what they would do until you're in it.

Are you fight, or are you flight?

I thought I'd come in guns blazing like a total badass, taking down the enemy with style. I never once imagined a scenario where I'm glued to a chair, a doe in the headlights, shaking like a leaf with no fucking clue what to do next.

This wasn't stored away in one of my brain files on how to react in dangerous situations.

Fuck.

It feels as if the weight of the world has me by the throat. Hunter's gaze rakes over my body, half rage, half lust. His monster peeks through behind the mask. He wants to hurt me just as badly as he wants to fuck me. Somehow, I'm not surprised. If I'd been in my right mind during our time together, I would have spotted the brightly flashing danger signs. Hunter is the worst kind of monster, the one you couldn't picture being a monster at all.

Every eye in the room is glued to my still seated body, watching this all play out on my face. Craving the chaos that is about to ensue. Mordred sits back, observing the scene with interest. I know what I should do. I know what the safe bet is, but I can't bring myself to grant my body to this incubus bastard. I will not sell my soul, not for my freedom, and not out of fear. Consequences be damned, I'll find another way.

There are a million words I'm trying to convey when I lock eyes with Sylas: *I'm sorry. Please understand. We were wrong. Mordred already knows. He's five steps ahead. When this goes down, I need you to do what needs to be done. Go to the ones I can't remember. Tell them everything. I trust you to get me out of the mess I'm about to make for myself. I need you to trust me, too.*

Even if he only understands that last part, that's enough. If he can get a message to the people I can't remember, I think I can do the rest. As I push against the dread pooling in my gut, a new plan takes shape inside my head. Taking a deep, calming breath, I pull my pieces tightly to myself. And then I stand, coming to Hunter's side and accepting his hand. A pleasant smile graces my lips as I stare at him in adoration while he makes his announcement.

"It is my greatest honor to announce my betrothal to the beautiful Princess Genevieve of the Shadow Court." He grins as he raises a champagne flute, flashing a satisfied smirk in my direction.

Oh, Hunter.

Hunter, Hunter, Hunter.

He thinks he's cornered me with this public revelation of who I am, or maybe he knows he hasn't shocked me at all? No matter. It's cute that he thinks he's bested me, both him and Mordred. I like to save the real fireworks for the pinnacle moment. I guess you could say I'm a real "go out with a bang" kind of girl.

The dinner crowd quiets as I swipe my spoon and tap on my champagne flute. All eyes settle on me again. Twice in one day? What a lucky woman I must be. This time I'll make sure I give them something to talk about.

Mordred's eyes give away the most delicious secrets. He doesn't even know it, but he's shown me his hand. Hunter is too dense to get what's coming next. He's a pawn, just like I am. The difference is that I'm not a sexual predator masquerading as a nice-guy-romantic-type. Instead, I wear my emotional scars on the outside for everyone to see, like armor.

Sylas's icy blue eyes glisten as he watches me with rapt attention. I'm sure to incline my head in his direction before I speak, hoping he got the unspoken message and knows what to do next.

"I'd like to make a toast!" I call out cheerfully.

Mordred's stare turns to poisonous barbs.

I smile at him sweetly and continue before I lose my nerve.

"Raise your glasses with me, in honor of my father, the God of War. And what a spectacular father he is! Although he must've misplaced the invitation to attend my childhood. That's a shame. I was such a spirited youngster." I exaggerate my bottom lip, sticking it out just a little before rearranging my facial expression back into a pleasant smile.

Hm. No clapping? I thought that was a magnificent speech.

"And to Hunter, my *betrothed*. He's a catch, ladies, am I right? Very sexy. Until you wake up one day and realize weeks have passed while he's had you under his thrall, doing goddess only knows what. He likes em' against their will, if you know what I mean. Anyway. Cheers!" I playfully wink at Hunter as I pour my champagne onto the floor.

The raging fury glinting in Hunter's golden eyes is almost orgasmic.

I regard him with a calm sort of rage. "Sweetheart, there's just this one tiny thing. How could I possibly agree to be your wife when I am already another man's Queen?"

Watching Hunter obliterate his "nice guy" persona in front of an influential audience. It's a thing of beauty. A genuine work of art, really, it is. My smile is positively beaming when he lunges for me, and Mordred is required to step in.

Hunter's declaration of my title just cemented my legitimacy as an heir to this festering hellhole, and I've just forced the king to protect me from his commander in front of his council.

Checkmate.

And may the goddess have mercy on me.

———◆———

I was expecting to be dragged away after dinner abruptly ended. What I didn't expect was waking up with a monster fucking headache and a case of the lightheaded wobbles. I did *not* expect to open my eyes inside a lair of terrors. And I didn't envision I'd be strapped to a thick wooden table like a godsdamned science experiment, but here I am.

At this point, I suppose the most sensible thing to do is to check my restraints, so I do. These are tight. There will be no death-defying Houdini stunts for me anytime soon. The good news is that I am on my own for the moment. The bad news is, my eyes are crusted over and blurred. A powdery film falls from my lids into my eyeballs as I blink. It stings like acid and the waterworks flow from my eyes. Eventually clearing the film away so I can see.

There are murky jars lined across a wall of shelving. I squint to see what's in them, but the soft tissue is so mutilated I can't tell what they are. Crude furs line the rough walls. A mortar and pestle sit on a workspace littered with bundled herbs hanging to dry. Live critters in small cages line another wall. It smells of moonwort and thyme. Bones of all shapes and sizes hang from the ceiling, swaying with no wind. I stretch my neck as far as I can, leaning my head backward to catch a look at what might be behind me—and a severed tongue all stitched up in a thick black cord hangs over my head.

That can't be a good sign.

The walls have been carved from obsidian, and it's unnaturally warm here, which tells me I'm somewhere burrowed inside the volcano's outer walls. Or maybe the underground part? I bet the Bone Keep has tunnels that run just like its hallways. Yes, that must be it. This means… tunnel access from the base of the volcano into the Bone Keep itself.

By the look of the random severed and stitched body parts that hang above me, my odds aren't favorable. Thane is planning to have a spectacularly unpleasant field day with me. I guess I only have myself to blame. It was either this or the alternative. I couldn't live with the weight of the alternative.

I don't know how bad it will get, but I already don't regret it. Stand for something or fall for anything. Right? I've spent a few weeks getting to know myself. Searching for my scattered parts. There are so many I still need to find, but I know one thing is for sure. Queen Genevieve isn't anyone's bitch.

"I had hoped to avoid this messy business, child." Mordred's voice cuts through the silence.

I suck in a breath, startled, but determined not to show it. "And what messy business would that be? Father."

That word tastes like ash on my tongue. Father.

"You have a mouth like your mother's." Mordred sneers. He says the word *mother* like it's rotted inside his mouth.

My veins swell with heat. If a single look could have killed Mordred. He would be in a thousand chunks of meat right now. Dragon food. Because I know. I fucking know it! Mordred hurt my mother. When I raise my arms to rip him to shreds, I am reminded that they have strapped my body down. He leans closer when he sees me struggling against the restraints. It's as if he wants a better look at the show.

He wants a show? Grab the popcorn, Motherfucker!

Leaning my head as far as I can, I feign interest. "And what can you tell me about my mother?"

Mordred steps closer, leaning down, wearing a cruel grin. He's about to deliver another emotional wrecking ball, I'm sure. But before he can cut another barb under my skin, I haul my head back and spit on him. It is the ultimate sign of disrespect, and I hope he feels every bit of it.

"I see." Mordred brings his handkerchief to his chin, removing the evidence of my refusal.

My smile radiates the hatred swelling in my soul. "You have seen nothing yet."

"Yes. Just like her mother, indeed. Don't you think so, Thane?" Mordred calls to his muse like a besotted fool, a vicious glint in his crimson irises. She appears out of the darkness in the corner. It's pretty fucking creepy. When she glides across the rock floor like a deranged Grim Reaper, I understand my circumstances more clearly.

It was a mistake to think that the Bone Keep was hell's basement.

It wasn't.

"And like her mother, she will break." Thane's husky voice floats in the air as she runs her daggered claws across Mordred's chest. He trembles at her touch, closing his eyes and leaning into her.

Gross, and good luck!

There's nothing else to say. It won't matter. My hand was forced, so I made my choice. Now I will suffer the consequences. Hopefully, it doesn't lead me to an early grave, but if it does? Then I'll go out in style. Without giving them a single fucking inch.

CHAPTER TWENTY TWO

THANE'S LAIR

DAGGER TIPPED NAILS DRAG against my skin, soaking me in paralyzing fear. I don't know how long I've been in this chamber of dread. Time has lost meaning. My hope for survival is dwindling. Thane chuckles as she uses her knife-like fingernails to cut into my skin. She slices down my wrist and then watches with interest as my flesh splits.

My blood trickles into her waiting pestle. She whispers words of vile darkness into the air. The bed of herbs sizzles on contact, coaxing tendrils of yellow tinged smoke to dance for her. She smiles. Her otherworldly beauty is a hypnotizing force.

One look at that face, and it doesn't take a genius to figure out why she wears a veil. Those sparkling hazel eyes, her plump heart-shaped lips, the symmetrical angles of her nose and jaw... looking upon her could bring even the strongest men, and some women, to their knees. If she were to roam the castle uncovered, I have no doubt it would cause a bloodbath. And she would love every second. A monster lurks under her impeccably smooth skin. Evil. Pure, unfiltered, soul eating evil. Her beauty is a toxin. She draws you in and then poisons your mind. She digs her talons deep and twists my thoughts into a living nightmare.

Thane takes her time with me. Laying everything out just right, all of her tools were in meticulous order. She is thorough in her execution of pain, precise with her cuts, and even more careful with her timing. And then she drinks the essence of your soul. She loves the screams; her breathing grows shallow, her skin flushes, and she makes sure not to rush. Drawing it out and savoring the sound while she digs through your mind.

"Let's poke around in your darkest of hells, Genevieve. I wonder what I shall find. Hmm?" her voice is filled with anticipation.

I think I may be sick.

It's strange to say my blood aches, but it does. Of course, this isn't our first round of her sick game. So, I already know when to brace myself. But it doesn't matter. When Thane thrusts her wicked fingers into her blood-soaked concoction, I scream. Just like she likes it. An ear-splitting, nosebleed, soul wrenching wail. And then I'm plunged back into Thane's world.

Hours of genuflecting have torn my knees to bits, leaving them bloodied. Muscles tremble out of pain or fear. A cocktail of misery. But I cannot move. Not until I've done what my mentor has asked of me.

A tall, dark man bent before me, his beady eyes boring into my middle. Impossibly cold. He sneers, revealing jagged teeth, and he tells me to kill. Kill. Kill. Kill. He points to the man on the ground. Mud clings to his skin, his clothing is modest, and he has kind eyes. In denial, the man shakes his head, pleads, begs, and cries. I've never seen a grown man cry before.

"When you can prove your worth and do as you are told. You may stand, Genevieve." The tall man instructs.

My mentor leaves me behind the bars of a cell, locked inside with a grown man, twice my size. I remain on my knees, bleeding on a piss filled rock floor. My only way out, the last salvation for me, is to kill. Kill if I want to live.

The crying man's trembling eases the moment my mentor is gone. After all, what damage could a little girl do?

I wish I didn't know the answer to that.

They made me for this; I was born to kill. And the more I fight it, the stronger the darkness calls. I'm crying now. I've joined the crying man. When I lift my palms to his cheeks, he thinks I'm offering to ease his pain.

I am. It will only hurt for a second. I know how to make it fast. That's how I make my way through. It's how I survive.

"Genevieve!" a muffled voice cries out from somewhere far away, but it doesn't belong here. Nobody belongs here.

I grab the crying man's face, reassuring him with my eyes. I won't make you suffer.

He shakes and bleeds. Eyes, nose, mouth. He bleeds. And when I lift my hands, I see red, red, red. The little girl with the bloodstained hands.

I'm choking; I can't breathe.

I'm dying. No.

No, wait. I'm not dying.

Thane's lair…

Just kidding, I only wish I was dying. Almost everything hurts. Being tossed from one reality to another may cause my brain to burst. I attempt to clear my head. Who am I? *Genevieve.* Where am I? *The Bone Keep.* Why am I here? – *Because I am a Queen.*

"Nasty one there. Hmm, executioner? Feel that power, savor it. This is what you are, a murderer." Thane's husky voice grates my ears.

She caresses my pain now, coaxing every drop to the surface. The hollowness in my chest expands. I executed people, so many people. I'm a killer. Even as a child, I was a killer. I was rotten from the start. Dark. Evil. Wrong.

Thane toys with the memories I've buried, the ones dug in so deep I never knew they existed. My insides will crack, and I'll implode on myself at any minute. So I understand what Sylas meant when he said Thane would stir fry my brain. And if I'm being honest, he downplayed it. The stir fry was mild. This is more like one of those things that pulverizes garlic cloves. I guess that's a harder thing to say to someone. It would be like saying, 'Congratulations! You're screwed.'

To the best of my ability, I force myself not to feel anything.

My smirk is venomous. "So, I was nine years old when I became a dark witchling puppet. What a fascinating setup for a villain arc. You can have the television rights if that's what this is about. Are we done yet, bitch?"

"You will control your mouth!" Mordred sits in a leather chair in the corner. His hands grip the armrests as if he'll rip them apart.

"Yes, daddy," I sneer, looking him straight in the eye.

Mordred huffs as he crosses the cavern in just a few steps. I am not surprised by the blow to my face and the consequent bloom of agony that follows. As I mentioned, we have been at this for a while, reliving my torture sessions — sorry, I mean *training* sessions — and recounting the lives I have stolen. Those are Thane's favorite ways to break me. Mordred's style is a bit more old-school. Fists. Boot tips. Broken bones.

I vowed not to give a single inch, but I falter somewhere between the fourth and seventh replay of 'The Child Spawn of Satan' starring... me.

I start to wonder, what could it hurt? Are my secrets all that dangerous? I doubt it. I've got to be pretty uninspiring if nobody has come crashing through these walls to rescue me, right?

If these are my people, these memories. Where are they? Maybe I really am what Thane is trying to convince me to embrace. Perhaps I am the monster, and I should just let her end it. From what it seems, my whole life has been pain. One misery after another. When does it stop being worth the fight?

Almost instantly, my heart flutters. A familiar wave of heat washes over me. I don't know if he's real or if he's something I created to survive, and I don't care. Just one glimpse of those intense turquoise eyes, and I'm ready to risk it all. If he's a figment of my vivid imagination, meant to grant a reprieve from the horrors of the Shadowlands, it's working. It's almost like I can hear his voice whispering along my bones... *fight, do not yield, this is your destiny.*

Fuck destiny. But I want to stay alive long enough to know that I'm not a ticking time bomb and haven't been hallucinating. So I need to see it through. Not for destiny, not for the Gods, but because there's a deep inkling within me—I have something they want, and as long as I don't give it to them, they're screwed.

I'm the one with the power here, which makes my inner darkness positively giddy. Spite. Now *that's* a reason to stay alive when everybody expects you to die.

I spit out the blood pooling in my mouth from a split lip, aiming for Mordred's fancy shoes. "You can kick my ass, but I'll never give you what you want."

"How do you know? I haven't told you what I want."
Mordred grinds his jaw.

I meet his enraged eyes, pinning him with my stare, and
then I laugh. "You think I don't see right through you,
Mordred? Kill me. I dare you."

If looks could kill...

"THANE!" Mordred bellows. And I know I shouldn't,
but I can't keep the satisfaction off my face as I watch him
unravel.

Thane answers like a good pet, gliding back to my side. It
makes me wonder what ties her to him. He wouldn't know
what love is if it walked up and cut off his balls. So, it's not
that. It makes sense why he's besotted with her. Power, most
likely. But why is she loyal to him? I have a feeling that's the
million-dollar question.

Too bad I don't have very long to contemplate the
possibilities because she gets back to work, knocking my
skull around in a metaphorical blender. But this time, she's
even more erratic, almost desperate.

"Aw, is someone not pleasing her master?" I taunt.

The pressure in my head intensifies. I can still feel the
chunks of my soul she's already devoured; they're trapped
inside her web. The malevolent glint in her eye is horrifying,
and I can't control the way my body trembles. I know
whatever is coming next is going to be brutal. That my jaw
clenches so hard I almost bite off my tongue when she creates
the illusion that my skin crawls with fire ants. She's no longer
trying to finesse the information out of me. She's forcing it.

I choke out between gasps of agony. "You'll... never be
beautiful when... you're hideous on the inside, Thane."

Blood seeps from my nose. The unbearable pressure inside
my skull threatens to explode. Thane buries her claws deeper.
Sweat breaks out in my hairline; I'm pushing back as hard
as possible, but she's about to rip me apart. No one can

withstand such pain, supernatural or otherwise. My body lifts off the table as the agony intensifies. Silent screams fill the emptiness, and her nail scours my insides. It feels like she's erasing me, and I shove back with all my might. Thane recoils. I notice a slight tremble in her hands.

A tiny drop of black liquid edges her nostril, and I smile. Unable to deny the satisfaction. Even if this is my last day. Even if I'm destined to fall right here, I've gotten in a few good blows. I made her work her ass off for it, and in the end. No matter how hard she pushes, Thane will never find what she's looking for.

I close my eyes, and a pair of endless turquoise storms follow me into the darkness.

CHAPTER TWENTY THREE

VIVI

I'VE BEEN HERE BEFORE, somewhere in between. The last time I found myself inside the darkness was in the Culpepper Library as I opened a book that I had no business touching. The damned thing teleported me through the looking glass and straight to hell, complete with wild horned beasts and a sexy, dark-haired man without a face.

While drifting in this darkness, bits and pieces of memory float by. Fitting together like the edges of a puzzle and coming back in slow, staggered steps. The manor, a little green woman who loved me more than life itself. A bar. A wolf. My familiar... I have a familiar. A sob builds in my throat. The moment that thought hits, so does the soul-deep longing. Where is my familiar? There was an office, a lot of blood, and a fire. And Bronwyn. Holy shit, we really did know each other! I demanded to see the truth inside that office. The truth from... from who?

From Deacon.

My heart constricts, and I just may drown in happiness. I remember him. I remember his hair gel, his musky cologne, and the way he laid into me when I misbehaved, which was all the time. The rich smell of whiskey clung to his jacket.

Then, everything falls apart in an instant because another memory plows into me like a truck. Deacon is dead. He told me he loved me, and Lincoln was there too. He loved us both, and he died. Was killed. No, murdered.

Deacon was murdered.

Someone grabs me. Even though I had power, it wasn't enough. An ear-piercing sob erupts from my throat as the chasm in my chest widens. Mordred isn't my father. He's a monster! My father is dead. He's gone, and my heart doesn't know the difference between when he left us and now. The pain is fresh, like being stabbed in the gut. I always said that hearts are the wildest of beasts. That's why they're kept in cages.

Maybe mine has been broken from the start.

The darkness envelops me as I float in misery. My question is: will this be my new reality, or is it just a pre-show to whatever horror comes next? In truth, I have no idea where we go after death. Some say you're reunited with loved ones, but I guess that's meaningless if I can't remember them. Some go up, some go down. Maybe it's Valhalla. Perhaps it's just a parking lot somewhere in Texas when it's a hundred degrees outside.

What if this is it? No fire, no brimstone, just an endless existence with nothing but your thoughts to keep you company. Who needs fire and brimstone when you can float into nothingness and torture yourself for eternity with all the deeds you would do anything to forget? I would call that an effective way to make someone wish they were never born…

"Child." A familiar female voice accompanies the darkness, and for a moment, she overpowers it.

We sit in the greenest grass on the lawns of a beautiful manor. She's watching the sunset and hasn't spoken yet, so I admire the sunset too. The silence feels silky. I want to curl my toes in it.

"Do you know who I am?"

I contemplate that for a moment. "You're my mother."

"You always were so bright, my love." The woman who looks so much like me smiles.

"Are you dead?" I blurt, more than ask. I'm not even sure why I said it, but now that I have, I'm afraid of the answer.

The woman regards me, her violet eyes softening. "You're not asking the right question."

I'm not sure why that makes me giggle, but it does.

"We are running out of time, child. You must resist Thane. You already know how."

"I do?"

"You always have, sweet girl. Survive and then find me."

Everything fades away, and I'm plunged back into the void, surrounded by darkness and completely alone. I must float there for hours, perhaps days? There's no way to tell, and without any beasts or men without faces, I fall into exhaustion. My awareness slips in and out. A shadow below me in the distance catches my attention when I open my eyes again. The shadow is faintly glowing. There is a light. Is that *the* light? The one we're supposed to go to when the grim reaper tags our asses.

Getting closer, the light becomes more steady, brighter. I am gripped by dread at what could happen next, but this is my only chance to escape the between. Screw it, I'm going into the light.

There is no door, no portal to the afterlife as I approach the light. I don't think this is the light I thought it was. This is a more intimate, familiar space. The blinding light is not my one-way ticket to the hell pits...

Holy shit, it's mine! A radiating ember flutters in the center of my heart, flickering but clinging to its flame. It's the source of my power. And then, suddenly, my mother's words make perfect sense.

"You already know how," she said.

That's right, I do know. I know what to do. Lifting my hands above my head, I flatten my palms against each other and swan dive into the glowing light. Although I feel the heat licking at my skin, I don't burn. I dive past the first layer, the second, and the third. The heat intensifies with each layer until I genuinely feel like I'm in a tunnel leading to something at the other end.

Down, down, down. Into the depths of all my pieces, melding them. Demon. Witch. Goddess. Daughter. Sister. Friend. Lover. Queen.

I finally reach solid ground, the place from which all my power emanates. Purple flame caresses my leg as it winds up my calf. I feel the same on my face, my arms, and across my body. As if I were being hugged by an old friend, the flames enveloped me. I don't jerk away or try to avoid the truth this time. When my body erupts, this time, I am whole.

I've merged with my magic. Now we are one, and we have some unfinished business. Getting leverage is difficult, so I crouch down, gather my leg power, and then leap. I'm back in the tunnel, through the flames, picking up strength. I smash through Thane's hold over me, and now it's my turn to do some damage.

Thane screams and thrashes as I enter her flow of magic, burning my way past her hold on me, scorching everything in my path. She wants to throw around nightmares, but I can kill with far less.

There is no limit to how quick or painful I can make it, or how long I can drag it out. Thane underestimated me. Hearing her screams is bliss. I blow through the last bit of her power and open my arms, burning hotter than the sun. A raging inferno nobody will ever exploit again. I burn endlessly. Furiously drowning out Thane's cries. I burn until something inside me cracks, filled with a ferocious vengeance. The walls of Thane's power crumble. She pulls away, trying to escape my wrath, but I can only laugh.

I let the sound of my voice invade her mind. "Not this time, sorceress. Surprise! I'm a bigger fish."

One final burst of supercharged flame and something slips into place. A lock opens, and memories cascade. Emotions reverberate through me, flooding all my senses. And I remember. I remember everything! My mother. Her sacrifice. Living out my days at the Gravestone, content and happy. The Academy. Deacon, Marlow, Lincoln, Rowena, Calypso.

My sister...

My knees buckled. I can't recall when the sobbing started. There is so much happening all at once. There is torture, hatred, pain, and death. Willa, Iris, Amethyst, and Ansel. Jagger, Anise, and the twins. I remember him then, the supernatural force that is Killian, the Dark King of the Netherworld. The broken prince who gathered up my pieces and reattached them. That insufferable lying prick who says the prettiest things, but he writes his deepest secrets on my lips.

Anger, longing, hatred, lust, pain... love.

As if he were standing next to me, I feel a sharp tug in my middle. Our connection has been restored. Anyone's magical hold must have been swept away by the flames. With the raging storm in his eyes, Killian turns and hypnotizes me. I lean into his touch as his fingers gently brush my cheek.

"You're real."

"I'm real."

I half-laugh, half-sob. "I thought you were a dream."

"I've been called worse," Killian smirks, kissing my forehead.

My teeth scrape my bottom lip, and my heart lunges against its cage. I want him. In phantom form, in any form I can get. I want him more than I want to fucking breathe, but we're all in danger, and this is my one shot.

"There's a tunnel from the base of the volcano into the Bone Keep, Killian. I don't know how difficult it will be to get past the thousands of night creatures who guard this keep, but the rumors are false. It's not impenetrable."

His brow lifts and a devious grin overtakes his handsome face. "Is that so?"

"What happens next?" I ask, a slight tremble in my voice.

"Now, you go back to that cave and play dead, Kitten. Rave about that pretty wedding dress you will never wear. Bow, smile, nod. Knowing the whole while that you are a Queen, and you will have your vengeance soon. You outshine the stars, Genevieve. Stay alive. I'm coming for you." He presses his soft lips to mine, and my doubts melt away.

Killian was a mystery to me before. I accused him of manipulating me and playing with my emotions. However, in recent weeks, I've found myself in the hands of an entirely different incubus. He is everything I accused Killian of being, and worse. My only way to survive him was to imagine a man I wished with all my heart was real. Now I know that he was standing in front of me all along, with that cocky smirk and a filthy mouth.

Yeah, Killian watched me get my ass kicked in a dungeon and didn't stop them. He kidnapped me, too. So what if he stalked my entire life and sold me out to my tyrant sperm donor? There's a laundry list of despicable things he's done to me, and I to him. But I'm done keeping score.

Killian is a God, a demon, and an incubus. Next in line to inherit the full power of the God of Death. He is ruthless. He is a murderer. He's most of the things Mordred accused him of and quite a few more, and I don't care. Because he loves his people, loves this realm, and loves me.

I'm not one to listen worth a damn. But this time, I'll do what he asks. Then, when the time is right, we'll take them down. Together.

***

Upon returning to consciousness, the first thing I notice is my body, mentally checking each limb for pain. It's genuinely shocking when I realize I feel better. No, not better. I feel great! I could get through a yoga class without a cramp in my ass cheek. I could run a marathon. I haven't felt so alive in years!

A thought scratches the back of my psyche. It's strange, but I have this memory from when I was a child. I was walking among some apple trees at Bloodgood Manor. Rowena follows behind, quietly watching as I find a wounded rabbit. A feeling washed over me, a deep longing to ease its suffering. When my hands ignited, I reached out to touch it.

As Rowena gasped, I grabbed the poor thing. I didn't burn it alive, as she was terrified that I would do. Instead, those flames engulfed that rabbit, entered its body through its ears, and then sputtered out. And then I watched the bunny jump and run away, healed.

Completely healed.

Those memories were hidden from me, repressed behind a door. My flames must have penetrated my subconscious and unlocked a spell. But now I know it. I know it in my bones. I can use my flames for destruction or for healing. I am not just one thing. I cannot be confined to one box. There is no doubt that I am a monster from the darkest depths of whatever hell I came from. And yet, I am a healer too.

Keeping my eyes closed, I hear voices echo through the cavern. I don't want to give away that I am awake.

"We did it. Her will is broken, her memories wiped clean. She almost killed Thane in the process. Her power is more extensive than we imagined, but she will be compliant and moldable going forward. She will be the ideal wife." Mordred speaks to someone unknown.

"Don't worry, our deal still stands. I just want to breed the dumb bitch while I siphon her power. You can still have the children for your test tubes." Hunter replies.

He's going to die for that.

CHAPTER TWENTY FOUR

VIVI

"OOH, IT'S BEAUTIFUL!" I nearly gag at the mountain of tulle and ruffles that sit before me. On what planet is this a wedding dress? It looks like a demented cupcake.

Stay alive. I'm coming for you…

I could kick Killian in the shins for this. Who needs a curse when you have an irrationally sexy incubus who is bossier than he has any right to be? Ugh. So, I lie about the dress. I follow the directions like a good little pet. I drink the fucking tea and then burn it out of my system right in front of their faces.

"You think this will make your marriage any easier? Whore. He's going to tear you apart, and I will love the show." Marta gives me her usual sneer.

People say things when they think they have compromised your mental capacity. It's fascinating. As I chuckle, I realize that I've learned a great deal at the Bone Keep, but Marta has remained a mystery. Why was she so hateful towards me? No fucking clue. Probably for no reason at all. Marta seems like the type. Cruelty and violence for the thrill of it. It's not because she's a banshee, but because she's twisted in the head.

Soon enough, she'll apologize.

"Una, may I see the dress for this evening's festivities?" I smile, my hands crossed daintily on my lap.

"Of course." She shakes her head, barely restraining the snort I know she wants to let loose.

Una knows I'm free to do as I please, with no leash to hold me and total control over my memories. But, for some reason, having "our little secret" amuses Una. I imagine it's the feeling of having one-upped a miserable bully she's endured for goddess knows how long. As much as I fucking hate bullies, I'm willing to indulge her with a few extra swipes at Marta when I can get away with them.

I'm taking Una with me when this place falls. She's too good for them.

"You have no need of that dress until tonight, *princess.* Una, get the sundress." Marta orders. "Hunter likes her in pink."

Pink. Really? The poor thing is just asking me to remove the air from her miserable lungs. Una's shoulders slump, and she does as instructed. When she stands before me, dress in hand, without complaint, I look her in the eyes and lift my arms, reassuring her... not much longer.

A soft knock at the door breaks eye contact, and before anyone can answer, it is already open. Hunter behaves as if he owns the place, and I understand why he thinks that. Now that I'm willing and compliant, he's taking all the liberties. Especially when he comes into my room as I am getting dressed. His beady eyes soak me in as if he owns my body.

"Hello, Sweetness. You look... delicious this morning."

Fuck you.

"Why, thank you, Hunter! Marta was just saying how much you enjoy me in pink."

I feel his golden eyes linger on my curves. He lost all sense of decency and gentlemanly behavior when he became too comfortable with my false submission. Now I spend most of my days trying to keep Hunter's roaming hands out from under my skirts, and bile rising in my throat. So far, I've invoked the "not until our wedding night" clause to keep him away. But he's a stubborn little deviant. Every day, his advances become bolder.

I hear a phantom growl ricocheting through the bond and feel a trace of Killian. Obviously, he can listen to or see me, and he's put everything together. That's good. He deserves a bit of punishment. If I have to experience it in person, he can feel it secondhand. Hunter is not a threat to me. I could drop him in a matter of seconds. Killian's tantrum is about me being touched by someone else. My Dark King of the Netherworld is still a possessive alpha-hole, but I will fix that when I get home.

Smiling, I send a love note down the bond. *"If you don't like it, come and claim me, darling."*

The scorching heat lapping at my center is all the response I need. He figured out how to be present without *actually* being present. That sneaky fucking genius. He hacked the godsdamned bond! What was his secret? I would love to know. I admit that a small part of me wants to know for selfish reasons. What would it be like to be a fly on Killian's wall? I imagine it would be incredibly informational.

"What the fuck is wrong with her?" Hunter's grating voice interrupts my illusion. "I thought she was supposed to be done with this black out shit. Instead, she's staring at the wall like a worthless figurine!"

Una's timid voice shakes. "I'm not sure. It's only been a few days… maybe… maybe it takes a bit to rewire a brain?"

Marta laughs. "You wanted the bitch broken. Here you go. Careful what you ask for, huh? On the bright side, you can experiment on this one, and I doubt she'd even know. Drink her pain and her pussy, Hunter. A two for one special."

"Shut the fuck up, Marta!" Hunter grinds his jaw.

That's interesting. Hunter likes to take things without permission, but he can't get his dick hard if they're not cowering and afraid. He's the type who likes them crying, begging, and bleeding.

I'm looking forward to seeing his face once he realizes I've defeated him. I want him to know it was me before he's ripped down to the lowest pits of the Netherworld and feasted on for eternity.

I paste an empty smile on my lips. "What's wrong, Hunter? I can change the dress if you'd like."

He spins toward me, face red as clown shoes. A gamut of emotions plays out on his face. In fact, he wants to hurt me almost as badly as he wants to fuck me, but he doesn't want to break me in front of the audience. Tsk. Tsk. That's a tough spot to be in. *What will he do?* I wonder to myself.

His throat bobs as he swallows thickly, replacing the nasty glare with an affectionate gaze. "The dress is perfect, sweetness. Let's get down to breakfast, shall we? It's a busy day."

Victory! I'm under his skin, and he can't fucking stand it. I will make it my mission to drive Hunter batshit crazy before we part ways. While walking through the now-familiar corridors, I nod at him warmly and take his hand. I smile at myself while practically purring.

This is just too easy.

The moment I melded all my pieces together, I embraced everything they made me. I became a goddess. A witch. A demon. At any given moment, I am whatever I need to be. Nothing more, nothing less. My dark side no longer scares me. It has its place. How could I be when I have so much fun with my demon side?

As usual, breakfast is a disappointment. Although I admit, it's mildly entertaining to watch the assholes on parade discuss tactical plans at the table. Mordred's ego is impressive, quite honestly. His absolute faith in his sorceress, his legion, and even some of his staff. He expects blind loyalty so fervently that he's created a smokescreen for himself. All that betrayal, and he hasn't learned a thing, huh? That seems suspicious.

Speaking of Thane. I haven't seen or heard anything about her since our last girl chat went south. I wonder if I pissed Thane off, and she's purposely being kept away from me. Or is it something more sinister?

Secrets, secrets are no fun. Secrets, secrets hurt someone.
I'm kidding. I know the answer already.

Una is quiet, like a little mouse. Nobody pays attention to what they say when she's in the room. So, I already know that Thane, as we know her, is burnt toast. I've done too much damage to her body for her to remain inside it. So, they're working on shoving her spirit into Thane 2.0–the not as hot, but the best we can do for now version.

Ask me if I feel bad? Then, I'll tell you the answer.

After breakfast, the walking begins. After the walk, it's time for twisted tea with the worst father in the world. Then it's time for (you guessed it) more walking. I'm glad I was a mindless drone during most of my time here. Being ignorant, I didn't feel nearly as itchy.

Hunter strolls beside me, content to walk in silence. Who am I to argue? Hunter is more interesting when he is silent. Plus, I find myself occupied. From now on, everything must go according to plan. Just one wrong move, Genevieve, even one, and it's all over.

Literally.

You might think of it like this: when I was born, The Oracles installed a kind of panic button within my magic, except that the panic button is really an apocalypse button.

So the cockroaches will have their pick of this realm if I use it.

Of course, I don't want that to happen. I want everything to go according to plan, but the flames have uncovered another secret. I understand what the prophecy means, and I know my purpose, should Mordred gain the upper hand.

He cannot succeed, and *that* is why I come with a panic button. Suddenly Willa's frequent use of the words *harbinger of death* and *abomination* makes a lot more sense. I knew that old bat was crazy... like a fox. With any luck, I'll live to tell her to her face.

"You are aware of how you are expected to behave this evening."

Oh good, Hunter is talking to me.

Technically, that wasn't a question. Does that mean it doesn't require an answer?

"ANSWER ME!" he roars.

Temper, temper. All you had to do was ask.

"Of course, I understand." I lower my eyes, watching my feet move closer to my door.

Hunter stops in my archway, bending down to eye level. "If you embarrass me, I will make you wish you had never laid eyes on me."

Too late, but please. Continue.

"Now, get in that room and wash up. Make sure you shave and exfoliate, Genevieve. You'll be in my room tonight. I think an engagement party is close enough, don't you?"

Shit. Shit. Double fucking shit.

"I couldn't agree more, Hunter," I reply huskily and slip into my room.

Or maybe it should be called Kalliope's room since that was who lived here before it was converted into my tiny prison. I realized it the first night I was back there, all my memories intact. I found the notebook. Those words. And those sketches. This was my sister's room, and she yearned for someone to save her from it, just like I do.

It has always seemed as if Kalli was loyal to Mordred. Until recently, I hadn't even considered the possibility that she was trapped, too. We lived the same lives but in different cages. I know in my heart Mordred gave her that tea. He stole her ability to make her own choices. She was dissatisfied with him, and he threw her away like trash. He's never even mentioned Kalliope. There's no sign that she's ever been here. Used and erased, like he plans to do with me.

The shadows move in the corner. I brace myself for the pop in my ears when Sylas materializes.

"Hey, Little Monster." He smirks.

"Hey, Big Asshat." I grin.

Sylas chuckles, and I cover his fat mouth with my hand.

"Just because you saved my sister's life doesn't mean I won't kick your ass if you get us caught," I whisper.

"Una was worried. She said the walk with Hunter was unusually long. She wanted me to check on you." He replies.

"Did he?"

"No, no, nothing like that."

The relief on Sylas's face warms my heart, which makes what I'm going to say next even harder. "I have to play my part, and so do you. No more visits, it's too dangerous. Just stick to the plan and be ready."

"I understand." He looks me over, smiles, and then melts back into the shadows.

As I sigh, I take advantage of the few moments I'll have before Una and Marta rush in with everything they need to scrub and polish me to perfection. Then, they will stuff me into another dress, place a mask over my face, and escort me to the main event. The masquerade.

CHAPTER TWENTY FIVE

THE MASQUERADE

THE FEEL OF THIS dress on my skin is positively sinful. It moves across my legs like warm butter as I make my way down the hall. I'm not one to swoon over much of anything, but a dress? That's unheard of. Until today. But listen—vintage black lace, a see-through scalloped neckline highlighting the curve of my collarbone, high-low cut with my thighs exposed, a full flowing skirt brushes the back of my calves. Blood-red lips and a black lace filigree mask tied delicately under my hairline. I'm lethal in this dress, a deadly demon goddess witch from hell.

I take my time observing the gathering before I enter. It's difficult to hold back the snort in the back of my throat when I really thought my outburst at the dinner would save me from this. I should have known better. Sometimes my mouth overrides my common sense, and I miss what's right in front of me. There was only one way this would go down; I would have chosen something other than an engagement party.

The decadent hall is lit with thousands of candles in all shapes and sizes, lined on shelves, and arranged in pyramid forms. The shiny black gallery is swathed in golden-hued drapes of silk; twinkle lights swoop from the ceiling like miniature half-moons. There are tables dotted throughout the space, covered in iridescent fabrics and gemstones.

It's breathtaking. What a shame.

"Welcome!" a commanding voice calls out to the gathering.

Voices hush. A blanket of midnight falls over them. A dim light grows near a platform, a throne. And Mordred, standing regally next to Hunter. Waiting for total submission of the crowd before they continue with their speech. My stomach twists and nausea clings to my tongue.

"As is tradition, for one night only, you will remain anonymous if you are in this hall. Until the stroke of midnight, when we will unmask and reveal ourselves to the objects of our attention. Then, if your partner accepts, you are free to play out your wildest fantasies until dawn. We do this as an offering and in celebration of the future of our people. The doors will close in five minutes should you change your mind. Let the masquerade begin!" Hunter hasn't taken his eyes off me the entire time Mordred spoke. His intentions aren't hard to figure out.

How I'm going to dodge him for the next two hours? That's what's going to be hard to figure out! My eyes dart, scanning the hall, watching the dark corners. Willing their secrets to show themselves to me. In five minutes, these doors will close. There will be guards posted, and I still haven't found what I'm looking for.

He won't let this happen to you, Vivi. Relax, he'll come.

I've been waiting for Killian since he entered my consciousness and told me to stay alive, that he was coming for me. Biding my time, gathering as much intel as possible. Waiting. Waiting on him. What am I doing? He has to know the Masquerade is tonight. I *know* Killian knows what that means, what Hunter plans to do. With me. So, this is his last chance for that rescue he promised for all intents and purposes. And I don't feel him.

I don't feel him, I don't see him, and the doors are closing. I have to escape this castle. I bite the inside of my cheek, my breath catches in my chest, and I'm doing my best to keep the moisture out of my eyes. What good does falling apart do? But I have survived. I've stayed alive; I've done everything right. The things I let slide. They gutted me, humiliated me, and chipped away at my self-respect. But I did them because he was coming...

A string quartet begins with a haunting melody, a classical cover of *Bittersweet Symphony*. I make my way through the shadows, eyes on Hunter. He's searching the dancefloor, sniffing out his prey. I think I can keep this avoidance dance going for a while, just until I come up with another plan. If the lights are low, I can stay in the shadows. Stay hidden. My hands shake, and I suck in a deep, shuddering breath.

No, nope. Knock that shit off right now, Vivi Graves! Hiding, cowering in the shadows is not your style. Moments ago, you were a badass demon witch from hell. If one man not showing up can strip that from you? Then you don't deserve to have it. Now get out on that dance floor and don't let him take anything you're not willing to give him!

"Fuck this. I need a drink." I mutter to nobody in particular.

I snatch a glass of champagne from the tray of a waiter passing by and chug it. Then, setting the empty glass on the tray of the next waiter to pass me and grabbing a new one. It's like double fisting, but incognito.

Sipping on this glass, I enter the dance floor. The sexual chemistry emanating from everyone smacks me hard. That was not what I was expecting at all. It throws me off guard, not to mention the flutters beneath my dress. Warm hands graze my hip, and I go along with it, swaying my hips and then moving to the next pair of roaming eyes. Allowing the dance to take over, letting my power swell. Feeding it.

If I could just stay here a little while...

He pulls my backside into his grasp with a rough grip, stinging my skin. I can feel his hardness pressed against me, his heavy breaths on my neck. Honey and something foul. It takes all of my resolve not to punch him in the nose, but this is a long game. So finally, taking a thick breath, I lean into it.

When I hear a sharp inhale, I smirk. "Hello, Hunter."

His hands roam my sides, fingers grazing underneath my breasts. I picture every one of those fingers broken, nails ripped out for good measure.

"You're like a drug, sweetness. I crave you, and I get what I want." His fingers trail down my arm, and I can tell he's feeding his seductive power into me. But I guess Hunter doesn't have enough juice to run my motor. "Tonight, we show everyone who this pussy belongs to."

He thinks he achieved something there, doesn't he? It might have worked, too, if I hadn't heard what he really thinks of me. Had I not already snooped between his ears and discovered his lust for violence and brutality. Most especially in the bedroom. Hunter has no idea that he's going to strike out, but we'll save that for later.

"Is that right?" I sway, chuckling to myself in what I hope is a sexy manner.

Hunter growls under his breath. "I own you."

Yeah, sure you do, buddy.

As I spin towards him, I offer him a saucy wink, place a kiss on his cheek, and then I dissolve into the crowd. Suddenly, my breathing is irregular, and I feel the panic rise in my chest. His touch makes me sick. I'll kill him before he reaches for my panties. I swear it.

My attention is drawn to a tickle on the back of my neck. Though familiar, it's hard to say for sure. My gut says to find a stationary spot, out of sight, but with an excellent visual. I'm not sure where that thought came from. Although I'm not sure it was my idea, it's a smart one - so I followed through.

The best vantage point is closest to the doors. There is dim light, but it doesn't quite reach into the corner. A massive velvet drape hangs from floor to ceiling. Also obscured by the light. As I spin slowly towards the crowd, I realize I am right. I can see the entire room. Awareness lights up my insides as I gracefully sway backward into the shadowed corner.

After one more step, my back hits something warm. Smoky jasmine fills my nose, and every cell in my body vibrates with heat. I feel his hand move over my hip, erasing Hunter's touch left minutes ago. He proceeds to massage every spot on my skin that has been tainted by Hunter's filthy hands. When he reaches my neck and gently wraps his fingers around my throat. I melt.

Killian brings his lips to my ear lobe and whispers. "Hello, Kitten. Did you miss me?"

"You have no idea," I whisper back, relief washing over me.

The feeling of lust overwhelms me like a tsunami. I cannot get enough of Killian's hands. He is everywhere. While he caresses my neck softly in the shadows, he stands behind me, both hands rocking my hips into his. Yet I feel hands on my thigh, down my arm, and fisted in my hair. He is saturating me with phantom power. My pussy clenches with an ache for him.

Killian groans, pressing against me. "You smell so good, my murderous little Poison Princess."

I spin around, and our lips collide. The world fades away. Light and sound no longer exist. Neither do the Shadowlings nor the hall. It is just him and me. In a universe we created. He undoes me and stitches me back together. Ruins me and saves my soul. He tears down my walls and invades my heart time and time again. The minute he looked at me, I was lost to him, all swirling galaxies and raging storms. He turned my world upside down the moment he stepped into Enchanted Brew. The way he clung to me, even in the middle of a kidnapping, like I was his salvation. The way my soul felt about him, I knew back then. Deep down, I knew Killian was my mate.

I release a shaky breath. The pressure between my legs is painful, too much to bear. "I need you, Killian."

When he growls at me, I go feral, and I'm in the air, my legs wrapping around his waist. I need him so badly that my hips move on their own, seeking what they want. I have lost all control. When his finger presses against my clit, I nearly scream. Killian smirks, putting his hand over my mouth to stifle the sound as he stares deeply into my eyes. Then, rhythmically, he swirls and rocks me with his finger.

"Yes. More." I've been reduced to one-word sentences.

The bass in his voice travels straight to the core of my being when he chuckles. As he adds another finger, I clench around him. This is driving me mad. Our mouths find their way back together as we match our tongues' rhythms to our bodies. His fingers. If he doesn't fuck me, I'm going to die. It is a primal need that I can't fully comprehend. The desire to be marked is overwhelming. I need him to claim me as his for eternity. I want everyone to look at me and know who owns my heart. That he didn't steal my soul.

I gave it to him.

His smooth voice calms my frenzy. "Relax, Kitten. I'm going to mark you for days. I plan to mark you so deep you'll never get me out from under your skin. So, lean back and let me fix this for you."

"Oh, my goddess, I'm going to pass out." My voice is hoarse with need.

Putting my trust in his arms, I lean back. To the beat of his hips, his fingers rock against mine. A powerful heat builds in my center, ready to explode at any moment. As I face him again, Killian looks me directly in the eye, saying everything and nothing simultaneously.

"Come for me." His deep voice cuts through my chest. I can't help but obey. I rock back and forth, unable to catch my breath as I shatter against his hand. Soundlessly falling into ecstasy.

There will never be another man. Not for me. Killian is my north star. He kisses me softly as he gently removes his fingers, bringing them to his lips and sucking them clean. "There's more where that came from when we get out of here, my love. Are you ready to make a scene?"

The mischievous glint in his eye makes me burn. Do I want to cause an unholy, vengeful riot in this house of horrors with the sexiest man I've ever seen in my life? Oh, fuck yes. My red lipstick smirk is all trouble. "Absolutely, I am."

CHAPTER TWENTY SIX

VIVI

"HUNTER IS MINE," I growl.

Killian chuckles. "I would never ask you to be less than what you are, Kitten. A sexy, brilliant, vicious little beast. I'll take pleasure in watching him suffer."

I can feel his erection brushing against me, and maybe it's fucked up that the idea of me murdering a man for putting his hands where they don't belong makes him hard. I don't know, and I don't care anymore. He's my kind of twisted, and I think it's fucking hot.

"Please tell me we're not here without backup." I plead.

"You wound me, Genevieve." Killian purrs low in his chest. The look in his eyes promises dark things, things I cannot wait to get home to.

Just then, the lights move to spotlight the stage, and there stands Hunter—microphone in hand. The sound of his voice makes my inner monster murderous, and now that I know I have a way out. That karma I've been talking about is making house calls.

Hunter drones on about some tradition or another. I don't give a shit. I was so busy drowning out his voice, I didn't even notice Killian was no longer standing behind me. Shit! Godsdammit, fuck. I said he was mine! I make my way along the outer wall, trying to get as close to the edge as possible. Killian has been here for under two hours; he's already ruined my panties and then pissed me off.

"And now, we count down to masks off. 10, 9, 8, 7..." Hunter's voice steals through the barricade I've tried to raise inside my head. I'm almost there, just a few more steps.

I spy Killian moments before he makes a leap for the stage. "3, 2, 1...."

Boom! It happens so fast; that I take a second to process what I just saw. Hunter was about to remove his mask. Killian flew onto the stage like a cracked-out batman, and just as the countdown ends, the Dark King's fist plowed into Hunter's nose. Blood spurts into the crowd in a sickening crunch, and everything comes to a screeching halt.

So much for discreet, I guess?

I honestly hadn't noticed that I'd moved closer to them. My body has a mind of its own near Killian. Laws of nature don't apply. So, when he turns around and smirks like a Cheshire cat and puts his hands in the air, unphased. I'm speechless.

"I apologize. I couldn't help myself, but I didn't use magic, I swear."

He winks, and my insides go wild. How can I be angry with that stupid fucking handsome face? I sigh, shaking my head with a whisper of a grin on the corner of my lip and motion for the microphone.

Jagger and Lincoln step out from behind the stage and take hold of Hunter's arms, dropping the mic to the floor. My chest heaves, and I'm torn between squealing like a total girl and jumping into both of their arms for a split second. Fuck this stupid stage and Hunter, too. There are more pressing matters. My teary-eyed hellos will have to wait.

Killian bends to grab the microphone, handing it to me, and I steal a quick glance at Lincoln. I've always hated public speaking. I'm a choke artist. But, back in Thornfall, Lincoln would dare me to get up at open mic night and talk or sing. The fucker knew I could *never* turn down a dare. And he would sit on that ratty old couch at The Brew every time, watching me freeze, cheering me on.

He has that look now, holding Hunter still with a twinkle in his eye. Telling me he's right here, and it's okay to speak.

My heart swells, and I nod, bringing the mic to my lips. "Okay. So, um. Hello! My name is Genevieve Graves. You all probably know me as something else, but I'm Mordred's daughter…."

I don't remember what I was going to say. There are barbs of panic climbing up my throat, and I lose my point. I glance at Killian, and he's patiently waiting for me to find my strength. He doesn't appear to be in a rush, which makes me wonder why Mordred isn't raising hell right now? But it mostly makes me feel safe. Looking to my opposite side. Linc's forest-colored eyes are steady and calm. He raises two fingers on his free hand, our made-up childhood sign language. Telling me he knows I've got this.

With a shaky breath, I raise my chin and continue. "My name is Queen Genevieve of the Netherworld, Soulbound Mate to the Dark King. I am also one of the two heirs to this Bone Keep. They brought me here against my will. My memory was altered with magic, and when I figured it out, they took me to Thane's Lair, and I was tortured to the brink of death."

A few gasps filter through the air.

"If you had nothing to do with that. I wish you no harm. You may stay and help us rid this keep of the filth allowed to fester here. Or you are free to go."

Killian's eyes widen. I don't even bother looking at Jagger or Linc. One will laugh, and the other will be pissed. I love them both, but they're super predictable.

There's a buzzing sound coming from the crowd now. My heart hammers against my ribs for several reasons. What if they all leave? What if they all stay? These are my people, as warped as they have become. They're Kalliope's people, and for some silly reason, I care.

The enormous doors open, and I realize it's Sylas and Bronwyn—giving them an exit if they choose to take it. A small stream of people file out, primarily women. Looking around the room, it's like my old life and this farce I've been living in has collided. I mean, I guess it has. So, I shouldn't be so choked up right now. Ansel has Marta by the throat. His lumberjack-looking ass seems bored. Mordred is in a chair, with Anise behind him. I'm not sure what she's doing with her Siren call, but he's not moving, so that's a plus. Una stands to their left, her midnight eyes swirling and black hair dancing in the wind.

A commotion brings my attention back to the stage. Hunter is struggling against Linc and Jagger. I can tell he's using his power. Which sucks, because I was hoping he still hadn't noticed it was disabled.

"Kitten? I'm not trying to rush you, but I would find great pleasure in watching you handle this situation. It's just a suggestion." His voice is gravelly, and it's a suggestion, alright.

Everything about him is *suggestive*.

"Fine."

I smile and swagger toward Hunter. Sizing him up like prey, hoping he feels every ounce of fear it invokes, I bring my face close to his, our noses only an inch apart. "I've studied you, Hunter. When you thought you could control me, I was smarter than you, better in every way. You think women are prey. Objects to be hunted, fucked, smacked around."

He rears his head back, and I sidestep. Easily missing the headbutt he was aiming at my face.

"Tsk. Tsk. Now, that wasn't very nice." I reprimand, lifting my palms and calling the flames. Of course, they listen beautifully now that all of my monsters have made friends, now that I'm so much more than Hunter bargained for.

He's fighting now, sweat beading on his forehead. He hurls his threats, his taunts, his rage. And when he tires of that, he begs. Ahh, that's what I was waiting for. Finally, Hunter is on his knees, seeing the error of his ways.

"Apologize."

He spits blood at my face, painting my cheeks with red and clear liquid freckles. An audible growl comes from behind me, raising the hairs on everyone in this room with the electrical storm he's about to unleash.

Hunter is already on his knees, but Jagger shoves his head further. "You will bow to my queen. And she said, apologize!"

"Fuck off, dragon bastard! You're only out of hiding because daddy can't whip you for showing your face!" Hunter screams at Jagger.

"Shh," I whisper, putting my finger up to my lip. I'm slow and deliberate in my movements, kneeling closer until our noses touch. "That was a mistake."

I bring my hands to his cheeks, engulfing us both. My flames enter through his mouth, nose, and ears. Ready to eat him alive. They lick and tear at his shell, ready to incinerate him, when I realize his taste. Sage and citrus. Hunter is also next in line for the powers of a god. Now I know why Mordred wanted him to pump me full of babies to steal. Sick fuck. Good thing he's only the *next* in line. He doesn't have them yet.

"Scream for me, Hunter." I pour mockery and derision into my words. Isn't that what he wanted me to do? Scream around his cock... anger flares. And then I set my hungry flames loose, breathing fire into him and back into myself like oxygen.

I can feel it this time when I light up like a glow-worm. He screams, and it feeds me. Like a musical note that lifts you up and frees you from your chains. He screams until there's nothing left but bones and ash at my feet.

Killian's electric heat moves up my spine. His breath strokes my skin, building a bonfire between my thighs as he whispers into my ear. "Vicious, sexy creature. Are you trying to make me explode?"

Good goddess, if he can do half of the things he's done to me in those dreams in real life...

"Keep it in your pants, Bro. We have company." Jagger throws ice water on both of our fantasies. Then he chuckles and shakes his head. "Trying to fuck in the middle of a battle like a couple of horny teenagers."

A loud bang rings out from somewhere in the castle, and heavy footsteps echo into the hall. A shit load of heavy footsteps. My eyes dart to Mordred, and he's grinning like a mastermind about to see the fruits of his labor.

"Right. Like I said, we have company." Jagger repeats.

I look at Killian, eyes wide and panicked. "We need to get out of here. Now! It's a trap."

"Shift, go! Get the others." I call Lincoln and Jagger.

The shadowling abominations Mordred calls a legion begin to file in through the double doors. Why didn't I see it before? One exit. He chose this hall I'd never been in before, strategically. Shit. Shit! We're sitting ducks.

"We will have to fight our way to those doors and out that gate," I tell Killian.

His answering rumble is all I need to hear. "Ready?"

CHAPTER TWENTY SEVEN

THE SHADOWLANDS

IT DOESN'T TAKE LONG for everything to go from bad to almost comically worse. Thank the goddess for whatever happened to Thane because if the obsidian was still blocking our magic, we'd all be strung up on the gates right about now. Even so, a group of supernatural fuckups (powerful ones, but misfit fuckups all the same) up against a never-ending legion of actual monsters? Let's be real. The odds are shit.

A goblin warrior with greenish skin and sharp ass spear leaps toward me. He jabs, but narrowly misses my neck. Duck and roll never seemed as important as Deacon made it out to be, but like always, he was right. I got the duck part without a problem. I had a little difficulty with the roll part, though. Now I'm pressed against a wall. Trapped.

Goddess, if I could just not get trampled, that would be great.

Somewhere in the chaos, I hear Jagger's loud mouth talking shit. I didn't realize he wouldn't be able to shift until we found a way out of this hall. His size makes it impossible. Right now, all he has is brute strength, and I'm to blame. The boot implanted in my ribcage steals the air from my lungs as my chest heaves. A sharp pain radiates down my spine and into my legs, causing me to twitch. Finally, I push myself up off the floor out of sheer spite.

"Motherfucker!" I screech, whipping a fireball at the bull shifter who just had his hoof on my side. His fur goes up in flames, and I grin as I watch. "Mmm. Smells like steak!"

"Genevieve?! Genevieve!!" Killian's voice travels over the sound of clanging metal and guttural shouting.

And I understand he has my back, or he might be nostalgic and protective toward me. We can talk about that later, but this is a fucking liability for now. Jagger needs help right now. Ansel and Linc are nowhere to be found. Anise is losing her grip on Mordred. Everything is falling apart, and the last thing we need is the King of the Netherworld becoming distracted by me.

"I got it, babe!" I shout.

"Babe?" He calls back.

Seriously? He's flirting right now. This is exactly what I'm talking about. This is the shit that's going to get someone killed.

I break free from the wall and run for it. Running past Killian towards Jagger's voice. My heart stops when I see his legs dangling in the air, and Marta has him by the throat. Dark veins crawl along her skin. Mordred's experiments have made her not just a banshee but a monstrosity. She is draining the life from my friend.

I can feel my pulse pounding in my ears. Whoosh, whoosh. That's the only sound I hear. The scream that erupts from my throat when my eyes lock on Marta's face is inhuman. I'll tear her skin off her bones! Let's see who's a whore now? My palms ignite with a raise of my hands, and I aim for her chest. When I'm about to unleash hell on her, pain bursts across my head.

Fuck! That fucking hurt. I lift my fingers to my ear, and warm liquid coats my fingertips. There's a lurch in my stomach. I don't feel so good.

"Up you go! Warrior princess. I don't know why you insist on meeting like this. They always knock you flat on your ass, and here I am, always standing over you. Saving it." Linc smiles, not wasting any time scooping me up and getting out of harm's way.

"Jagger!" I wheeze.

Linc shrugs, looking in that general direction. "I think it's handled."

Trying to figure out what the hell he's talking about, I strain my head. I watched Marta drain Jagger like an inhuman vacuum cleaner. He must be mistaken. Twisting hurts like a bitch, but I feel better as I lock eyes with Jagger. His feet are on the ground, rubbing his neck, but he's okay. Huh? Obviously, I have a head injury.

Marta's scream tears my eyes away from Jagger, and I don't know if I am horrified or turned on? Killian suspends Marta with his shadows in the air. They enfold her like hands grasping her shoulders. As if by magic, one of the "fingers" on his oversized shadow hands becomes a point. An extremely sharp point. He stabs through Marta's thigh, and she screams again.

Holy. Shit. The shadows are solid? At a time like this, I know this is wrong. I know it makes me a shameless hussy to even think about it. Still, my imagination spirals straight to hell in gasoline-soaked fantasies. What other things can the shadows do? I feel my thighs tighten and my abdomen heat up.

Killian's eyes go twisted galaxies, and my chest tightens. His shadows appear as multiple hooks, like an octopus, but more sinister. He huffs once and tears Marta in half. Her body slams to the ground in a sick crunch as he turns away.

Fuck shit, dammit! Why was that so hot? I need a therapist. A cold shower. And to get the hell up out of here so I can jump my man until he's begging for mercy and trying to crawl away from me.

Anise taps my shoulder, scaring me half to death. "Your sperm donor got away."

"He what?!" I raise my voice, but the moment I set my eyes on her bloodied face, I shut my mouth. "It's okay, Anise. Where's Ansel? Let's bail. This is a lame party, anyway."

A huge body crashes through the table next to us. Something big as a damn polar bear lies on the ground, knocked unconscious. "At your service, my Queen."

"Oh, for star's sake! How many times do I have to tell you to stop saying that weird shit?" I chuckle. Leave it to Ansel to body-slam a fucking bear and still manage to sound like two stick figures rubbing against each other. Unsalted french fries. Goddess love him. He's the best soggy cardboard of a person that I could ever imagine.

Since everyone is standing in front of me, casually fighting off errant monsters. I signal for Linc to put me down. As soon as my feet touch the polished obsidian floor, agony burns through my side. I take a deep breath and bite the sides of my cheeks so hard that I taste copper. "So, what do you say we raze this hall to the ground?"

"Fuck yeah, Little Monster," Jagger smirks, looking at Lincoln as he nods. Anise bounces, Ansel lifts his chin, and Killian looks at me like it's his birthday and I'm the gift-wrapped cherry on top.

Well, I guess that's settled.

As we hold hands, Killian and I instinctively know what to do. The bond solidifies, filling me with buzzing energy. As the pain in my ribs diminishes, the humming intensifies. Every part of me feels his presence. Finally, the wild magic engulfs us, and my head falls back.

"Her eyes are glowing blue!" Anise shrieks.

"Can you hear me?" I hear his voice loud and clear inside of my head.

"Wait, Killian? Yes. Yes, I can hear you."

"Do you feel that humming?"

"It feels like a swarm of bees trying to get out of my stomach," I say.

"Let it grow, and when you feel you may split in two, set them free. Okay, Kitten?"

"Okay, babe," I respond

"Careful, Kitten. I could get used to that." I can feel his smirk through our bond.

The buzzing builds and builds some more. Low humming is now an ear-splitting noise that threatens to destroy my eardrums and sanity, but it's not enough. At least not yet. My body vibrates like a supernova about to implode. Amid the clashes and grunting sounds, my adrenaline spikes. Goddess, please help me save my friends. I can't let it go yet. Just. A. Few. More...

Awareness blooms, and I sense a dark presence. A powerful, supernaturally pissed off, pitch dark presence. Sylas.

"Killian, wait." I groan out, hardly able to speak. "Sylas. Bronwyn. Una."

His eyebrows shoot up. "Bronwyn? She's here?"

I nod, sweat pouring from my forehead and dripping from my nose. But where are they? There are bodies and weapons everywhere. The floor is covered in entrails, and the goddess knows what else. Neither Killian nor I can stop what we've started, and I can't hold on for much longer. I only hope that Sylas and Bronwyn can feel the energy changing and will take shelter.

As I watch Killian's forehead crease, I can tell he's struggling with the same decision. We put ourselves in danger for the people we love. In small ways that add up over time. And there are the significant ways, like the mother you see on TV who stands in front of a bullet for their child. This is one of those moments.

Killian, we have to end this.

I know.

As the humming intensifies, it reaches a crescendo. My body vibrates on a different plane of existence, as if all my atoms will rearrange and come back together. Blue fills my vision as I observe our surroundings. Yet, I only see death, hatred, and pain. The corners of my eyes sting from tears. So many lives wasted. This is wrong, and we must eliminate it. I raise my body from the ground as a brilliant blue light emanates from my chest.

Set it free, my love.

And I let go.

———— ◆ ————

As Obsidian cracks, fissures appear in the walls. For a moment, I drain the oxygen from the room. Then BOOM, my body explodes, and the walls burst out into the tar-filled courtyard. Bodies are thrown everywhere. When my feet reach the floor, only a small portion of it is left. My friends are all standing on a round section of polished obsidian.

There are only a few beats before we need to act, because we are still very much in danger. Remember the rows and rows of zombified super troopers Mordred squirreled away behind the gates? We stand in the middle of them, surrounded, and although I can see the gates from here, it will be the fight of our lives to get there.

I guess I had my Dr. Jean Gray moment. When Iris warned me about what would happen if I didn't learn to control it, she wasn't kidding. If we can get through this, I will listen from now on. If that ever happened at the Night Fortress, if I ever lost control. No, I can't even think about it.

Whether I'm scared or feeling adrenaline, my hands tremble. It's hard for me to tell. Could it be a mix, or perhaps it's because I just turned myself into a fucking bomb? It doesn't matter. I don't have time to be in shock.

"When you said to wait outside the doors, a little warning would have been nice." Dante chastises Killian. Or is it me? As he and Bane approach, gasping for breath.

I didn't even know they were here. I scan my eyes over them, checking for injuries. When I'm satisfied that everything is fine at surface level, I turn to the rest of the group to do the same thing. After a few moments, I'm interrupted by an affectionate chuff and something rough rubbing against my calf.

"Calypso!" I drop to my knees, hugging my hellcat with all my might. "Are you okay?"

She looks at me like what I've just asked is offensive, whipping her tail and lifting her proud feline head. I think I even heard a snort.

"Stay in pairs. Fight like hell. Get through those gates by any means necessary!" Killian calls out an order to our people and then looks at me with a whisper of a smirk on his lips. "I'll deal with you when we get home."

"Please do," I murmur, then grab the dagger from my thigh, leaping into action.

There are at least a hundred zombified monsters between us and that gate. Again, terrible odds. But they were worse inside the hall, and we made it this far. I have no intention of failing now. I crouch, slash, kick, and stand. Check my surroundings. Look for ways to provide backup. Slash, kick, punch, cut again, crouch, kick, stand. We're trying to stay as close as possible to each other, fighting as one. Slash, punch, fireball, kick, stand.

We're getting closer. Closer than I imagined in such a short time. This is working. We're almost there. I don't see guards outside the gate, which is either stupid on Mordred's part or another trap. We'll cross that bridge when we get there, but we *are* getting there.

In the distance, I spy silver hair, and my heart stutters. I madly search for lavender, but Bronwyn is so short it would be impossible to see her from this far. I have a split second to make a choice.

A hundred more yards to the gate and freedom for everyone I love. The people who came to rescue me, who knew their lives were at stake. Or do I go back to Bronwyn? Our beginning was rocky, but I don't have any doubt that she's my friend. Killian loves her like family. I know because the look on his face when he thought she betrayed him was gut wrenching.

"Lincoln," I say his name, and his head whips to me, waiting. "There's something I have to do."

His forest-green eyes flash with terror, and he then looks at Anise. I nod, knowing that the realization will come to him. Before, we were inseparable besties for life, but now he has a new duty. Someone that loves him and depends on him. He cannot chase me into danger headfirst anymore, and that's okay with me because I don't need him to.

His eyes are rimmed with red. "You better fucking come back, Viv. I promised Marlow."

"What's this?" Killian makes his way to my back, shoving his electric bolt into the chest of a humongous bird and kicking it out of the way.

I point behind us at the silver hair bobbing among the throng. "He's Bronwyn's mate, and he's fighting."

Realization dawns on his face almost immediately. Killian looks at the rest of our crew fighting fiercely to get to the gate and then back at me.

Send them away, Killian. Order them. We'll take Calypso.
"To the gates!" Killian calls out an order. "Do not look back
and be ready. We'll meet you with Bronwyn."

—◦—

Killian and I work as one, the bond enabling us to anticipate
and mirror each other's movements. We make it to the area
when I last saw Sylas with little resistance, but I don't see him
now.

"Here."

Killian and I have reverted to one-word sentences. We
don't need more than that. The bond tells us all we'd ever
need to know.

"Search."

We both focus on the surrounding area, Calypso at my
side, fending off anyone who gets within two feet of us. I see
nothing but tar, blood, weapons, bones, and meat. Where is
Sylas? They are mates. Barring an act of nature, Sylas will
not be far from her... but how can we find them? I take
my frustration out on a vaguely fishlike woman who comes
barreling toward me, fangs exposed. Holding her throat, I
forced my flames down, incinerating her.

My lips curl, and I snarl. "SYLAS!"

If I can't spot him, I'll just have to make a scene until he
finds me. This should not take long. My violet flames and
frantic shouting act like beacons, drawing blood-streaked
silver and purple hair toward us. Calypso roars, knocking
monsters aside, clearing a path for Killian and me. When a
pair of brown eyes latch on me, I exhale an audible breath.

"Bronwyn," I whisper, holding back tears.

Then I see it. Sylas is propped up on her shoulder. Blood
flows out of his side, and it does not look good. She
looks terrified, her eyes broken. I spring into action, sliding

through the crimson-colored mud to my knees. I rip the train from my dress and lay it down.

"Put him down," I tell Bronwyn, and she does.

They designed me for destruction, an expertly crafted killing machine. However, not all of my flesh and blood came from him, and although I have a mother who is likely as sinister as he is, she is the queen of witches. I got my magic from her, and she wasn't all evil.

I remember when tears of love fell down her cheeks as she looked at me. There's no denying that my mother is a vengeful goddess. But unlike Mordred, she could love with that selfless, crazy type of devotion. That's why I am confident I can do this because I inherited the trait from her. My hands can heal him.

Calypso and Killian guard me as I place my palms on Sylas's chest, whispering. "This is going to hurt, my friend."

The power flows through my palms into his veins, searching for damage, knitting muscle and nerve back together. Searing the insides of his veins, charring the death from his bones, drawing it out of his body and into me.

It takes several minutes, but it's working! Bronwyn sits next to me, shaking in silence. Holding her breath. Sylas sputters, and blood sprays from his mouth as he inhales a shaky breath, opening his eyes wide.

"He's okay." I exhale as my vision blurs and I collapse.

Movement jars me awake. Running, Killian is running. "Stay with me, Kitten. You burned your flames out, but you're going to be okay. Just stay with me!"

I'm slung over his shoulder, watching Sylas and Bronwyn running behind us. Calypso is at Killian's side. Turning my head, I can see the gates. He's right. We *are* almost there. We did it. I lay back on Killian's shoulder, looking behind us when everything slows to a crawl. A man steps onto the path we cleared in front of Bronwyn. His long sword just out, hitting Bronwyn in the throat, nearly removing her head.

Her body drops, and I wail. "No!"

Sylas roars, and the sky turns black. Monsters fall where they stand like he just ripped the souls from their bodies. Killian whirls, taking in the scene as I struggle from his arms and topple over my feet to get to her body. I slam my palms into her chest, willing the flames to rise.

"Work! Godsdammit. Fucking work!!" I scream into the air, begging gods and goddesses. Demons and monsters. Anyone who will answer my call.

I pound my palms on her chest, each time more frantically. Finally, my tears fell over her still face. Her beautiful brown eyes staring back, empty. "No! We're here, Bronwyn. We made it! Wake up, wake up right now. We have so much to catch up on, you can't…."

The cyclone churning above us sounds like a freight train. My body convulses between the soul wrecking tears and the paralyzing fear. Sylas is doing this. I don't understand. What the hell is he?

"If I could just talk to him, tell him I'm sorry." I cry out.

Killian kneels, placing his hand under my chin and lifting my head until our eyes meet. Tears stream down his face, too. And the sight of him in pain rocks me to the core. I would do anything to take the sorrow from his eyes.

"We must live to fight another day, Genevieve. She's gone. Let her go." He whispers, leaning his forehead to mine. And then I'm in the air, watching Bronwyn's body get smaller as we run further away.

Jagger's screech echoes above when we make it through the gate, and massive clawed feet slam into the ground next to us. Lincoln reaches down, holding out his hand with bloodshot eyes. "Get on, Viv."

CHAPTER TWENTY EIGHT

THE NIGHT FORTRESS

THERE WAS A TIME I was convinced I would never make it back to this bed. But I'm here now, mostly in one piece. I remember my fucked-up life and the people I love who help make it bearable. It took a month, but it happened. My very own dark prince came and rescued me from the castle. If it were under any other circumstances, I'd be overjoyed.

But I can't feel a thing.

An overwhelming sense of danger, powerlessness, and fear. That's what creates trauma, they say. Loss of control. And I guess that's correct, but it's not why I haven't left my bed in a week. The truth is, I'm paralyzed.

When the thing that you thought could never happen, happens. What then? Because now anything is possible. We assign that phrase to the good stuff. "Anything is possible! Reach for the moon. If you miss, you'll land among the stars."

It gives us a sense of having some control over our futures. But what about when the thing that's possible is watching your guardian die, your familiar, your friends? What about being tortured? Fighting for your life and losing. What happens after you wake up and realize that the boogeyman is real?

We faced Mordred and lost. No matter how strong the Netherling forces are, it is no guarantee. Thane is still alive. Of that, there is no doubt in my mind. Mordred has escaped. I have broken my promise to Una. I did not free her. I did not take her home with me. I'm not even sure if she is still alive.

Sylas...

My breath catches as I lie on my side in a mountain of blankets, a tear rolling down my cheek as I clutch my pillow. Sylas risked everything twice to protect me. But, in return, he lost his mate. While I am not an expert in fae culture, everyone knows what it means when your mate bond is severed. You roam this plane with a piece of your soul ripped away, a gaping wound that never heals. It is a fate worse than death.

Sylas and I are not friends. Not really. I worry about him, though. According to reports, he caused some damage with that cyclone of anguish, but he disappeared. Not even the high priestesses could find him.

To escape my thoughts, I build walls. I build walls with blankets and junk food. Walls inside my head and walls around my heart. I murdered her once, but it turned out it wasn't her. It doesn't change what I did. I don't deserve to think about Bronwyn. I can't think about how I could have done something different, regained my memories faster, and planned better. There must have been something I could have done. Would've. Could've. Should've. Doesn't make a bit of difference.

I drench my pillow in fresh tears. It's at least ninety percent salt by now, but I won't let Maius have it. People try to visit, although I wish they wouldn't. Outside my door, I hear their voices attempting to console me. I tune them out.

Whenever I'm not sinking into the pits of despair, I stare at the double lounge chairs Killian put in my room. That was when he imagined his future and saw me in it. Side by side. With two chairs. On two thrones. Sharing two hearts. I doubt he feels that way about me now. I failed him, too. His love for Bronwyn was like his love for a child, a prodigy. A child prodigy. He was her Deacon, and I got her killed because I have powers I cannot control. If I had held some of it back, if I hadn't used it all on Sylas. But I didn't think. I just reacted. I went headfirst, full throttle, no helmet, into the fray without a plan.

Reckless. Headstrong. Impulsive. When I felt them through Killian's bond, those words burned into my heart.

In his grief, he blamed me and cursed my name while his heart broke. And he's right. I am all of those things. I couldn't endure feeling his suffering for one minute longer, so I turned it off. My magic blocked our bond, and I can't reverse it because I don't know how I did it in the first place.

Vivi Graves—Professional Destroyer of Lives. It has a certain ring to it, I suppose. Screw it. I need ice cream.

Suddenly, the door opens. Ansel is grinning like an asshole as the ladies of the Night Fortress file into the room. Fucking Ansel! When did he get sassy? Where has all his stale cornbread personality disappeared to? Can't anything just stay the same? He's cornflakes. Unsweetened fucking cornflakes, godsdamnit! I told him I was not fit for company and didn't want anyone to see me like this. Nobody with a penis in this room except Grim, especially Killian. He's made good on that, at least. But... every night this week, Marlow, Anise, Amethyst, Sybil, and Kalli barge in with chocolate, alcohol, and movies with zero romance.

His ass would be fired if he weren't such a giant and didn't make me feel so safe posted outside my door! Ugh. Why?

"Hey, sexy bitch. How do you feel about 'John Wick'?" Marlow plops on my bed, crinkling her nose, when she hears a crumpling sound underneath her, and pulls out a candy bar wrapper.

"Whatever," I reply.

Anise snorts, "You look like shit. You *almost* look worse than my brother!"

"Anise!" Amethyst hisses.

"What? She does! You smell, Genevieve." She gives me sad eyes.

Amethyst looks at Sybil, exasperated. "That's not what I meant, Anise."

"Can everybody just agree? This is a no-man zone. Except for John Wick's fine ass. He can have a sleepover any time." Marlow jokes.

"No sleepovers," I grumble.

"Yeah, yeah, yeah. I hear ya, Vivi. But you *have to* get in the tub. That's the deal." She grins.

If looks could burn, she would need a small to medium sized band-aid right now.

"Fine."

"Good, then it's settled! Hello, John Let-Us-See-Your-Wick." Marlow winks and tosses me a peanut butter cup. I would have laughed at that if I could properly locate my emotions.

Leave it to Marlow to make it weird.

We sit in comfortable silence. I mean, minus the fact that I would rather wallow in self-pity alone. It's not terrible to wallow in support if I don't have a choice, I guess. Instead, I find myself staring at Kalli. She wasn't with the rescue team at the Bone Keep. I want to ask her why, but I'm not sure I want to hear her explanation. Everything in my world has cracked, and my foundation is crumbling. If I lose Kalli, too, I'll be under the rubble.

As the movie ends, Marlow delivers on her threat to remain rooted to the spot if I don't get up and take a soak in the whirlpool tub (which she doesn't have, and I should be thankful for). I know her better than I know myself. She won't stop until she drives me batty or pisses me off enough that I do it out of spite.

Damn her for knowing my secrets.

I fling off the blankets that cover my third-day nightgown and try to run my fingers through my knotted hair. Finally, I groan in frustration when I can't get my fingers through the bird's nest on the back of my head and stomp off to the bathroom.

When I leave the bathroom, I don't smell like a stale gym bag. Other than Calypso, who is never far from my side, and Grim, who is always near hers, the room is empty. My bed has been cleaned, and I notice that my sheets and blankets have changed, and pizza crusts and wrappers have been discarded. It's the most basic act of kindness, but I'm overwhelmed by powerful emotion. I have nothing to offer them in return, nothing at all.

Tears unexpectedly stream from my eyes. Do people love me even when I'm unlovable? They're willing to take care of me when I have lost the will to care for myself? Fuck. I've been so broken for so long it didn't even occur to me that such a phenomenon exists or that anyone would find me worthy of it.

I'm so exhausted I think my brain could melt, and if I am afflicted with any more feelings tonight, I may rip my hair out and scream. So, I curl up in bed and snuggle into the fresh sheets, willing my mind to shut the fuck up and leave me alone. As Calypso purrs on her new giant kitty bed, I finally drift off into oblivion.

My bare feet touch the cold floor as I stand, baring my legs to the chilled evening air. The door between my room and Killian's is open. A cranberry scented draft pulls me closer, and without thinking, I go to him.

He stands with his back to me on his balcony. His broad shoulders glow in the moonlight, and my heart aches.

"I was wondering when you'd come," Killian speaks as if he's conversing with the clouds in the sky, back still turned away from me.

My chest is heavy, and my soul is tired. So very weary. I stand in his doorway, feet from him, unable to move closer. Even in my imagined dream world, his despair overwhelms me. It seems I'm only good at causing him pain and him in return. That's just what we do. Destined to hurt each other for eternity. He deserves so much more than that.

I blink, and he is no longer on the balcony. Instead, I can feel the warmth of his chest pressing against my back, his expert fingertips brushing against my shoulder.

"Come back to me, Genevieve."

In a flash, I'm back in my body, still sleepy and unsure of what just happened. The lure of respite pulls me back under, but I feel a dip in my mattress just before I drift off. Then my body is enveloped in warmth. Slender fingers grasp mine. And for the first time in a week, the pain lessens, and I sigh into a peaceful slumber.

Besides someone snoring like a goddamn torture device, there's a foot in my butt crack. I didn't anticipate waking up to this. Am I dreaming? Someone is in my bed. Someone is in my bed, with their foot in my ass and holding my hand?

I opened my eyes wide. Then I noticed something on my face. Swiping my arm over my eyes, I noticed something else on my face. White hair, so much white hair everywhere! It's in my mouth. What the fuck? What is Kalliope doing in my bed?

It was real. How did my sister get into my room in the middle of the night, climb into my bed, and hold my hand as I slept? I'm having trouble loading my brain.

"You snore." Kalliope's voice is raspy.

"I snore?! You sound like a chainsaw."

Both of us are trying to untangle hair and limbs wrapped around each other's faces, arms, and legs. Kalli's foot slips as she tries to lift it, and she kicks me in the vagina. A giggle builds in my chest, sparked by the ridiculous look on her face. Before I realize what's happening, I'm laughing like a goddamned hyena. I'm breathless, my belly aching, and my eyes wet with tears.

"Stop. Stop! I'm gonna pee." Kalliope snorts and then covers her mouth, laughing even harder.

"Don't you dare piss in my bed!" My giggle-scream is obnoxious, which sets off another round of uncontrollable laughter. We're rolling around on the bed, yanking each other's hair and slapping each other. It is hilarious and precisely what I needed.

When I hear Killian's adjoining door open, I freeze. Staring at Kalli as my pulse races and my eyes are glued open. Totally freaked out deer in the headlights.

"Nope. Turn around and go back the way you came, Killian!" Her bright green eyes narrow on him for a few heartbeats, and then I hear the click of a latch.

Kalliope's eyes turn back to me. "You're clear. The dark one went back to his hideout."

I release the breath I was holding, letting my muscles relax, and my head falls to my pillow. All sense of humor erased. I stare at the ceiling. "Thank you, I don't think I can face him yet." Kalli nods, watching me. The following words fall from my lips before I can censor myself. "Kalliope, why weren't you there to help me escape?"

Her lips press into a thin line, anger showing in her forehead creases. "King Dickhead wouldn't let me come. He was right. The best place for me was far from Mordred. But fuck him anyway. The overbearing peacock!"

He made her stay back to keep her safe, and I want to know how he accomplished that?

"So, are you going to make your bed into a trash bin and lay in it for another week? Or are you going to face your shit?" Kalliope stands, placing her hands on her hips.

"Harsh!" I whine, a little offended.

A disappointed Kalli simply shakes her head. "Perhaps the Bone Keep can wait, and your people are not particularly concerned that the Queen has returned but is somehow still missing. Their King has become an emo boy lunatic. Morale must be high right now."

What a bitch! She has a few valid points, but what can I do? Just get dressed as if nothing happened and go down to face them all, knowing that I'm the reason Bronwyn will never return home. Then what? Look at Killian and say, "Whoops, sorry about blocking our bond."

Yeah, that should be a hoot.

"I fucked up, Kalli." I sigh.

She twists her face with a disgusted look. "And who hasn't?"

We both sit with our thoughts for a few moments, and then Kalli marches over and yanks my arm up and out. "Fuck this. Pull your head out of your ass and find your fucking courage. You have ten minutes to locate clothes or go down to dinner naked."

⚬

My sister bullied me into this, and I have no idea how she did it. She has that big sister's stern face, and it gets results. I cower as I approach the black marble pillars that lead to the outdoor gardens and the pavilion, where the band of misfits is gathered. So naturally, I'm flipping the fuck out on the inside.

I check my pits for sweat stains as I smooth my hands down a simple white summer dress. I'm sweating like an assassin about to be tried. For now, Kalli stands by my side patiently, but I'm confident that won't last. Today, she has definitely pushed me. I know she will shove harder if she thinks I need it... and that's when I decided I'd rather die than be put in the spotlight by my bossy sister. Nobody forces my hand again after what just happened in the Bone Keep, not even my trouble-making sibling.

I imagine a steel rod replacing my spine. Bulletproof, baby! It's not the first time they've paraded me in front of a crowd that hates me. Shit, Faustus did it in an actual parade every year since I was ten! This is doable. This is fine. Take one step, and the other will follow. Go ahead and move forward...

I can hear boisterous laughter emanating from the gazebo, but I don't understand why? I can feel my blood curdling. Maybe I do understand. Seven days have passed. How can they laugh like it's no big deal? How can they keep going without... me? I'm not trying to be selfish here. The truth is, I can't stop it. Since I can't keep up with my rollercoaster emotions, they change tracks faster than I can comprehend.

One more loud chuckle sets my feet on the move.

Don't think I didn't notice Kalli smirking, either.

It looks like every dysfunctional family dinner I've been to since I entered the Netherworld as I come up the path. The way Jagger talks about something is so animated it makes him look like a cartoon. Marlow mocks him for it. Anise twirls a fork across her knuckles as she stares off into space.

Linc stares at her as if she had painted the stars in the sky by hand. It's only natural that the twins are creepy because they're the twins. Selene quietly chuckles at their antics. And Killian is... staring right at me.

My heart feels that euphoric tickle. The flutters. Cardiac arrhythmia. Whatever. This boy is so fucking beautiful it hurts. In anticipation of another epic shipwreck, I lift my chin and stare into the storm. There is none. All eyes are on me, and if Kalli weren't clutching my hand and Killian wasn't holding my gaze, it would be awkward. There appears to be a pause, as if the universe has taken a break. A sense of tension permeates the air. Eyes bouncing between us, anticipating what may come next.

Killian softens his eyes as he strides toward us. The steel rod I envisioned in my spine slips for a hot second. I am shaking like a leaf, not knowing what to expect. When he reaches me, his face is filled with relief. I am swept into Killian's arms, my legs hanging over his forearms. He kisses me like a man who has been starving for a long time, and I am his salvation. It's so easy to melt into his arms, like coming home.

"Somebody pass me a cigarette. This is getting intense!" Marlow shouts, coaxing a laugh out of everyone.

His lips never leave mine as he smiles widely. I feel him peer into my soul as he holds my forehead close to his. Then he runs his tongue along his teeth, pulling me back to him. As his mouth embraces mine, it is hot and consuming. Suddenly, I feel lifted off the ground. He squeezes his hands into the sides of my ass, and I wrap my legs around him. All the while, we continue to kiss.

"Gods damn!" Jagger bites out.

I'm afraid I might cry when Killian removes his lips from mine. Having his heat taken away from me is unbearable. I grab at the back of his neck to pull him closer, but there is nothing there when I reach. Instead, I find him leaning back when I open my eyes, smiling at me. He lowers me down to my seat at the table.

"Uhm. Welcome back, Viv!" Lincoln chuckles while Anise bounces next to him with a crooked smile.

"Hey." Am I blushing? Fuck, I'm definitely blushing.

Amethyst gives me a mischievous grin. "I thought Sybil was insatiable, but that was... more water for the table. Anyone?"

"Yes! Yup, great call. I'll, umm, I'll go fetch us some." Sybil blurts, and Amethyst looks at her with renewed interest. "Amethyst is coming with me!" She exclaims again, and the two of them are up and out of their chairs with a quickness I have rarely encountered. They can't even keep their hands off each other long enough to get out of sight.

"Something tells me that *water* is going to take a while." Kalli snorts.

"Indeed." Killian chuckles.

They settled back into the conversation they were having before I interrupted. Turns out they were talking about Bronwyn. Killian had recounted a time when she was young and training, when he had sent her out on a mission to recover a coin from one of the lord's homes. They burned her hair from her head, but she had that coin! Linc tells a quick story about the night creature that attacked him, and how Bronwyn jumped in and healed his wounds. That was one of the scariest nights of my life. We all reminisce about the good times and share a meal while talking.

I feel a lightness in my chest when I see the people who have become a part of my family here. Together. Never in a million years did I think this would become a reality for me. This is everything. I take another bite of pumpkin pie and a swig of spiced wine. I'm just taking it all in. This is my place. This is where I belong.

"Well, it's getting late." Jagger tries and cannot keep a straight face. I'm not surprised when everyone else agrees, even Kalli. Especially Kalli.

I figured it out a while ago. This was a setup, and I'm going to be alone in the gardens with Killian at sunset any minute.

CHAPTER TWENTY NINE

KILLIAN

FROM CERTAIN ANGLES, HER midnight hair appears blue. It makes my cock twitch like a teenage boy when I see her nervous quirk on her rosy lips. It makes me want to kiss those lips until we're breathless and ripping into each other. Peeling away layers. Taking each other to bare bones and fucking like the monsters we are. I want to adore her and make her feel that she's the most precious thing I've ever held in my hands. I ache to feel her tongue skim over mine and drink her moans into my mouth.

I'm standing before her, staring now, like a man obsessed. Who am I kidding? I *am* obsessed.

For a moment, her cautious eyes meet mine before she glances away and bites at her bottom lip. Does she know what that does to me? Keeping my hands moving through my hair, I worry about what she's thinking. It is hard for me not to touch her, but her body language seems hesitant. It's like she's coming out of shock and running headfirst into reality.

"In my dreams, what you did? The things we did to… each other. Was it real, Killian?" her voice falters.

Is that why she's hesitant? Have I never explained how it works to her? I rummage through my memory. I'm not sure I have. She's not human, so Genevieve shouldn't think like one, but she does. It's a fact I keep forgetting.

Gods, I'm a dick.

"Every single word. Every touch, kitten. I'm sorry I never explained it to you."

Her gaze casts downward, and the rumble in my chest is instinctual. This is my firecracker, my crazy girl, my poison princess. The most fearless, awe-inspiring woman I have ever met stands in front of me, weak and unsure. It makes my insides burn to imagine someone stifling that wild, fearsome beauty. I want to resurrect that motherfucker and murder him myself. This time slowly, with more screaming.

Hunter, this sorry excuse of an incubus. Using his influence to force his will upon her. Taking advantage, breaking her spirit, putting his filthy fucking hands on my mate. I can't control the flinch that this thought invokes. It's no wonder she doesn't want to look me in the eye. I've been an asshole more often than I've been kind to her. Stubborn pride and a misguided sense of duty made me a bad guy. And then she encounters him. The worst sort of my kind, the lowest of the low. Genevieve has every reason to hate me.

"Could you feel the things I did to you? Or is it a one-way thing?" She asks.

Clearing my throat, I am woefully unprepared. I had thought about what I would say to her once we returned to the Night Fortress. How would I handle her anger? I expected fury and fire. I didn't expect we'd be coming home without Bronwyn. Instead, everything from the moment we returned has been off-kilter. How do I deal with this? I have no idea how to handle this. My chest tightens as an odd and unfamiliar sensation sweeps through me.

"I sense your arousal, your thoughts in an abstract manner. I cannot read your mind, but I can feel what I am doing to your... you might call it an aura. I feel enough to be efficient in delivering pleasure." I try to be as direct as possible. Genevieve complains that I hold secrets.

Her face falls as if she's sad. "So, your gift isn't for your own pleasure."

This line of questioning is befuddling.

"No, Genevieve. I am not created to receive, but to give."

Stepping closer, she pauses. It's as if she's making an important decision, and then her eyes turn a darker purple. I feel her breasts crush against my chest, igniting me with her heat. Her lips touch mine, searching, questioning. An enthralling groan rises from the base of my spine. Every time I think I have her figured out, she surprises me. She always surprises me.

She pushes her tongue against my lips, looking for access. I'm more than happy to provide it. If I could, I would taste her lips forever. When neither of us can breathe evenly, we slowly pull away, our foreheads pressed together. Together, we share the same air, breathing into each other's mouths, and I bask in the closeness. I want this with her. From the top of my head to the depths of my soul, she can have it all.

Fuck. When did I become such a romantic? It's her. The murderous, gorgeous, raw, mystical thing that drives me fucking mad. She makes me wild. She makes me possessive. She makes me feel alive.

As her kiss deepens, her hips shift against mine, and I am hard as concrete. I press my fingers into the delicate skin of her cheeks over the fabric of her dress, holding us both still. Taking a moment to catch my breath before I lost myself and disappointed us both.

"I want to make you feel it." She whispers.

I resist the urge to bite my knuckle and groan into my fist.

The moment she grabs my hand and leads me through the hedge maze, my heart races. This version of Genevieve. She intrigues me, but I have no idea what to make of her. It seems like she pulls me from one section of the maze to another. Even though I've lived here my entire life, she's got me confused. Lost. We stop in a small alcove where a seat has been cut into the hedge. Genevieve presses herself against me and walks me backward until the hedge reaches my legs, and I sit down.

Her cheeks are flushed, but she isn't second-guessing herself. Her eyes hold the kind of determination that makes my insides tremble. She stands over me. My mouth is watering just thinking about tasting her, but it's clear she's in charge now. I keep my hands at my sides.

Genevieve sinks to her knees on the browning grass. Then she unzips my pants and releases my raging erection in one smooth motion. I suck in a sharp breath through my teeth. It's no secret that I've had women before, but they've only ever been a source of energy or a way to pass the time. But not like this, not like her.

I can't help groaning when her pretty pink tongue flicks at the slick mess she's already coaxed from my tip. While I want to close my eyes, I can't seem to stop myself. My mind is full of sexual tension as I watch her work my cock. She barely fits her delicate hands around my girth as she clasps me close. Her throat bobs, and she swallows as if to brace herself.

"Genevieve." I'm not sure how to word this. "You don't have to…."

"Shut. Up," she growls and takes me inside her mouth.

She holds me there. Near her throat opening, but not inside it. Her tongue moves back and forth along the underside of my cock, exploring, teasing, and adjusting to my size. When she pulls me out and swipes her tongue across my ridge, my legs tremble. While I can't imagine what the meadows feel like, this has got to be close.

I watch her midnight hair move as she guides herself up and down my shaft, savoring every sensation. "You're so fucking beautiful, Kitten."

Her eyes glance up, questioning, but she continues to move. Her gaze is fixed on my face as she twists her hand and gently sucks on my tip. "Oh, gods. Just like that, you're so fucking perfect. Just like that."

"Mmm." She hums around my cock, looking at me, asking for something.

"Do you want me to...?" I tentatively thrust deeper into her mouth, and her eyes light up.

Oh. Fuck. She's going to kill me.

I twist my fingers through the hair at the nape of her neck, making a fist and pulling just enough to cause pressure but not pain. Then she moans, guiding her head down my shaft, squeezing her thighs together.

She likes this, my dirty goddess.

"You want me to fuck your mouth, Kitten?" She pushes her lips further down my cock in response.

This woman is a fucking deity. I fist her hair and then slam her mouth down on me. She gags around my length, and I hold her there for a moment, feeling her throat spasm. When I guide her head back up, her eyes are wild with lust, and her hips are grinding.

"Fuck. Fuck. Fuck. That feels so good. You feel so fucking good, Genevieve." I don't even know what I'm saying. I just want to praise her like the goddess she is.

She dives back down like a wild cat, devouring me. She has me enthralled with her wildness. Then, shoving my hand back into her hair, I give her what she wants.

It should be submissive to see a woman on her knees, but this is not submissive. It is pure power, the power she holds over me. My demon wants to mark her. It's an instinct. And her demon? She wants me vulnerable before her, completely under her control. Currently, she owns me. Body, mind, and spirit. I would destroy worlds, trap a star, steal the fucking moon if it made her happy.

"You're gonna make me come, Kitten." I groan, and she nods eagerly.

She pumps me with her hands, mouth, and tongue. Setting a feverish pace until my entire body vibrates with the need to spill into her. My equal. My mate. Genevieve senses the twitching of my cock, the tightening of my balls. She locks her hypnotizing violet eyes with mine, saying everything and nothing at the same time. She's not only a witch or a goddess, but she's also merged. Her demon needs to see what she has done to me. It's what female demons do while choosing a mate. She needs to watch me come undone inside her velvety mouth, taste me, and then she will decide if I am worthy of her mark.

Fuck, that is the hottest thing I've ever seen.

My release hits me hard, and by surprise, I throw my head back, and I swear I can see stars as she drinks me down, milking every drop with the tip of her tongue.

As soon as my body stops convulsing, I haul her to her feet and crush her mouth against mine. Pouring every ounce of my being into her, worshiping her mouth as she just worshipped my cock.

As Genevieve lays her head on my shoulder, her breathing is finally even. She asks. "Are you taking me to our bed?"

Our bed.

"As you wish, my queen."

CHAPTER THIRTY

VIVI

THERE WAS A SLIGHT lift of the haze between the gardens and here, and I'm still trying to decide if this is real. Killian is looking at me like I'm in the center of the universe. His expression is open, even tender. Could it be that I'm just fucked up? Maybe I'm traumatized. But I'm waiting for him to transform into a pumpkin or a monster. Say something asshole-like and pull out one of his famous cocky smirks. Storm out in a burst of pissy shadows or throw a king-sized tantrum.

The moment he re-enters his chambers. *Our* chambers? I'm fuzzy on the details of that. When I said it, I wasn't thinking straight. Anyway, Killian's eyes have not changed, but what's even more alarming is that he is carrying two glasses and a bottle of wine.

Did he go into the kitchens or wine cellar and get them himself? Do you mean to tell me he didn't ask a servant or make a charming face and sucker someone into it? Instead, he went down the stairs and got it for me? I don't even know where the kitchens or wine cellars are.

Maybe he's possessed…

"Are you trying to unlock the mysteries of the great pyramids inside your head right now?" Killian quirks his brow.

Damn. Busted. I need to learn how to keep my thoughts from leaking onto my face.

"I was trying to unlock the mystery of *you*, Killian."

Having miraculously lost his shirt, he strides over and sits on the edge of his bed. Then, holding out a glass to me, he offers to pour it. This I agree to. I mean, why not? Compared to everything else, alcohol seems sensible. But have you seen this mess? Right now, things are seriously strange.

Kilian places the bottle on his nightstand, then he scoots up to the pillow holding a glass of wine. "The mystery of me," he whispers. "Mmm. And I wonder what sorts of discoveries you've made."

"Not a fucking thing." I meant to have a stern expression, to let him know I mean business, but the openness in his eyes catches me off guard, and I smile.

Godsdammit! What kind of incubus bullshit is this? After everything I just experienced, I'm tempted to strangle him. As I narrow my eyes, I feel for any tingle of power (now that I know what it feels like), but there's nothing.

"Oh, that's why your forehead has a crease the width of the river Styx?" I'm taken aback by his knowing look.

Sighing, I take a sip of the wine. It's my favorite, blackberry. My mind tries to mash up my thoughts and words coherently, but every time I speak, it falls flat. I must look crazy.

The tip of Killian's thumb runs along my jaw as he leans closer to me. There's something different about his touch. I'm not sure what it is, but it makes me pissed off! He guides my jaw upwards and catches my lip between his teeth while biting down. My thighs clench, and I have to rely on all my willpower to avoid rubbing myself against Killian's leg. I may have it bad for him, but I will not resort to leg humping. There's a line. We've got to draw it.

What has gotten into me?

"Wait. Just wait. I manipulated you into publicly lashing me, and I then got myself kidnapped and nearly married off. I accused you of using me for power. Bronwyn is dead." My eyes prickle with unshed tears. "Killian, I blocked our bond, and you're not even broody or screaming at me. What's your angle?"

His face is tinged with an emotion that I cannot identify. When he looks back at me, he says, "I don't care."

Wait, what?

"What do you mean, you don't care?" I raise my voice, ready for the confrontation that I'm sure will follow.

But Killian only sighs and moves closer so that we're lying side by side, facing each other. And he speaks. "The moment I saw you in that river, none of it mattered to me. You have been missing for several weeks, and I have felt as if my body was being ripped apart. So, no. You could set this fortress to flames right now, and I wouldn't be angry with you because you are alive! You are next to me, breathing. Bronwyn is not your fault."

His chest is rising and falling more aggressively now, but it's not because he is angry. Instead, his eyes sparkle with desire, and I can feel it in the air. Warm, silky liquid drips along my folds as I twitch my hips. Fuck. The only thing keeping my hands off his muscular chest is the glass of wine, which is fortunate because I still have one more thing to say. It would be nice if I could stop my brain from short-circuiting long enough to say it.

As I stumble through my thoughts, Killian interrupts me. He says, "Genevieve, I smell your need. And I'm sure you can feel mine. I just told you I can't live without you, and I don't care what sort of havoc you conjure in your wake. Raze an army of the dead if you want to. Build a new wing on the fortress, build ten. Start a godsdamned war for all I care! I'll hand you the throne to do it. It's all yours. But if I am not inside you soon, I may die."

I can't help but giggle at that. I mean, seriously. He'll die? I've heard many ridiculous things in my life, but that is top ten for sure.

"Her laugh is like a knife to the heart." Killian dramatically brings one hand to his chest, smiling as he plucks the wine glass from my hand.

He has dimples.

The Dark King of the Netherworld has fucking dimples. I'm glad that I didn't see those before now. They make him look young and carefree. I think I might be in love with those dimples.

I shake my head. "You're insane."

"And you'll have me anyway?" he smirks. The sound of his voice hits me right in my core, and I forget all about what I was going to say.

As if someone flipped a light switch, Killian and I closed the distance between us. Our kisses are slow and sensual. Maddeningly so. Even though my insides are on fire, he takes his sweet time. As I buck my hips, he grabs them. Pinning me to the bed.

The sound of his voice is low and unbelievably sexy. "Genevieve, I'm about to make love to you slowly. You will feel every inch of me, and there will be no denying that you are mine."

Holy. Shit. I don't think he's bluffing.

My fingers can't resist grasping at his dark green bedding. The intensity of his gaze as he positions himself above me is overwhelming. Literally breathtaking. As in, I forgot how to breathe.

He has a haphazard piece of inky hair hanging over his forehead, and his skin is flushed. Smooth as silk, polished, broody Killian is smoking. But this Killian?

The otherworldly handsome, vulnerable, tender man. The Netherworld's Dark King, stripped of the mask. He is fucking devastating.

I enjoy the feel of his skin under my fingers as my hands move across the back of his shoulders. Then I gasp in pure pleasure. His stormy eyes never leave mine.

"I love you. I fucking love you." He murmurs into my ear.

I think I've died and ascended to the Netherworld equivalent of paradise. The weight of his body on me, the delicious friction of every movement, sends waves of pleasure to every nerve ending. Unlike anything I've ever experienced before. This isn't just sex; it's an awakening. This is the divine masculine meeting the divine feminine. A collision of stars.

It all seems so intense, and I can only whisper. "You are the only man I will ever love."

"Mine." He rumbles low in his chest.

He glides both of us in a synchronized rhythm. Gradually increasing the intensity and depth of his strokes. My tongue runs along the smooth skin of his neck, tasting the salty sweetness of his sweat. A tickling sensation spreads from my navel to my lady bits, like a shaken two-liter of cola. Pressure builds, enveloping me in another sensation.

Killian.

A strangled whimper escapes his throat as his eyes widen.

Genevieve?

I can feel the magnitude of his emotions as he kisses me deeply. The movement in his hips intensifies, driven by passion. "Our bond. Fuck, it feels so amazing."

As soon as the demon slithers into my consciousness, I can tell. Wild instinct takes over and possesses me. I want it. What do I want? No, I *need* it. Before my power rips me apart.

"Killian…" I mutter breathlessly. "Something's wrong."

His pace slows, searching, and he lets out an erotic groan and says, "Goddamn. Your demon wants to mark me. Holy fuck, that's hot."

"Is that something bad?"

"It's how you let the world know you've accepted your mate."

My mate. Much more than a husband or even a king. An actual soul connection. Permanent. Indestructible. Forever. This is a weird conversation to have while in the throes of passion, with him still hard as steel pumping inside me...

I place my hands on either side of his face. "Do you want that?"

He is more demon than man now as his eyes flash midnight galaxies. "I am yours."

Did an ancient demon of death just tell me he likes me?

I don't have time to think about that because the moment my demon recognizes the change in his voice, she goes berserk. My body heats to an unbearable temperature, bursts of violet flame shoot from my hands, and I have this overwhelming desire to fuck until he begs for mercy. Killian freezes. That is a solid plan because I'm not sure merging means I have complete control. This demoness inside me is a wee bit sketchy. I'm not sure if I'd rather fuck him until he's dry or eat him alive. That's concerning.

Killian's chest rumbles in response to my monster. Comforting her. He teasingly rocks my walls around his cock. No friction, no friction, no friction. I slam down on him, taking what I want and burying him entirely. My body contracts, stretching, molding itself around him. The rumble coming from my chest catches me off guard. I didn't know I could make that sound, but my toes curl when he answers with one of his own.

He slowly drags his shaft against my inner walls with a growl, provoking my pleasure until his tip hovers at my entrance, barely brushing my clit. He has drowned me in emptiness. My body is writhing now. Beckoning, welcoming him. Throbbing, I look at the point where our bodies meet.

"Please." I whimper.

"Please, what?" He hits me right on the clit with his silky voice.

"I need you to fuck me, Killian. Hard."

He does. Oh, my goddess. He. Does. I feel his body slam into me brutally, painfully, gloriously. The ultimate pleasure/pain. His skin slapping against mine sends me into a primal state. My nails dig into his back as he pistons himself deeper than anyone has ever been. The way he moans and the carnal groans. It's like an aphrodisiac. Every sound he makes sends me further into a trance. The moment that familiar tightness coils low in my belly, spreading outward, I am wild with the need to be filled by my mate.

My breaths are labored, husky. "I need it. Please, Killian."

As he pounds into me, sweat drips from his brow to my lip, and I run my tongue over the salty liquid as he watches. Then, finally, his mouth slants, and he asks, "You want me to come in your pussy, Kitten?"

"Yes! Yes! Yes! I scream as he flips me up and onto his lap, striking me from a different angle. A really, *really* good angle.

"I need you. Oh, fuck. Oh, my fucking... Ohhh!" My words turn into brain soup, followed by uncontrollable moaning.

As I buck against my king recklessly, his hands grip my throat, and I moan in exhilaration. Almost there. He pulls all the way out, lets me feel the excruciating emptiness, then dives back into me with all his strength. My orgasm explodes violently, and I shatter against Killian. My legs shake, and I'm chasing my breath, but the urge is overpowering. I bite down on his shoulder, and I'm coming again. Hard. Killian roars as he spills into me and pins his teeth into my collarbone.

Marked.

Immediately, Killian gets up from the bed, and my heart sinks. Is this it? Ruin me for every other man who ever existed and disappear. What the fuck? My chest hurts, my walls are down, and I can't control my tears after something so intimate. I hear the distant sound of a sink running. Am I being oversensitive? Perhaps he just had to use the restroom. There is some shit to clean up in the trust department on both sides. I get that. But I can't handle him walking away from me right now.

I hear his footsteps, and my heart skips.

Please don't go out that door...

His handsome face pops back into view, and I swear my soul leaves my body. And, of course, he feels it right away. My fear, nervousness, and anxiety. The look in his eyes is pure love as he holds up a washcloth. "I wanted to clean you."

Oh, my stars. New obsession unlocked.

"I'm sorry. I'm trying to do better." I mutter, recognizing that I may have hurt him with my assumptions.

"I will never leave you, Genevieve. We are mated and bonded. There is nowhere in the world you could go that I wouldn't be able to find you, and it works the same for me. I am yours, Kitten. And you are mine." Killian climbs back into bed, kissing me lightly along my legs as he washes me with the warm rag.

It feels like years since I've taken off my armor, maybe more than just years. Have I ever not had armor on? This is the first time I've ever felt safe and cared for. I let my walls drop and cry from the depths of my soul. Letting it all out, mourning everything I've ever lost. He doesn't judge me. He doesn't rush it or try to fix anything. Instead, Killian rubs my back while I cry it out. Kissing the tears away.

Hours later, while wrapped in each other's arms. Content and lazy. Killian brings his lips to my forehead and whispers. "Be my queen, Genevieve. For real."

CHAPTER THIRTY ONE

SURPRISE, SURPRISE

WHEN I WOKE UP, I was alone. Feeling the satisfying ache in my tight muscles after an incredible night of Killian-guided sexcapades, I stretch out across his dark sheets. I know he isn't here before I open my eyes, but I'm trying something new. Actually, it's brand new. Trust. Killian told me he wouldn't let me go and asked me to believe him.

Opening my eyes, I am relieved to discover it's cloudy. Of course, no day in the Netherworld is hot or uncomfortable (that's a myth), but something about a cloudy day in the middle of fall fulfills my soul. I breathe deeply and release the tension. Between Killian's unmistakable smoky jasmine scent enveloping me and the aroma of changing leaves blended with apples... I could stay here forever.

Moments after the thought enters my mind, Marlow and Kalli burst through the door and pounce. They're in good spirits. Why? Smiles like that raise my suspicions, and I can't help but lift my brows. "I see you two have become friends during my absence. Either I'm thrilled or terrified about that. Which is it?"

Kalliope grins slyly, confirming my suspicion.

These bitches really are up to something.

"Get up and put that amazing ass in the tub! You're going to be late, Vivi!" Marlow squeals.

"Late to what?"

"Bath. Now. Your dress is hanging on the back of the door." Kalli orders, hand on her hip and lips pursed like a mother hen.

"Okay, Okay. Fine. I'll play along. Fuck, you're bossy!" I whine, dragging my ass out of bed and into Killian's bathroom. My tub is great, but his is even better.

After drawing the bathwater, I urinate for the fifth time in the last twelve hours. What?! Last night was crazy, and nobody has time for a UTI. Stay hydrated! The steam from the hot water fills the room. I notice new vials and glass containers sitting on the ledge of his tub.

Was this Killian's idea? He's being so cute that it's disgusting.

Slipping underneath the oiled and scented petals, I wash the last few weeks from my skin. This feeling engulfs me, perhaps pride. Or maybe a sense of accomplishment. My goodness, I've been through some seriously fucked up shit. I know there's more to come, but I made it this far. And that's a godsdamned miracle.

"Do you hear that, Deacon? I made it, old man. Help me get to the finish line. And take care of my friend. She's special, okay." I whisper to the empty room.

I feel my stomach heat, and flames burst from my fingertips like tiny ballet dancers. I've come a long way from the days when I would combust in my sleep and burn my bedding. It seems like a lifetime ago.

Things are different now. And I'm different, too. I suppose that's the point of living through hell, isn't it? Nothing changes if everything stays the same. And yet we fear change the most. Here's my theory. It's the fear of the unknown that fucks us up. It's not about change. It's about the what-ifs.

But I could hypothetically what-if myself into oblivion and still not achieve the life I desire. Why bother? Sometimes you have to take the risk. Jump, and hope there is a net of strong friends to catch you if you face plant.

I'm distracted from my musings by a spazzy knock on the door. I call to whoever is having caffeine jitters on the other side. "Do we have a secret knocking code that you have not taught me, or is someone out there having a seizure?"

Marlow huffs, "Oh, my fucking fuck, Vivi! You're killing me. Put on that damn dress and let us in your hair. Never mind, we're coming in."

She sounds like an impatient toddler waiting for cotton candy at the carnival. These two are acting peculiar and twitchy.

"What the hell is going on?" I ask, standing buck naked and with my titties out. "Kalli, why aren't you being a snarky asshole? Lowe, why are you wound so fucking tight?"

They glance at each other and chuckle. The sarcastic assholes.

"For once in your tight-assed life, would it be possible just to go with the flow? You might be surprised. Get. Dressed. Hooker." Marlow smiles.

Honestly, I'm done. I was just talking to myself about this, and now these crackpots are trying to test me. The gods have jokes today.

As I climb from the bath, all the women in the fortress crowd into Killian's bathroom. Okay, maybe not all. The spacious room suddenly feels cramped. There are hands in my hair and on my face. Everyone here has seen a lot more of me than they bargained for. I feel tempted to throw a fit when Selene walks in, leaking sunshine from every pore, and removes a dress from an old-fashioned-looking garment bag, her eyes rimmed with moisture.

"Pretty Girl. I see you're still stirring up trouble?" She nods, motioning for me to lift my arms as she drapes the dress over me.

I hold back a squeal as I look in the mirror. It's breathtaking! A black corset bodice with sparkling crystals and an open back. They covered the skirt in sheer floral lace appliques, while fluffy tulle glitters beneath. It fits me like a glove. I feel like a fallen star. My hair and makeup feel like a team effort, but I barely notice.

I can't help but stare in the mirror, taking in the dress, appreciating the light foundation, but loving the dramatic smokey eye. Then, a pair of bright green eyes appear behind me. Kalli hooks me with a knowing smirk. "Don't forget your red lipstick, sis."

⚬

Normally I'd say I'm intelligent, but I'm standing here under a canopy of twinkle lights and gothic chandeliers. I'm wearing what looks almost like a wedding dress now that I'm paying attention. In retrospect, I should have figured it out a lot faster.

It is a small gathering, just close friends and family. Set up in the forgotten garden where our mothers were once friends, or at least not enemies. The decoration is minimal, but the meaning is not lost on me. Killian told me his secrets here. There, he bared his soul to me, and I saw the love inside his turquoise storms for the first time.

Anise stands beside me, hardly bouncing at all, and whispers. "He did everything."

"The dress too?" I whisper back, and she shakes her head in agreement. Yes.

There's no time to think because everyone stands, looking past my shoulder. I can feel him, of course. I can always feel him.

Killian slides into the spot next to me and winks. "I thought you'd appreciate walking down the aisle together, and goddess knows no one can speak for you. However, I didn't think you'd want to be given away by someone other than yourself."

"You thought right." I smile.

On the inside, butterflies are having a rave in my stomach. I search the faces of our guests: Marlow, Kalliope, Anise, Amethyst, Sybil, Selene, Bane, Dante, Lincoln, Ansel, Calypso, and Grim. We're what's left of the band of mystical fuckups. Bronwyn's absence is felt. It's written under the hopeful smiles of our friends and family, but it's there. Just as I know that Deacon's absence is marked in both Marlow and Linc.

I lean into Killian and question. "Where is Jagger?"

The smirk on his face has me curious to see what these two oddballs have in store for us. Only the Goddess knows. As I stand here in a pretty black dress next to my mate, it feels a bit awkward. Everyone is on their feet, staring. Waiting. Fluttering nerves take over. Spotlights make me nervous...

"Hey." Killian's voice is calm and sexy. "He's late. I apologize. Is that what I'm feeling? Or do you not want this?"

The bond.

This will take some getting used to, but if he's going to know everything I'm feeling with no context, I might as well answer him. "I want this."

When Jagger arrives, disheveled and bleeding. I give Killian a questioning glance. I said I'd trust him, and I do. But also, what the fuck? Jagger grins like an idiot and asks if we're quote—'Ready to get this party started?'

There are no declarations of love or outrageous promises in our vows. It's just an agreement between two souls not to fuck each other up too badly and a commitment not to run away when things get serious. Now our hearts are connected; we have nothing to prove. And when it comes time to exchange tokens of our love? I draw my dagger from its sheath and cut a lock of hair, a powerful talisman in witchling culture. Killian places a ring on my finger, but it is not just any ring. When Jagger whipped it out of his pocket, I realized why he looks like roadkill.

This ring is from the Realm Draconis, which isn't supposed to exist.

Killian runs his fingers across the back of my hand, sending shivers into my spine. "One grand gesture! Just the one, I promise."

He takes me into his arms and kisses away all my common sense. He makes me dizzy just by his presence.

"Hot damn." Jagger whistles. "I can't believe this show is free! Before you get X-rated in a plant cemetery, though, you're pronounced man and wife! Or lady person and dude person? Partners? Queen Genevieve and King Killian? I don't fucking know. Congrats! Food and liquor in the hall!"

That gets an uproar of laughter out of everyone, and suddenly they're piling out. This is the second time that Killian and I are alone in a Netherworld Garden in two days. This is helpful since I find it impossible to keep my hands to myself. So before our guests have even left sight, I'm wrapped around his waist, watching him grind his pleasure against my folds while pinned against a tree.

"Happy honeymoon, my love." Killian nibbles my ear lobe while his thick shaft glides me into ecstasy.

My words come out in broken, breathless pieces, "How... ah, shit... how did you figure it out? Oh, my gods... yes. Fuck. Yes!"

"I know you, Kitten. You'll be knee deep in trouble before we finish dinner." He chuckles.

"Probably."

Killian flips me over and grabs me from behind. His warm hands dig into my hips, creating a delicious ache I can't get enough of. Then, as he chants my name and kisses my neck, he tenses up and spills himself into me. When we finally enter the hall to join our celebration, we're disheveled, breathless, and totally satisfied.

Our "reception dinner" wasn't any different from the boisterous dinners we have every night. Apparently, Killian had it stuck in his mind that we include earth realm customs along with the Netherworld. But, of course, I don't have the heart to tell him that witchlings don't do any of these things, except the attaching our souls to one another in the presence of nature. So, I guess we included it.

While everyone is carrying on separate conversations, I look at Killian's smiling face, and I feel like I've come home. I stand to make a toast, and the table quiets. "Hey. So, um. Thank you. I'm terrible at these speech type things, but I... well, I guess I can say we... we appreciate everything you've sacrificed to get here."

I feel dumb. This is so uncomfortable and not me.

"Okay. You know what? Let me back that up. Thank you! Killian and I have our shit to work through, but I'm honored to be your queen. Now that we have that out of the way. Let's talk war."

Killian's answering smirk bolsters my confidence.

"So, here's what I learned at the Bone Keep."

I recount everything I can remember, pissed that I didn't grab those notebooks before I busted out. "Mordred engineers his legion. Engineers, as in, injecting them with a mixture of science and magic. I think he breeds them, too, maybe even speeds up the aging process. The point is, he has a lot more forces than we thought."

The table is paying attention now.

"Thane is his secret weapon. She spells the obsidian. It's her magic that alters Mordred's experiments. I injured her while in her lair, and when I left, she hadn't been seen for days. I don't know if she's alive or dead."

Kalli interrupts. "She's not dead. Thane is a goddess. Mordred has bodies on backup for her. She'll just come back with a different face."

Killian clears his throat and turns his attention toward Kalliope. "Is Thane the sorceress who cursed my father?"

"A version of her, but that's not the right question. Was it Thane's magic that created the curse? That's the question. And the answer is yes," Kalli responds.

An idea pops into my head. Well, the beginning of an idea, anyway. "Would it be fair to say that if we take Thane out, Mordred falls?"

"Good luck taking her out! Hundreds have tried. You'd have to be a...." Kaliope's eyes damn near bugged out of her skull.

I wait a moment to see if she will finish that sentence, and when she doesn't, I get nosy. "You'd have to be a *what*, Kalli?"

My sister's eyes shoot to Killian, and I'm thoroughly confused.

"You'd have to be a God Killer, my love. The rest is for another time and a much stiffer drink." He rubs my leg reassuringly, so I let it go for now. But only because I have a bombshell of my own to drop.

The old Vivi would have kept it quiet and dove headfirst into trouble on her own. Although I've said it before, I am planning to change it. That was about the time I ran off on my own and got caught by Mordred. However, Deacon always said that words are just ideas without action. So far, they have only been words. Tonight, it's time to put those ideas into action.

"To defeat Mordred and his forces, we're going to need the entire might of the Netherworld. We'll need the witches and warlocks, too. This is everybody's fight." So I present the first part of my proposal, and everyone agrees.

Good. It'll make the next part easier.

"Killian and I are leaving tonight; we're going to the Academy to recruit some powerful witches to our cause. And I have some unfinished business I must attend to before entering this battle with any hope of winning." I state.

The way Killian handled it was smooth as butter. I did not tell him what I was going to say or that I would turn him into an accessory for whatever I had planned. Yet his expression never changed, and instead of being irritated, his eyes were filled with curiosity.

"Yes. Jagger, Dante, Bane: start preparations while the Queen and I visit the Earth Realm. Anise and Lincoln try to contact the other orders. Dante, Bane? You know where I need you to go." He gives orders.

Bringing my lips to his ear, I whisper. "Let's go kill a curse, my king."

CHAPTER THIRTY TWO

GRAVESTONE ACADEMY

I AM GROWING FOND of Willa's office. She has a clean, crisp, modern library atmosphere going on. The chairs are comfortable, and I'm getting used to it. Killian sits next to me, completely still. If his chest wasn't moving, I would think he was a statue or a dead person. I grab his hand and rub his palm in lazy circles. I know this is pushing his boundaries right now. But I can't reveal my unfinished business yet. He will understand soon.

"Dear girl! It is so nice to see you again. Glad to hear about your safe return. And you're married too! Congratulations to you both!" Iris enters the office and goes straight for grandma hugs. The look on Killian's face as he receives one of Iris's hugs is priceless. The poor guy doesn't know what he's been missing. His expression is far from comfortable. I'd say it's more of a horrified-slash-I might vomit combo.

He is the damn mascot for 'I wasn't hugged enough as a child.' Not that I have a lot of room to talk, I'm just making an observation.

Iris smells like gingerbread today, and it summons a memory of Marlow and me. Here at the Academy, on the east end of the lawns, sharing gingerbread cookies. We got them for Mabon Celebration, right before the… Festival of Light.

Goddess, it's been a year? An entire year. Wow! It feels like yesterday and a thousand years at the same time. But, I guess it's true what they say: a lot *can* happen in a year. More than I ever thought conceivable, and some things I was sure were impossible.

"Hey, Iris!" I secretly love the feel of her honest to goddess smile. It lifts my spirits, but I'll deny it every time. "We're just waiting on Willa to give an update. Would you mind staying? I have something I'd like to speak about after."

"Of course, dear." Iris smiles and takes a seat.

Willa enters like a bull shifter in an antique shop. Madder than hellfire and headed straight for me. Shit!

"Genevieve Evanora Graves! You are a reckless, insolent monster of a girl, but I have never believed you to be stupid." She trained her milky eyes on me; her crooked finger is in my face. "But what could possess you to leave the security of the fortress and go straight into Mordred's arms, other than stupidity?"

"Well, it's Morningstar now. My last name, I mean. And I love you too, Willa!" I can't keep the toothy grin from my lips this time. Goddess, help me.

Willa's nostrils flare, and I brace myself for the tiny spiders. But instead, she huffs and turns on her heel toward her desk. "Reckless monster of a girl!"

Even Killian has difficulty keeping the amusement from breaking through his cool facade. I can tell because his eye is twitching.

"Let's get this shit show on the road." I kick off the conversation. "We've got to make moves, and soon. We do not have the luxury of time, so here's the rundown. Mordred is creating warriors, a lot of them. Thane is not just a sorceress. She's a goddess. A petty, scary, vengeful one—and she can't die. We need her to die. See the dilemma? If we can accomplish that, then we can take the Bone Keep and restore the Netherworld. But this is too much for just the Nether realm. This is everybody's problem because he will not stop at one portal or realm. We need witches, Willa. In serious numbers. Both mixed order and pure blooded. It's time to come together and fight."

Iris and Willa exchange a loaded glance. I have no clue what it meant, but it signified something. Finally, Willa answers, "Have Amethyst and Lincoln get us the word when the time comes? We'll be there."

"I want to thank you both," Killian's smooth, charming voice fills the room. "On behalf of the Netherworld and its inhabitants."

He's so much better at this shit than I am, case in point. Hold my beer…

"Yes, thank you so much. Iris, I need you to take me to the Cove of Myths."

I really know how to kill a vibe, let me tell you. If there were a kill-the-vibe competition? First place, baby! Winner, winner.

I glance at Killian's face first since this is the moment he's been anticipating, and it's here... but I'm unsure how he'll react. Either by pure dumb luck or much to my pleasure. Killian seems relaxed, flirty even. I'm not sure we have the stamina or the time for what I see in his eyes.

Whew, cool down, Vivi. Not the time or place.

"Iris? Did you hear what I asked?" I speak up, wondering if maybe I've stunned her.

She clears her throat, glancing at Willa for half a moment, and then nods. "Who am I to deny a queen?"

"Come on, now! It's not like that. This isn't an order. Well… I don't think it is? I'll find a way in myself if I must.

Shit. That sounds like an order. But it's not! You don't have to, but I will get into that cavern at all costs, even if it means exploding every underground catacomb until I find it." I explain, then think about what I just said.

Willa raises a brow.

"That's not a threat! Fuck, that sounded like a threat. I'm so fucking bad at this." I slap my hand to my forehead to the tune of Killian laughing.

Full on, uncontrollably, holding his stomach and laughing at me. If it wasn't the most captivating thing I've ever seen, I'd be pissed.

"My queen has a unique communication style. We're working on it." Killian forms a short (bullshit) sentence through his shoulder-shaking laughter.

Fine, let's cross 'Inter Realm Relations' off the list of things I'm qualified for.

<hr />

It feels like déjà vu. It is still one of the most elaborate caverns I have ever seen. Cream-colored fabric was strung throughout, and candles with melted wax were on every surface. Yet, it's still dim and haunting in a way that feels like it's touching the soul. This cavern is alive. Roses, a hint of incense, and ancient magic. It is a sacred place.

When I think about why I am here, it makes my breath catch. I hadn't allowed myself to contemplate it. It seemed more sensible to bury it until it is in your face, and you have to deal with it. The plan worked. But now that I am facing it, I'm freaking the fuck out.

I knew I would want him here for this, and what that would mean to him. It will be one of the most challenging moments of my life, and I want him to share it with me. I said he would understand soon, and I meant it.

As we approach the carved stone staircase, Killian squeezes my hand. Air is forced out of my lungs, and my heart beats uncontrollably. A woman dressed in red cotton voile stands at the base of the stone staircase. But not just *a* woman, *the* woman.

My seat is the same as last time, in the spiral in the center of the cavern. As she languidly approaches us, my lip trembles. He releases a small pulse into my skin, not enough to tingle, just enough to calm me. That's a handy skill to have, I admit. I can't control my tremors or the sweat pooling in my palms, but Killian doesn't falter. I feel grounded and balanced under his fingers. More and more, I understand *why* he is my soul-bound mate.

The Oracle reaches us, bending her knees to meet us at eye level. "Genevieve," her haunting voice beckons from behind the veil she wears over the lower half of her face.

The tears are falling before I can catch them. My body shakes. "Mom?"

Killian's body stills.

"I figured out who she was while I was being tortured," I whisper to him between shaky, tear-filled breaths.

"Killian Morningstar, the Light Bringer."

Now it's time for my eyes to bug out. She just called him a what? A light bringer? Has she *seen* him?

"Oracle." He bows his head briefly.

Her smile is warm, and I think I can see pieces of myself behind that veil for a moment. Pieces of her. The woman I remember at Bloodgood manor, the mother who loved me enough to give me away.

"Will you allow me to touch your hand, Genevieve?" her voice floats through the cavern.

I don't know if I'm capable of speaking right now. There's a river rushing toward me, and the dam may break if I speak. Killian senses it through the bond. The way he is wrapping his muscular arm around my body tells me a lot. Defending. Protecting. Even if that means shielding me from my own emotions.

He clears his throat. "She's ready."

My mother runs her hand along my cheek, crying. "It's time." Her voice shakes as the walls of my childhood home echo with violence and death. "One day, you will understand why, and you will forgive me—my sweet one. But until the day comes, know that everything I've done is for love." She places her hand on my temple.

How did I forget this? These are the last words my mother said to me.

Another scene hits me in the gut like a ton of bricks. I'm lying in filth, mostly dead, on the floor of the academy dungeon. And I hear her voice.

"You must listen, Daughter of Oracles. Take these and when the time is right, use them."

"Why do you keep calling me that? Daughter of Oracles. What does it mean?"

"All in time, Sweet One, all in time."

My mother was with me. She protected me. Tears flood my eyes, and everything blurs. She didn't abandon me. She sacrificed herself. And then saved me in her next incarnation.

"It's best I start at the beginning." She speaks. "I am not a virtuous goddess, Genevieve. I am what they created me to be. A temptress, an agent of chaos, and a protector of warriors."

Her eyes move to Killian, a slight grin on her lips.

So, she was protecting him too? I don't understand.

"We'll get to that, Vivi. Everything in time. I am your mortal mother, and you are my child. I am the Mother of Witches. The Dark Goddess. Queen of Night. Some call me Hecate. Now I am an old one, as intended."

"Hecate? Then who is Evanora Bloodgood?" I ask.

"She's the woman who gave you life. She is me."

I *think* I understand, with the whole body-hopping-goddess-spirit thing.

She nods to Killian. "Your father is a tyrant who deserves eternal sleep, but he helped erase us from the Netherworld and keep us in hiding. Your mother was kind to me, Killian Morningstar. You have her temperament, Netherworld King. That's why they chose you."

They? Chosen for what?

My mother turns her attention back to me. "Mordred found us, my sweet girl. Your memories of that day were scrubbed by me. I did what any mother would do. I cloaked you, scrubbed your memories, and lent as much of my power as your fragile body could handle. Then, I put that amulet around your neck and sent you off to Thornfall with my closest confidante and the only man I've ever loved."

She's leaving out the part where she died in the process. And I fucking knew it!! I knew my mother and Deacon were in love.

"Mom? I know you're an all-knowing Oracle, and you're probably already... I think I just need to say it to you, for me. Or maybe for you? Deacon is dead. He died protecting me. And Rowena has been missing for a very long time. I don't think she survived Faustus."

"Deacon is at peace. He died doing the only thing he ever wanted to do. He died loving you enough for the both of us, just like I asked him to. And one thing to remember about the fae folk, Genevieve. Never count them out." She smirks.

Killian rubs my arms. Comforting me, she looks at him. "You have the future of the Netherworld in your hands, Killian Morningstar. And you have the love of my daughter. Together, you can change everything, but there is something you must do first." She gives him a sly look.

"Okay, so I'm just the third wheel? What does he have to do?" I ask.

Both Killian and my mother train their eyes on me, their gazes soft but firm.

"He has his destiny too, sweet one." My mother replies warmly.

This is an emotional fucking rollercoaster. I am sitting in front of my mother, and yeah, she's not perfect. She's been villainous and manipulative. Who hasn't at some point in their lives? So maybe she wasn't created to be the mother of the year. That makes it even more impactful that when she sensed my father wanted to use me, harm me. So she gave up her crusade for more power.

She chose me.

"You mastered your gifts. Remove the enchantments on yourself, your magic, your memories. You are fierce and loyal. You fight harder than anyone I've met for the people who have shown you kindness. You are who I hoped you'd be. I am so proud of you, Genevieve." And now, tears dot her eyes. "It's time."

"It's time for what?" I ask, a bit of panic seeping into my voice.

My mother responds. "For you to gain your birthright."

No. No! Wait, that's the body hopping spirit goddess thing.

"What will happen to you?" the anguish leaks through my words because I already know. This is goodbye.

"I will serve my destiny. I carried you in my body. I knew what you would be, Genevieve, and the Oracles tasked me to keep you safe. In return, they gave me salvation from my past. Now? I'll live out my eternity in peace, and you will be The Dark Goddess, Mother of Witches, Queen of Night, Hecate. Whatever you choose to be called makes no difference."

"I feel like I just got you back."

"I never left, darling." She whispers and then presses her hands into my chest.

My body lifts off the ground, filled to the brim with power. Suspended in the air, I'm glowing. It hurts, but I can't feel it past the pain of losing my mother again. This time, the pain is different. I'm gutted, and it will take some time to be okay with this.

After the power sinks into my bones and my body lowers to the ground, I collapse into Killian, and he holds me while I sob.

CHAPTER THIRTY THREE

THE NIGHT FORTRESS

LAST NIGHT, I HAD no desire to see or talk to anyone, including myself. So calypso and I headed to the blanket mountain after skipping dinner. What a surprise it was when Lincoln Blackwood got past Ansel (I wonder how that happened?), and he invaded my depression fort.

"Building a nest, Viv?" Linc's comedian smile is the thing I didn't know I needed.

I laugh and shove him in the chest. "It's not a *nest*. It's a depression fort. You have a terrible eye for design."

"My mistake. I like what you've done with the place."

"Your good looks and boyish charm are the only things keeping you from the wrath of my flames, Lincoln Blackwood!" I joke.

"So, you want to talk about it? Your husband is down in the hall looking like someone took his sword away. Kicked puppy vibes, Viv." He stares until I crack. Damn him for knowing me so well.

"I met my mom."

Linc chokes on his own tongue. "I'm sorry, I think I misheard. Did you say your *mom*? No fucking way! Where's Lowe? Have you told her yet?"

That doesn't mean I wasn't going to share it with my friends or that I was trying to avoid Killian. But when I am overwhelmed, I tuck myself into a cozy corner and hide. That needs to change. I'm working on it. You know, hyper independence can be a sign of trauma. So, there's that. And perfection is overrated.

"Yeah, I… I just needed to work out my shit for a minute." I stutter.

Linc regards me with a suspicious glint. "Well, you know I'm down for a sheet burning party. Or an ice cream fueled cry fest. Loud music scream-a-thon. You pick the meltdown; I clean up the aftermath. Just like old times!"

"While that's tempting, I think I'll be alright. Give me an hour to pull my shit together? Then I'd like us all to meet in the war room. Can you facilitate that?" I ask and then add. "Oh, and *wonder bread* out there is fired. He's a terrible security guard, letting the rabble come right on in and climb into my fort."

"Ansel!" Lincoln shouts, and my door cracks. "Our queen says you're a terrible guard. Fired, even!"

Ansel chuckles. "Thank the gods, it worked!"

"Out! Both of you." I giggle as I lob a pillow at my door, missing Ansel by a long shot.

Linc agrees, with a condition. If I'm not meeting them within the hour, he's sending in the *real* menaces.

The ladies of the Night Fortress.

———◇———

There's no way to describe how good it feels to be back in my whirlpool, covered in rose oil and bubbles. With my head resting on the ledge of my marble tub, I take a moment to think. We've all been through a hell of a storm since the loud-jukebox karaoke nights at the Gravestone, but the tidal wave is now upon us. The next storm could change everything, and I only hope it's for the better.

Amethyst and Sybil were two throwaway witches who lived most of their lives hiding in a cave system because they were different. Suppose we survive this. What kind of future will they build together? Amethyst is a born warrior and a brilliant strategist. Sybil rarely says more than a few words a day. However, she sees everything. I hope they live out loud somewhere in the sun. And Marlow, it doesn't take a genius to see the love in her eyes when Jagger is nearby. I want that for them. I want to be the crazy auntie of some unruly Netherling beasties. I would love to throw outrageous birthday parties and watch Killian play with nieces and nephews.

Maybe we'll have our own little beasties. Perhaps we won't. It wouldn't matter to me.

Linc, what else can I say? That man is somebody's dream husband. I've always said that. Maybe years ago, a part of me wished I could change myself and be his endgame. That was, until Killian walked through the Gravestone doors. To be honest, I had not considered Anise for Lincoln. As much as I do my best not to count her out, I'm guilty of it. Thank the goddess Lincoln saw in Anise what I have always seen. Few others do. Anise is a riot of beauty and chaos. There is so much more to her than meets the eye. So fierce. So loyal. Broken. But, of course, it would be Lincoln who could see through the antics to her heart. It would be Lincoln who could help her heal. It should have been obvious to me.

And Kalli. A strong, beautiful, traumatized, yet still fucking standing woman. My big sister. She makes me want to be like her one day. But more than anything, I want a chance to reclaim what they stole from us. We are sisters. We are a family. Our blood flows through each other's veins, and I want ample time to relax and breathe so I can enjoy it.

On the horizon is a storm that threatens all of it. In an instant, everything I love could be gone. We must stop Mordred and Thane. The future depends on it.

The very thought of Mordred, Thane, and Hunter makes my body shiver. But I should thank those piles of shit for teaching me something. Killian is an incubus, so I never trusted him. Initially, I thought he was slippery (and he is), but it wasn't until I met Hunter that I realized how dangerous an incubus who doesn't respect you can be. With one hundred percent certainty, I knew Killian would never do the things Hunter did to me. I learned a lot from Hunter. Too bad I can't march through those gates and kill him again.

My bathwater started boiling before I realized I'd gotten so worked up.

Argh. Anyway. I'm ready to get out of this bath and into a fight with the Shadowlands. Mordred is about to receive a Netherworld-sized ass-whooping.

***

It feels great to be back in my leggings, knee-high boots, and tank top. The smallest things can make all the difference. I never imagined that I would miss these halls and their Tim Burton-esque qualities, but as I continue on the same path I've taken a hundred times before, it becomes harder and harder to ignore. I feel at home here. From the beautiful main hall to the walkway outside the gardens to the east wing with the library and offices. Despite just being together yesterday for the ceremony, I am excited to see everyone in the same place again. Maybe it's because I feel like I have lost a lot of time. This alternate version of myself is confusing me. Since when am I miss perky and feeling excited about things?

I guess the answer to that is—when I lost it all. Fuck. This fortress drives me nuts almost as much as the people in it, but this is my circus. These are my monkeys. Actually, my shitheads. For better or worse, and all the bullshit in between.

"Morning bitches!!" I call out as I shove the door to Killian's office/war room, expecting the band of misfits sprawled over Killian's fancy furniture.

What I got were Killian and his mom.

"I'm sorry to meet you this way, but I must insist we have a conversation." Selene is the first to speak. And my eyes rapidly move to Killian, reading his expression. Waiting for... reassurance? I don't know. His eyes are a stormy turquoise. He's not angry. Does he know what she wants to talk about? Or are we being reverse parent trapped?

Killian's return gaze says he's not altogether sure what's happening, but he has an inkling.

Selene shifts in her seat, then changes her mind and stands, pacing. Killian and I look at each other, puzzled. Is she nervous?

"Queen Genevieve, it was me. I was the one who stole your dagger before you were taken." Selene's shoulders slump as the words come out.

Okay. That's not the best news I've ever received, but not the worst.

"Why?" I lean my head to the side as Killian's fingers touch the small of my back.

Selene lends me a sad smile. "Our match was one of convenience, but I loved my king more than anything. Sometimes I think more than even myself." Her eyes scan the floor momentarily as if that truth was difficult to part with. "But I love my son more."

"Mother, what did you do?" Killian's voice was feather soft.

She inhales, and something like determination overtakes her. "I did what I had to do."

"What does that mean?" Killian continues, "What you had to do? I don't understand! He's been asleep for a decade, Mother. Were you trying to wake him up? You know what he'll do to Genevieve! He was already doing it from his slumber, him, and that wretched curse. That's why I had him bound, mother!"

Killian has his father bound. Like, magically? I guess that would make sense. I haven't been attacked by any stray logs in quite a while. Then, suddenly, a vision materializes, or more specifically, part of a vision. I remember the hallway and the maiden, the dream-like state, and the blood flowing from my arm. I woke up with a scratch. It was the same morning my dagger went missing. And then I was taken, so the dagger was the least of my worries…

"You're the one who put him in eternal sleep." Killian states. It's not an accusation; it's a fact.

A whisper of a smile crosses her lips. "I had a little help."

"My mother. She helped you put him down, didn't she? But she wouldn't have done it out of the kindness of her heart. Unless… unless you were friends."

"You're a bright woman, Genevieve. Perfect for my son in every way." Her eyes gleam with something I can't quite place. "The night the Oracle visited your mother, she came to me too. Both with the same message, about our first-born children. And the prophecy they would fulfill."

No fucking way! I'm… I… wait a minute. The prophecy isn't about Kalliope and me? But it has to be. Everyone said… Fuck, nobody knows what it means.

Unless you're the person who received it.

"Hecate. I'm sorry, Evanora. I know that name resonates with you the most. She came to me after her visit from the Oracle. She had no clue I'd had a similar visit. We repeated the words together, '*One made of darkness. One made of light.*

Air burns to Ash. Shadows take flight. When light pierces night, a new dawn will rise.' And after that, it was irrefutable."

The garden. That's where they practiced, right under the king's nose.

"You and my mother put him in eternal sleep. I'm assuming this was after he helped us out of the realm. But you didn't put the killing curse on Killian, and my mother didn't put a killing curse on me. So, who enacted the killing curse?" I ask.

"Thane." She replies, lips in a thin line.

I look at Killian, wondering what's knocking around in his head. He knew some of this already, I can tell. But I'm done worrying about what he knew and when. None of it was ever malicious. I can sense that through the bond.

Killian clears his throat. "Why did he need to be put under eternal sleep, mother? Why did you have to choose between him and me?"

"Your father would never allow Genevieve to live. He had no intention of allowing his only son to wed Mordred's daughter. His wounded pride wouldn't allow such a slight. We didn't know if that would activate the curse, but he stood firm. Your father had to be stopped." Selene's face softens.

"And what about the dozens of times he whipped Jagger? When he drowned Anise's mother? I won't even speak of the twins. He ran my siblings off the major fortress and ordered them killed on sight! When I had to smuggle a crimson haired infant into the fucking harem so he couldn't find her. Why wasn't he stopped then?" Killian's voice is an octave higher than usual, and my heart breaks. I've never seen him allow himself to hurt so openly.

"I failed them, Killian. And for that, I am sorry." Selene takes his hand in hers, and he looks like he may yank it back.

Please don't, Killian. She did the best she could.

When he stills, I'm a little stunned. He heard me. I was only thinking about it, but he heard me.

Selene grabs the opportunity to steer the conversation again. "Genevieve, I stole that dagger, and I cut your arm so the blade would absorb your blood."

"Why?"

"Because your blood is the key. Genevieve, your blood infused with this blade can kill a God." Her face is solemn now. "I didn't realize it wouldn't be enough, that it would have to be you who wields the dagger."

"Why would you want me to kill the man you love?" I could never, but then again—I'm not a mother.

Selene deflates, and I think I see the passage of time underneath her eyes for the first time. These secrets have aged her and weighed on her soul for a long time.

"Because my son is my world, but The Dark King of the Netherworld has a weak spot. One that only I know, and now you. Killian is not immortal until my husband is dead. He does not have his full power, and to go to war without it..." Selene sobs.

And I gasp. "Killian Morningstar! You *knew* this? Every time you have thrown your body in front of death while it's speeding toward me, you knew. I can't just bring you back from the dead! Why would you be so?"

"Reckless?" Killian interrupts with his signature smirk.

Fuck. He's got me dead to rights. I'd do the same fucking thing for him without a second thought. For Marlow, Linc, Kalli. For all of them. I would throw myself in front of a meteor to keep them safe because I love them.

I focus back on Selene. "So, you want me to kill the God of Death?"

CHAPTER THIRTY FOUR

VIVI

FUCKING SPELLS AND CURSES! So, I'm a god killer? I didn't intend to run off after hearing the news. Suddenly, I felt like I was boiling, and I was running out of air. I stepped outside, and the next thing I know, I'm pacing a hole in the floor of my room. I can't stop myself. It's like my brain has shorted out. My thoughts are moving so quickly that I can barely keep up. I know I should act. What other choice can there be? He's dangerous. He cannot be allowed to wake. The Band-Aid Killian slapped on it keeps the killing curse away for now—but there is no way that's going to last.

Kilian will ride into battle a mortal if I don't do this. He'll be superhuman and harder to kill, yes. But still mortal. And why shouldn't I do it joyfully? Especially after what he did to the man I love. FOUR men I love! Not to mention a redheaded princess who deserves the world.

Killian will tell me to do it. I know he will.

But what about in ten years? Or twenty? We will stand in a dining hall, screaming at each other from all our resentment? Will I lose my husband? How do Jagger, Anise, Dante, and Bane feel about it? I can't just kill people's fathers without talking to them – at the very least. But how does such a conversation even go? "Hi, friends. I need to stab your dad with a dagger to erase him from the fabric of space and time. Are you going to be pissed with me about it?"

I mean, come on!

Calypso paces the floor next to me, on edge, and I feel shitty about that, too. She plays off my emotions, and I know it. What I choose for me, I also choose for her. Fuck!

It is one of those times when I need to consult the Goddess of Night or Frank. Somebody! There is no Goddess of the Night this time, as I *am* the Dark Goddess. My decisions are mine alone. And I don't know what to do.

"Hey, Psycho." My sister's voice makes its way past the hysteria. "First, stop moving. You're making me dizzy. Sit!"

As if on command, I do exactly what she says.

"Alright. So, you're freaking out, and I'm sure I know why. So, I'm going to talk you off the ledge, and then we won't have to commit you. Okay? I don't know what this looks like from your point of view, but from ours, you look like you're having a nervous breakdown, Vivi."

Ours?

My eyes search the room, and there he is. Standing in the doorway between our rooms. Holding his emotions close to the vest, I can't tell what he's thinking or feeling, but he seems content to let Kalliope take the reins and tame my crazy.

"Will you hate me?" I stare him in the eye, looking for truth.

Killian sighs, running his hand through his hair. He's rumpled, and it is sexy. Watching him lose control is my new obsession. "Kitten, you must. You are not safe with Aedonius alive. Even in eternal sleep."

That's the first time I've ever heard him say his father's name out loud.

My voice lowers to a whisper. "That is not what I asked you."

Killian moves from the doorway to standing impossibly close within seconds. So close, I can feel his warm breath on my forehead. "I could never hate you, but I will hate myself if you don't do this and something happens to you. After this, I'll be able to protect you."

I roll my eyes. "You know that I'm the Goddess of Night with my full powers, and I was quite capable of taking care of myself even before that? So don't underestimate me."

"My beautiful, murderous creature. I would never." He grabs my hips and plants his sinful mouth on mine, caressing my tongue with his and stealing the breath from my lungs.

Kalliope's feet shuffle. "Ugh. Get a room!"

Killian chuckles. "You're in it, Sweetheart."

"Oh, for star's sake! I want to see Killian's siblings; can you round them up, Kalli? Have them meet us in here?" I flash her an apologetic smile.

"Take your time." Killian captures my eyes and bites down on his lower lip.

Fuck, that's so hot.

Kalliope barely makes it to the door before his hands and lips are everywhere, spreading lightning through my veins. He's pressing against me like he can make the fabric of his slacks dissolve by thought alone. His voice is husky and filled with dark promises when he latches his teeth into my ear and rumbles. "I can't wait. Tell me yes, Kitten."

"Yes."

Within seconds, I've got my leggings ripped off at the crotch, one hand inside my bra, squeezing my breasts and rolling my nipples between his fingers as he uses the other hand to undo the buttons on his pants and free his thick cock. I can't resist looking back at it. It's so perfect. I want to see it. His cock throbs and twitches in search of the warm folds that belong to him. Goddess, he is so turned on. And it's turning *me* on.

What has gotten into him? Or me, for that matter.

He's on his knees behind me, dragging his hot tongue across my warm slit without warning, and my knees buckle as I moan.

"You taste like fucking heaven." His muffled voice is filled with desire. Taking his fingers, he spreads me open so he can have better access and then presses his tongue flat against my clit. As I writhe, my body begging for more pressure, he licks upwards and then sucks on my clit.

As I fall face first onto my bed, Killian's hands are on my hips, digging his long fingers into my flesh. He wraps an arm around my waist and lifts me onto the middle of the bed, pushing me flat into the pillows. In one fluid motion, he sinks into me and buries himself.

"Yes! Oh, my goddess. Please." I cry out.

The nearly inaudible moans coming from him drive me fucking wild. He glides into me rhythmically at first, a perfect fit sliding against every part of me. "Fuck, Vivi, you feel so good. I need you; I fucking need you."

He only calls me Vivi when he doesn't know he's doing it.

"Then take me." I moan.

Killian's hips move faster, hitting my ass cheeks with force. But he's holding back, and I want more.

"Stop trying to protect me and fuck me!" I moan, reaching back and digging my nails into the sides of his thighs as he growls.

"You sure about that?" he smiles as he flips me over to face him, eyes of swirling midnight, jagged teeth, and his claws protruding. He's losing control of his demon.

Half-shifted, Killian looks down at me. I know what he's thinking. He's afraid that I won't want it when I see his darkness. He is fearful of me rejecting him. But that couldn't be further from the truth. My hands grasp the sides of his head, and I bring his lips to mine - careful of his fangs, but not at all apprehensive. I kiss him as if he's the only man who's ever existed, and I do it while keeping my eyes open.

"You are mine." I snarl, letting my demon come out to play, too.

When I see his control snap, I smile. Then, as he slams into me, his teeth clamp down on my shoulder, and I scream in pleasure. I'm mindless and trembling as he pumps himself against my silky insides. Panting out words I cannot understand.

"Are you ready to come for me, Kitten?"

"Yes. Yes, please, yes!" my voice sounds strangled.

Killian smirks, eyeing me like a steak dinner. "And what will you scream, Kitten?"

"Your name." I pant.

"Good girl," he says as he lifts my hips and spears me in the right place, pumping and grinding his length so that it hits every spot.

I love the way he watches me, how he just called me a good girl, and how he dominates me. Killian's intensity increases, his deep penetration and grinding more punishing than before. There is no other feeling like it, and my eyes roll back in my head. "Look at me, Vivi. Look in my eyes and come for me."

A wave of soul-rending pleasure envelops me from my feet to my scalp. I am riding a wave of rapture mingled with pain, love, and beautiful destruction. It's too much to bear. I scream his name like he's air, and I'm drowning.

— ◦ —

We lay under the covers in absolute bliss. Killian has a thing for cleaning me up and spoiling me afterward. The last time it was a washcloth and a glass of champagne. This time, he cleaned up his mess with his tongue and then smothered me in delicate kisses.

My Dirty Dark King. I love it.

"I need you to be serious right now," I attempt to gain his attention for the fifth time. Killian's stormy blue eyes flick up from the kisses he's determined to place on every inch of my skin, and he beams at me.

He could ruin my life with that smile, and I would thank him.

But not right now. I know it's our honeymoon, but there are some pressing issues we must deal with. "Your siblings are going to be in this room any second." I huff, and he smiles again.

I think he's sex drunk or something.

"And? We're covered up." He gives me that cocky smirk.

I'm not going to pretend to understand whatever I'm feeling through our bond. It's possessive, but not in an alpha-hole way, more like an excited boy who wants everyone to see his most precious work of art.

I don't have time to argue because, as always, I'm right. The doors open, and Anise, Lincoln, Jagger, Marlow, Dante, and Bane file in. Standing at the end of my bed. The bed I am freshly fucked and still naked in.

Kill me now.

But Killian sits us up, making sure he wrapped the sheets around anything I don't want them to see, and he wraps his arm around my bare shoulder. "Your queen would like to have a word."

With that, everyone in the room is snickering, holding in their laughter, or snorting. I want to kiss Killian for knowing I was uncomfortable and bringing the attention to himself.

I clear my throat, and my cheeks flush. "I have a feeling you already knew this first part before I found out… whatever. That's not what I want to talk about. This morning, Selene told Killian and me that she's the one who stole my dagger and cut my arm. My blood and the daggers are the keys. Put them together, and I can kill a god. Selene wants me to kill the King of the Netherworld."

There were a few small gasps, but not the reaction I was expecting. Looking at Anise, the answer is written in the bitter rage on her stunning face. She wants him dead. Jagger looks ambivalent, but Marlow is holding his arm as though he needs support.

"Jagger? This is a vote. I care what you think." I remind him we are friends first, queen and subject second.

He's silent for a few moments, and then he sighs. "Killian will be mortal until father dies? Is that true, bro?"

Killian nods in affirmation.

"He's not taking my brother from me. So kill him, Little Monster. He's a piece of shit anyhow." Jagger crosses his arms against his chest.

I have no love for him, Genevieve.

Bane answers in my mind.

He's a dick, save our brother.

And that's Dante.

"The twins are on board," I announce, since not everyone has heard their opinion.

Marlow is fidgeting. When she gets squirrelly, it's not typically a good sign. "Do I get a vote here? Or maybe not a vote since I already killed my father. But can I ask questions?"

"I also have questions." Lincoln chimes in.

Oh, dear goddess, these two.

"Of course, Weirdos! Don't start treating me like a queen. You've seen me blackout drunk crying into my toilet. And you have had to change how many pairs of my burned-up sheets? Fuck. Quit being strange." I wheeze.

Marlow isn't impressed. She gets that way for me. "Will you be in danger? Can he kill you while you're killing him?"

Oh shit, I did not think of that. But, of course, Marlow would.

"I don't know."

"No," Lincoln answers, panic in his eyes.

"Every one of you has taken chances with your lives for me, for each other. I've already done it a hundred times over. You're not immortal, Linc. But are the wolves going to be on that battlefield? I already know they are. One of these kingdoms is falling, and I cannot guarantee it won't be ours."

He doesn't look happy, but Anise gets it, and I can tell by the twitch of her fingers that she's taking the edge off that shifter temper of his. Linc grinds his teeth. "Fine, but I want to be there when you do it."

"Me too." Marlow chimes in.

"And me," Jagger says.

"Everyone wants to be there. Got it. Are we in agreement, then?"

A chorus of nods seals my fate.

CHAPTER THIRTY FIVE

A TIME TO DIE

IT'S NOT LIKE WE have much time to waste. The longer we wait, the better the chance Mordred has of reviving Thane. As a result, there was no pause between the conversation we just had and being led out to THE DOOR. I'll admit, I am trembling like crazy. I find it unsettling that there is no time to prepare, but that's my life, isn't it? *There is no time to prepare.* It might as well be my middle name.

Kalli stands on one side of me, ready to rip anyone apart who gets too close. What a transformation from at each other's throats to double trouble. When the two of us are on the same team, we're explosive. As for our enemies... good luck.

Despite leading the way, I notice Killian checking across his shoulder frequently. He is watching me like a hawk for signs of distress, so of course I'm hiding them. Some things are better left to sisters, and this is one of them. I would think about Killian the entire time if I were walking in front of him, trying to figure out if he really meant what he was saying.

Overthinking at its finest.

No, it's better to be next to Kalli and Marlow. As expected, Calypso is stuck to me like glue. She has been since I arrived back at the Fortress. I have no complaints; she is the calm in my storm despite her own chaotic nature. Perhaps we cancel each other out.

I cannot help myself when we reach the door. My heart pounds, my hands tremble, and I hesitate. The memory of the maiden, the bleeding walls, my hand through my sister's rotting chest cavity. What does that mean? The door opening, feeling the darkness emanating from the space, the shadows moving, and the hallucinations that follow in my dream. I shiver. More like nightmare. It wasn't real, it wasn't an omen, and I'm not bitching out now. Fuck that. I can do this.

As we turn the corner, and I find myself standing in front of the door of my literal nightmares. It opens. Just like that. A violet flame only. No magic mojo, not even an F-bomb. Almost like this creepy-ass wing of the Night Fortress is daring me to confront it. Good. Game on, Aedonious. My pace quickens when I reach Killian's side. I'm not waiting for anyone else to enter before me. No way in hell.

When I cross the threshold, it's like stepping into a cathedral. It feels like we've entered another world. The chapel has five floor-to-ceiling stained glass windows depicting angels, demons, flames, and blood. My attention is drawn to one window. It pulls at my heart - drawing me in. The Oracle, one of the many, or few? I believe the Oracle is collective. The stained glass depicts a mosaic of a man and a woman embracing, standing face to face as if in love, yet her shadow floats away from him. The stained glass is center-lit with gold. It's not a light, it's a swaddled blanket. They sacrificed an infant to the night.

Is this the story of me?

The Daughter of Oracles. I thought it simply meant that my mother wasn't dead, at least not completely. Since she was an oracle, and I am her daughter, we solved the mystery. But there's more to it than that, and I'm just now putting it all together. Mordred created me, yes. The question is, who or what inspired him to do so? He is the God of War, not Frankenstein. The Oracles created me for this moment. At this very moment, I'm witnessing déjà vu in a thousand-year-old stained-glass window.

Almost as if to ask permission, Killian brushes his warm hand over mine. I reply by slipping my fingers between his. "It's about me."

"It's about us." He corrects me. "I haven't been through these doors since he was cursed, not since the day you disappeared. I was here. This is what I was doing. I was standing in this cathedral after so many years of refusing to enter, looking at this window. At what it means, at what it always has meant. I looked him in the face for the first time. I was so hurt after the public lashing, and I thought by coming here I could decide. Do you know what that decision was?"

"What was it?" I ask.

"If I could destroy my father to save you."

My throat feels dry. I swallow past the grit in my throat. "And?"

"Whenever my mother told stories about this window, I despised it. She said it was my destiny. I hated the thought of my future being planned out, of having no options. I hated it even more because I have always felt it. Here, in my chest. Genevieve, you have been mine in every lifetime." His gaze returns to the stained glass. "And I would sacrifice worlds for you."

My heart bucks against my ribs, begging to escape and throw itself at his boots.

"Smooth talker." I squeeze his fingers tighter and grin.

"Are you ready?" Killian stares into my eyes as if he were trying to become an incubus lie detector.

Looking over my shoulder at the pack of weirdos who have become my family, I see nothing but strength and support in their expressions. My love is beside me. Calypso is at my back, and my family is behind me. If this were my last moment, I couldn't imagine going out on a better note. Except for this *one* thing.

"Kalli?" the shake in my voice refuses to be ignored. "Will you?"

Perhaps for the first time in her life, those bright green eyes are not filled with sarcastic venom. Without a word, she stands by my side, fingers intertwined. Kalli on one hand, Killian on the other. I walk toward my destiny.

From the doorway, a cobalt rug runs down through the center, splitting into two paths. Banners droop with gilded tapestries hanging on either side of a glass coffin. The banners each have a miniature luster hanging between them; some have been lit, illuminating my father-in-law's face.

Aedonious.

I see Killian in him. He is older and more severe, but I see him. Even in a dark magic-induced coma, Aedonious is handsome. What a tragic fate for Selene, to fall in love with a man like this. He's nothing like his father, but she gave him the absolute best of herself. I can't pretend to understand the universe or its reasons. Goddess knows none of it makes sense. I just think it's fucked up.

Killian smiles sadly as he hands me the other dagger and says, "It's time."

I glance behind me again, trying to memorize the faces of the people I care about the most. Considering how unpredictable life can be. Okay, plus double checking that no one objects. I catch Jagger's eye and he nods.

I slash my palm more forcefully than necessary, eager for the pain. Smearing blood on the knife as it rises from the wound and watching it disappear into the blade.

"Because I could not stop for death. He kindly stopped for me." Kalliope muses to herself.

Emily Dickinson. The poetry at the Bone Keep, it was Kalliope.

Killian lifts the glass, revealing his father's body. I swear it feels like time stands still. Like in the movies when everyone is paused but you. This is it, the moment of ... truth? Destiny? Stupidity? Fate? Fuck if I know, but I'm tired of wondering. I raise my arms high over my head and plunge my blood-soaked dagger deep into Aedonious's chest.

And Killian screams...

He grits his teeth and cries out, jagged sparks of electric blue pouring through his veins, lifting his body off the ground. Suddenly, every nerve in my body takes over, causing my insides to twitch. I collapse to my knees, unconcerned about what is happening around me. My chest fills with a gut-wrenching scream, ready to unleash itself upon the world.

"Don't touch him!!" I hear Lincoln's voice as if it's filtered through static, but I don't listen because Killian won't hurt me.

As I lay my hands on his heart, I open our bond wide. Every moment, every emotion, all our memories hit him all at once. Our eyes meeting across the bar, the sound of the stuck door in a coffee shop, and his fingers trailing my skin in an alleyway. I had been beaten, and he saved me. Every stolen moment, where our resolve cracked, and we crashed into each other like tidal waves. Our binding night.

As I open even further, we're both thrown into a vision. As he raises his arms to the sky, the blue lightning surges through him, using him as a conduit. It's hurting him. I launch myself toward his back and throw my arms around his waist without a second thought. Clinging tightly.

My body is on the floor, laying protectively over Killian. It's like a human shield (okay, not really a *human* shield) surrounding him. Calypso is pacing, snarling... she is guarding us.

The fuck! Have we been lying here for a long time? As I sit up, my gaze falls upon Killian's pale face. He looks like crap, but he's breathing. It wasn't until after that I noticed everyone was watching us. Jagger looks like he's about to vomit. Selene is holding a hysterical Anise. Lincoln seems helpless while rubbing Marlow's back. And Marlow is watching Kalli, who appears to be steaming pissed. This is a shit show, and it's best we get on with it before any more catastrophes occur.

I lean down and whisper into Killian's ear. "It's time to wake up, my king."

Killian's eyes open as if summoned, searching for me. An electric blue glow has replaced his intense stormy eyes. As our stares lock, he delves into the pits of my blackened soul.

He is the God of Death.

And I am his Dark Goddess.

CHAPTER THIRTY SIX

JUDGMENT DAY

NOT LONG AGO, I passed through this towering gate with its two enormous black obsidian snakes; however, that was quite a different story. My life has changed dramatically since then. I suppose Thane has something to do with that. After all, she brought all my monsters together during one of her torture sessions. Perhaps I'll thank her face to face. But this time? Hell is with me.

We have all the power of the Netherworld, a couple hundred powerful witches, and twice that many shifters. While I'm not sure if it's enough, we cannot afford to doubt it. The stakes are just too high. As of today, Mordred and Thane will be eliminated, and the Bone Keep and land surrounding it will be seized. Or we die trying.

It's as simple and as complicated as that.

Marlow and Sybil are using magic to protect the entrances to the night fortress. Anise, Dante, and Bane remained back if Mordred gets any slick ideas about attacking the Night Fortress while we're here to mess his world up. Willa and Iris are both here with us. They have the academy under lockdown with their own mages and witchling security.

Osric is here with the unified shifter clans. Jagger has his forces trained to perfection. We all have our roles to play, there are plans in place, and we're as prepared as we're going to get.

So why do I still have this nagging feeling in my chest? It's like the feeling you get before leaving the house without your keys. When you walk into the kitchen and can't remember why you went there. Something feels misaligned, displaced. Regardless of what it is, it's causing my stomach to swarm with hornets.

"Killian, do you trust me?"

He regards me with curiosity. "Yes, Kitten. Is there something you need to tell me?"

"What if I told you I had a feeling? Not magic, not psychic, just a regular human-like intuition in my gut that something isn't right. But I can't tell you what it is or if there's anything we can do about it."

His hands move to his jaw, rubbing against his two-day stubble. "I would say that you are an incredibly intuitive woman, and we should heed that warning."

"How?"

"Jagger," Killian responds as his lip curves as the dragon boy comes over. "You know that thing you love to do? The one thing I always say *not* to do?"

When I tell you Jagger's eyes light up, I'm talking like a toddler with a cheesy poof. Which piques my interest, because what the fuck was that?

"What are you two…?" Jagger disappears right in front of me.

Killian brushes my arm, whispering. "It's our best-kept secret."

Holy unicorn shit. Jagger can fly incognito! Like a full-on invisibility cloak, but without the cloak part. No way, I did not just see that! I thought we were friends, and he never said a damn word. Does Marlow know? Oh, my goddess.

"It wasn't my secret to disclose." Killian's quiet voice reminds me. "He'll make sure the message gets to the right people."

Fuck, my nerves are fried. The last-minute jitters have led to me smothering my familiar with protective love...

Lippy, do whatever you have to do to stay alive.

The resounding huff is a welcome sound. Of course, she is defiant, but that's the comforting part. I can always count on her. As the sun sets every night, Calypso is always a pain in the ass.

Killian squeezes my hand. "Are you ready?"

I nod, "Ready."

"Let's rattle the Netherworld, my Dark Queen." His eyes glow neon.

Now it's my turn to shine, so I close my eyes and feel the well of power that resides deep within me. I am calling it to me, promising to release the chaos it craves. Violet flames and glow-worm eyes shimmer with ferocity as my body lights up.

"Fuck, that's so sexy," Killian growls.

I wink and crouch into a fighting stance. After I do, everyone follows suit.

"Knock, knock. Mordred!" Killian roars as the sky opens for him, and then Jagger lets the first firebomb loose on the front gates.

———◆———

Within minutes the gates are down. Our two forces clash so violently that I have lost sight of everyone except Kalliope and Calypso. In the gigantic courtyard, wounded fighters are strewn everywhere. A barrage of sounds fills the air.

Explosions of magic, war cries, and the screams of the wounded. I always wondered how they managed to survive battles like this in medieval movies. When there is so much destruction and carnage, it is impossible to tell what's in front of you, and the enemy is coming from all sides. My imagination could not have prepared me for this. The sight is nightmare-inducing.

If I'm such a magical being, you may wonder why I fight with daggers and not throwing power around like Captain Big Dick energy. The answer is simple. Mordred hasn't shown his face yet, and I learn from my mistakes. When I went nuclear, I was inexperienced and worked off pure emotion. Bronwyn died as a result, and it isn't something I intend to do again.

My trainer was one of the finest warriors in this realm. I can defend myself, and until I see that shitty excuse for a sperm donor's soulless red eyes, I am not releasing my deep well of power. My magic stays exactly where it is, allowing the pressure to build until it's time to release it. Plus, Kalliope and I work well as a team on the battlefield. Who knew?

I feel the massive hooves of a Nightmare (undead warhorse) kick violently into the pit of my stomach. My muscles tense as the pain bursts through my torso and rips the air from my lungs. Attempting to regain my senses, I stumble back with a groan. However, the moment I raise my arm to strike, he kicks me to the ground again.

Calypso leaps, her jaws open wide, her fangs gleaming, and tears his throat out as she hurls fluids into my face.

"We have to get closer to the main entrance, Kalli!"

I see wolves fighting in that area and witches hurling spells as a backup. In the background, I see neon blue, and, despite most of the substance coming from the ground being on fire, I think I recognize Jagger's firebombs.

While Kalli is struggling with a night creature, I'm still trying to get on my feet. Deacon always told me, "In a fight to the death, don't be the one flat on your back."

He had all this wisdom, and I'm not saying I didn't listen. I'm just saying I should have heard him a bit more.

"Push, Vivi! Dammit!" Kalliope cries out. Her hands are too full to come help me.

I need to release a small amount of power to get back on my feet. The sharp shooting pain nearly makes me drop. I broke a rib. What the fuck is it with me getting my ribs broken during fights? Honestly. This is ridiculous!

To tell the truth, this situation has deteriorated from terrible to disastrous. There are not enough of us. Mordred appears to have doubled the number of abominations in just the few days I have been absent. Something about that doesn't feel right. What am I missing?

Kalli and I trek through the filth and blood, scrambling over dead bodies and dodging fire. Shoving and hacking at mindless night creatures that stare back at us with empty eyes.

Empty eyes... wait... I have it. I've got it! This is Thane. These ghost servants, these catatonic abominations lining the entire estate. She controls them.

"Kalliope!" I call out to her, but it's too loud, and she doesn't hear me.

"Hey, asshole. Focus, listen!" I break through our link.

"I hear ya. A little busy right now...."

"No, listen, it's Thane. She's controlling them. Fuck the fighting. Get to the door. We need to get inside!"

"Power up, sis. Let's do this quickly."

I understand what she means. Blaze a straight path forward with our power. It's a gamble. We will be weakened before the main event if we use too much. But what if we don't? We may not have the main event.

My hands slam to the ground, looking for any sign of life. I need to send my power deeper than I've ever been. They are there, though. Seeds, soil, and water. Now we're talking!

"Come to me," I whisper, and the ground rumbles beneath our feet. "Kalli, power up and run!"

I burst into flame and take off at breakneck speed. Calypso is fast on my heels. I watch mutant plants rise from the ground, ripping the creatures to shreds. They encase some of the night creatures in the soil. Buried alive. It's brutal. Entrails are literally raining down on me, and I'm equally nauseated and astonished by the sight.

The doors are now within our sights and the group we were separated from. Ansel's wolf would be recognizable anywhere, and Amethyst is taller than most men. Both Iris and Willa look closely at one another, flicking their wrists like they're shooing away insects as night creatures turn to ash.

Um, that's fucking wicked.

Killian and Jagger are tag teaming the largest concentration of guards at the entrance. Just successfully kicking the living hell out of them. I should have a clear path soon. We'll be fine — it'll be over soon. I repeat that mantra until I am within inches of Willa. I ignore the pain and focus on her. Nearly. Almost. Just a few steps left...

Initially, I feel a mild tingling in my back, like a scratchy sweater against my skin. The feeling quickly intensifies into a panic. They're behind me. I have no idea how. I simply know it, like I know how to breathe. Mordred and Thane are behind us, and we are surrounded.

In moments like this, people share stories of how their lives flash before their eyes. I wish I could say that's what happened to me. Sadly, it wasn't the case. My decision took about a second, but time only stands still for so long, and then you're out of luck. I turn to meet my father's eyes and face the moment they created me for. But not as a helpless lamb. This time I'm his executioner.

I can't be Genevieve, the daughter, because I'm the only one who can undo this. They made me to right this wrong. I have never been more sure of anything in my entire life.

"Hello, Mordred," I call him with more confidence than I feel.

Thane stands next to him, wearing the face of another person. I suppose it doesn't matter now that she has ditched the lace-covering. There is no ethereal quality, no instant lust, no striking beauty, and her body is scarred. Thanks to me.

"Genevieve, my dear." His voice makes me sick. "And my precious Kalliope, I'm so glad to see the two of you getting acquainted."

Kalliope looks up and flinches. My loud-mouthed, stubborn, tough-as-nails sister cringes in her own father's presence. Fire slams through my veins, burning everything it touches, and I spit venom. "You don't deserve to say her fucking name!"

I feel the heat at my back calm the inferno raging inside me. My king, my soul bonded mate. I feel him. I can *always*-feel him.

"You think to come and do what, Genevieve? Take my castle?" he sneers.

So sure of himself... there is something he's hiding.

"Oh no, I don't want your castle. But my sister, on the other hand. This is her home, and I know this is a spoiler alert—but this is about to be *her* castle." I smile brilliantly.

"Vivi!" Kalliope hisses.

"What, sis? Did I blow the surprise? I'm sorry. I've just been so excited to share the news with dear old dad." I'm going for petulant child vibes here.

Kalli, get behind me. Power up. I know what I'm doing, trust me. Please.

Mordred's face is cherry red. The veins in his neck are protruding. He is rapidly losing the gentlemanly façade he hides behind. It's like I'm watching him unravel. He doesn't even know he's taken the bait.

"I think you should redecorate though, Kalli. It's depressing in there." I snicker, and Mordred lunges for me.

The rest occurs in a slow-motion similar to an action movie. I pull my dagger from its sheath and slice my palm. Mordred reaches for the dagger and in one stroke of pure luck, I could slip it between his ribcage just under his pecs, right into his heart. Mordred's eyes widen as he stares at the dagger and then back at me. Astonished at what he was seeing. I don't blame him either. I'm also hesitant to believe it. As I hold the hilt, I swing my other hand around and pelt him with flames. Stalling, waiting, while his blood flows out from behind the dagger, but he's not falling.

Panic floods me. I did it right. I did exactly what I was supposed to do. So why isn't it working? Fuck. Fuck. Fuck. I steal a second to glance at Killian. He's got blue veins writing under his skin, ready and waiting. But *he is* waiting...

He doesn't know either. Shit! Mordred's hand juts down and clasps around my throat, lifting me in the air by my neck as my feet flail. He looks at Killian with smug satisfaction. "Make a move, and I'll snap her pretty neck. That dagger works with my bloodline, by the way. Not just hers."

Boom. Gotcha, motherfucker!

"Kalli, can you hear me?" I call through our link.

"10-4."

"It's both of us. There are two daggers, because there are two of us. The other one is on my thigh. Grab it, cut your palm, and let it drink your blood, stab right where I did. Make sure you hit his heart. Can you do this?"

"I can do this."

Perfect time for a distraction.

"Fuck. You." I mouth, mainly because my air supply is cut off and for maximum dramatic effect. And then I go Firestarter.

Thank the goddess for the mate bond because I didn't have to use words to tell Killian to take the Keep. I thought about it hard enough and knew he would pick up what I was putting down. I am not a damsel in distress. I do not need him to stand behind me and oversee. The castle is wide open for the taking, which is his chance.

The commotion makes it easy for Kalli to sneak up to my thigh and pull out the second dagger. It is even easier for her to slice her hand and coat it with her blood. Mordred does not notice her until she inserts the dagger into his heart. Which, I suspect, has been the case her entire life.

Not so invisible anymore now. Is she DAD?

When Mordred's grip on my throat slips, I look toward Kalliope covered in gore, and I smirk. "I guess the way to a man's heart is between his fifth and sixth rib."

I didn't hear the scream until it was too late. I never even questioned where she was this whole time. We were going to find her and take her home with us. But I should have foreseen this. Thane got to her, and she isn't herself anymore.

When Una's ungodly screaming hits a fever pitch, I hear another deeper voice's primal scream. "Viv, NO!"

And then I'm on the ground, pinned down by Una's corpse, with no idea what the fuck is going on. I can't pick out one voice among all the noise. Everybody is shouting. Everyone is fighting. I'm stuck under a corpse, getting my ass trampled. Could this day get any worse?

As I struggle through the mud, I grab a root and pull my body halfway out from under Marta, allowing me to open my eyes. I didn't believe it at first. I asked the universe if it could worsen, which is a cruel joke. I will not accept it. No, because I cannot gaze into Lincoln's lifeless forest green eyes with a sword piercing his chest.

A sword that was meant for me.

If that's Lincoln on the ground next to me. If that's... if he is, I think I'm going to get sick. My head is spinning; I can't feel anything. So tell me this isn't real. No, this can't be happening. He's my best fucking friend! Blackwood Alpha. He'll make the perfect husband, and his pups will be adorable. Remember?

He's going to be in love, happy...

Anise. Marlow. Oh, goddess, please no.

When I pull my legs from under Marta, I scream in grief. My grief turns into rage. As I stare down at her, I am consumed by it. She will be too. I snap my finger and reduce her to fucking ash. Mordred lies motionless, bloodied on the ground, as my eyes dart to him. Two daggers protrude from his ribs, and my screaming intensifies. My hands are scalding hot, and this fire is white.

"You're the light, my queen." Killian's voice soothes the raging monster within. His gentle hand on my arm steadies me.

I look into his neon blue eyes and say, "Not yet."

I could feel Thane reaching into the obsidian, but not for the reasons I had imagined. She was never spelling obsidian itself. These are tunnels. They surround the whole grounds, and they're full of night creatures. She's charging up the rest of the legion. A literal legion of the fucking dead.

The sound of my screech is unhinged and inhuman. I point at Thane. "YOU! You murdered him! I will rip your fucked-up soul apart and devour it for dinner!"

I don't remember when I started crying. Perhaps I have been crying all my life. It seems like it. My vision is hazy. I

can't see what's in front of me. In any case, I am gearing up
to unleash my full crazy.

Willa touches my shoulder. "Your skull is half-caved in.
Wild, reckless girl! Tatiana, come heal her."

It's no wonder I feel lightheaded; I think I'll lie down now.
Tatiana's hands are freezing, and it feels lovely on my skin.
Do you think she knows I'm burning?

This is like watching a dream happen from the outside.
Someone else's dream is projected on a screen. Killian
decimated twenty men at a time, wielding the weather to his
advantage and commanding lightning like a second skin.
Beautiful. The stormy-eyed king. Whoop. That's why his
eyes are so stormy! It makes sense. But for each twenty, there
are a hundred more.

I think I'm dying.

Once again, everyone is fighting, and wolves have entered
the Bone Keep. I can see them through the open doors.
Jagger is like that awesome pilot guy from the movie. That is
all I can make out of my scrambled brain. Jets. The fast ones.
But it isn't enough. What's up with the howling? What an
awful sound. Anguish, I can feel it. I can taste it. Lincoln...
he was the Alpha.

I can feel my heart cracking in two. Maybe dying isn't so
bad after all.

Thane. The sorceress Thane. She's toe-to-toe with the
witches, throwing everything they've got at her. It doesn't
look good. Mordred was eliminated, but it does not matter
because we failed. The man was a piece of shit, but he was
never the real threat. His secret weapon was his mistress,
hiding in plain sight. She outsmarted us all.

"Horns! I hear horns!" someone shouts.

I listen more closely.

Those aren't horns. They're fae trumpets. Fae trumpets!

"Tatiana?" I motion to the blonde-haired healing witch, "The Fae are here."

I watch them file in on their wraithlike hooved beasts, eyes rimmed in technicolor and long silver hair. Not just any fae, *royal* fae. Rowena used to tell stories about the fae princelings. She was their caretaker once upon a time before she became mine...

Rowena!!

I search the hordes of fae for green skin, and there she is. On the front of a warrior's horse, looking for me, too. Her eyes well up, and she jumps down from the beast.

"My darling, Vivi! Sorry I'm late."

I can't hold back the sob but manage to mutter. "Better late than dead."

"Isn't that the truth." She kisses my forehead. "It's over, Vivi. Won't be long now. You did it; you're safe. We're all safe now." She places her glowing fingers at my temples, healing me.

CHAPTER THIRTY SEVEN

GRAVESTONE ACADEMY

THE QUIET RAIN AND overcast sky accentuate the somber atmosphere. Killian stands solemnly, his hand resting on my back, dressed in his finest suit. As for me, I am dressed in black.

Osric and Ansel prepare Lincoln on the ceremonial pyre, consecrating their fallen Alpha, honoring the spirit of the valiant dead according to shifter custom. They speak the words and burn the herbs to send their warriors to live among their ancestors. This usually happens in a closed ceremony. Yet Marlow and I are just as much his "clan" as the shifters who honor him, and thankfully, the elders of shifter clans around the world have realized the error of using archaic customs that were created to divide our orders.

In the last year, if we've learned anything, it's that hate is bred by division. The very thing Lincoln Blackwood fought against. What he ultimately died for.

That's why Marlow, Ansel, and I petitioned for Linc's last rites to be conducted on the grounds of Gravestone Academy. Each fallen soul who helped to make this institution a reality will have a permanent memorial there.

A new hope for the future, without forgetting those who helped us get here.

As I approach Osric, my eyes swell with tears. My body trembles and I glance over my shoulder at Killian, at my chosen family. Trying to find courage. Each one of them is glued to me, their eyes full of support. Then I turn back toward the last resting place of my best friend, so peacefully laid upon a bed of pine and forest.

"It's time, my queen," Ansel whispers. I close my eyes, straighten my back, and summon the strength.

And then I step forward.

My fingertips ignite, and as I lean down to light the fire. I whisper, "I hope you know you're an asshole for leaving me like this, but you will forever be my favorite song."

As the pyre burns, I try to keep my composure. I promised myself I would sit with him until there was nothing left, no matter how difficult it was or how long it took. Because Lincoln would have done it for me. As the deep well of anguish slides up my throat and the first raw sob claws its way out, Marlow rushes to hold me. I clasped her hand around mine. Calypso curls up next to us on the ground, and we let it all out.

From the corner of my eye, I spot Killian, Jagger, Kalliope, Anise, Dante, and Bane. Ansel, Osric, Rowena, Willa, and Iris. Even Amethyst and Sybil stand behind us in support. In the distance, I think I see a dark figure hidden between two trees. Sylas. But before I can grab his attention or invite him to join us, he's disappeared.

The serene gaze of Anise catches my attention once again. Everyone has been worried about her. Would she be able to cope with such a loss? But in typical Anise fashion, she shocked us all. She's probably the strongest person here, and I just want her to know how much he loved her. As her eyes shift toward mine, I realize I've been staring. But the slight smile she gives me as she caresses her stomach rocks me to my very core.

Anise is going to be a mother. She's already comforting the wolf prince of the Blackwood Clan in her womb. That explains why Ansel has been following her around like a weirdo. He's Linc's second, and he would have sensed it. He has a responsibility to protect the wolf prince, so Anise will always be safe. She deserves it. And now she has the chance. Anise never got to know the love of her mother. She was not to blame for that, and I can see it in her eyes. She wants to give this child everything she never had, how deeply in love she already is.

Lincoln Blackwood, you sly devil.

He always had to have the last word.

CHAPTER THIRTY EIGHT

FAREWELL

I'VE DREADED THIS DAY for the last week. It's been so nice to have everyone under the same roof as our guests at the Night Fortress. We'd spent the week of mourning together. With a side of laughter and reminiscing. Even planning some decisions regarding the futures of the realms. Bonds were formed, which turned into alliances. Built not on money or power, but friendship and mutual respect.

I got to spend time with Rowena, which was something I didn't know I needed so badly. She told me of her harrowing journey back to the Fae realm, and how long it took her to unify the princes. Bron, Bairn, and Baela had a hand in their "change of heart" from what I understand. Which is hilarious, because now I can't stop picturing the very handsome fae princes with hot pink skin or spikes growing from their faces. I told her about everything I'd been through to get to this place, and about how I saw my mother (her friend) for the first and last time. We shared some tears about that, and some wistful thought about whether Evanora Graves and Deacon Harwell are living happily ever after in an alternate universe.

Everyone has been fawning all over Anise, of course. The little wolf prince has become something of a beacon for all of us. A bit of sunshine in the aftermath of so much pain. But alas, all good things must come to an end. Or so I've been told. And it's time to say our goodbyes.

Killian and I stand before the garden portal. Me in a ridiculous dress with stupid puffy frills. Killian in a sleek suit and an obnoxious crown. I can't help but think of all the other times he and I stood here, under very different circumstances. Me leaving him. Him leaving me. Now here we are, the King and Queen of the Netherworld. Bidding our guests safe travels.

Wild, right?

"Vivi, my dear girl, promise me you'll visit me in the fae realm. And bring that delicious man you've caught yourself along too." Rowena pinches my cheeks, apparently not giving a single fuck that I'm a queen. I love it, my very own sassy fairy grandmother.

"I promise." I chuckle, giving her a kiss on the cheek as she steps into the churning kaleidoscope of purples and black. Killian wraps his arm around my waist and kisses my neck, chuckling with me.

Next, it's Willa and Iris. Headed back to the Academy and the bright minds of the future. While they were here, a badass arrangement was made. You see, I had no idea how old Willa really was, so when she mentioned staying on for a few years until the Academy is established and then turning it over to Marlow—I was shocked. Marlow, on the other hand, was ecstatic. And now that I think of it, I don't know why I hadn't pictured it sooner. Marlow and Jagger running the academy while Iris makes Willa purple lemonade on a tropical beach. What a sight to imagine! I can't wait to see it play out in real life. In a few years… I still need my bestie bitch by my side for a while.

After saying goodbye to Iris and Willa, it's Kalliope's turn. I'd be lying if I said this one doesn't hurt a little harder. And I know she's just a trip across the scary bog of doom, but it's not the same as having her here. With me. But she has work to do in the Shadowlands. She needs to go home, because Kalliope is going to be the one who restores the Netherworld. If there was ever a hero in this story, it's her. And I'll be at her side every step of the way. Two Queens. Two Kingdoms. One unshakable bond.

I'm still secretly a little pissed she's taking Amethyst and Sybil with her. But then I remember how the Shadowlands is going to be run by a Queen with no plans for a king, and an all-woman council...

And then I'm fine again.

I'm hope they'll rename the Bone Keep to something cool like Fort Badass Girl Power, and wear leather jackets.

Kalli and I don't really do the hugging thing, so I smirk instead and make my voice sound like my nose is plugged. "See you in a few weeks, asshole."

To which she laughs and replies as she's walking away. "I'll be sure to lock the doors, psycho."

And I wouldn't have it any other way.

There was a time I was convinced that I'd go with Kalli to the Bone Keep. The castle I am co-heir to. It's supposed to be my home. But through all my trials I've realized it's where I was conceived. Yes. But it was never my home.

Killian's warmth slides up my back as he presses himself into me, knowing full well what he's doing to my lady bits. He's smug about it, of course, and then he whispers. "I've got a fireplace waiting in our room for that itchy dress."

Laughing out loud, I lift up on my toes and kiss the man of all my dreams and nightmares combined.

I didn't have a home until I met the cocky-mouthed swaggering jackass standing next to me. We've been through hell and back, literally. He and I. And I'm not naïve enough to say it will be smooth sailing from here. In fact, I can promise it won't. But his demon plays well with mine, and isn't that all we really want at the end of the day? Someone who sees your darkest parts and says, "I love you anyway."

The End

Vivi and Killian's story has come to an end, but maybe. Just maybe, we'll see them again?
Stay tuned for Sylas's Story in the Nightshade Trilogy.
.Book One is Coming Fall 2022!

Did you enjoy your reading experience? Please help a girl get the word out and leave a review!

For exclusive content, hilarious memes, the first look at new releases, and fellow bookworms doing bookworm things.

Come to the dark side
!
Join my author group on Facebook –
Darwin's Darklings

.

ABOUT THE AUTHOR

AN AUTHOR BY DAY AND a werewolf by night. Amber is a lover of coffee, books, nature, and all things dark and witchy. Not necessarily in that order.

She currently resides in Wisconsin with her rock band husband, a few beastly children and a house full of familiars.

Made in United States
Troutdale, OR
09/10/2023

12798081R10193